DARKNESS PEERING

The Stuntman's Daughter: Stories

BANTAM BOOKS

NEW YORK TORONTO LONDON

SYDNEY AUCKLAND

DARKNESS

PEERING

ALICE BLANCHARD

DARKNESS PEERING
A Bantam Book/August 1999

Book design by Laurie Jewell

Library of Congress Cataloging-in-Publication Data
Blanchard, Alice.
Darkness peering / Alice Blanchard.
p.   cm.
ISBN 0-553-11153-1
I. Title.
PS3552.L36512D3   1999   99-24823
813'.54—dc21   CIP

Published simultaneously in the United States and Canada

Bantam Books are published by Bantam Books, a division of Random House, Inc. Its
trademark, consisting of the words "Bantam Books" and the portrayal of a rooster, is
Registered in U.S. Patent and Trademark Office and in other countries. Marca
Registrada. Bantam Books, 1540 Broadway, New York, New York 10036.

PRINTED IN THE UNITED STATES OF AMERICA

BVG   10   9   8   7   6   5   4   3   2   1

FOR DOUG,
whose love sustains me,
and in memory of
BEVERLY LEWIS,
whose wisdom graces
these pages.

Deep into that darkness peering, long I stood
there wondering, fearing.
Doubting, dreaming dreams no mortal ever
dared to dream before.

I

INDIAN SUMMER, 1980

1

POLICE CHIEF NALEN STORROW FOUND THE DEAD GIRL LYING faceup in a rust-colored runoff pond on the westernmost corner of Old Mo Heppenheimer's cow pasture. Her milky eyes were open to the morning sky, one hand suspended as if brushing away insects. The sun was shining down, warming tiny black tadpoles in the shallows at her feet. A king snake was coiled in the muddy hollow under one arm, and a daddy longlegs crawled across her extended fingers.

"Git." Nalen waved his hand and the king snake slithered into the duckweed. He followed its progress until it vanished, then realized he was biting the inside of his cheek hard enough to draw blood. He looked away for an instant, heart thudding dully in his chest. A dense forest abutted the pasture, balsam firs releasing their aromatic fragrance from sap blisters on their trunks, leafy ferns thriving along with golden saxifrage and wild iris at the forest's edge. The day was hot, the sun high, and the silence was so thick you'd've thought the sky didn't have any air in it.

Steeling himself, he rolled up his pant legs and waded into the shallow pond, mud sucking at his shoes. He probed the cadaver's scalp, neck, arms, chest and legs, careful not to shift her position before the photographs were taken. A foul smell lingered in the air above the body like smoke in a bar. He could find no entrance or exit wounds, no blunt injuries, no ligature marks, although he detected finger markings around the throat. Livor mortis had set in, rendering the underside of her body a reddish purple due to the accumulation of blood in the small vessels. Her elbows were blanched, as were the backs of her legs due to compression of the vessels in this area. Rigor mortis was fully developed, pinning the time of death to between twelve and twenty-four hours. The girl's face appeared congested and cyanotic, with fine petechial hemorrhages on her eyelids and across the bridge of her nose. There were also contusions and fingernail abrasions on her neck near the larynx.

Nalen recognized the dead girl from her pictures: Melissa D'Agostino, age fourteen, missing since the previous afternoon. Shy, chubby, mentally retarded. Her left hand, fisted shut, rested on her belly. Her face with its characteristic Down's syndrome eyes, its triangular nose and protruding tongue, was pallid in the strong sunlight, and dark curls as thick as sausages clung to her forehead. She wore laced yellow sneakers and her pink shorts and short-sleeved polka-dot top were bunched up in back from being dragged a short distance.

Nalen took a step back and scanned the horizon, a mild breeze lifting his thinning brown hair. He'd been a Boston patrolman for fifteen years before moving his wife and kids to this sleepy community five years ago to become its chief of police. Flowering Dogwood, Maine. Population eighteen thousand. Nobody locked their doors here. This was a small town, and he was the top man in a small-town police department, and the sight of the dead girl shook him in ways he hadn't been shaken in quite some time.

Here, in this isolated stretch where Old Mo let his Holsteins and Guernseys graze, local teenagers hung out late at night, smoking pot and getting drunk. Across the street was a dead-end dirt road, a lover's lane, and further east was the Triangle, the town's poorest neighborhood, whose cramped streets of dilapidated houses grew weedlike around the industrial section where the old sawmill and ceramic plant were located. Flowering Dogwood had prospered in the early nineteenth century, becoming Maine's sixth-largest municipality. The town's boots and shoes were renowned for their craftsmanship, and the dense, compact, fine-grained wood of the flowering dogwood was unequaled for the making of shuttles for weaving. By the late 1800s, however, Flowering Dogwood's fortunes had begun to decline, and nowadays the town was known mostly for its historical import, its ceramics and handcrafted furniture.

But what really distinguished this little community from other tradition-steeped New England towns was its school for the blind. The sidewalks were wide for pedestrian traffic and the streetlights were outfitted with little alarms that whooped whenever the walk light went on. Seeing-eye dogs were bred and trained locally and the historical society had fought to preserve the eighteenth-century house belonging to the school's founder.

Turning his attention back to the scene, Nalen searched the area for footprints and found a partial in the mud. The toe print was unclear and didn't have any tread, making it virtually useless. Nearby rested a branch the perpetrator must've used to wipe away his other footprints. That was smart. Nalen felt the hairs rise on the back of his neck.

A siren whelped, and Lieutenant Jim McKissack's dusty '72 AMC Javelin pulled onto the field, bumping over furrows. McKissack slammed on the brakes and the car fishtailed, stopping just short of a barbed wire fence where cattle craning their necks toward the sweeter, taller grasses reared back. McKissack and Detective Hughie Boudreau got out and headed across the field toward Nalen, a study in contrasts.

Jim McKissack was tall and good-looking, a ladies' man with a gruff sort of charm, a meticulous dresser—everything Hughie Boudreau was not. Hughie was short and rumpled, fine-boned, almost girlish, with a mustache that looked penciled on. He had a head of prematurely graying hair and reminded Nalen of a kid on his first roller-coaster ride, eyes constantly roving. Hughie was married and considered himself a good Christian, whereas McKissack was the type of guy who'd sell his own grandmother to the cannibals if it would help him solve a case. The kind of cop who smoked a cigar and wore sunglasses at five o'clock in the morning.

"Criminy." Hughie froze a few yards away.

"Our missing person," Nalen said.

"Jesus Cockadoodle Christ." His eyes looked stapled open.

McKissack smirked. "Lemme adjust the hue, Boudreau. You're looking a little green."

"Watch out, there's a partial right in front of you," Nalen said, and Hughie spun around and vomited in the grass.

McKissack radiated vigor as he strode toward the runoff pond. Parting the black-root rushes and broad-leaved cattails, he stood studying the dead girl with the same kind of impatient intensity he brought to every case. "What d'you think, Chief?"

"Strangulation, would be my guess."

McKissack shook his head. "Petechiae could also be present for heart failure or severe vomiting."

"Yeah, but the signs of cyanosis are most striking on the neck. See those contusions and fingernail markings? He used more force than necessary to subdue the victim."

Hughie was making retching sounds like a door being torn off its hinges.

"Who the hell would strangle a retarded kid?"

"Some severely inadequate person," Nalen said softly, since the angrier he got, the gentler his voice grew. He stared at the victim's face. During manual strangulation, the perp commonly altered his grasp of the neck, resulting in intermittent compression of the veins and arteries with waves of blood coursing in and out of the head, accompanying peaks and valleys in blood pressure that resulted in the rupturing of blood vessels. The petechial hemorrhages on the victim's eyelids and over the bridge of her nose were due to ruptured capillaries.

McKissack quickly unlaced his expensive Italian shoes and left them like two footprints on the muddy bank. "You think we've got a pedophile on our hands?"

"I doubt it."

McKissack glanced up. "You don't think this was a sexual homicide?"

"Let's wait for the autopsy."

"Give me your best guess, Chief."

Nalen thought for a moment. "She was strangled in the field, then dragged down to the pond."

"No rape? No molestation?"

"Look at her clothes. Nothing's twisted up or unbuttoned or put on backwards."

"Still . . . I've got a hunch." McKissack lit a cigarette. "She was a very trusting person, according to her mother. She might've done a few things willingly . . . you know, not knowing any better."

"I doubt it," Nalen said.

McKissack picked up the muddy branch and turned it over. "He erased his own footprints?"

"Except for that partial there."

"I was hoping we'd find her alive." Hughie straightened up and wiped his mouth on his sleeve. "My wife and I were on our knees last night . . ."

"Whatever floats your boat," McKissack said, and Hughie spun around, his face an ugly mottled color.

"We were praying, you ignoramus! You should try it sometime, McKissack, it just might do you some good."

"Yeah, well, it didn't do her any good, did it?" He glanced sharply at the corpse.

"Gentlemen." Nalen snapped open his notebook, fingers cramping white around his pen, and started ticking off points on his mental checklist: they'd have to write a description of the scene, make sketches, take pictures. He'd already formed an opinion. The medical examiner was due any minute now, and Nalen was anxious to confirm his suspicions. He figured the girl had been dead for at least fourteen hours, strangled to death by a pair of unforgiving hands. If they were lucky, they'd get fingernail scrapings.

He went to his squad car, opened the trunk and got out a roll of yellow police tape. With measured steps, he cordoned off the area, looping the tape around the swamp rose and cattails, making the perimeter as wide as possible. In the distance, people were already beginning to congregate by the side of the road, some of them crossing into the pasture.

"Hughie?"

"Yes, Chief?"

"Keep those rubbernecks back, would you?"

"Sure thing, Chief."

"Take a look at this," McKissack said as they bent over the body together. There was a contusion on the back of the girl's skull, and Nalen wondered how he'd missed it.

"The perp must've struck her from behind," McKissack conjectured, "then raped her. Then strangled her. Then dragged her down here and dumped her."

"Nothing's amiss with her clothes, McKissack. Why rape somebody, then rebutton their shorts?"

"I dunno. Smells like rape to me."

"Let's wait for the autopsy."

"I bet I'm right."

"This isn't about right or wrong." Nalen's head was throbbing, and every shining blade of grass seemed to reflect the full glare of the sun. He took off his hat, mopped his brow. McKissack wasn't a bad cop, just a little arrogant. He tried to macho it. He didn't want help, and because of that, he would fail. They'd argued more than once over procedure. Still, Nalen figured that, with the proper guidance, McKissack could turn out to be one of the best. In the meantime, he spent half his time at the scene playing mind games with McKissack, the other half playing nursemaid to Hughie, when all he wanted was to keep things rolling, keep his team moving, no time to contemplate the tragedy here. No time to acknowledge this was somebody's little girl.

Nalen stooped to pick up a cigarette butt. "Goddammit, McKissack. This yours?"

"Sorry, Chief."

"Now that's just irresponsible." He pocketed the butt and continued searching the perimeter, where he found a three-inch-long piece of red thread, a matchbook from Dale's Discount Hardware and over a dozen glass shards, beer-bottle green. He sealed these items in evidence bags, then knelt to examine the body again. Stuck to the bottom of the girl's right sneaker, wedged into the tread, was a small piece of yellow lined notepaper. He removed it gingerly and held it in his palm, letting it dry slightly before opening it. Torn haphazardly in the shape of Italy, it was approximately two inches by one inch. He slipped it into an evidence bag, then knelt to take a soil sample.

While he was scraping the mud off a rock, the image of the girl's broken body flashed through his mind, and his stomach lurched. A sharp pain gripped his skull. Nauseated, he rested his head between his knees and took deep, shuddering breaths.

"You okay, Chief?" McKissack took the evidence bags from him. "I'll finish up. Go catch your breath."

Grateful, Nalen raised his head to the light and sat for a while, lost in thought, as if he were waiting for a turkey sandwich.

A car horn blared, an oddly comical sound in the bright morning air, and the medical examiner's platinum Mercedes 280CE coupé came cata-humping across the field.

"That guy changes cars the way some people change underwear," McKissack muttered as Archie Fortuna got out and, with a ceremonious flourish, snapped on a pair of latex gloves. He had delicate hands for such a big man. Archie was all dancing belly— a balding, fortyish indoor enthusiast who barreled toward the scene with the kind of eagerness most people reserved for sex or steak dinners.

"Howdy doody, Chief." Archie's breath was infamous for its alleged ability to drop a Doberman at six paces. "Whaddaya got?"

"Looks like she was struck on the head and then strangled," Nalen said. "Possibly dragged from a car, although I think she was killed right here in this field."

Archie clapped his hands with professional zeal. "Let's have a look-see."

They bent over the corpse together, shoes sinking into the muck. Archie had a lover's touch. When he turned the girl's body over, a hundred tiny beads of dew rolled off her skin.

"Petechial hemorrhages," he said.

"Mm-hm."

"Finger markings around the throat. Possible blow to the skull. See this reddish area? Look for a blunt instrument . . . a rock, maybe. You called this one, Chief." Archie grunted as he straightened up and squinted at the sun, dark eyes disappearing behind greasy folds of flesh. "Take any prints?"

"Couldn't. Skin's too wrinkled."

"Not to worry. I'll finish back at the lab."

Nalen tried not to think about the process Archie would use to obtain the girl's prints for identification purposes. He'd seen it done once before; Archie would peel off little ovals of skin, place the flaps over his own fingertips, and then, using an ink pad, press them to the blotter.

Archie let out a muffled belch. "Mongoloid, huh?"

"Down's syndrome, they call it."

"Makes you sick, doesn't it?" He raised the dead girl's fist and delicately pried her fingers apart, and to the astonishment of both of them, a tiny silver bell fell out.

"What the doohickey's this?" Archie held it to the light.

"Looks like a cat bell," Nalen said, and Archie dropped it into his palm, where it rolled to a stop with a little tinkling sound.

2

NALEN CROSSED THE D'AGOSTINOS' FRONT YARD, NOTING THE weed-choked foundation and rusty watering can, the cracked slate slabs leading toward the sagging front porch. Out back, the lawn sloped sharply toward the woods, where birch trees shot up from the ground like jet contrails. He could hear the cries of the neighborhood children; they sounded like gulls. The air was fragrant with azaleas and sweet william, pregnant with the promise of rain.

Picking up the morning paper, he rang the doorbell. "It's Nalen Storrow," he said through the screen, and Frances D'Agostino let him in. She was in her mid-forties, built solid, with weathered skin and a heavy brass-colored braid slung over her shoulder. He handed her the newspaper.

"Hello, Frances."

Hope flashed in her eyes. "Did you find her?"

He shook his head and all hope died. "I mean . . ." He fumbled for the right words. "Well . . . I need to talk to you and Marty, if he's home."

"Something's wrong, isn't it?" She had the dried-out stare of an old woman.

"May I come in?"

Silently, resentfully, she stepped aside.

He took a seat on the living room sofa, removed his hat and leaned against an embroidered pillow that said "There's no place like home." The house was neat as a pin. Just yesterday, he'd issued a bulletin and placed Melissa D'Agostino's name in state police files. He'd taken down a report—physical description, medical history, access to bank accounts. He'd called the county hospital, just in case, and formed a search party. Now the search was over. They could all go home. Except that, for the D'Agostinos, this place would never really feel like home again.

"Marty, Chief's here!" Frances hollered up the stairs, then moved awkwardly into the living room, her wary eyes on him.

The air smelled warm and moist, something meaty boiling away on the stove. "Smells good," he said politely.

"Pot roast." Frances rubbed an arthritic hand across her belly. "Stomach's been cramping up on me. Hope I don't get cystitis again. Hate those sulfa pills. Oh, here you are, honey."

Marty D'Agostino strode into the living room and sat down opposite Nalen in a plaid armchair. Marty had a resonant voice, an imposing frame and a shock of spiky gray hair. He was an accountant for an insurance firm in Manchester, New Hampshire, and commuted four hours back and forth to work each day. When Melissa was a toddler, Marty had refused the doctors' suggestion that he commit her to an institution; instead, he'd insisted on mainstreaming her into the public schools, an uncommon request in 1970. Heroism came in all shapes and sizes, Nalen thought, as Frances sank onto the sofa beside him.

Marty's lower lip trembled. "She's dead, isn't she?"

In the second or so it took him to respond, Nalen wished he could've made something up. A better ending. *And silence sounds no worse than cheers, after death has stopped the ears.* He cleared his throat. "I'm afraid so."

He could hear the air going out of their lungs. The living room was all patches of color embroidered with their stunned faces. Frances's arthritic fingers clutched the sofa cushions.

"Where'd you find her?" Marty asked.

"Out on Black Hill Road."

"Could you be more specific?"

"Off the road a ways . . . lying in a runoff pond."

"What d'you mean?" Marty was glaring at Nalen now.

Frances hoisted herself off the sofa, went over to a bookcase and reached for a photo album on the top shelf, lacy yellow slip showing beneath her floral-patterned dress. She dropped the album in Nalen's lap. "There's my baby," she said, pointing at a family portrait.

Marty fearlessly held Nalen's eye. "How did my daughter die? Did she drown?"

"We think there might've been foul play."

Marty sat back.

Frances leaned over and thumbed through the photo album's thick black pages. "I don't understand," she said softly, "who'd want to hurt my baby?" She tapped one arthritic finger against a snapshot of her daughter. Melissa had a face like a big, sweet pie. She mugged for the camera, her round cheeks like two cupped hands framing her short squat nose with its triangular nostrils. Her eyes sparkled with mischief and she exuded so much warmth and curiosity, it wasn't difficult to imagine how easily she might've fallen prey.

Marty's face reddened, all its angled planes pinched with pain. He slammed his fist against his knee. "What d'you mean, 'foul play'?" His words fired off like darts.

"We won't know for sure until after the autopsy. I can give you more information then."

"Give me more information *now*," Marty insisted, his steely gaze boring into Nalen. "Was she drowned in this pond? Is that what you're saying? Somebody drowned my Melissa?"

"No, sir," Nalen said softly.

"What then, for chrissakes?" Waves of anger peeled off him like heat from an oven. "What happened to my daughter?"

"We think she was strangled."

Frances clutched her braid, lowered her head and wept. Nalen could feel each sob like a body blow. He didn't know whether to put an arm around her or not. He was usually good at this sort of thing, but the murder of a child was different. The murder of a child was inexplicable, unforgivable.

"You're sure it's our Melissa?" Marty pleaded, eyes like two watery coins. "You're absolutely certain?"

Nalen set the photo album carefully on the coffee table and stood up. "We need you to come down and identify her for us, Marty."

Marty bowed his head. Frances was shuddering, eerie grunting sounds emitting from her lungs. Nalen noticed his hands were shaking. It wasn't fair. He remembered his father's words just then. *Life's a comedy to those who think, a tragedy to those who feel.*

"Marty . . . Frances . . ." Nalen looked at each of them in turn. "We're going to solve this case. I promise you."

"You know . . ." Marty rose on tall unsteady legs. "Melissa always told the truth. Children tell the truth, you know. Us adults . . . we're good at self-deception, but not kids. Why do you think they call it the 'unadulterated' truth?"

"Well, you're right about that." Nalen moved toward the door. Outside, a light rain was beginning to fall.

"Boy oh boy, she loved cows," Marty said. "You know Stinky Peppers? We'd go down to his farm and visit the cows. Melissa loved those cows with all her heart. Stinky let her name the calves. You ever been out to Stinky's place?"

"On occasion." Stinky had a habit of getting drunk and beating his third wife and their many children.

Frances gripped Nalen's hand, her fingers warm and rough. "Bless you, Chief. She's with the Lord now."

"Stop it, Frances," Marty said, eyes blinking in irritation.

Nalen felt this sore spot between them like a slippery drop down a granite gorge, icy as glacial meltwater.

"Almost forgot." Nalen pulled the cat bell out of his jacket pocket. "Do either of you recognize this?"

Marty studied it for a moment. "Itch had one of those on her collar."

"Itch?"

"Melissa's cat. Got killed six months ago." He looked away, embarrassed. "You know, that brouhaha with your boy."

Nalen felt his face flush, every cell in his body awake now. "And you haven't seen the cat collar since?"

"Nossir."

Nalen pocketed the bell.

"You know," Frances said, "when Melissa was born, I thought everybody else's baby was just a baby . . . but my little girl was a real human being. Isn't that funny?"

"I know what you mean," he said, thinking of Rachel.

3

THE MEDICAL EXAMINER'S BUILDING WITH ITS NONDESCRIPT brick facade was sandwiched in between the First Bank of Maine and the police station on Lagrange. Autopsies had been performed in the basement of this building for decades. The lobby smelled like a dentist's office and was decorated with the same quasi-cheerful decor—flowery wallpaper, tangerine upholstered sofas and chairs, side tables offering up neutral reading matter like *House & Garden* and *Popular Mechanics.*

"Hiya, Chief!" Archie Fortuna's irreplaceable assistant, Betty, greeted them with a warm, gracious smile. She tripled as receptionist, secretary and medical assistant, and Nalen liked her a lot. She had a tousled head of dark hair, intelligent eyes and a bright, energetic manner that served to neutralize the depressing atmosphere of the morgue. "I'll tell Archie you're here. Please, have a seat."

They sat in silence, Marty D'Agostino's face a mask of torment. The viewing room was all they would see today, but Nalen knew the rest of the building like his own sorry face—Archie's office with its tumble of files, its mini-fridge full of hummus-and-black-olive pita bread sandwiches; the medical lab with its formaldehyde smell and bottles of preserved body parts; the storage room, a jumble of black metal filing cabinets and cardboard boxes labeled 1919, 1920, 1921, and so on; and finally the basement morgue with its cement floor and stark lighting, its walk-in refrigerator, its body bags and gurneys and signs prohibiting eating and smoking. Nalen had witnessed over a hundred autopsies in his five years as police chief and remembered every single one of them—the man who drowned in his bathtub, people killed in car crashes, the high school cheerleader who OD'd, the SIDS case. He admired the way Archie bore up under tragedy, how even the most heart-wrenching case seemed to buoy him like an inner tube.

"Marty?" Archie greeted them at the door. "Chief? Would you come with me, please?"

They followed the rotund man in the white lab coat down a long corridor whose carpet was a lovely cowpie brown. Fluorescent lights flickered overhead with irritating irregularity. At the end of the corridor, they entered a cramped, dimly lit room where a gurney held the body of Melissa D'Agostino, white sheet pulled up to her shoulders. Her eyes were closed, her mouth sealed shut with some sort of adhesive—Nalen detected a smear of glue on her lips. She looked very peaceful, as if she were sleeping.

Archie turned to Marty D'Agostino. "We need you to ID her, then we'll leave you two alone for a moment."

Marty's eyes had almost disappeared behind their pouchy lids. He gave a curt nod. "That's my daughter."

"Thank you very much," Archie said, hitching his pants over his prodigious belly. "Chief?"

They stepped out into the corridor and kept their voices low. "I've got to testify this afternoon. Elderly female died of dehydration, family's suing the hospital. I've scheduled the autopsy for this evening. How's five o'clock sound?"

"Good."

"I've already performed a preliminary. No signs of penetration, no semen or blood or bruises on her lower extremities."

"So we can rule out rape?"

"Think so. Don't quote me yet. Got some good fingernail scrapings, but it looks like mostly dirt. State lab'll give us the results in about a week . . ."

Marty D'Agostino opened the door, his bony features sunken as if some internal structure had collapsed.

"My condolences," Archie said.

"She was a good girl."

"You okay? Need a lift home?" Nalen offered, even though Marty had come in his own car.

"I'm fine, Chief. Thanks for asking."

"Can I get you something?" Archie offered. "Iced tea?"

"I need to ask you gentlemen a favor."

They looked at him quizzically.

"Melissa was wearing a friendship bracelet when she disappeared. Frances and I would like it back."

"Friendship bracelet?"

"She made it herself at summer camp. Red and yellow yarn woven into a sort of diamond pattern. She kept it tied around her wrist. Never took it off."

Nalen and Archie traded a look. Then Nalen spoke up. "We didn't find anything like that on her, Marty."

"No?"

"I'm sorry." Nalen suddenly remembered the three-inch-long red thread he'd found inside the perimeter and wondered if it belonged to Melissa's friendship bracelet.

"She always wore it. Every day. Wouldn't leave the house without it."

"Maybe the perp took it as a souvenir?" Archie conjectured, and Nalen put his arm around Marty and walked him toward the door.

"I'll have my boys scour the area," he promised as they headed out to the parking lot. The whole town seemed to be silently suffering its loss, distant trees shooting into the sky like life's exposed wires.

4

ON HIS WAY HOME, NALEN STOPPED AT A GAS STATION TO use the john. His stomach growled. The toilet gurgled. He opened the dirty window facing the street and heard a child's scream. The sound froze his blood, but now the child was laughing and he relaxed a bit.

He gazed at his reflection in the fogged mirror—bags under his eyes despite the sleeping pills he swallowed nightly by the handful, sallow skin, fleshy middle-aged face that used to be lean from long-ago daily workouts, no time for that anymore—and told himself there was no connection, no connection at all . . .

Nalen pulled the cat bell out of his pocket. Six months ago, Hughie Boudreau had radioed in a disturbing call. Nalen met him at Ravenswood Road where the two men hiked about a quarter of a mile into the forest and came upon a clearing where a grisly scene assaulted their eyes: five decapitated cats, their heads stuck on stakes, broken bodies discarded in a pile at the base of a tree.

They soon found a suspect, Ozzie Rudd, the high school football coach's son. Ozzie had an insolent smirk and slicked-back hair and confessed that he and some friends had gotten drunk and teased some cats . . . maybe shot at them with a BB gun or something . . . but he swore on a stack of Bibles he'd never de-capitated anything in his life. Then, to Nalen's astonishment, he implicated Nalen's own son, Billy.

That night, fighting a burning knot in the pit of his stomach, Nalen drove his own flesh and blood to the station for an inter-view. Pale and trembling, Billy denied everything at first. Nalen knew he was lying because Billy had come home drunk a few nights prior, the same night the cats were slaughtered. But Billy kept stubbornly shaking his head, insisting, "No way, Dad!"

It turned out that four sixteen-year-olds—Billy and Ozzie and Neal Fliss and Boomer Blazo—had gotten drunk on illicitly purchased tequila, rounded up some stray cats from the neigh-borhood, carried them in a burlap sack into the woods and shot them to death with a BB gun. Ozzie and Neal did most of the shooting. The boys then left the dead cats where they'd fallen and drove to the Triangle, where Ozzie picked a fight with a boy named Eddy Tourneau, after which somebody called the cops and everybody scattered to the four winds. Despite vocifer-ous protests from a few fervent animal lovers, the crimes had drawn only misdemeanor charges. The judge handed down le-nient sentences—$500 fine, one year's probation. As added punishment, Nalen had grounded Billy for a month and made him do volunteer work at the blind school. But to this day, Nalen wasn't sure who'd decapitated those cats, or just how involved Billy had been, and the whole incident left an acrid taste in his mouth.

Now, splashing water on his face, Nalen wondered if there was any connection between the dead cats and Melissa D'Agostino. "Of course not, you idiot," he said aloud. "Give your head a shake." Melissa probably found the bell after her cat had disappeared and was carrying it around like a keepsake. That must be how it'd got-ten into her hand.

Billy was just an all-American boy drowning in raging hor-mones, Nalen told himself firmly, pushing any lingering doubts to the deep, slumbering part of his brain where all his miseries resided.

He drove home and parked in the driveway, smiling for the first time that day when his nine-year-old daughter, Rachel, came scooting across the lawn toward him. "How's my Pickle?" She squirmed in his arms, barefoot and giggling. "How's my girl?"

"I fell!" She pointed at her scraped knee. "Mommy says I can keep the scab. I'm gonna put it in an envelope."

"You are?" He laughed.

She tugged at the crotch of her creeping-up shorts and wriggled around until he let her go. Beautiful. She was stunning. Yellow hair twisting in the hot breeze. Blue-green eyes the color of the deepest part of the ocean.

"Where's your mom?"

They turned toward the house and there Faye stood, almost as if they'd willed her to appear. She was weeding the flower bed that bordered the house, hoe in hand, sun throwing glints of her light-colored hair back to him in brilliant flashes. She caught his smile and frowned. "Did you find her?"

"Um . . ." The words died on his lips.

Faye gave him a dark look. "Rachel, go inside and get a popsicle."

"Oh boy!" She scampered into the house, screen door slamming shut behind her like a gunshot.

Faye wore a sleeveless sand-colored dress and white sandals, her short, dirty-blond hair held in place by plastic kid's barrettes. Her face was flushed and it shocked him how pretty she looked. She had a small beige-colored mole high on her forehead and thin lips she was constantly rubbing the lipstick off of. "So she's dead?" Faye asked with grim suspicion.

"Yep."

"Was it an accident?"

"No, she was strangled."

Faye stiffened, and he knew she was thinking about the children.

"I just stopped by to see how you're doing," he said. "I've gotta head back to the station. Won't be home until late."

"Fine," she said, turning away from him, a mild breeze toying with her dress. He knew she hated his world, a world of hard information supported by physical evidence.

"We've only got forty-eight hours, give or take, before the trail grows cold."

She ignored him, pretending to wipe the dirt off her hands.

"Where's Billy?"

That got her attention. "Over at Gillian's. Why?"

"I need to talk to him."

Her eyes narrowed. "What about?"

"Just a few questions."

She pressed her lips together, a white circle forming around her mouth, and shivered like a horse after it's been running for a long time. "You're never going to forgive him, are you?"

"I forgive him. I just don't trust him."

"Great." She threw down her hoe. "It's not like he murdered somebody. Or are you going to blame him for that, too?"

"Faye." He walked up to her and ran his hand tentatively down one naked arm. Her skin was warm from the sun. "I'll give you a call tonight, okay?"

She jerked away from him. "What about us? Are we going to be all right? Is it safe here?"

"You'll be fine. Just lock the doors."

"Lock the doors?" He felt her anger like a blast of muggy laundromat air. "Great. I'll lock the doors, Nalen. I'll lock the doors. In the meantime, what exactly am I supposed to tell our children?"

He shrugged. "Tell them the truth."

"That's your area of expertise, isn't it? The truth? That's what you're forever getting to the bottom of. So why don't you tell them, Nalen? *You.*" She spat the word like a grapefruit seed.

He watched her march off, arms and legs oddly pale in the September sun. The date on this milk carton had definitely expired. She used to wet her fingers to put out candle flames, wash her feet in the damp grass. She had been his view for nearly eighteen years, the bull's-eye of his day; and all the while, a sense of privacy had been growing up around her. At some point, she'd lost her habit of wanting him.

"Faye, don't be mad."

She disappeared into the toolshed.

Nalen went inside the house and found Rachel planted in front of the TV in the living room, skinny legs swinging back and forth to the tune of some game show theme song. She licked a strawberry popsicle, her tongue turning obscenely red, and suddenly he envisioned her dead, sunk in the muck, those lovely, curious eyes open to the sun, flies feasting. His stomach lurched.

She swung her head around. "Daddy, it's *The Match Game!*"

He crouched down until he was eye-level. "Listen, Sweet Pickle," he said, "I've got something important to discuss with you."

"Is it about the missing girl?"

"Yes."

"She's retarded."

"Who told you that?"

"Everybody."

"Rachel," he said, taking her by the shoulders, "I've warned you not to talk to strangers, haven't I?"

She rolled her eyes. "Only about a million times."

"Well, not just strangers. You've got to be careful of people you know, too. I don't mean to scare you. I know this may sound strange, but you can't trust anyone. I don't want you going anyplace alone, understand? Always tell your mother where you plan to be, even if it's with a friend, even if it's just up the street. And if anybody starts acting, you know . . . funny . . ."

Her eyes grew round with wonder, and she drew her knees to

her chest, bare legs dusty from playing in the backyard where the grass grew spotty in patches.

"Some people can be dangerous. It's like with the wasps in the attic," he said. "You've gotta run away when they start dive-bombing for your head."

"Okay," she said, clearly puzzled.

"What I'm saying is . . . if a stranger or even someone you know . . . an adult . . . asks you to come with them—"

"You're scaring her," Faye said.

Nalen stood, knees creaking. Since when did his knees creak? He felt mildly dizzy, his vision narrowing so that, for an instant, Faye was the only thing he could see. He caught his breath and the world widened.

"Rachel, go wash up," Faye said.

"But Mom!"

"I said now."

"How about a kiss?" Nalen opened his arms. "I won't be home until way past your bedtime."

"Boo-hoo!" She made a dramatic face, then leapt into his arms and presented her strawberry-flavored mouth to be kissed.

He gave her a puckering, daddylike smooch, and she giggled and wiped her lips, wiping some of the dirt away. She slipped from his grip and ran up the stairs to splash water on her face and pick at her scab.

"This town was supposed to be safe," Faye said, still angry. "I thought that's why we moved here."

She looked radiant in her indignation, and he was once again reminded that all his love for her, all of his deep and desperate need, swung in a soft sack between his legs. "Well, I guess it's all my fault, then."

Her expression softened, hips propped against the doorframe. "You're just never around, is all."

"Sometimes it's more of a job than other times."

Her eyes took him in. "You look terrible, Nalen."

"I'm sorry I scared her."

"No, you're right. She needs to hear it. I could never do that. Steal her innocence from her. You're a lot braver than I am."

Sensing empathy in her voice, he hooked her by the elbow and drew her close. "You know what?"

"What."

"I've still got a crush on my wife."

She gave him a warm, melancholy smile. "Being married to you has given me ulcers."

"Being married to you," he said, "has given me a purpose."

The setting sun melted her face to honey and shadow. "Be careful," she whispered.

He kissed her softly, reluctant to let go. "Don't forget to lock up."

5

BACK AT THE MORGUE, NALEN PUT ON A SURGICAL MASK AND stood beside Archie as he opened the dead girl's rib cage with pruning shears from Dale's Discount Hardware. The medical examiner wore a standard-issue surgical gown, green surgical mask, shoe covers, and a pair of latex gloves and spoke into a microphone attached to a tape recorder tucked underneath the steel table. The dead girl lay naked on cold steel, her pear-shaped body the color and texture of cream cheese. She seemed small for fourteen; her breasts had just begun to develop, and the fuzz of darkish pubic hair sprouting from her genitals was just about the saddest thing he'd ever seen.

Archie worked for two hours, reducing Melissa D'Agostino to a series of statistics. "Fourteen-year-old white female, manually strangulated. Dissection of the throat reveals extensive hemorrhage into the musculature and bilateral fractures of the thyroid and cricoid cartilage. Four foot eight, ninety-six pounds. Fair-skinned, dark-haired. Eyes, green. Eyelids oblique in the manner of most Mongoloids. Stumpy, pudgy hands and feet. Ears small and rounded with a badly developed lobule . . ."

On and on it went. When Archie took swabs from the girl's vagina and anus, Nalen felt a sharp sympathetic pinch in his groin like a stuck zipper. An X-ray film of the victim's skull was attached to a light box on the wall, the cranium cracked like an egg.

"Cause of death was occlusion of the blood vessels supplying blood to the brain," Archie told Nalen. "Most people mistakenly think it's the lack of air that kills you, but it's really due to the lack of blood going to the brain." He spoke into the mike. "There's bruising on the middle fingernail of her left hand. X rays indicate an old injury to the right arm, a fracture that's long since healed."

"So she didn't fight back?"

"I don't think she saw it coming. He hit her on the back of the skull . . . perhaps with a large rock. Possibly a tire iron." He pried the jaws apart and, using tongs, pulled out the extra-long tongue. "She has a high-saddle palate and irregular, malformed teeth. Probably sucked on her tongue, a habit that encourages fissuring and swelling of the papillae. See here?"

Nalen glanced at the tongue, then looked away.

"Those bite marks are severe."

"So it's your opinion she was strangled to death?"

"You see the fingernail marks on both sides of the neck? Two hands were used and the victim was strangled from the front. Erythematous marks, here and here, are posterior to the sternocleidomastoid muscles. But then he shifted his thumbs around to the front, see here? The two thumbs were used to apply pressure to the larynx and trachea, which results in erythematous markings on the anterior aspect of the neck."

"Would the perp have scratch marks on him?"

"Depends." Archie ruminated. "Remember that strangulation

case a few years back with the two fellows outside the Peaked Hills Bar and Grille? Even though the victim struggled, the assailant didn't have a single scratch on him."

"If he does have injuries," Nalen said, "they'd most likely be on the backs of the hands and arms."

"Maybe the face."

"What about rape?"

"As far as I can tell, no. We'll get the lab results in a week or so and we'll know more then."

"Okay," Nalen said, whipping off his surgical mask and tossing it in the trash. "Call me if there's anything else."

"I'll keep you posted, Chief."

Nalen found Billy over at Gillian Dumont's and drove the boy back to the station, where they sat together in his office. There were citations on the wall, photographs of Nalen with the mayor, his master's degree in criminal justice, and a montage of crime scene photos from unsolved cases. His desk was piled high with interview forms, evidence vouchers and unfiled autopsy reports.

"Billy," Nalen began, "what do you know about this?" He handed Billy the cat bell and the boy blanched.

"I dunno." He handed it back.

"You've never seen it before?"

"Looks like a cat bell or something."

"I know what it is, Billy." Nalen stared at him over steepled fingers. "I want you to tell me the truth."

Billy was a tall drink of water, a string bean who'd shot up three inches in the past year alone. Faye couldn't keep up with his adolescent appetite, always driving to the store for more food and doubling the milkman's order. Nalen could feel his son's agitation in the way he scratched his elbows and legs. His slender nose was slightly crooked (he'd broken it falling out of an apple tree at age seven) and he'd bitten his nails to the quick. Now he kept tugging anxiously on his red sweatshirt, the one with Aerosmith stenciled on the front.

"You know something," Nalen said firmly, thinking he could scare the truth out of him, "so you'd better come out with it."

"Maybe it belongs to one of those cats?" Billy said innocently enough.

"The cats you boys killed?"

"I don't know . . . probably . . . maybe." He shrugged, emptying his face of all emotion. Nalen hated that face. It went all the way back to Billy's childhood, back to his infancy, practically, to when Nalen used to drink. Before Faye had given him her ultimatum.

"I thought you said they were strays, those cats?" Nalen asked.

"They were."

"So how could a stray have a cat bell?"

"I dunno."

"You don't know?" Nalen leaned back, leather chair squeaking. "Was one of those cats you killed wearing a collar?"

"One of 'em might've been."

"Answer the question, Billy. Yes or no."

"I don't remember."

"So this bell—"

"I said I don't remember!" Billy wiped under his eyes and tapped his fingers nervously on the arms of his chair. "Jeez, Dad, what're you dragging all this stuff up again for?"

"Why do you think I'm bringing it up?"

"I don't know." His pupils contracted. "I'm not a mind reader."

"Billy . . ." Nalen rubbed his eyes. "The girl who disappeared yesterday . . . she's dead."

Billy grew very still and wouldn't meet his father's gaze.

"If you know something," Nalen said, "if you goddamn know anything, Billy, you'd better tell me right now. Right here. In this room. Between the two of us."

Billy sat with his head bowed, eyes downcast, and didn't speak for a long time.

"Billy," Nalen said, tension burrowing into his windpipe, and Billy jumped. "Do you know anything about Melissa D'Agostino?"

His forehead wrinkled in a frown. "Just that . . . you know . . . what somebody told me afterward . . . that it was her cat."

Hairs pricked the scruff of Nalen's neck. "So this cat bell belonged to Melissa D'Agostino's cat?"

"I told you a million times, it wasn't me. It was Ozzie and Neal. They're the ones who shot those cats."

"And you know for a fact that one of the cats belonged to Melissa D'Agostino?"

"It's just something I heard."

"All right." He ran his fingers through his hair and noticed he was trembling. "Let me ask you this. Were any of those cats wearing a collar?"

"I don't remember."

"Think, Billy."

The boy shrugged. "Yeah, maybe."

"But when Detective Boudreau and I got to the scene, there weren't any collars on any of the cats."

Billy crossed his arms and stared sullenly at the floor.

"So I can assume that, between the time you boys shot those cats and the time Detective Boudreau and I got to the scene, somebody stole that cat collar. Am I right?"

Billy didn't answer. All Nalen could see was the tip of his nose and the crown of his head with its soft brown hair, and for an instant, he had an urge to pat his son's head, to stir that soft hair and tell him everything was going to be okay. Only it wasn't going to be okay. Far from it.

"Billy, did one of the boys take the cat collar? Did *you* take the cat collar?"

"No," he said defensively. "I just wanted to get the hell out of there."

"So Ozzie and Neal . . . they took turns shooting the cats, and Boomer . . . Boomer was letting the cats out of the sack one by one . . . and you were sort of corralling the cats so that Ozzie and Neal could get a good shot. Is that right?"

He winced. "That's about right."

"And afterward, when all the cats were dead, somebody took the cat collar as a sort of souvenir?"

"No," he said, voice cracking. "We were pretty fucked up, Dad. I know it's a disgusting thing to do, shooting innocent creatures and all—"

"Billy, let's nail this down."

He looked at his father with pudding-colored eyes. "I wouldn't hurt anyone, Dad."

Nalen exhaled in frustration.

"D'you believe me?"

"Yes."

"You believe I wouldn't hurt anyone? I mean, just because I did something stupid like, over six months ago . . . 'cause I mean, you don't hate me or anything, do you?"

"No, son, I don't hate you."

"But you think less of me."

"I don't think less of you." Nalen shifted in his chair and the leather squeaked, advertising his discomfort. He'd always been uncomfortable around Billy. Always. All Billy had to do was look at him sideways, and Nalen would inwardly cringe as if he were on trial.

Abuse, Faye had called it. But Nalen was merely imitating his own dad, a Boston cop, a hard-drinking, hardworking hard-liner who loved his family even as he beat them. Early in his marriage, Nalen had followed in the old man's footsteps, getting drunk with the boys after work at the Blue Wall, beer and shots and boilermakers, and he'd almost lost Faye and Billy due to his own stupidity. Almost lost his family. She had threatened to leave him, but then he'd done the impossible, quit cold turkey, no twelve-step program for Nalen Storrow, thank you very much. And yet . . . and yet maybe he had lost them, after all?

"You keep looking at me funny," Billy was saying now, and Nalen glanced away.

"I guess I'm trying to figure you out."

"So maybe I did something really stupid just to be part of something . . . that doesn't mean I'd hurt anyone, does it?"

"You tell me."

"I mean . . . jeesh. She was retarded and everything."

Nalen could hear the beating of his own heart. Leaning forward, he held Billy's eye. "Roll up your sleeves."

Billy's voice rose half an octave. "You think I killed her?"

"Tell me, son," he said, "tell me you don't know anything about Melissa D'Agostino's death. Tell me that right now."

Indignant and scared, Billy rolled up the sleeves of his sweatshirt and displayed his bare arms. They were the arms of a scrawny teenager, abrasion-free.

"Okay." Nalen sat back, inwardly relieved.

"Jesus, is she really dead?"

"She was killed yesterday."

"Wow." He briefly met Nalen's gaze. "What happened?"

"That's all you need to know for now."

"Jeez, Dad." His eyes welled with tears and he slumped in his seat. "I'd never hurt anyone . . ."

"I know you wouldn't," Nalen said, but he knew, he just knew Billy was holding something back.

That night, Ozzie Rudd's father brought Ozzie into the station for questioning, and they didn't get much out of him, either. They also questioned Boomer Blazo and Neal Fliss. Nobody knew anything about any cat bell, and nobody had seen Melissa D'Agostino since the day she disappeared; not since lunch that day at school, not since they'd done their usual messing around with the kids at the Geek Table. All the retards ate lunch together at one big table, and Ozzie and Boomer and Neal liked to tease them a little bit. Just a little, and that was the last anybody'd seen of Melissa D'Agostino.

Around 10:00 P.M., Hughie Boudreau, drenched with sweat and exhaustion, pulled Nalen aside and said in an urgent whisper, "Chief, we gotta talk."

"What is it, Hughie?"

"Earlier at the morgue . . . ?" He balled his fingers into a fist as if he were trying to summon the courage to put into words what had been bothering him all day long.

"I'm listening."

"I was walking around the gurney, you know? And the strangest thing happened." He lowered his voice. "I could've sworn she was watching me."

Nalen sighed, muscles bunching. "It's a common experience, Hughie. Don't worry about it." He patted Hughie's arm, but Hughie wouldn't let the matter drop.

"She followed me with her eyes, it seems like, no matter where I was standing in the room."

"That's a common illusion, Hughie. Don't let it spook you."

"You're the only one I can confide in," Hughie said, pallid and frail-looking. "I don't know what came over me, but the next thing I knew . . . I was sticking my tongue out at her."

"You were what?"

"I had to push her away, you know?" His face was crimson. "'Stop looking at me' kind of thing. I realize now she wasn't looking at me. I know that, Chief. Dead people don't look at you. I know what's real and what's not."

"Are you sure you can handle all the ramifications of this case, Hughie?" Nalen asked as gently as he could.

"Sure, Chief. I mean, it's not like I'm crazy or anything."

"No, you're not crazy, Hughie."

"Please don't take me off the case, Chief. I'm really ashamed of myself."

Nalen was concerned. Hughie hadn't joined the search party the previous afternoon because he'd driven off by himself after a bad fight with his wife. He'd gone all the way to the New York state line, his fury slowly draining at the wheel, and hadn't reported to work until around eight o'clock that evening. He'd been gone all afternoon, and this fact hadn't rung any bells with Nalen until now.

"Look," Nalen said, "we're all under enormous strain. Let's just forget about it, okay?"

"Okay."

"Go home, Hughie."

"I'll sneak downstairs and take a nap."

"Go home. You're exhausted."

"I'm fine."

"You're gonna make a mistake. You're not alert."

"All right." Hughie hung his head.

"And remember, my door's always open."

Nalen watched him shuffle off, thinking you could implode so subtly, nobody would even notice.

6

AROUND THREE IN THE MORNING, NALEN PARKED HIS DODGE Challenger in the driveway and crossed the front yard under a full moon that lit the toolshed and lawn chairs and made deep night seem like the dusty moments before dawn. All the lights in the house were off and the door was locked. He fumbled for his keys, let himself in.

Upstairs everybody was asleep. He crossed the moonlit hall

into Rachel's room, leaned over her bed and inhaled her sweet scent. Her lips parted with a bubble.

"Daddy?" She stirred in the sheets.

"What is it, sweetheart?"

"Is the retarded girl in heaven now?"

He sat on the edge of her bed, careful not to squash her feet. On her bedside table was a box of shells from their most recent trip to the seashore, a butterfly barrette, a Mickey Mouse key-chain. "Yes," he said, "I think she is."

"Daddy?"

"What, Pickle?"

"Tell me again how you get into heaven?"

He sighed, feeling the birdlike throb of her breath against his arm. "A long time ago, the Greeks believed that after you died, your soul went to heaven. And the gods put your heart on a big scale— your heart on one side of the scale, and a feather on the other side."

"What's the feather for?"

She already knew, but he told her anyway. "It's the symbol for truth. If your heart is full of lies and meanness and cruelty, it'll be much heavier than the feather and you'll get thrown back down to earth because you're not ready yet. But if your heart is as light as the feather . . . if it's empty of lies, and full of goodness and truth, then the gods will open the gates and you can waltz right in."

She wrinkled her nose. "Was the retarded girl's heart as light as a feather?"

"I think so, yes."

"How about mine, Daddy?"

Nalen kissed her cheek. "Don't worry, sweetheart. Yours is light as a huckleberry."

Nalen stripped in the dark, crawled between the pretzel-smelling sheets and drew Faye close. They lay for a while like that before she spoke, her voice scratchy with sleep. "Let's not fight."

"No, I don't want to fight anymore."

She was warm and tensile in his arms, moonlight from the window washing over the strange planes of her face. "Nalen?"

"Hi."

"I had this dream you drove off a cliff and died."

The room was so quiet, the clock sounded like a bass drum. "It's all right," he said. "We're gonna be fine."

"Are we?" Her exhausted eyes were on him. "Really?"

"Yeah."

"So what happened tonight?"

"Nothing much."

"Any suspects?"

"Not yet."

"Oh God, I feel sick." She rolled away from him and he lightly ran his hand along her bumpy spine, muscles bunching beneath her musk-smelling skin. "I almost called the precinct," she admitted.

"Sorry. I forgot. We were swamped."

"I hate you."

Very gently, he stroked the nape of her neck. "No, you don't."

"Yes, I do. I hate you."

"Faye . . ." he said, drawing out her name until it sounded like a prayer.

"You never listen."

"I'm listening now."

"No." She twisted around to face him, her worry and frustration palpable. "You keep shutting me out. You shut us all out, Nalen."

"No, I don't."

"Yes, you do. You don't realize it, but you do. There are days . . . whole days where you'll say maybe two words. I don't understand you."

He knew what she was talking about. She was talking about

his black moods. Whenever a black mood hit, he'd go for a walk in the woods or else down to the basement where he could be alone. Down in the basement, he'd sit in the semidark and think about the past. His mind whirred like a movie projector as he relived long-ago times with his brothers and mother and father. Mostly his father. Good ol' Pop, with his adrenaline-loaded sweat and his stinky boozy breath, cleaning his service revolver at the kitchen table. "You ready?" he'd ask. Nalen wouldn't blink as Sheldon Storrow slid a single bullet into the chamber, spun it and held the gun to his son's temple.

"You ready?"

Nalen would squirm like a pinned insect as Pop waited an eternal, gut-churning beat, Nalen's eyes swelling shut, his brain collapsing in fear . . . and then *click.* That particular flavor of hell. He'd piss his pants and get a lungful of cheap-beer-and-good-jukebox breath, and Pop would lean back laughing. "What'd I tell ya, son? You were born with a horseshoe up your ass."

Now Nalen took a deep breath. "I'm sorry, Faye," he said, coming up for air. "I don't mean to shut you out."

Her face crimped, and she stroked his cheek with her curled index finger. "I hate him for what he did to you."

"Pop? He had a rough life."

"Achh. See that?" She glowered. "Always leaping to his defense. This man who beat his wife and kids. And we're still suffering the aftereffects, me and the children. I'm glad the bastard's dead."

"You don't mean that."

"Yes, I do."

Something inside the house creaked, and he bolted upright, reaching for his service revolver and listening for the sound of footsteps or the creak of a door—but there was only silence. It was okay. They were safe. For now.

She was lying there, watching him, disgust stamped on her face. "You always expect the worst."

"No, I don't."

"It's like we're all biding our time until the sky comes crashing down around our heads."

He tried to laugh it off, but secretly he knew she was right. He was a pessimist's pessimist. He tucked his revolver back in the drawer of the bedside table and settled down beside her. Her breath smelled sweet-and-sour and her eyes glinted with Faye's own patented brand of fury. "I don't always live my life that way."

Her voice was small. "You need counseling."

"We're not having this discussion."

"Why can't you just acknowledge something's seriously wrong, Nalen?" Her rage flared. "We do not have the perfect marriage, you are not the perfect father, our children are suffering . . ."

"What time did Billy get home last night?" he asked, stopping her in midsentence. She looked at him with wary eyes.

"About six-thirty. Why?"

"Six-thirty?"

She sharpened her focus. "Why?"

"Did he go out later on?"

"He drove over to Gillian's around eight. Why?"

"When did he get back from Gillian's?"

"Where are you going with this, Nalen?"

"Nowhere. Just curious."

She stared at him. "He went out at eight o'clock and came back at ten-thirty, just like I asked him to."

Nalen chewed on his lower lip.

"What's so important?"

"I didn't say it was."

"Is Billy in trouble?" He wouldn't answer, and she grabbed his ears and twisted. "Tell me."

"Ow." His face grew hot. His ears stung, and he pried her hands off him. "It's probably nothing."

"Probably?"

His blood was thrumming through his veins and he was reminded of long-ago days early in their marriage when their love-making had been full of passion, passion verging on violence—not truly, not really—but something close to wrestling and a heated exchange of words, a torrent of emotions, the pivotal one being jealousy. Crazy jealousy. He remembered once inside their little apartment, the neighbors had called the cops and they'd had to explain that, no, Officer—sheepish and half naked—no, they'd just been *dancing*. And giggled about it later. And jokes down at the precinct.

And once Faye had been so furious, so raging lunatic jealous, she'd locked herself in the bathroom and threatened to slit her wrists. He'd been talking to another woman where they were supposed to meet for dinner, a little Italian place off Tremont Street, and she'd entered the restaurant looking like a million bucks, a real knockout; but when she saw him with the woman (who'd come up to him because he was in uniform, they were all over the place, those cop groupies), Faye spun around on her heels and stormed out, and he'd chased her down the sidewalk and all the way home, she crying bitterly, her betrayed face . . . and she'd locked herself in the bathroom and he'd had to kick the door in, and she'd stood there with a razor blade poised above her wrist . . . and he'd cried with her. The two of them holding each other on the cold tiled floor, him pledging his eternal love. And only later, much later, had she confessed that she'd only been pretending to slit her wrists, that she had in fact sustained that pose during the time it'd taken him to kick the door down . . .

Now Nalen was kissing her, his strong arms tentacled around her as she struggled against his weight.

"I'm still angry," she said as he rocked them off balance.

"I'm sorry, Faye. Don't hate me, Faye."

And finally her muscles relaxed, giving in, and he knew she would never stop resenting him, never stop feeling trapped, and that this—his burning hunger and her bitter resistance—was the sum total of their lives together.

FIVE PAST MIDNIGHT THE FOLLOWING SATURDAY, NALEN rubbed his face hard. "Okay, people," he said, exhaustion slurring his speech, "what've we got?"

They were seated around the conference table—Nalen and McKissack, Detective Sergeant Guy Fletcher, dispatcher Phillip Reingold, and Detectives Hughie Boudreau and Irving Nussbaum. A squat black bookcase crammed with mug shot binders leaned crookedly against the wall to their left, and a mini-fridge used for bag lunches hummed industriously to their right. The empty terrarium on top of the refrigerator had once housed a live tarantula until somebody'd sprayed it with a lethal dose of Windex; now there was nothing inside but a rubber octopus floating on a sea of rubber bands everybody took turns shooting into it. The carpet was a dingy, coffee-stained maroon.

"Anybody else want a cup?" Hughie helped himself to coffee from the machine, stirred in three heaping tablespoons of powdered nondairy creamer and sat back down.

"Okay." Nalen's stomach cramped at the thought of all that powdered creamer. "What've we got, people? What, what, what?"

"No abduction site," McKissack began. "No weapon. No eyewitnesses. No physical evidence." He rocked back smugly in his chair and chewed on a toothpick, since Nalen didn't allow smoking inside the station. McKissack claimed he needed to keep his mouth moving no matter what—pencil, chewing gum, finger. Claimed he had an oral fixation. "Oh, and did I mention . . . *no suspects?*"

"Well, gee whiz . . . thanks for nothing, Lieutenant," Nalen said, refusing to let his best detective's hard-bitten cynicism get the better of him. "Now let's see what we *do* have." He flipped open the case file. "We picked up some fibers on the victim's clothes. Dark green, synthetic. Ten percent wool, sixty percent rayon, thirty percent nylon."

"Wow, that eliminates one percent of the population," McKissack said with snide glee.

Nalen bristled to life. "What d'you want, McKissack? You want my fucking job? Here, take my fucking hat."

McKissack threw up his hands. "I don't want your job, Chief. They aren't paying you enough."

Nalen couldn't help smiling. That broke the tension.

"The sooner we wrap things up," he said, "the sooner we can all go home."

"She disappeared sometime shortly after school let out on Tuesday," Hughie Boudreau began. Stress had painted violet circles underneath his eyes. "The medical examiner's best guess for time of death is somewhere between five-thirty and six-thirty P.M. No later than six-thirty. That leaves four hours, give or take, still unaccounted for."

"There's our window," Nalen said. "Two-thirty to six-thirty P.M."

"It's like she disappeared off the face of the earth," Guy Fletcher said. At six-foot-four, Fletcher was 220 pounds of ripped muscle and Algonquin heritage inside an old biker jacket. "Nobody saw anything."

"These retarded kids are apparently highly ritualized in their behavior," Irving Nussbaum interrupted. Nussbaum sometimes joked he was the only Jew in Maine. Squat and balding, he'd gravitated here from New York City after having burnt out on big-city violence, just like Nalen. "Mom and Pop say Melissa was committed to her routine. Every morning when she brushed her teeth, she always touched the bathroom faucet twice before turning it on. She squeezed the toothpaste out carefully onto her toothbrush, then rolled up the bottom just like her daddy taught her to. In a similar vein, she had a specific route home she rarely deviated from."

"What I wanna know is," McKissack said, "what's a kid like that doing in high school?"

"It's called mainstreaming," Nalen said. "Go on, Irving."

"Trinka Parsons says every weekday at about quarter to three, Melissa walks past her house."

"Every day at two-forty P.M.," Hughie corrected him, "the Parsons' dog runs up to Melissa, and Melissa plays with her for a minute or two, then waves bye-bye to Trinka. Then she's on her way."

"She always exits the northern-facing doors at school, then heads south on Bellamy, right onto Addams, left on Crowing Heights, left on Spencer." Nussbaum scratched his chin. "Not once did she deviate from this route."

"Trinka Parsons thought Melissa was out sick on Tuesday," Hughie said, "because the dog kept wagging its tail and gazing longingly up the street, but Melissa never showed."

"The Parsons live on Crowing Heights, so that narrows it down to somewhere between Bellamy and Addams."

"What about the partial?" McKissack asked, propping his feet on the table. Nalen didn't mind people propping their feet on the conference table after midnight; it was the territorial way McKissack did it that bothered him. As if he owned the place.

"It's pretty nondescript." Nalen pinched the bridge of his nose, trying to squeeze more information out of his brain. "No tread, size nine or nine and a half . . ."

"Not a terribly big guy. That fits with the fact that the body was dragged rather than carried down to the pond," McKissack said.

"Nobody at school saw anything unusual." Hughie leafed through a stack of interview forms. "It's perplexing."

"It's like she was invisible," Fletcher said again, and Nalen detected the angry residue in his voice. "Nobody noticed her when she was there. Nobody noticed her when she was gone."

"What about the hotline?"

"We're getting plenty of calls," Phillip Reingold, the dispatcher, said. "Mostly asking if we've found any suspects yet. Folks are pretty scared."

"That all?"

"Plenty of leads. Most of 'em dead ends."

"Every lead's a dead end," McKissack growled. "I hate this."

"Any anonymous tips?" Nalen asked.

Phillip flipped through his logbook. "One caller says he saw a girl matching the victim's description walking through the Commerce City mall at around six o'clock Tuesday night . . ."

Nalen shook his head. "Doesn't fit the time frame."

"Another caller, this one female, spotted a girl matching the victim's description riding in the front seat of a green car heading south on Route 88 toward the exit at Foggy Bottom around 4:30 P.M."

"Green car? Could you be more specific?"

"A green sedan, maybe. She couldn't describe the driver except to say he was probably male. She noticed the girl because of her Down's syndrome."

McKissack shot a pencil into the terrarium, which bothered Nalen. The terrarium was meant for rubber bands only. That was the irritating thing about McKissack, he made up his own rules.

Nalen leaned forward. "Archie found the remains of a vanilla ice cream cone in her stomach. Now obviously she didn't get that walking home from school."

Hughie closed his eyes. "Bludgeoned and strangled," he whispered like some perverse prayer. "No blood or skin in the nail scrapings. No semen."

Nalen leaned back and sighed. His eye caught a memo tacked to the wall above the coffee machine: DUE TO COST CONSTRAINTS, THE LIGHT AT THE END OF THIS TUNNEL HAS BEEN TEMPORARILY DISCONNECTED. The town had recently laid off three patrol officers, leaving only two detectives under the supervision of a detective sergeant, ten patrol officers under the command of a sergeant, two secretaries, the dispatcher, Lieutenant McKissack and himself. The conference room was on the second floor. Down the hall was the squad room and the locker room. Downstairs were the jail cells and the dispatcher's station, and upstairs was Nalen's office, the detectives' suite and the storage rooms. The building was 150 years old, and sometimes you could hear the stairs creak when there was nobody else in the building.

Guy Fletcher wiped the hair out of his eyes, his frustration palpable. "We're gonna find this animal. One day we're gonna knock on his door, and this fucking animal's gonna get the death penalty."

Nalen tapped his fingers on the blowup photograph before him. Melissa smiled broadly into the camera, eyes wide and inquisitive. She was the essence of innocence. Her left hand was raised as if to wave hello, and Nalen spotted the bracelet—red and yellow yarn woven in a simple diamond pattern tied securely around her left wrist. The missing friendship bracelet.

Melissa D'Agostino had stuck close by her teachers in Special Ed. She liked birthday parties, caramel apples, and drawing pictures at school. Nalen had a sample of her artwork right in front of him—a purple monster with pinwheeling eyes and thick black brushstroke eyebrows hovering hungrily over three smaller figures—father, mother, little girl.

You always expect the worst.

"How much overtime do we have approval for?" McKissack asked, his edginess contagious. The whole room was vibrating now with his impatience. The men were clearly ready to go home.

"Keep track of your hours." Nalen gathered his papers. "I don't care how long it takes, I don't care if it takes us to the end of the next century, we're not eating this one."

"I don't know about you guys." McKissack landed in his chair with a thud. "But I could use a drink."

8

NALEN, MCKISSACK, PHILLIP REINGOLD AND HUGHIE BOU-dreau were seated at a booth inside a bar called Big Tee's. McKissack signaled the waitress for another pitcher. "More beer for the horses!" Nalen was drinking nonalcoholic O'Doul's beer. The fact that he no longer drank, didn't smoke and rarely swore set him apart, and he didn't like being set apart, but there you were.

McKissack was checking out a fake driver's license he'd seized from an underage, pimple-faced kid. The quality was poor—the edges didn't match and the glue showed. Ripping it up, McKissack said, "Vamoose," and the kid hightailed it out of there, trailing cops' laughter in his wake. "Stupid kid tries to pass in a police bar, of all places."

Nalen could taste the length of the day on his tongue. His jawbone ached, and suddenly he wanted nothing more than to crawl into bed with his wife. Her hands would be pressed together on her pillow like two pale leaves.

"It breaks you up," Hughie was saying, and Nalen could almost count the slender hairs that composed his scraggly mustache.

"I know, Hughie," Nalen nodded.

"It just breaks you up, that's all."

"I know."

"You get annoyed."

"Okay, Hughie."

"Chief," he said, eyes narrowing in the manner of a drunk's when he thinks he's about to say something profound, "sometimes I'm out there at four in the morning, y'know? And the whole town's asleep, and I can't help thinking to myself, these people don't realize . . . they don't realize there's bad guys running around, doing things at four in the morning. Drugs, prostitution, domestic violence . . . this town doesn't want to admit it has any problems. It doesn't want to admit that it has any weaknesses at all."

"Hughie." Nalen stifled a yawn. "I'm beat."

"Me, too, Chief. I'm beat, too. I'm beyond exhaustion. I'm be-yausted."

McKissack's eyes danced with amusement.

"I'm consumed," Hughie said. "Is that a word?"

"Yeah, so is asshole."

"Shut up, McKissack."

"Gentlemen, please."

They decided to order some food to sop up the alcohol. Nalen hadn't had a drop since 1970, but before then he used to haunt the bars after pounding the beat. All those brick sidewalks, all that snow and slush, all those hippie drug dealers and dead hookers and runaways. And then one night, he got drunk and threw his six-year-old son against the living room wall, and that was that. No more alcohol. It took him three months to convince Faye he meant what he said and that he could do it without AA or any of those self-help groups. Looking into Billy's face was reminder enough. The hurt and betrayal emanating from his son's eyes was like a blinding light you couldn't stare at for too long.

Now Nalen hunched over a plate of greasy fries and whacked the bottom of the ketchup bottle until the red stuff plopped out like hot fudge. Vera walked over to their table. Vera was a friend of McKissack's.

"Bet I can guess how old you are," she told Nalen, sizing him up. Her hair was like a soft knot of yarn, and she hid her freckles under too much makeup. She put her cigarette out in the ashtray on the table, carnival pink lipstick staining the filter. "Thirty-nine," she guessed.

"Forty-three," he said, grinning.

"Ooh. Close."

Vera grabbed McKissack's wrist and tried to yank him to his feet. A slow song was playing, but McKissack wouldn't budge. He sat like a boulder while Vera pleaded, "Just one little dance?"

"We're discussing police matters."

"Oh sure, Officer Shithead." She planted a lingering kiss on McKissack's lips. When she released him, he reeled backward and laughed. Vera lit another cigarette.

"What's Sheila going to say?" Hughie admonished them.

"I ain't married yet," McKissack said.

"Yeah, but you're engaged, aren't you?"

"Okay, c'mere." McKissack grabbed Vera around the waist and swung her onto his lap. She seemed comfortable there, her face flushing slightly.

"I've been having the weirdest dreams lately," she told them between puffs, "like I don't exist anymore. Not in this dimension anyway. I'm crossing a room, I take a step and start sinking into the floor." She took a sip of Nalen's O'Doul's, made a sour face and set it down with amazing gentleness. She had a pretty laugh.

McKissack kissed her mouth. "Oof, you're heavy."

She stood. "Go ahead, spoil the romance."

McKissack stretched his arms over the back of the booth, muscles hyperactive under his swarthy skin. "Don't talk to me about romance," he said.

"It's all we've got left, honey."

"Not if you use a condom."

"Christ, you're crude." She laughed. "You can all talk about me now," she said, walking away.

Nalen yawned, trying to pop his ears. It surprised him how some people didn't care about the murder anymore. Already yesterday's news. The haze in the bar was like a forgotten dream. He took out his wallet, a pitiful reminder of the kind of money he didn't make.

"I dunno." Hughie shook his head. "I've always been of the opinion that there's a little bit of good in everybody."

"Then let me remind you," McKissack said gruffly, "you haven't met everybody yet."

"So what d'you think happens when you die?" Hughie asked no one in particular.

"You're shitfaced." McKissack laughed.

"I believe you go to heaven if you're good. I honestly do."

"Yeah, right," McKissack said. "You and Santa and the Easter bunny. What's heaven, anyway? Angels floating on cottony clouds? Clouds can't hold anything up, they're just vapor. And if you could stick a million souls on the head of a pin, who'd need clouds anyway? And what I really want to know is, if all life is sacred, then do mosquitoes end up in heaven, too? Or just cats and dogs and things we like?"

Hughie laughed drunkenly. "I don't have the faintest fucking idea." He laughed until he nearly choked, and Nalen had to pat him on the back, then his shoulders slumped in a defeated sort of way and he said, "We're gonna nail this guy. Right, Chief?"

Counting out his money, Nalen pretended not to hear.

Hughie turned to McKissack. "We're gonna find him, right, McKissack?"

"Don't worry, Hughie," McKissack said with a wink. "The chief here could look up a bull's asshole and give you the price of butter."

"That's what I thought." Hughie nodded confidently.

"I guarantee you we will nail this guy," Nalen said, and in the silence that followed, you could hear an evidence bag drop.

"Look, look, look." Hughie passed out, his nose squashed flat against the tabletop, gold flecks buried in the pink Formica.

"I'll take him home," Nalen said.

Vera hurried over. "Uh-oh, he's dead." She giggled. "Quick, check his pulse."

"Hughie?"

"Come on, partner." Nalen helped him to his feet, and he and McKissack supported him between them.

People were smiling. Waving good night.

"See that, Chief?" Hughie said.

"You're a lot heavier than you look, Boudreau."

"You see it?"

"See what."

"Her eyes? Did you see her eyes, Chief?"

"Shut up, Hughie."

"You saw her eyes, too, didn't you?"

"You're skunked."

"You saw her eyes, too."

9

IN THE MIDDLE OF THE NIGHT, NALEN FELT A CAT WALKING across the foot of the bed, only they didn't own a cat. He bolted awake and yanked his pistol from its holster, heart hammering.

Melissa D'Agostino was seated at the foot of the bed, mattress bobbing as she restlessly shifted her weight. She looked just like her pictures—dark hair, green eyes, that endearing pie face. She sat perched on the end of his bed as if somebody had told her to wait there. She didn't seem to want anything from him.

Nalen realized he was dreaming. He tried to wake himself up, heart slamming around in his rib cage. He couldn't move his arms. "Wake up," he told himself, then felt two dead fingers on his forehead.

His eyes popped open. The room was checkered with shadows, vague forms appearing just beyond his range of vision. His arms and legs felt weighted with bricks. He struggled to sit up. Through slitted eyes, he saw a dark figure flit out into the hallway. Fully awake now, he reached for his .38 and leapt out of bed.

The floor was cool. Nalen headed down the hallway in a combat stance, head snapping at the slightest sound. Hands shaking.

Thwunk.

He spun around.

"Dad?" Billy came out of his bedroom, rubbing his eyes. He reminded Nalen so much of the sleepy kid who'd once crawled into bed with them because he thought there was a wolf in his closet. "Dad, what's wrong?"

Nalen stared blankly, then slowly lowered his pistol. The boy's expression did not change; he seemed unafraid, still half asleep. When he yawned, Nalen could see the velvety deep part of his throat.

"Nothing," Nalen said without smiling. "Go back to sleep."

10

NALEN'S STOMACH TURNED SOURLY AS HE BELCHED UP THE taste of the chili dog he'd had for supper. All his men were out in the field, so he was stuck doing phone duty. Several evidence bags were lined up on the desk before him—the dozen or so shards of green glass; the matchbook from Dale's Discount Hardware, no fingerprints; the length of red thread, perhaps from the girl's missing friendship bracelet; and the small piece of paper torn in the shape of Italy, some gummy substance on one side from where it had wedged itself into Melissa's sneaker tread.

Now the phone rang and he picked up. "Police department, how can I help you?"

"Hello?" came the hesitant, high-pitched voice of a teenage girl. "I have some information?"

"Go ahead, I'm listening."

"About the girl who was murdered?"

"Yes?" He leaned forward to scribble the time and date in his logbook. "Go on," he said as gently as he could so as not to alarm her.

"I'm not gonna turn anybody in or anything . . ."

"That's fine." Nalen listened with every fiber of his being. "Go ahead."

"Am I being recorded?"

"No, ma'am."

"I don't wanna give you my name . . ."

"You can remain anonymous if you'd like. Just say what's on your mind."

"Okay." She hesitated. "This guy . . . he's a good person underneath, but sometimes he does stupid things . . ."

"I'm listening."

"He picked her up . . ."

"Melissa D'Agostino?"

"Yeah, he picked her up after school and we . . . he drove her over to Commerce City . . ."

"He who?"

"Excuse me?"

"Who picked her up and drove her to Commerce City?"

"This guy I know."

"What's his name?"

"All he did was buy her an ice cream cone. That's all. He wouldn't kill anybody. A few other guys came along for the ride . . ."

"Could you give me some names?"

"We . . . they were just goofing on her, that's all. Just goofing. They bought her an ice cream cone. You know how people are. They didn't do anything bad to her, I swear to God."

"What's the name of this boy who drove her to Commerce City?"

There was a long pause.

"If you know something, miss, I sure as heck wish you'd share it with me. You'd be doing the right thing."

Her voice was barely audible now. "Ozzie Rudd."

Goose bumps rose on his body like a sudden sprinkling of rain. "Ozzie Rudd?"

"I think," she said, "this was a mistake."

"Wait—"

The line went dead.

11

NALEN SPED TOWARD ROOSEVELT HIGH, WHERE GILLIAN Dumont's mother said that Billy and Gillian had gone. It was nine o'clock, the sky was overcast and the school seemed deserted. He circled the parking lot, then got out and crossed the athletic field toward the bleachers. Resting his palm against a diseased maple tree, he scanned the back of the school building. A couple of second-floor windows were decorated with construction-paper flowers, and he wondered if that was Special Ed or the art department. The athletic field was well lit, bleachers casting spidery shadows.

Nalen's ears pricked as he heard distant melodic laughter. He cocked his head. A girl was laughing. Breaking into a run, he charged around the side of the building, beaming his flashlight. As he rounded the corner, a girl screamed.

Nalen bolted after the two figures. Two kids were running up the block ahead of him. "Police, freeze!" He was nearly out of breath when he hooked the boy by the back of his T-shirt and flung him to the ground, then jumped on top of him.

Billy stared up at his father, terrified.

The girl stopped running and stood about ten yards away. Her face was small and pale, her eyes stoned-looking. "Don't hurt him!" She kept brushing her long hair off her face.

"What'd you run for?" Nalen screamed in Billy's face, yanking him to his feet.

"I'm sorry, Dad." Billy cowered.

"Why the hell did you run away?" he demanded to know. Billy's eyes were red-rimmed.

"Dad, we didn't know it was you."

Nalen grabbed him by the T-shirt and shook him hard. "Don't you ever run from the police again, you hear me? You know better than that, Billy!"

"Ouch, you're hurting me!"

Nalen released the boy, who stumbled backward.

Gillian stood shivering in the damp night air. "We were smoking. *Cigarettes.*" She looked at Billy. "That's why we ran."

"I don't think so." Patting Billy down, Nalen found a joint and a Bic lighter in his pants pockets. "What the hell is this?"

"Pot," Billy answered matter-of-factly.

"That's mine." Gillian stepped forward. She was playing with a necklace made of painted wooden beads. Her hair was almost white, the kind of blond that wasn't ashamed to show off its roots. She bit her lips sensually, as if she'd seen too many perfume ads on TV. "I asked Billy to hold it for me. If you're gonna arrest someone arrest me."

Nalen looked at her, then at his son. Tears welled in Billy's eyes and his shoulders sagged beneath his too-big T-shirt. Nalen pocketed the joint and grabbed Billy's arm, practically tearing it out of its socket as he pulled him away from his overprotective girlfriend.

"All right now," Nalen hissed, "I know you know more than you're letting on."

"Huh?"

"About Melissa D'Agostino. Ozzie Rudd picked her up after school last Tuesday and drove her over to Commerce City, didn't he? Tell me the truth, Billy. Were you involved?"

"No way, Dad . . ."

"Billy." He resisted a terrible urge to hit him. "Cut the crap. Either you tell me the truth right now, or I'm arresting you for possession. Simple as that."

Billy stared at him with wounded eyes.

"Billy?" Gillian cried, and Nalen turned to her.

"Stay back, young lady."

She did as she was told.

"Dad . . ."

"Tell me."

"Dad . . . I don't—"

"Tell me!"

Billy's mouth contorted and blinding tears spilled from his eyes as he confessed, "All right, all right . . . *I was there* . . ."

Nalen felt the words like an electric shock and almost lost his balance, horror cinching up his gut. He stared hopelessly at his tormented son. "What d'you mean, *you were there?*"

"You wanted the truth, right? So I'm telling you the truth!" Billy cried. "Ozzie picked her up on Bellamy Road and a bunch of us drove to Commerce City together. It was no big deal. We got some ice cream and cruised around for a while, that's all. We were just goofing on her, Dad."

Just goofing on her. Nalen could barely fathom the cruelty contained within those four little words. Nothing on God's green earth was less merciful than a child. "Who else was involved?"

"This junior named Michelle. She rode in the Grey Ghost with me, and Neal and Boomer took Boomer's dad's car, and Ozzie and Dolly took Melissa in the Green Hornet. *Nothing happened.*"

"Is that why you kept it from me? Because nothing happened?"

"I knew you wouldn't believe me. I can tell you still think I decapitated those cats."

"I never said as much, did I?"

"We were just having a little fun. I kept telling them not to. I told them we should let her go, and finally we drove back and Ozzie let her out."

"Let her out where?"

"You know . . . Black Hill Road."

"Let her out on Black Hill Road?"

"Yeah, and then we took off. So we're innocent."

"You let her out all alone on some deserted street?" Nalen slapped his son across the face, and Billy screamed.

"Billy!" Gillian ran to him.

"I didn't kill her!" Billy shrieked, and Nalen hated him just then. Tasting his own sour breath, he loosened his tie. He could see stars swimming in his field of vision . . . red stars. The boy's face was pale and blank, Billy's patented emotionless expression, and Nalen hated him for being a constant reminder of his former self . . . of his lack of control. Physical, flesh-and-blood evidence of his buried, abusive past.

"I didn't!" Billy protested from somewhere far away. A nasty desperation clawed at Nalen's insides, and he spun around and vomited in the grass. He vomited until he got the dry heaves. The beatings would often come after the vomiting, beatings accompanied by the smell of bile and alcohol. Nalen almost blacked out, and then a pair of cool hands were propping him up against a tree. He caught himself on the damp bark. Gillian was tapping his face, whispering, "Yoo hoo, Chief Storrow?"

He groaned.

"Hey. Hello. You okay?" She put her hands on his face.

"Stop." He shoved her away and she stumbled backward, then righted herself. She regarded him with skeptical eyes. He glanced around for his son. "Where's Billy?"

She stared at him. "Are you sure you're okay?"

"Gillian," he said, straining for the most normal tone of voice he could muster, "you'll only get yourselves into worse trouble. Come down to the station and we'll straighten things out."

"You never believed him," she said with an adolescent's obstinate contempt, her eyes sparking with candor. "He didn't hurt Melissa D'Agostino. He came over to my house. He was with me from five-thirty to six-thirty that night, so he couldn't have done anything, right? How could you even think such a thing? Billy wouldn't hurt a living soul!"

Nalen drew himself upright, then saw stars and collapsed back against the tree. He felt helpless. Ridiculous.

"You're sweating all over the place," she called from across the road. She was moving swiftly away, under cover of darkness. "I hope you're okay and everything!" Then she was gone.

It took Nalen several aching minutes to drag his carcass back to his car. He sagged in his seat, breathing laboriously and wondering how he was going to tell Faye. His hands trembled as if he'd been squeezing oranges. This was awful. He wanted to go home and cower under the covers like a little boy, but there would be no cowering. He knew what had to be done.

Head pounding, he keyed the ignition, and a squirrel, caught in his high beams, danced around a small circle of space.

12

NALEN STOOD IN THE KITCHEN AND LISTENED TO THE WIND howling through the scrub pines. Half past nine, nobody was home. Faye had taken Rachel to her first piano recital, yet another event in his children's lives he had missed. Another reason for Faye's anger to fester. Billy was off somewhere conspiring with Gillian. His son, now permanently lost to him.

Nalen's chest muscles constricted around his rib cage and an acid taste burned the back of his throat. The kitchen's overhead fluorescent bulb cast sickly shadows down the green walls and across the dingy linoleum. He'd just come in from outdoors where he'd inspected Billy's car—the Grey Ghost, a '76 Chevy Impala—and found nothing. Now, knowing what had to be done, he headed up the stairs.

Billy's room smelled of soiled socks. Nalen stood for a moment on the threshold, gut seizing. Surely it couldn't be true. Billy was innocent. He hadn't hurt Melissa D'Agostino, he'd simply gone along for the ride. He'd been morally wrong, ethically wrong, but legally innocent. He hadn't decapitated those cats. Billy wasn't capable of such depravity. Was he?

Nalen stepped cautiously into the room, booby-trapped with comic books and eight-track tapes and a tangle of clothes. If Billy was innocent, then why had he repeatedly lied? And why had Gillian insisted they'd spent Tuesday evening together from 5:30 to 6:30? Her little speech sounded forced. Almost coached.

Taking a deep breath, he began to methodically search the room for clues. A warrantless search. Illegal. His stomach clenched. He could barely admit to himself what it was he was looking for—Melissa's friendship bracelet. After stirring through the detritus of this teenage wasteland, Nalen discovered in the far reaches of the closet a pair of muddy sneakers, their treads worn down to nonexistence, size nine and a half. Jesus. It took a moment for this to register. He examined the sneakers carefully, turning them over in his hands. Not that it proved anything. What teenage boy didn't have a pair of muddy sneakers in his closet?

Nalen set the sneakers aside and continued poking and prodding around his son's bedroom. Parental betrayal, professional betrayal. He couldn't find the bracelet anywhere—bureau drawers, bedside table, bookshelves, foot locker. His heart momentarily lightened. The boy's desk was a disaster area of textbooks, crumpled papers, empty milk cartons, leaky pens and nubby pencils. He flipped through an algebra book, then noticed a yellow lined pad covered with doodles. The top page was torn, a small piece missing. The missing piece was in the shape of Italy. The boot.

Nalen froze as if he'd caught a gang of bullets in his heart. He picked up the pad and studied it, as if by staring at it he might make it go away. He'd lost touch with Billy a long time ago. Lost touch with his concerns, his preoccupations. Billy was like a little mystery he kept stubbornly trying to find the keys to. Occasionally he caught the boy staring at him with a mixture of resentment and longing, and he would try to think of something fatherly to say, something wise or profound, but the words eluded him. How did you explain to a sixteen-year-old that it hurt to look into his eyes because he reminded you of your own shameful past?

Nalen examined the notepad, its top page ripped across the midsection, the small, torn-away portion located in the lower right-hand corner. Had Melissa been inside Billy's car? Had this notepad been on the floor of the car? Had Billy startled or scared her, compelling her to break away and run into the field? Had Billy pursued her there?

Now the house shook with wind and his breath quickened as he tore the top page out of the yellow lined pad, balled it up and took it downstairs with him. Holding the paper over the kitchen sink, he lit it on fire, then ran the cold water, watching ashes swirl down the drain. Everything hurt. His brain felt broken. He thought of his father, pinned beneath the wreckage of his police cruiser after a high-speed chase gone bad. Had his father in his dying moments realized he'd let his son down? Did he admit to himself he'd caused damage? Did he think of death, in those last few precious moments, as *a little sleep, a little slumber, a little folding of the hands?*

Nalen went outside and crossed the darkened backyard into the alfalfa field, sweet and legume-smelling. He scaled the rusty barbed wire fence and sat on a low stone wall facing the swamp, where gentian and wood sorrel grew on the spongy bog surface. Every once in a while, he brought Billy down here with him, and they'd count the stars in the great big sky and try in vain to hold a conversation. In the distance, beneath a brilliant cheese-colored moon, he could make out the windswept fir-clad ridges of the surrounding mountains, and closer and all around these fields and jumbled boulders, the black dense woods.

What a brutal night, stars nailed to an indifferent sky. He took the cat bell out of his pocket and flung it as far as he could into the swamp. He thought he heard the rustling of the upland lady fern as the cat bell landed, but it could've been his imagination. The wind picked up, a dull roar in his ears, and he drew his service revolver. Perhaps some other persevering do-gooder would find Billy guilty of murder, but it wasn't going to be him. His chest rose and fell, rose and fell, and suddenly it occurred to him that he'd lived his entire life as if someone were holding a gun to his head.

You ready?

He remembered many years ago putting his arms around his wife and feeling her pregnancy, her waist thick with new life. She eventually gave him a son. And now his son looked at him as if he were a stranger.

He shut his eyes. His wife sank against his chest, her flesh much weaker and softer than it gave the impression of being. "I'm sorry," he told her, imagining her bruised and hurting all over. He didn't want to hurt anyone. He'd never had an extramarital affair. He'd never wanted another woman. His body was in perfect health. Maddeningly alive. Blood coursing through his veins, lungs expanding and contracting, heart pounding . . . thub-dub . . . thub-dub . . .

You ready?

He listened to the wind, the horrible lonely sound of it. His hands were steady. He placed the cold barrel in his mouth, gazed for a moment at the stars, the brightest ones representing the people he loved most in this world—wife, daughter, son. And when the stars became smears of light, he pulled the trigger.

EIGHTEEN YEARS LATER

1

DETECTIVE RACHEL STORROW WAS ON HER WAY HOME WHEN
the call came in. "Possible forty-five," the dispatcher's voice
blurted between hisses of static, and Rachel's hands gripped the
wheel. A forty-five meant a corpse.

She made a U-turn in the middle of Pumpkin Run Road, tires
chirping as she headed back across town. She'd spent the better
part of the day knee-deep in garbage, looking for the gun a victim
claimed her husband had shot her with. He confessed he'd
thrown his Saturday Night Special in the town dump, but they
hadn't been able to locate it yet.

Rachel's clothes reeked, the fabric clammy with sweat. A fetid
aroma of wet cardboard and rotten lettuce filled the car, the kind
of smell that lingered for days. She'd been on her way home to
take a hot bath, but that would have to wait.

Cruising the familiar neighborhood, she glanced into windows of passing houses and felt a twinge of nostalgia for their
buttery light, their illusion of safety; she caught a glimpse of a
mother tugging a curtain shut, a child changing channels on the
TV, cozy scenes of domestic bliss she'd left behind forever like
old children's books. People didn't realize how vulnerable they
were. If they knew Flowering Dogwood the way she knew it,
they'd turn their homes into armed fortresses.

Now she came up behind a tractor hauling a load of manure,
doing fifteen miles an hour, and flashed her high beams until the
driver pulled over to let her pass. She waved at Neal Fliss, an
old friend of her brother's. They hadn't spoken in years, not
since Billy had gone off to Amherst, and now Neal was a dairy
farmer like his old man—exactly what he'd once sworn he'd

never be—and married with three kids. He was shirtless, smoking a cigarette, baseball cap smashed flat on his head, and she couldn't believe she'd once had a major crush on him.

Pumpkin Run Road traveled through dense woods of white pine and birch, their tangled branches catching in her headlight beams. The road slowly descended into the rolling valley, a stunning view of the White Mountains looming on the horizon. As she approached Holderness Street, the white-steepled First Congregational Church rose above the town center, a lovely green fronted by elegant Federal and Colonial-style houses. This was the nicest part of downtown, the part that poverty, progress and unemployment hadn't touched.

Rachel pulled into the parking lot, then crossed the blacktop toward the church's back door. The September moon was a sliver, clouds like lichens growing over a granite-colored sky. Rachel knocked on the door, and the Reverend answered. "Wow, that was fast."

"Hi, Reverend."

"C'mon in, Rachel." Hughie Boudreau had once been a cop, way back when her father was still alive, but at some point along the way he'd had a spiritual awakening and had decided to join the ministry. His Sunday sermons were quite popular, according to what she heard. At forty-five, Hughie had a shock of polar-bear-white hair, dainty features and a restless gaze that had once upset her, but now she rather liked him. The Reverend Hughie Boudreau had presided over her mother's funeral three years ago.

"We got a call about a dead body," Rachel said.

"One of my homeless folks. Right this way." He led her through his private residence toward the rear of the church, and they passed his wife, a petite brunette with a pert smile, now talking on the phone. She waved at Rachel, who waved back.

"You remember that little girl who got murdered about eighteen years ago?" the Reverend asked as he opened the carved mahogany stairwell door. "The little girl with Down's syndrome?"

"Vaguely," Rachel said, recalling how she and her friends used to tease Melissa D'Agostino. If you got too close, you could smell her, people said. She smelled dirty. She sucked her thumb and looked like a baby monster. And once, in the girls' room at Fischer Elementary School, Melissa had asked Rachel in a plaintive voice, "Would you be my friend?" In response, Rachel had run away.

"Well," Hughie continued, "the gentleman downstairs is her father."

The basement of the First Congregational Church had been converted into a homeless mission of sorts, partitioned off in an attempt to provide privacy for the dozen or so men, women, and children who'd taken up residence and were now sleeping soundly on their cots. They tiptoed past this snoring flock, detoured through a spotless kitchen into a small private room where an elderly man lay curled in a fetal position on a narrow bed, clean white sheets tucked securely under his chin as if he were somebody's child.

"He had his own room?" Rachel asked.

"I considered Marty to be a permanent resident. He died in his sleep, looks like to me."

The room was spartan, the furniture mostly secondhand. Books littered the rickety bedside table. On the dresser was a photograph of a man, woman and child—Melissa as a toddler. Her mother held her with supreme tenderness and delicacy, as if she were made of handblown glass, and everyone was smiling.

Rev. Boudreau picked up the picture from the dresser. "After his daughter was murdered, his wife, Frances, just fell apart and had to be committed. In one fell swoop, Marty lost everything . . . his family, his job, his home."

"And that's when you took him in?"

"Heavens, no. He rode the rails for several years. I don't know what happened to him during that time. We never discussed it."

Rachel checked for a pulse. The old man's skin was cold and livor mortis was evident, indicating he'd been dead for at least a couple of hours. After a brief inspection, she said, "And the murder of his daughter . . . that case was never solved?"

"I have my suspicions." He looked at her oddly. "You don't remember any of this, do you?"

She shook her head, an old sadness reasserting itself. "My father committed suicide right around that time."

"Oh yes," he said tenderly. "I remember."

When Rachel was young, there were scary things she wasn't supposed to talk about. Secrets. Bad things. Like Billy killing those cats. Like her father's dark moods and her mother's anger. Like the retarded girl. Rachel and her friends used to take turns acting out the murder. Rachel often played the victim, and her best friend, Anne Marie, would wrap her hands around Rachel's throat and squeeze, and once Rachel almost blacked out. There was a murderer loose in town, but then her father shot himself, and none of her friends ever mentioned Melissa D'Agostino again.

After Rachel's father committed suicide, a hole opened up inside of her. She couldn't stop thinking about the last few seconds of his life. She hoped he wasn't in any pain when the gun went off. She hoped he blinked out like a light. As the years passed, the hole inside her filled up with tears and guilt, and then one day she stopped thinking about it altogether.

Her mother had been inconsolable. Her mother's sorrow had stretched across the landscape like a blanket of snow, smothering all color, suffocating the world.

"You said you had your suspicions, Reverend?"

He glanced down at Marty D'Agostino's body and sighed. "Ozzie Rudd. Perhaps a few others."

"Are you serious?"

"I wouldn't kid about a thing like that."

"But no suspect was ever arrested, isn't that right?"

"Correct." He shrugged. "The evidence was circumstantial, at best. No confessions. No eyewitnesses. You have to realize, these kids were all from influential families. The D.A. wouldn't touch it."

"What makes you so sure it was Ozzie?"

"I'm not sure. It's just a hunch. Ozzie Rudd admitted to us that he and some friends picked Melissa up after school on the day of the murder. And that they later dropped her off at Black Hill Road."

Her stomach knotted. "What friends?"

He gave a pained expression. "It's all in the case file."

"You're not suggesting I reopen the case, are you, Reverend?"

"I'm not suggesting anything."

She didn't know much about Billy and the cats. Her parents had protected her from the truth, and she'd buried the memory like a shameful thought. She didn't feel sorry for herself for having lost her father so young. Instead she locked the mystery away in her heart and kept it there, snug. Her private fury. Daddy was gone. He had given so much, and yet he'd taken away even more.

Rachel shook her head, refusing to accept it. "Ozzie Rudd wouldn't hurt a flea."

His smile was kind. "Your father was a good man, Rachel. Melissa D'Agostino's death troubled him a great deal. You know, he didn't drink, didn't smoke . . . didn't have the kind of vices most people use to numb their pain with."

She blinked back the tears that had inexplicably sprung to her eyes. "Do you know why my father killed himself, Reverend?"

"It's the grip of Satan," he whispered, his slender fingers encircling her wrist. "He's got a grip on this world like you wouldn't believe."

With a shiver, she reclaimed her hand.

2

RACHEL GOT TO THE STATION AROUND MIDNIGHT. THE OVER-head fluorescent light in the storage room kept flickering on and off as she rummaged through stacks of dusty cardboard boxes until she found what she was looking for. She pulled out Melissa D'Agostino's case file, its worn seams held together by silver duct tape, a round orange sticker on the front indicating that the case remained unsolved. She felt the kind of elation and sense of discovery she'd rarely experienced in her four short years on the force and didn't stop reading until three hours later, when she went home exhausted.

At eight o'clock the following morning, Rachel walked into the chief's office and shut the door behind her. Police Chief Jim McKissack, at fifty, was a brash combative man with a voice as scratchy as beard burn. He was leaning back in his chair, talking on the phone. When he saw her, he took his feet off his desk and shot forward. "Yeah," he said into the receiver, "okay . . . call me back this afternoon." He hung up.

She dropped the case file on his desk. "I can't believe you never told me about this."

He glanced at the file. "I didn't think it was relevant."

"Not relevant?" Her face flushed. "Not relevant that my brother came *this close* to being a murder suspect?"

McKissack shrugged. "Put a police officer in a dark room with a sixteen-year-old boy and you could probably get him to say he was on the grassy knoll in 1963."

"So you don't think Billy had anything to do with it?"

"I didn't say that." He gestured for her to sit, but she kept pacing back and forth in front of his desk. The office was warm.

Stuffy. She studied his impassive face and wondered if he was deliberately trying to provoke her. His eyes were the solid color of dusk, without any specks or flaws in the iris.

"So what *are* you saying, McKissack?"

"That he was guilty of being an impressionable kid who hung out with the wrong crowd. Siddown, you're making me seasick."

She slumped in the wooden captain's chair, trying to solve in an instant what had remained a mystery for almost eighteen years. "The cats were this big deal in our house. I remember my father being so outraged, and Billy just moping around and basically feeling rotten. My friends and I would scare each other to death with decapitated-cat stories, but after a while, nobody mentioned it anymore, and sometimes I thought I must've dreamt it."

"Oh it's true, all right." McKissack lit a cigarette and gazed at her over the curl of smoke. His hard-muscled body was full of compressed, unreleased energy. She didn't know how to bridge the gap between them. They'd ended their affair three months ago. McKissack was married, and she knew his wife, Sheila. She liked Sheila, and she'd met his kids, ages ten, twelve, and fourteen. Good kids. A wonderful family. Still, her desire for him was as smooth and light as water.

"I've always had a sense there was some connection between my father's suicide and the dead cats, but I couldn't be sure. I had this vague feeling it had something to do with the retarded girl, too, but I didn't know how, exactly." She stood up and leaned against his desk. "You don't honestly think the two cases are related, do you?"

He considered her question, eyes narrowing. "I think there's a connection because it was the same kids involved, yeah. And we found a cat bell in Melissa D'Agostino's hand . . ."

"That disappeared, I know. You don't think—?"

"I'll tell you what I think if you'll sit down a minute." His tall forehead and alert eyes contrasted sharply with the rigidity of his jaw and those deep parenthetical lines around his lips, lips she had once kissed and which, if she admitted it to herself, she still wanted to kiss. "I think one of the boys who was there that night went back and decapitated those cats. I don't think it was your brother, though. I think Ozzie Rudd killed Melissa D'Agostino."

"That's ridiculous." She tried to picture the soft-spoken truck driver—her brother's childhood friend, the football coach's son, now a devoted father himself—killing someone . . . anyone . . . but couldn't. She'd known Ozzie since they were kids and he'd always been kind to her, giving her an occasional Milky Way bar or a bottle of toilet water.

"I disagree." McKissack sat forward. "I think Ozzie Rudd shot those cats, then went back later on and decapitated them for kicks. I think he dropped Melissa D'Agostino off at Black Hill Road, then returned later on to strangle her. I think he's one sick fuck."

"So why wasn't he arrested?"

"He had an alibi, if the girl is to be believed." An old rage flared in his eyes, then dissolved into resigned bitterness. "We couldn't make a strong enough case to satisfy the D.A."

"Ozzie's no murderer."

He shrugged. "You asked."

Her stomach constricted as she held his eye. "I'd like to re-open the case."

"What for?"

"We owe it to her parents."

He crossed his arms, and the body language book she once read would've said he was shutting her out, being noninclusive. A lowered chin meant insecurity, folded arms meant distrust. "We don't have the manpower. We don't have the funds."

"Please," she begged. She'd never asked him for a favor before. He rubbed his eyes, smoke ribboning from his nose, and she wondered if he missed her as much as she missed him. She could feel the heat emitting from his body. He couldn't help himself, he radiated vigor.

"Rachel. I'd strongly advise against this. You never know what you might uncover."

"Like what? The truth?"

Wearing a slightly defeated look, he tamped out his cigarette. "Do it on your own time."

"Thanks," she said, grateful. "I promise it won't interfere with my regular duties."

He leaned back in his chair. His desk was old wood. Oak. "I got my picture in the paper right after the murder. Somebody cut out the article, but I had to throw it away. I didn't want to be reminded." His lips, pressed against one another, grew pale. "Doesn't matter how many homicides you handle, you never get used to the death of a child."

She picked up the file. "All the more reason to find out what happened."

He gave her a wry smile. "You're more like your father than you know."

3

EVERY MORNING AT 8:30, BILLY STORROW WAITED FOR CLAIRE Castillo to join him in the lobby of Pelletier Hall, where together they greeted their students. Claire taught the lowest-functioning class of juniors and seniors at Winfield School for the Blind and Special Needs, and Billy was her teacher's aide. Their students ranged in age from sixteen to eighteen and most lived on campus in cottages named after characters from Beatrix Potter books. The double doors of Pelletier Hall—a grab bag of nineteenth-century architecture—opened into an ornate lobby with two banks of grillwork elevators and a central staircase. The lobby glittered with glazed terra-cotta tile beneath a domed stained glass skylight, and Corinthian pillars supported the fourteen-foot ceilings. Billy spotted Claire among the throng of students pouring into the lobby and waved.

"Hi, you," she said, slightly out of breath from walking up the front steps. Her cheeks were flushed, and her long red hair was shiny and brushed off her face, and he felt light-headed just standing next to her.

"Hey," he said as casually as he could.

"I can't believe it's Monday already."

"Do anything fun over the weekend?"

"Naw, just sat around in my underwear, mostly."

He was backed against the stairs, carved mahogany balustrade supporting his spine. Oh fuck, he wanted to say. Jesus. She was the most beautiful woman he'd ever known, with hair the faded red of an overlaundered shirt. She had to have the longest legs in the world, which today's calf-length brown skirt partially hid, and she never seemed to care about the runs in her panty hose.

"You?" she asked.

"Huh?"

"What'd you do this weekend, work on your novel?"

"Oh. Yeah," he lied.

"I'd love to read it sometime."

"Let me think about it," he said. He hadn't written a thing, not one blessed word.

"I understand," she said with a sweet, understanding smile, and he felt like the worst kind of fraud. "Artists are sensitive."

Now one of their students came barreling across the lobby toward them, swinging his cane, and Billy narrowly prevented him from crashing into them. "Whoa, Gus, where's the fire?"

"I dunno." Gus had lived at Winfield since he'd lost his sight in an automobile accident at the age of five. All the bones in his face had been painstakingly reconstructed, leaving him with the look of someone who'd collided with a brick wall, disbelief stitched into every expression. His blond hair was cut so short you could see the pink, exposed skin of his scalp.

"You almost whacked into us," Billy said.

"I did?"

"You're like a lethal weapon with that thing."

Gus had a snuffy little laugh.

"It isn't funny," Claire snapped, ever the disciplinarian.

"I know."

"Then why are you laughing?" But before Gus could respond, she hunched her shoulders and gave a few hacking coughs. Claire had asthma, and twice she'd wheezed so violently in Billy's presence he was afraid she might choke to death. She reached into her leather bag and pulled out her inhaler. "You've gotta be more careful, Gus," she said between coughs, spraying the medicine directly into her mouth. It took a few moments for the attack to subside, then she continued as if nothing had happened. "There are other people in the world besides you, you know," she said, eyes shiny bright with tears.

"I know." Gus crossed his arms defensively.

Her features softened. "Pretty sick of my lectures, huh?"

"No." Gus had a charming smile, two of his front teeth missing. He was supposed to wear a bridge but hated the thing and was constantly losing it. Once Billy found two front teeth sticking out of the soil of a rubber plant in the cafeteria.

Now Luke came sauntering toward them, a towering teenager over six and a half feet tall. He wore an extremely nerdy outfit chosen with great care and carried a boom box. On certain days, he would only respond if you called him Elvis. He loved rockabilly music and was constantly snapping his fingers to the incessant beat inside his head. He'd been born three months premature and had lost all vision in both eyes after being removed from the incubator.

Billy touched Luke's arm to let him know they were there. "Hey, Elvis."

"I'm not the King today."

"Oh. Hi, Luke."

Taller than his teacher by several inches, Luke reached down to pat Billy playfully on the head. "How's the weather down there, Teach?"

"Ha ha . . . funny guy." Billy slid Luke's hand down over his face so Luke could feel him grinning. "How was your weekend, buddy?"

Luke's smile snuck up on one side. "I got a Supremes tape."

"Ooh. Ow. I love the Supremes!" Claire swiveled her hips and snapped her fingers, her voice endearingly off-key. *"Love child . . . never meant to be . . ."*

"Is that you, Ms. Castillo?" Luke asked.

"Yeah, it's me. And here comes Gabie and Tony and Eric."

"Where's Brigette?"

"Here I am!" She tugged on Billy's jacket sleeve.

"Oops. Sorry, honey. I didn't see you." Brigette, a petite albino teenager, was low-sighted but could see well enough to get around without a cane. The students at Winfield had varying degrees of vision loss; many were partially sighted, meaning they could see shapes, or lights and shadows, or narrow bands of images. Enrollment had dropped in recent years due to mainstreaming and medical advances. Meningitis could be cured with antibiotics now and fewer babies were being born blind from their mother's rubella. The future of Winfield rested in the hands of crack babies and premature births, and only the most complicated cases were sent here—behavioral problems, head injuries, deaf-blind, severely impaired. Billy loved every single one of them.

"You guys ready? Let's go."

They were heading up the stairs when Billy spotted his sister entering the lobby. At twenty-seven, Rachel was strikingly pretty despite the conservative gray pantsuits she always wore. Her leather holster showed beneath her jacket, her Smith & Wesson .38-caliber revolver entirely inappropriate in the school's sun-drenched lobby.

"Hey," Billy called out, and she met him at the bottom of the stairs. She had their mother's tall milky forehead and imperious chin, which was offset by her sweet smile. Her blond hair was pulled into a ponytail so tight her eyes seemed slanted, and he still had a hard time thinking of her as a cop.

If Billy thought about it, he had to admit he was jealous. She'd followed in their father's footsteps, whereas he wasn't even a full-fledged teacher, just a teacher's aide. It was a constant source of embarrassment for him. Not that he'd ever wanted to be a cop. Billy had higher aspirations. After graduating from college, where he'd majored in English, Billy moved around a lot—from Cambridge, Massachusetts, to Seattle, from Buffalo to New Mexico. Over the years, he kept trying to settle down and write that novel, but to date he hadn't written a thing. Instead, he'd ended up waiting tables and working in bookstores, searching all across America for good material. Three years ago, right before their mother died of breast cancer, he finally returned home, feeling like a failure. Lately, he'd been considering writing a book about the blind.

"Listen, Billy, we need to talk," Rachel said.

"Class is just starting. What's up?"

"Nothing's up," she said, but her voice was pinched. "We need to talk, is all."

"Lunch?"

"Sounds good."

"Noon at the picnic tables out back?"

"Sure. See you then."

"Hey. Everything okay?"

"Yeah," she said a little too brightly, and he knew she was lying. "Everything's fine."

4

BY MIDMORNING, THE SUN WAS HEATING THE BACKS OF THE students' heads. Gus and Luke were dozing, and Eric was brailling secrets into Brigette's tiny hand. Billy knew they'd lost them somewhere between 1775 and 1783, but Claire kept charging gamely ahead, refusing to accept that her class would never truly grasp their country's complicated history.

"Okay, now, the American colonists were protesting what?" Claire prompted. The desks formed a horseshoe, and she paced back and forth in front of them, clutching the delicate gold crucifix at her throat. She was a lapsed Catholic who for some reason clung to the trappings of the Church. "What were they protesting? Anyone? Eric?"

"Huh?" Eric sat abruptly forward. He had an unruly red mane, a freckled face, large feet and an even bigger heart. He was the brightest kid in this class of especially slow learners, and Claire couldn't help constantly turning to him for answers. She and Billy had a running dispute about it. How would the others learn if Eric kept bailing them out?

"What were the American colonists protesting?" Claire asked again, cheeks flushed from the excitement of teaching.

"Um . . . the British?"

"That's right, they were protesting British domination, and that was what started the Revolutionary War. Okay?"

She looked around at their blank, upturned faces. Billy caught her eye and smiled encouragingly, despite the fact that he knew it was hopeless. Sixty percent of the students at Winfield were handicapped beyond their blindness; many suffered some degree of delayed development, a polite term for mental retardation.

Here at Winfield, the brochure explained, each child was measured against himself, not some outside norm. The best many of these students could hope for after graduation was a room in a state-funded community residence and a menial job, although there were notable success stories: a professor of history at the University of Maine, a state senator, a printer of large-type books, the owner of a dry cleaning establishment, an innkeeper. *Blindness doesn't mean limitation.*

"In 1775," Claire continued, fingering the gold cross at her throat, "we fought to gain our independence from what country? Gus? Am I boring you, Gus?"

So far their relationship hadn't progressed the way Billy had hoped it would. At first, he hadn't liked Claire very much. She struck him as arrogant, a bit of a snob. She was a strict disciplinarian in the classroom and a cipher outside of it. She listened to his problems and gave him advice, but shied away from revealing too much about herself. Whenever he probed too deeply into her past, she clammed up, lips pressed shut like the licked flap of an envelope. All Billy wanted to do was witness her loss of control.

"Anyone? Brigette?"

"Yes?" Brigette sat fingering her pencil and gazing at the brilliant slash of sunlight slanting across the blackboard. She had milky white skin, cottony white hair and flickering pink eyes that seemed to take everything in—although that wasn't quite true. Brigette had a doughnut-shaped field of vision, which meant that objects swirled before her like planets disappearing into a black hole. Unlike Gus, to whom light and shape were but distant memories, Brigette could differentiate between shades of gray and vibrant shapes. She carried a ring of keys that rattled noisily, so you always knew when Brigette was coming. The keys didn't open anything she owned.

"Brigette?" Claire said. "What are you thinking?"

"This weekend I'm going swimming," she said in her high, childlike voice.

"That's fine," Claire said, "but we were talking about the American Revolution. Do you know what the American Revolution is, Brigette?"

Brigette stared at the blackboard, then finally admitted, "I don't know."

Claire glanced helplessly over at Billy and threw up her hands. "Maybe now's a good time," she said, "to practice our handwriting?"

"I think that's a great idea." Billy sounded more gung ho than he'd intended, and Claire frowned at him. She was always frowning at him. She found fault with Billy's leniency, his tendency to cut the students too much slack. "If we don't push them," she said, "we'll never find out what they're truly capable of."

"Do souls need eyes in order to see?" Brigette suddenly asked, and Billy and Claire stared at her.

The other children fell silent.

"Excuse me, honey," Claire said, "but where did that come from?"

"My grandma died this weekend."

"Oh my God." Claire knelt down beside her and gave her a hug. "I'm so sorry, sweetie."

"Do they?" Brigette asked, hugging Claire back.

"Do souls need eyes in order to see?" Claire glanced at Billy, her beautiful almond-shaped eyes filling with tears. "No, you don't need eyes in heaven."

"So when I go to heaven, will I be able to see like everybody else?"

"Yes," Claire said.

"No kidding?" Luke perked up. "Me, too?"

"Yes," Claire answered, and a fresh surge of desire rattled through Billy, throat thickening with a strange blend of sorrow and yearning. She wore stockings even on the hottest days. She wore sleeveless blouses, sweat collecting in half-moons under each armhole. Whenever she kicked off her shoes, the faint smell of baby powder wafted toward him. She had narrow feet with bright red nails showing through the cinnamon-colored nylon.

"Why did Grandma have to die?" Brigette asked.

"We don't know why people die." Claire held Brigette's pale, delicate hand. "Not really. It makes life more precious, though, for those of us who survive. Your grandma's spirit will live on. You'll never forget her, will you?"

"No," came Brigette's soft reply.

"Is there anything special you remember about her?"

She thought for a moment, then said, "She liked cherry cough drops."

"See?" Claire smiled. "From now on, whenever you have a cherry cough drop, you'll remember your grandma."

Luke rubbed the bridge of his nose as if it irritated him to be there. His boom box was on the floor by his feet. "Am I going to die?" he asked.

Claire glanced over at Billy, who tried to think of something wise to say. He opened his mouth, then shut it again.

"Am I?"

"We're all going to die eventually, Luke," Claire said. "But hopefully we can all die like Brigette's grandmother . . . of old age."

"She died in a car accident," Brigette announced to the room, and the children shifted uneasily in their chairs.

"That does it," Luke said, his large, bony hands caressing his Braille book. "I'm never getting into a car again."

"Luke," Billy said, "most cars don't have accidents."

"That one did."

"Yes, it did. But most cars don't."

"How d'you know?"

"Because. They just don't."

Claire grimaced.

"I don't care, I'm not riding in a car ever again," Luke said with finality.

"Look . . . guys . . ." Claire said. "It's like a leaf falling from a tree. Just because one leaf falls today doesn't mean they all have to fall today, does it? Some leaves drop off early, but then others hang on until winter."

The children seemed puzzled by this analogy. They were probably the most innocent teenagers who'd ever walked the face of the earth, or at least America. They didn't smoke pot, get drunk, take drugs, or have sex (as far as Billy knew). They didn't drive cars or go on dates unchaperoned. They were rare adolescents, their innocence intact.

"Forget it," Gus said. "I'll walk." His face beneath its blond fringe of hair looked squooshed-in, like a sat-on rubber doll's.

"Gus," Billy gently chided.

"What?" He blinked. He was wearing bright red Reeboks and a T-shirt with the Simpson family stumbling across the front. "You can *die* in a car crash."

"Yeah, and a safe could drop on your head," Billy said, but the irony was lost on them.

Gus seemed alarmed. "It could?"

Brigette stood up, walked over to Billy and reached for a hug, and Billy gladly obliged, something else Claire disapproved of. *If we treat her like a little girl, she'll never grow up. She'll never take on adult responsibilities. We should treat her like a young lady.* But Billy secretly loved Brigette's hugs, which she generously offered to anyone. Her girlish heart was pure.

"Brigette," Claire said, "is there anything else you'd like to tell us?"

"Grandma's dead," she said, calmly removing the ruby ring her father had given her for her sixteenth birthday, then sliding it back on her tiny finger again.

5

HIS SISTER WAS WAITING FOR HIM AT ONE OF THE PICNIC tables grouped on a long, undulating green behind Pelletier Hall. The picnic area overlooked the ivy-covered, eighteen-acre campus with its rambling footpaths and towering oak trees. Built in 1862, the Main Building soared above the green with its stately white facade and bell tower. Further south, slate-roofed brick cottages were arranged around quadrangles with playgrounds in the middle. Migrating birds flecked the sky, the leaves were beginning to turn, and a sense of timelessness permeated the campus.

Rachel was golden-haired like their mother, whereas Billy was dark like their father, yet they resembled each other more than they did either parent. Sometimes when he looked at her he saw himself, her face his mirror image. It was disturbing. She didn't seem to be as aware of their similarities as he was. She didn't seem to fathom the depth of his feelings for her. For Billy, the family was deeply rooted inside of him. It was who he was. He could still hear his father's voice in his head, belittling him.

"Hey, Sis."

"Hi, Billy." Her look made him nervous. "Thanks for meeting me."

"No problem."

She had bought a cranberry juice from the machine in the rec room and was playing with the bendy straw. The smell of nasturtiums and freshly mown grass wafted toward them. Daisy chains of kids filled the nearby playgrounds with their shuffling gaits, their anonymity behind dark glasses, their telescope canes. They groped for one another, shouted, laughed, collided in a tangle of waving arms and roving eyes, while the college students hired to look after them patiently untangled and redirected, consoled with exhausted competence.

Rachel got right to the point. "We're reopening the Melissa D'Agostino case."

His gut churned, his brain a jangle of raw nerves. Something about his posture didn't feel right; his shoulders slumped, and he tried to straighten up, but a coil was unfurling deep inside him. "Okay," he said cautiously.

"I just wanted you to know."

"Okay," he said, at a loss.

"Billy," she said, "I've read the case file. I know all about your involvement. I'd like to ask you some questions."

He rubbed his eyes, trying not to look as upset as he actually was. "I answered everybody's questions eighteen years ago," he said softly. "It's all in the report."

"I'm sorry." She smiled encouragingly at him. "I know you didn't have anything to do with Melissa D'Agostino's death. I just thought maybe I could jar your memory . . . squeeze out a few more details?"

A sudden swirl of cold air blew past them, and Billy folded his arms. Blackbirds fluttered up whenever the children got too close. His toes were cold. He tilted his face toward the sun, wanting to watch the clouds fly by. She didn't remember how bad it could get sometimes, with their mother crying and their father storming out of the house. She didn't remember how little their father trusted him. The fights. She didn't understand the craziness. She was too young, and her youth had protected her from all hurts, big and small.

"I remember," he said, "a lot of things."

"Like what?"

"Like discovering Dad's body."

She looked at him oddly and he got that misunderstood feeling again. After he'd moved back home three years ago, after he'd finally admitted defeat and come crawling back to this god-forsaken town, he'd lived briefly with Rachel and their mother and immediately resented their relationship, hated the secrets that flowed between them. There were watercolors on the walls, and girlish things and warm touches, and he felt excluded from the *insiderness* of the house. The exclusivity of its domesticity, the sense that it was somebody else's place, not his, that he was a mere visitor. And the other stuff, the old secrets, the bad things he didn't want to think about. After their mother died, he rented a place of his own across town, far from all the painful memories.

"You wouldn't talk to me about anything after Dad died," Rachel said, an old hurt bruising the delicate skin around her ocean-colored eyes.

"Well, I'm talking to you now."

"You never cried. I remember you'd sit for hours without moving. You'd stare at the TV . . ."

"I know."

"Daddy was gone. He just disappeared from my life, and it felt like suddenly you were gone, too."

"I know," he said softly. "It was an effort to think."

"I remember crying a lot. But you. Not one tear."

"Whenever I started to feel something," he said, "I'd just focus on whatever I was doing at the time. Like homework or sports."

Her eyes held him with their intensity. "I lost you both."

He exhaled sharply. "After Dad died, I had nothing but contempt for other people. I'm not proud of the fact that I distanced myself from you. I guess I was punishing myself. Sometimes in the dead of winter, I'd walk around without a coat just to prove how tough I was. I was contemptuous because it sealed away the hurt. You can understand that, right?"

She gave a reluctant nod.

"I remember that night . . . Dad's car was in the driveway, but he wasn't inside the house."

She winced as if she didn't want him going in that direction, but it was too late.

"You were watching TV. Mom called the station, but they said he'd left hours ago. I'll never forget the look on her face . . . as if she had a premonition or something. She said we had to find him."

"I don't remember any of this."

"She wanted to protect you. You were nine years old, for crying out loud. We went outside, and I sort of wandered down to the back field . . . down by the swamp, remember? Dad and I would go down there sometimes and look at the stars. He'd try to talk to me. I don't know why he bothered." Billy swallowed hard. "And there he was."

Her gaze was like a tug, urging him to continue.

"I could see, like . . . everything. The blood and . . ."

"Okay." She looked away, but he wouldn't stop.

"The back of his head was blown off, and there was blood dripping from his ears, and I couldn't catch my breath. I kept thinking, *holy shit* . . ." He rubbed his face, but the itchiness stayed on his skin. "I had nightmares for years. I still have nightmares."

"Billy, that's enough." Her eyes welled with tears. Even though she was seven years younger, she seemed older. Wiser. Billy had always been a late bloomer, that was his problem. He was ten years behind everybody else. *Billy* wasn't even a man's name. It was a boy's name.

"Sorry," he said, "but you asked."

"Not about that!" Her anger was palpable. She wiped her nose with her sleeve, and he knew that she loved him very much, but that over the years he'd lost some of his luster in her eyes. He remembered a time when he'd been her favorite person in the whole wide world, but now she could see the cracks in the armor.

"The worst of it was, I didn't feel anything . . . here." He smacked his chest. "At the funeral, it was like I was standing fifty feet away. I didn't know these people. Who were they? Some guy would come up and put his arm around me and I didn't know who the hell he was. In church, during the service, Mom grabbed my hand. She was sobbing and I could feel her shoulder sort of jerking against mine, and it . . . repulsed me. All that emotion. I remember looking down at her hand as if it were an object. And there was nobody to turn to. I felt so alone."

"I'm sorry, Billy," she said, her face finally opening up to him, her heart embracing him with pity.

"I remember exactly where he died. I could go down there and point it out to you. His blood was like paint on the grass. For the longest time, I'd go down there and stand in that exact spot and expect to find something . . . an answer, maybe." His own words buzzed in his ears. "You know how I've been nagging you to sell the house?" he said, and she smiled the way only his little sister could. "I'm glad you didn't listen to me. I mean, I really think you should sell it, it's a fucking museum. But part of me doesn't want to lose touch with the past, you know? Isn't that dumb?"

"No." She made a move to comfort him, but he wasn't crying.

"Remember the look he'd get in his eyes?"

"Like nobody was home."

"He'd go down to the basement and you couldn't disturb him."

"Not for hours."

She was shivering now, drawing her coat around her. Billy was so proud of her. She didn't have to do anything, he'd still be outrageously proud of her. He'd taken care of her, growing up. He'd been her best bud and they'd played silly games, hiding in the woods, pretending to be Indians. Her face was beautiful in the noontime sun, strong and fiercely determined.

"Dad used to say 'Shoot straight.' " She shuddered. "Isn't that weird?"

"Prophetic and weird."

" 'Shoot straight.' "

"You know what the obituary said? 'He died unexpectedly.' "

She closed her eyes for a moment. "It pisses me off."

"What?"

"Why'd he have to kill himself like that?"

He stroked her cheek. "It wasn't us, Pickle."

"What was it, then?"

"I don't know, but I don't think it was us."

6

THE DREAM WAS ALWAYS THE SAME. HIS FATHER WAS UP ON the roof, walking as easily as you'd cross a floor. Nalen Storrow walked to the edge of the roof, looked down at Billy with his ice-blue eyes, gold badge glinting in the sun, and said, "A conscience doesn't come with a dimmer switch, son." Then he began to glow as if lit from within. Eyes smoldering, he leapt into the sky and disappeared. And in his hand, Billy found his father's revolver. His heart pounded as he pointed the gun at his own head and pulled the trigger, and his bones dissolved and his brains came rushing out the back of his skull as he crashed to the ground.

Billy woke up drenched in sweat. The bed was damp, the sheets stifling. He kicked them off, sat up, rubbed his eyes. His hands were trembling. "Stupid fuck," he said. "Stupid shit . . . stupid fuck . . ."

He switched on the light. Three in the morning. He got up and started reshelving some of the books stacked haphazardly around the room. He stacked them alphabetically by author. He'd made the floor-to-ceiling scrub pine bookshelves himself.

A distant memory came to him. He must've been three or four years old when he found a moldy old baseball in the backyard and brought it inside to show his father. Nalen Storrow snatched the baseball away and chopped it in half with a hatchet. Only Billy couldn't be sure if it'd actually happened that way or if perhaps he had dreamt it. He wasn't sure of anything anymore.

Now the familiar nagging thoughts, bad thoughts, corrosive, tried to pry their way into his brain, and he did what he always did whenever that happened. He picked up a book among the stacks of books that littered the house and skimmed its pages. He didn't usually buy self-help books, but this one was about the children of alcoholics. He paused to read a random paragraph: *Some children grow up to become "super-coping adults," extremely diplomatic and capable of working very hard for little reward; people who set out to save others.*

That was Rachel, he thought. Whereas Billy fit the category of *those who had low self-worth and difficulty maintaining intimate relationships.* That was him, no self-esteem. Just a big emptiness inside he kept trying to fill up with a human being.

Billy didn't know who he was; he didn't fit into the world. He browsed and reshelved until dawn cracked the horizon; this was the way he dealt with his nightmares.

7

RACHEL'S CONVERSATION WITH BILLY HAD LEFT HER FEELING raw, angry and confused. For the first time, she understood what McKissack was talking about and she hated him for being right. She was too close to the case, and the hard weight of this knowledge sat inside her like a stone. She'd recognized pain in the sharp, cracked color of her brother's eyes and that had stopped her from questioning him further. Still, she wasn't ready to give up just yet.

Looking downrange at the target, she attempted to create in her mind a potentially life-threatening situation. She told herself she had no backup. It was just her and the perp and her life was in danger. What should she do? Her heart pumped rhythmically as she tried to imagine the perp's face but couldn't. He was a cipher. A face in shadow.

She'd been a patrol officer for three years now, a detective third grade just over a year, and yet she'd never shot at a suspect, never killed anyone. On Boy Range back at the police academy, she'd learned to shoot at the body-shaped targets stapled to stanchions across the range. The bullets were caught in sand piles behind the stanchions embedded in concrete. In her headset and goggles, she stood with the other recruits in the ready position, gun drawn, arm extended. "On the whistle, fire two rounds." Unload and reload with the speed loader. Fire off four rounds in fifteen seconds.

And always at the back of her mind was the question: What did it feel like to get shot? What did it feel like to turn your gun on yourself? To take your own life? Head ripped apart at the pressure of your own finger?

No, don't think about that now. Stay focused.

She imagined the perp several yards away, pointing a gun in her face. She needed to remain calm. She bent her knees, turned to the left and dumped her speed loader, slammed in a new one. Trigger control. Take it easy. She fired off six rounds.

Rachel liked her gun, liked the feel of it in her hand, the weight of it. Her gun was an extension of her sense of safety. She carried eighteen rounds of ammunition at all times: six rounds in the revolver, six in each of the two speed loaders she kept inside her purse.

Now she aligned the rear and front sights, then allowed her vision to refocus on the front sight and the distant target, choosing the Weaver stance, placing her feet in a professional boxer-type position and keeping a forty-five-degree angle to the target. More shots. The acrid smell of gunpowder. Two rounds supported, four seconds. Combat-unload and reload with the speed loader. Align the target in your rear and front sights. Squeeze the trigger.

She'd always wanted to be a cop, ever since she could remember. She'd loved her father's uniform, his gold shield, his shiny black shoes. He kept his gun loaded in the bedside table and she was forbidden to go near it, but sometimes she snuck into her parents' room and played with the ammunition he kept in his sock drawer.

Now she took a step back and arched her neck. Squinted at the target. Good grouping, probably in the high nineties. Not bad.

"Why the Weaver?" It was McKissack, coming up behind her on Charley Range. She'd know that voice anywhere. It crept up her spine and curled her toes.

"There's less of me exposed to my adversary. Greater mobility while on the run."

"Disadvantages?"

"Difficult to perform while under stress."

He squinted at the target. "Good grouping, Storrow."

"Thanks, Jim."

He flashed her a look that made her jump inside her own skin.

"I'm sorry," she whispered, and his features softened. "I don't know what to call you anymore. Not even when we're alone. Should I call you Chief?"

"Frankly, I don't know what I want," he admitted.

She reholstered her weapon.

"In a gunfight," he said, "you have no way of knowing when you're about to be fired on. So you take cover wherever you can find it. You have to respond quickly. There's not much time to establish sight alignment, and you usually end up returning fire instinctively, by pointing and shooting."

She gave him a puzzled look.

"Some things you can never prepare yourself for, Rachel," he said and walked away.

8

SINCE OZZIE RUDD'S DAUGHTER ATTENDED WINFIELD SCHOOL for the Blind, Rachel had made an appointment to meet him inside the Main Building on Friday afternoon around three o'clock when classes let out. You weren't supposed to drive your vehicle over twenty miles per hour inside the campus gates. Rachel parked behind the Main Building and entered the front lobby, where she greeted the receptionist, a large woman with navy blue nail polish and vampirish eye shadow whose nametag said *Cassandra*.

"I'm supposed to meet Ozzie Rudd here."

"Oh yeah." Cassandra removed a can of Static Guard from her purse and sprayed her clothes with it, a plume of toxic chemicals misting the air. "Cut through the library. Take any door on your right and proceed all the way down the hall to the very end. Room 138."

"Thanks," Rachel said with a dry cough.

In the library, a crystal chandelier illuminated what many of the children could not see—glass cases full of stuffed animals and shelves crammed with Braille books. The library's interior brick walls had been polished smooth from decades of handling by sightless children. The venetian blinds were dented at about the same height—that of a child's groping hand. The white walls were also smudged, a dirty gray trail leading from one end of the room to the other.

Rachel passed a small group of children gathered in front of one of the glass cases, where a boy with deep-set eyes was counting the fangs on a Bengal tiger, its jaws opened wide enough to swallow him whole. Taking the nearest door on her right, she walked down a long corridor to Room 138 and knocked on the door. The teacher, a perky brunette in a blue cardigan, swung around and smiled at her through the glass. "Can I help you?"

"I'm Detective Storrow. I was supposed to meet Ozzie Rudd here at three." She glanced apologetically at her watch. "I'm a little early."

"C'mon in. My name's Peggy Morrissey."

About a dozen eight-to-ten-year-olds turned toward her as the door thwunked shut behind her, their eyes alternately milky or roving or piercingly focused. Some of the children had visible deformities, whereas others were perfectly normal-looking. A boy in a wheelchair, his arms twisted like pretzels, directed his motorized chair by manipulating a lever attached to his chin. Moving slowly toward her, he parked a few feet away to gaze at her through his Coke-bottle lenses. She assumed he could make out the general shape of her, that from his point of view, she'd entered the classroom and stirred up the shadows.

"This is Bradley," Peggy Morrissey said. "Bradley, say hello to Detective Storrow. She's a police officer."

"Hello," the boy said.

"Hello, Bradley."

Peggy walked away, leaving them alone together. Bradley had the cockeyed look of a Picasso portrait, eyes slightly crossed, face stretched out where it shouldn't be, cheekbones two triangles under the artist's brush. A sweep of black hair drifted across his eyes, and a tangerine button on his sweatshirt announced "I have permission to roam." He jerked his head and the wheelchair shot forward half a foot. "You a cop?"

"I'm a detective, yes."

"Do you have a gun?"

"I have my service weapon."

"What's a service weapon?"

"It's a gun."

He had an exuberant laugh, one that came deep from his belly, air pushing through his nose with foghorn force. His fingers were twisted rigidly together, like Play-Doh that's been left out overnight.

"I like your laugh," she told him.

"You do?" He seemed delighted.

In a far corner, the other children were cleaning up after an art project. Water ran in the sink as they took turns washing their hands and groping for the paper towel dispenser.

"What're you doin'?" Bradley asked her.

"I'm supposed to be meeting someone."

"Who?"

"A man."

He looked confused. "What man?"

"His name is Ozzie Rudd."

"Colette's father?"

"Yes," she said.

He stared at the floor for a moment, then burst into song. *"Oh I . . . had the time of my li-ife . . . and I owe it all to you-ouuu . . . !"* There was no self-consciousness in his singing. No artifice. His face filled like a sail with joy.

Now another student tapped her way toward them, a little girl of about eight. She walked hunched over, arms clutching invisible bundles, head bowed, eyes squeezed shut. In one hand, she carried a cane carved out of a branch, its pointed tip dulled from months of skittering across the school's tiled floors. She put her hand on Bradley's head and probed his face with soft fingers, and Bradley laughed.

"Hi, Colette."

She gave a delighted squeal, her overall strap sliding off one shoulder, Roger Rabbit peeking out from the turquoise T-shirt. "Hi, Bradley poop."

"You're a poop."

They both giggled helplessly.

The door opened behind them and in walked Ozzie Rudd. Rachel hadn't seen him in quite a while, and his appearance shocked her. There were circles under his faded blue eyes and his forehead was taller than she remembered. She could tell he was holding in his gut. He wore a plaid flannel shirt and straight-leg jeans but still had the honey-and-whiskey voice that appealed so to women.

"Hi, Rach."

"Hi, Ozzie."

"You meet Colette?" He lifted his daughter into his arms and, squealing with delight, Colette traced his weathered face with eager hands and kissed the tip of his nose. He laughed as he bounced her in his arms. "Oof, you're getting big."

"Hi, Daddy!"

"Have a good week?"

"Yup!"

"Where's your homework?"

"We didn't get any!"

"No homework, huh?"

"Nope." Her eyes were marbled and deep-socketed, the irises like runny gray eggs, and she swung her head to and fro as if responding to some inner rhythm.

"What's this then?" he teased, opening his daughter's backpack and pulling out a heavy Braille book. Her hand groped for it, her delicate fingers ruffling its pages.

"Oops!" She giggled. "Homework!"

"Well, whaddya know?" He smiled, then turned toward her teacher. "See you later, Ms. Morrissey."

"Have a great weekend, you two."

"Bye-bye!"

Rachel followed them out the door, back through the library and into the parking lot where Ozzie's eighteen-wheeler was parked.

"She knows when I pull up to the building," he said, "because my truck rattles the windowpanes and shakes the walls, and she can feel it through the bones of her feet and her bottom, if she's sitting down. Can't you, honey?"

"Yup."

"She knows when Daddy's here." He set his daughter down and guided her toward the eighteen-wheeler, where he placed her hands on the auxiliary tank.

"Hello, truck!" she said, slapping it heartily.

"Truck says hello back." He smiled proudly as she headed clockwise around it, touching the semitrailer's mud flaps, the sliding tandem wheels, the marker light. She reached underneath the bed to pat the auxiliary tank and support leg crank, then paused a long while above the kingpin to caress the embossed name, *Long Ranger,* with her fingertips. Giggling, she tugged at the front of her overalls.

"What's so funny, pumpkin?"

"I'm not a pumpkin, Daddy!" Her breath came out in puffs: ah-ah-ah! "I'm not round and cold like a pumpkin!"

"No, but you smell like wheat paste." He gathered her in his arms again and hugged her tight until she squealed, then lifted her into the cab. He turned to Rachel. "Ever been to the Drop Off?"

She frowned. "We need to talk in private, Ozzie."

"Don't worry," he said. "Where we're going, Colette has lots of friends." ❧

9

OZZIE COULDN'T IMAGINE WHAT IT WAS LIKE TO BE BLIND, although he'd tried. He once squeezed his eyes shut and wandered around the house, where suddenly points and hardnesses leapt out at him, where the chalky feel of paint on the walls shocked him, where creases in the surface of his old wooden desk became ruts, ditches. The refrigerator was a tall, cold monster, the can opener a jutting weapon, newspapers spread across the floor slippery traps. He barely lasted five minutes, and even then he kept cheating, opening his eyes in surprise and alarm. It was so freaky, like drinking hot coffee with a mouth full of Novocain.

Ozzie transported farm equipment from one state to the next, sometimes moonlighting as a mover, but every Friday afternoon he picked up Colette and took her to the park, then out to dinner. Back home, she'd hunker down on the couch and giggle at the things he handed her—peach, stick of chewing gum, a fuzzy new toy. They'd spend the evening together and the whole rest of the weekend, then he'd drop her off at his ex-wife's house on Sunday night before heading out on another run. He'd miss her the entire week until they could be together again.

Ozzie was so proud of his daughter, he could burst. She knew the truck forward and backward, knew the fuel tank and battery boxes, the compressed-air tanks and every single lug on each of the hubcaps. She circled her hands over the headlights, played the grille like a harp, smacked the hood, plied the windshield wipers; and once he got a ladder and showed her the tractor hood with its cab lights and air horn, its vertical exhaust. Slowly, very slowly, he was teaching her to check the oil and water, to fill the tanks with fuel. Anxious to learn, she'd ask him, "What's this for, Daddy? Daddy, what's this?" In her coveralls and shitkickers, she seemed like a natural.

When Colette was a little girl, Ozzie would come home exhausted from a long haul and she'd probe his face and hair and throat, sniff his neck and clothes as if she were trying to memorize him all over again. He'd hand her a doughnut or a sticky bear claw wrapped in wax paper, and she'd hunker down on the floor to devour it, his chocolate-faced girl. With her animal nose, just a bud of a thing on her face, she'd attack the knees of his jeans during supper, his caked sneakers, sweaty socks, the pens in his pockets, his worn leather wallet, handkerchief, silver coins. Her darting tongue knew the taste of aluminum, dust, rubber, balsa wood. And those ears, two pink flaps. And the milky unknowingness of her eyes.

She would dart beneath the table and zigzag between the straightback chairs, worrying around the house with her constant touch-touch. She'd clack the furniture with her wooden cane, its tip as sensitive as a tongue. She smelled things long before anyone else could, like the fire that took the Garsons' house, or the dead mouse in the cellar, or what her father'd had for lunch that day.

When he tucked her in at night, he would bury his nose in her neck and snuff and huffle. She had that little-girl odor, her smelly toes and belly button lint, earwax coming out in yellow clumps on the Q-Tip, jagged white-blond hair full of sand and sweat and whatever else she'd gotten into that day—her mother's perfume, her mother's soap, bananas from her fingers. Mae used to cut her bangs and they would come out crooked because Colette refused to sit still. She'd grit her teeth and shake her head, not wanting a haircut, determined to have her own way.

"Daddy's girl," he'd whisper.

There were nights, long ago, when the three of them would sit out on the porch, long summer nights with the mosquitoes out, and the fireflies glowing green. The growing darkness would absorb them into it, along with trees, grass, awnings, rakes, mailbox, porch. The night would dissolve Mae's face, and she'd become part of the cricket noise, the whirling of gnats. Without any moon, they'd all three be blind.

And Colette, sitting between their feet, would get up and move with grace as if the day were still broad with light; she'd pace between her parents on her little footpads, playing some sort of private, foolish game. Pad-pad-pad, she touched her mother's knee, then her father's, back and forth, while a crow cawed somewhere in the hidden landscape, and Holsteins grazed in the alfalfa fields, and far off, swimmers splashed and shouted in the public part of the lake.

Mae with her full lips and a lisp so soft, you'd suspect you'd imagined it, and those too-large eyes, that gentle accepting smile, and that big bottom, short legs, and the amazing way it all fit together. Her hair was short, with French bangs cut like a suburban dust ruffle over bedroom eyes.

During long-ago summer nights, they lay naked in bed, their clothes scattered across the floor, their little girl sound asleep upstairs, wrapped in her blindness. Colette dreamed about whatever she'd touched that day, whatever she smelled or tasted, maybe even what she imagined she saw—shapes so strange, no scientist could figure them out.

Lovely Mae, wrapped in her sweat and smelling of the iced tea she made with mint from her garden, store-bought lemons, Lipton tea bags, and water from their well. On her hands, his skin smell; on her breath, zucchini and cucumbers; on her face, specks of dirt from her busy day; and that exhausted, trapped odor between her legs would come at him like a knife thrown by an expert. He'd hold her as if he were falling out of a boat.

The well-house pump would click on and hum its dutiful churn. Tomorrow, he would push his little girl on her tire swing. Teasing, he'd snatch something away, like the accordion straw she sucked her soda through, or her little red cane, or a favorite toy—and she would squeal until he handed it back. Then she'd scurry behind a chair, or else beneath the piano, or in the dark space between the kitchen cabinet and refrigerator where he thought no little girl could fit.

There was a picture of Colette on her birthday pony. He kept it in his wallet. Four years old, she straddled the dappled mare, kicking her heels against its sides, but that horse wouldn't move, would not budge. Colette's hands were drawn crablike toward her chest and her head was lowered, and you wouldn't know it, but she was smiling.

In another picture, she sat at the kitchen table before half a dozen cupcakes Mae had baked, a birthday candle stuck in each. Her eyes, illuminated by the candles' flames, did not see a thing. In the picture, she blew a crooked birthday wish, and Ozzie, behind her, appeared anxious for every single candle to go out.

Now Ozzie, Colette and Detective Rachel Storrow were seated at a square table that trembled whenever Colette patted its gold-speckled surface. The Drop Off was a real greasy spoon, knife and fork. Ozzie bent down to slide a wad of napkins under one of the shortened legs, his shirt untucking from its waistband. As he sat up, red-faced, Suzi with an i swiveled over to their table and wet a sharpened pencil with her tongue. A well-preserved sixty-year-old and lifelong waitress, Suzi loved Colette like her own granddaughter.

"Well, hello there, Cocoa Puffs," Suzi said, her gaze sliding coyly between Ozzie and Rachel. "How's my favorite customer?"

Colette made a musical, high-pitched sound and reached for Suzi's hand. "Got any ice cream, Suzi?"

"Well, honey. We just may have a few DoveBars kicking

around in the freezer." Suzi winked at Ozzie. "Mind if I kidnap your daughter?"

"Yay!" Colette slid out of the booth.

Suzi wiggled her hips with exaggerated impatience. "And what can I get you folks?"

"Two coffees."

She smiled as she sashayed away from them. "C'mon, Colette, let's go bug Earl."

The diner smelled of bacon fat and confectioners' sugar, a weariness wafting in from the street. Ozzie's shoes pinched and his bones ached from his long week on the road. He'd been a truck driver for fifteen years but still wasn't used to hurling himself toward unknown destinations marked on gas station maps. The hot, gritty highway took him places he'd never been before, numbing his brain with the constant state of passing through. He took little white pills to keep him awake during long night shifts through towns called Sleepy Hollow and Tallulah. There was beer to comfort him, and roadside diners, and wait-resses with beauty-queen smiles and sagging bottoms. There were hash browns and the CB and Smokey to watch out for. The delirium of too much road, the merging of broken white lines, the bored faces of nighttime travelers in their low-slung cars. From his cab, Ozzie would catch an occasional glimpse of dirty business going on inside a passing convertible; the gleeful head of a dog outside a car window, its floppy ears akimbo; the faces of too many children smeared across the back of a station wagon window like insect splatters.

"Well," Rachel began clumsily, hesitantly. She'd always had a generous face and wry humorous eyes that were right now rather dull and serious. She hardly wore any makeup—just a little plum-colored lipstick, maybe some blush. She might be a cop, but she was as pretty as a peach. "Your daughter is adorable."

"She's something else."

Another waitress brought their coffees. Ozzie could see Co-lette and Suzi through the half-open kitchen door. Colette was touching Earl the chef's face—that big bear of a man became putty in her sticky hands.

"I'll get right to the point," Rachel said. "I'm reopening the Melissa D'Agostino case."

"Oh." Ozzie stared down at his coffee, which he liked with lots of cream and sugar. He thought for some strange reason that maybe she wanted to see him because she'd had a dream about him recently. Sometimes he had dreams about people he hadn't seen in ages, and that made him want to talk to them again.

"I need to ask you a few questions, Ozzie."

"Shoot." He caught himself and winced. "Oh gosh, I'm sorry."

"No, don't apologize . . ."

"I'm always sticking my foot in it."

"Forget it." She smiled kindly. Sweetly. He'd always had a little crush on Billy's sister, and it shocked him when she'd gone off to the police academy, shocked him even more when she returned nine months later a full-fledged cop. Now here they were, and he wondered where her suspicions lay.

"Ask any question you want," he said, trying to be cooperative.

"I've been reading the case file," she began, "and it really both-ers me that this cat bell was found in the victim's fist. You know what I mean? Suspicion points to that earlier incident, the inci-dent with the cats."

"Yeah." He nodded sheepishly. "The cats."

"You boys . . . you killed those cats. You confessed to that. But it was never resolved who decapitated the animals after they were dead."

"No." He shook his head. "That was never resolved."

"You don't know who did it, do you?"

He blew on his coffee, then took a careful sip. They had a ten-dency to overheat the coffee here, and sometimes it tasted burnt. "No," he said. "I'd swear on a stack of Bibles."

"I know," she said. "I believe you. But I'm trying to figure out if there's some bit of information . . . some tiny detail you may have forgotten to tell the police at the time."

"No," he said. "I confessed to shooting those cats, but I don't know who went back and decapitated them."

"Wait . . ." She was staring at him. "Went back?"

"What?"

"You said, '. . . went back and decapitated them.' How do you know somebody went back?"

"Are you trying to trick me?" he asked angrily. He didn't have to talk to her.

"No. I'm just saying—"

"Because this is something that was resolved years ago. I mean, we got our misdemeanors, we confessed. We paid for what we did. I went through a whole bushel of bullshit over that one. My dad beat the crap outta me. I don't know why I said 'went back' just now. It's a figure of speech. The cops . . . your dad tried to paint me into a corner with that one, but I swear to Christ, Rachel, I told him the truth. I told the whole fucking truth and nothing but, pardon my French."

"That's all right," she said. "I speak French fluently."

He had to smile. "Look," he said, "I was a jerk back then. All screwed up. Dad was one tough bastard. That's what we used to call him. One Tough Bastard. He had a hide as thick as cement. You could never get through to him, didn't matter what you said or did. I guess I just wanted to piss him off, you know? Remind him I was there."

She nodded. She hadn't taken one sip of her coffee yet.

"I was always getting into trouble. Shooting those cats . . . I have to tell you, that was satisfying. This may sound sick, but I honestly thought every living organism on the planet was against me. Have you ever felt that way? Like the whole wide world hates your guts?"

"I can imagine."

"You know, I was young and stupid. But I'd swear on a stack of Bibles I never decapitated any cats. And I had nothing to do with Melissa D'Agostino's murder. They couldn't pin that on me. I cooperated totally—gave them a blood sample, whatever . . ." He drained his cup of coffee and signaled the waitress, and she produced a fresh pot.

"Thanks, I'm set," Rachel said, and the waitress walked away.

"You know, I don't think I ever told your dad this . . . but I liked Melissa. I instigated the whole trip, but the point wasn't to make fun of anybody. I mean, yes, I admit it . . . I'm ashamed to admit it . . . I thought she was a hoot. I got a big kick out of her. Billy's the one who chickened out, after we'd driven to Commerce City and all . . . after the ice creams . . . he started saying we're gonna get in trouble. He put the fear of God in the rest of us, and so we panicked. We dropped her off. Just dropped her off . . ." His voice faded, and he thought about the stupidity of that act and how, if anybody ever attempted to do something as cruel and heartless to Colette, he'd hunt them down and shoot them dead. He often wondered why Marty D'Agostino had never come after him. Never confronted him. "Listen," he said, voice thick with phlegm, "I do feel somewhat responsible. I mean, we just dumped her in the middle of nowhere."

Rachel nodded, then said, "You had an alibi, this girl . . . Dolly?"

"She's gone."

"Gone?"

"Passed away five years ago. Breast cancer."

Rachel grew solemn. "My mom, too."

"I know. I heard." He didn't think he ought to, but he reached out and patted her hand, and Rachel smiled; it was the same smile she'd always given him as a kid—an imp's smile. He remembered once she skinned her knee, and he put magic fairy dust on it to take the sting out, and she smiled through her tears and told him how she was going to keep the scab. She was saving her scabs and locks of her hair and fingernail clippings in a paper envelope, for when she was old, she said. That had just about slayed him.

"There were witnesses who saw us together that night," Ozzie said. "Me and Dolly at the Dairy Joy. It must be in the case file."

"Yeah, it's there."

"Rachel," he said softly, "I was an asshole. I had a lot of pent-up rage. I still struggle with it. But I'm no killer."

"I know," she said, but he wasn't convinced she believed him.

10

RACHEL STOOD IN THE KITCHEN REALIZING BILLY WAS RIGHT, the house was a museum. Nothing had changed since their mother's death three years ago. The teakettle waited patiently on the back burner; dusty candles bookended the table's center-piece of silk flowers; the living room chairs still held the shapes of their bodies; the salmon-colored couch emitted a faint whiff of Storrow sweat. Through the kitchen window, she could see a fat blue jay chasing the other birds away from the feeder—*legitimate birds,* her mother had called them.

Emotionally drained, Rachel removed her gun and holster, then sat at the table, recalling the day her father had brought it home in pieces from Sears Roebuck, and her mother's delight as her hand caressed the "distressed" wood, a new invention at the time—they beat the wood with chains to give it that pocked effect. Her father's sweat and straining muscles as he put the table together, the effort showing on his weathered face, his plea-sure at its completion, the mischievous way he'd cupped her mother's bottom in his broad hands.

There were still miniature half-moons embedded in the

linoleum from where Billy used to tilt his chair back. Rachel half expected to hear her mother's voice, the whistling sound she made through her nose during the last few years of her life. The clink of a spoon against china. *Do you think someone comes for you at the moment of death? Comes to take you to a new world? Do you think death is an adventure, like Sir James Barrie says? "An awfully big adventure"?*

How still the house was. Even the staircase spoke to her of her parents' long-ago presence, the squeak of the sixth tread as her father snuck home late at night, the murmur of the banister where he ran his hand, trying not to make a sound. She remembered eating sun-ripened tomatoes from her mother's garden, running over beetles with her bicycle, playing with her brother's electric train set in the hot dusty attic, stalking bullfrogs in the swamp—big fat frogs like bleating human hearts. Now all she could hear was the song of the red-winged blackbird.

Upstairs in the bathroom, Rachel gazed out the window. The grass was dying, leaves turning saffron in the tawny light of Indian summer. The yard descended sharply into open farmland, giving way to fields and pastures, then rising steeply into woods beneath a sky of steely clouds. Beyond the fields and humped green hills, in the great distance, were the White Mountains. Majestic. Magisterial. Conspiring in their silence.

Rachel washed her hands with a sliver of oatmeal soap. Her mother had died in the hospital, away from the house, away from her things, surrounded by strangers in uniforms. A swift, merciful passing, the Reverend had called it. Little did he know.

She opened the medicine chest, still crammed with her mother's things: milk of magnesia, Pepto-Bismol, Preparation H, a tall can of ozone-depleting hair spray, a tube of lipstick—that same fireball red she'd used all her life despite its passing in and out of fashion; no powder or rouge or eye shadow for her, just that double slash of red. Rachel recalled how much her mother hated perfumes or anything scented, how other people's colognes made her sneeze. She was allergic to wool and wouldn't wear jewelry. Buying presents for Faye Storrow had always been a difficult proposition. She recalled stumbling after their father as he hurtled through drugstore after department store in search of some perfect, nonexistent gift. Birthdays, Christmases . . . her father running up and down the aisles, asking, "What about this? Rachel? Billy? C'mon, kids, help me out!"

Now Rachel noticed a strand of gray hair stuck to the paint on the wall behind the towel rack and wondered if it could possibly be her mother's. God, this house really was a museum. A shrine. With a little shiver, she turned on the faucet and washed the hair down the drain.

Now a car pulled up out front, and she went downstairs to see who it was. Jim McKissack stood on the doorstep. "Can I come in?"

She opened the door, apprehension curling at the corners of her mind. He entered with flawless movements. His clothes, as always, looked freshly pressed, but there was nothing starched or stiff about him. McKissack's physicality was unavoidable, and her body began to hum with the kind of synchronicity she always felt whenever he was near. Inside the station, they could keep up the pretense of professional detachment, but outside it was hopeless.

"I wanted to see how you were doing," he said.

"Beer?"

"No, thanks."

"Well, I'm gonna have one. Been a long day."

He hesitated in the doorway, probably wondering what the hell he was doing there. She studied his face, but McKissack was impossible to read. They'd mutually broken off their affair in order to spare everyone else's feelings, but they'd forgotten about their own. As for Rachel, her desire for him lingered in her cerebellum right next to her everlasting shame.

"How's the case going?" he asked.

"You were right."

"About what?"

"About opening old wounds."

"You can always quit," he told her. "No dishonor in it."

"I can't quit, Jim."

A fly buzzed lethargically around their heads, and he snatched it out of the air. She laughed with surprise as he opened his fist and wiped dead fly remains off his hand.

"One of my many talents. Impressed?"

"Shit, yeah," she said, laughing.

"I ever tell you? I used to catch bees in a jelly jar. I'd put the jar on my bedside table and watch them die a slow, torturous death. I wanted to kill every single bee on the face of the planet. I thought they were evil incarnate. Guess because one of 'em stung me once."

Rachel smiled. "You're still trying to rid the planet of evil, aren't you?"

He gazed at her without speaking, as if she knew his heart.

"McKissack . . ."

"I think maybe I should go . . ."

When she touched him, he moaned as if he hadn't been touched in a very long time. He kissed her with his warm salty lips, and she could feel his cock harden through their clothes. When he smoothed one hand down between her thighs, her insides cramped. The nape of her neck tickled, and she imagined all the hairs on her head, every single strand, standing on end. The shock of his touch both petrified and fascinated her. When he touched her there, it was almost as if he could read her mind.

"Please," she whispered, losing blood in her head. She was going to faint. The kitchen grew dim, and she swayed a little on her feet.

"I couldn't concentrate today," he admitted. "I couldn't stop thinking about you." It startled her, how handsome his face was, all flushed and agitated.

"Maybe we should talk?" She moved away from him in a narrow escape. Pulse quickening, she opened the refrigerator door, the smell of sour milk wafting toward her. She needed a beer. She reached for the six-pack behind the chicken carcass, dry meat clinging to a construction of grayish bones.

"Rachel," he said, but she played deaf.

The beer's coolness passed through the bottle into her fingertips; she took a lingering drink. "I don't want to hurt anyone, McKissack."

He stood in the pantry doorway, hands dug deep in his pockets. His eyes were as gray as the fur of a Korat—a smooth, mist-soaked gray. "I'll have a beer."

"Here." She handed him one, their bottles clinking together.

"Thanks." He took a swig.

Wiping her mouth with the back of her hand, she said, "We both know what kind of mistake this is."

He took another swig, Adam's apple jutting like the whitened knuckle of a flexed finger. Falling silent, he gazed at her body.

"Screw you," she said.

In one swift motion, he set his beer on the countertop and reached for her. Folding her in his arms, he kissed her. "Take this off," he said, tugging at her T-shirt. His hands slipped under her black T-shirt and fondled her breasts.

"McKissack . . ."

He sank to his knees and pressed his face against her stomach. "Oh, God." He sounded stricken. "My cock feels so heavy."

She rested her hand lightly on top of his head, his emotional turmoil at once pleasing and disturbing, her own inner confusion exhausting her. And even though she knew it was wrong to want him, she gave in to it, let her muscles and tendons and nerves relax into wanting him.

Cupping her ass in his hands, he pressed his nose to the crotch of her jeans. Inhaling deeply, he said, "Jesus, I remember when you were just a kid with braces. I guess that makes me a dirty old man. I can't help it, Rachel, I want you. All I could think about today was fucking you."

Captivated by the pleasant cadence of his threat, she let him undress her. When she went to unbutton his shirt, he pushed her hands away, saying, "Don't." Her breasts brushed up against the warmth of his clothes, and he emitted a heat she could feel in her bones.

"Wait," she said. "Look at me . . ."

She looked into his eyes, the pale stain of stucco. He had just quit smoking, and she could smell the staleness of his breath, its urgency. Beads of sweat formed on the indentation of his upper lip, the fleshy part of his mouth that she most loved.

"What?" he whispered, desperate. Before she could speak, he pushed her up against the refrigerator, which hummed and clicked at her backside. Pressing his cold beer bottle between her breasts, he made her gasp. Her heart sang as the wind picked up, rushing through the trees outside the house, wind whistling in the rafters. Slowly, very slowly, he drew the lip of the bottle between her breasts and down toward her navel, bisecting her.

Wrapping her arms around his neck, she sucked on his lower lip until she could almost taste blood. He smoothed his hand between her thighs. She shivered and rubbed the wetness of her skin against him, and he unzipped his pants, the fabric caressing her thighs. He hoisted her up and locked her firmly against the refrigerator, its contents clanging and spilling over— a jar of mayonnaise, a bottle of ketchup. Fanning her fingers, she gripped his backside, and all the rubber magnets slid off the refrigerator door.

His breath caught in ascending steps of frustration. He kept his lips poised inches from her mouth, making her work for each kiss. They knocked against the refrigerator, rattling its base and making the floorboards squeak.

"Oh, God."

"Tell me this is what you want."

Her hair veiled her face. A bag of peaches slid off the top of the refrigerator and landed at their feet, peaches rolling across the floor.

"Say it."

"I'm afraid."

"Don't be. I'll stop whenever you say." He held her still and gazed into her eyes. "Do you trust me?"

She clung to his neck as he carried her out of the pantry, step-ping tentatively over the peaches. Tomorrow they'd be bruised, each one with its own soft, dark, sour-tasting spot.

11

"I DON'T KNOW WHAT I'D DO IF I LOST YOU, RACHEL," MCKIS-sack said. They were lying on the living room floor and he'd chivalrously draped his camel's hair coat over their naked bodies.

She looked at him. "You never had me, McKissack."

He couldn't help smiling, and she guessed he knew the truth, that she was his, absolutely. One hundred percent.

"You don't have to do this, you know," he said. "It's not like you owe it to him or anything."

"Owe it to who?"

"Your father."

She bit her lower lip, feeling the hot flush of anger ride up her neck and cheeks. "I'm not doing this for him."

He stroked her jawline with his thumb, his face oddly composed, as if he had a fever and didn't know it. "All I'm saying is . . . it's not like there's a reason he killed himself, and if there is a reason, it's not like you're necessarily going to find out."

"Why are you so against this?"

"I don't want to see you hurt."

"Maybe all I'm after is the truth?"

"Truth," he snorted. "I teach my kids to tell the truth. Be honest. Remember, George Washington never told a lie. Around the age of eight, they realize most people don't want the truth. Most people want nice, polite lies."

She looked at him. "I think you should go now."

He held her eye. "I don't want to."

"You can't stay. Your wife's probably worried sick."

"I'm not in love with her, Rachel. I'm in love with you."

She sat up and, reaching for her T-shirt, pulled it down over her head. They'd just made love and already her insides were aching from the loss of him. "You know, Jim, whenever I resist the impulse to make love to you . . . whenever I bury this constant desire I have for you . . . I know I'm doing your kids a big favor. I'm doing something good."

He watched her put on her socks. "It's gotten to the point that whenever I'm away from you, Rachel, I only want to be with you."

"All right, stop. Just shut up." The back of her throat burned. "I'm not going to tear their father away from them the way my father was torn away from me, okay?"

She waited for him to leave, but he brushed the hair off her face, and she felt an uncontrollable urge to weep. Closing her eyes, she lowered her head against his chest.

Soothingly, he stroked her backside. "You're right," he whispered.

"I am?"

"Yes."

"So what're we going to do?"

"I don't know." He rocked her for a while. "My kids are what I wake up for in the morning. They're my whole life."

She wiped her wet face. "My heart feels heavy."

"Like my cock?"

"No, bad heavy. Like I've done something wrong. Like I'm never going to get into heaven."

"I thought you didn't believe in heaven?"

"I don't. Not really. My father used to say you could only get into heaven if you told the truth. So I guess I believe in the truth."

He snorted. "The truth's subjective."

She thought for a moment. "If you pick up a ball, the truth is you picked up the ball. It didn't leap into your hands. Nobody else picked it up. It didn't grow from your fingertips. You picked it up, and now you're responsible for the next action you take. Either you toss it to somebody else or crush the air out of it. But whatever you do next, that's the truth. You can lie all you want, but if I saw you pick up the ball, then I know the truth."

"Okay, fine," he said, wiping the tears from her eyes. "Then this . . ." He leaned forward and kissed her forehead. ". . . is the truth. And this . . ." He kissed her lips. ". . . is the truth. And this . . ." He guided her hand to his groin. "Is the truth."

She knew she'd never be as whole as when she was with him. His mouth tasted sweet. She pretended for an instant that he was free, no obligations. He had stirred up the calm center of her, and now nothing else mattered. Morality melted away. Flesh dissolved. The frosted earth heaved. She slid with him to the floor, while outside the treetops churned in the cold ringing night.

12

THE FOLLOWING FRIDAY, BILLY STOOD IN THE LOBBY OF PEL-letier Hall, waiting to say good-bye to his students. It was three o'clock, October already, the lobby chaotic with noise and color. On the countertop above the receptionist's desk was a ragged pile of stray gloves and sweaters and jackets. Spotting a piece of paper on the floor, he stooped to retrieve it. Somebody had written in bold block letters AIR MAIL, GO FAST! He added it to the pile.

Now he could see Gabie heading toward him. At sixteen, she had the best vision of any of his students but was cripplingly shy. She had Crouzon's syndrome, a congenital defect that affects the skull and facial bones. In Crouzon, parts of the skull's plates become fused, restricting the brain's growth and deforming the midface, creating vision and hearing problems. Gabie had a beaklike nose, shallow eye sockets, and a dished-in face. Her forehead was flattened, and her lower jaw jutted cartoonishly, her mouth never completely closing over her overcrowded teeth. Billy used to have trouble understanding her, but now he could make out her guttural utterings with ease.

"So, Gabie, how was cooking class?"

"Good." She took his hand and made him sit beside her on the lobby's only sofa. All the sofas at Winfield were oatmeal-colored. They faced the potted amaryllis, its bloodred blossoms opening like obscene mouths.

"What did you make today?" he asked.

"Pizza."

"Cheese or pepperoni?"

She giggled, a thick-tongued clucking. She had a shy, furtive manner and a boyish haircut, her voice emitting awkwardly from her malformed mouth. Even though she could see fairly well, her eyes never made direct contact.

"How'd it go?" he asked.

"Pretty good."

"Save me a piece?"

"Nope."

"No?" He feigned disappointment.

Again, the giggle.

"Hey, that's a pretty sweater." She was wearing a navy blue cardigan with a Ninja Turtle pin holding it closed. "It's really windy out, though. Are you sure you're warm enough? Where's your jacket?"

"I dunno."

He was used to her monosyllabic responses. She squeezed his hand again. "You don't know where your jacket is?"

"I don't need one."

"You don't?"

"Nope."

"Sure?"

"Yeah."

"All right. Up to you."

Claire was standing a short distance away, observing them. Making mental notes. Her lips, pressed together, reminded him of a scar. Billy freed himself from Gabie's grip, and she reached into her clunky pocketbook and pulled out her gray woolen cap. Her mother had knitted her the cap last Christmas, and Gabie wore it year round, winter or spring, rain or shine, come hell or high water. Now she drew it down over her forehead so that it completely covered her eyes, and Billy suspected that, subconsciously at least, she was trying to disguise herself.

"Aw, Gabie, not the hat again," he groaned.

"Why not?"

"You look like a convict."

"No, I don't." Giggle, giggle.

"You're too pretty to be wearing that thing. We need to get you a new hat or something."

"You said it was cold out."

"Touché."

That giggle again.

Billy heard Brigette's keys rattling before she came into view—small, slender, white as a ghost. She scooted in between them on the sofa. "Is *your* grandmother dead?" she asked Billy in her childish voice.

"Yes, Brigette," he said. "She died a few years ago."

"She did?"

"I really loved her. She used to take her teeth out."

Gabie giggled.

Brigette's eyebrows lifted with wonder. "She did?"

"Yeah, she had false teeth, and she'd put them in a glass of water at night so she could sleep without swallowing them."

"That's weird." Brigette clutched Billy's hand, her gaze drifting sideways across his face, and he wondered what she saw, how he might look to her. "Wanna come visit me this weekend?" she asked. "We could go swimming."

Claire frowned and tapped her pencil noisily against her clipboard. Gabie shifted in her seat and pulled the gray wool cap down to her nose.

"It's too cold to go swimming, Brigette," Billy said.

"Oh." She wrinkled her nose with disappointment.

"Maybe next summer, huh?"

"Okay."

Claire's complexion darkened. "Here's your cottage aide, Brigette. Gabie, pull that hat back off your eyes. Got everything, Brigette?"

Gabie reached for the walls with outstretched arms, pretending to be blind. During the wintertime, some of the blind students pulled their hats down over their faces just like Gabie was doing, and Billy would panic, fearing they might hurt themselves. Then it would hit him.

"Gabie," Claire warned, and Gabie dropped the act. "Bye, Brigette, see you Monday."

"Bye!" Brigette chirped, waving at them while her cottage aide, a freckled pixie of a woman, escorted her down the front steps toward the cottages.

Gabie's van pulled up out front, and Claire took her by the arm. "Gabie, you're not blind, you're visually impaired."

Gabie grunted.

"Your van's here. Pull that hat back up."

Gabie reluctantly rolled the cap back above her eyebrows. She lived with a foster family because her mother used to beat her, and several of her front teeth were capped.

"Got your stuff? See you Monday," Claire said.

"Bye." Gabie moved gracefully out the front door.

"My man," Billy said, giving Luke a high five.

"Hey," Gus said on his way out, "what am I? Chopped liver?"

Claire and Billy exchanged a smile, and Billy high-fived Gus, then Eric and Gabie and Tony were caught up in the stream of children pouring out the door, and suddenly the lobby was empty, dust settling in the golden silence, and Billy and Claire were alone.

"I wish you'd stop encouraging that," Claire said.

"Encouraging what?"

"Brigette. She thinks you're her boyfriend."

"No, she doesn't. She knows the difference."

Billy braced himself for an argument, but Claire merely shrugged him off and went to check her mail. Billy followed her with his gaze. The mailboxes were back behind the stairs, between the woodworking shop and the bulletin board. Claire reached into her box and pulled out her mail, along with the red envelope Billy had noticed earlier. Every so often, she received a mysterious red envelope addressed to Ms. Claire Castillo in childish block letters with no return address. Once he'd even held it to the light but couldn't make anything out through the thick, high-grade paper.

She read it quickly, then slipped it in with the other papers and books she clutched to her chest. They'd never discussed the red envelopes. Claire had never opened her love life up for dissection the way Billy did. He knew she'd once had a serious boyfriend and that they'd broken up a few years ago. He knew she hadn't dated in quite some time. "The last man who touched me," she once joked, "was looking for tumors."

Now Claire touched Billy's arm, warmth passing from her fingertips. "We need to talk."

"Okay." His heart skipped a beat.

They sat at one of the wobbly cafeteria tables, Claire sipping herbal tea, Billy chugging a Yoo-Hoo. Claire's hand rested on a pile of lesson plans. She had delicate wrists and fragrant skin.

"You're encouraging something you shouldn't be encouraging," she said.

"Don't be ridiculous."

"Brigette has a crush on you. Gabie does, too, but she can handle it."

"Big deal. I used to have crushes on some of my teachers."

"What's the matter with you?" Her eyes narrowed as if he were a dense fog. "She's sixteen years old . . . almost a woman. Mentally retarded or not, she has feelings."

"Claire, I think you're overreacting."

"Overreacting?" She looked about ready to strike him. "These kids don't need a buddy, Billy. They need a teacher."

"You're really into this distance thing."

"That's an incredibly offensive thing to say."

"I'm sorry, I just don't happen to agree with you."

"Okay, so we disagree, fine. I can handle that. What I can't handle is you sitting there, holding hands with her. You two shouldn't be holding hands, Billy. The lines are growing fuzzy."

"Maybe for you. Not for Brigette."

"How can you be so goddamn sure?"

"Because she's just a kid."

"Exactly my point, she's *not* a kid. She's a young lady. And don't you ever tell me I'm overreacting again."

"I'm sorry. I just don't see what the problem is. Brigette and I have our little chats."

"It's not what you say, it's your body language. You held hands."

"I hold everybody's hand." The truth was, he welcomed the children's hugs and handshakes. That didn't make him a pedophile—didn't make him weird or anything—he simply appreciated their openness and innocence and trust. Most of the women he met, as soon as he told them what he did for a living, completely lost interest. He could feel their withering contempt, but the blind kids thought Billy was cool. Their love, their unconditional love, was like an opening for him into the human world. These kids . . . *his kids* . . . made him feel alive.

"Look, Billy, this is a school. An institute of learning. We're supposed to be preparing them for the real world. It's great that you show affection and everything, but I've seen what happens to these kids after they graduate. The real world eats them for breakfast. It doesn't embrace them, it recoils from them. They've got to learn how to deal with rejection."

"So you want me to be their drill sergeant, is that it?"

"You've missed my point completely."

"Shape up or ship out?"

"Discipline and unconditional love are two extremes. We should fall somewhere in between, don't you think?"

"Okay, fine. You've thought about this a little longer than I have. I'll try to set some limits."

"Fine." She stood abruptly, papers spilling to the floor. Billy bent to retrieve the red envelope and she snatched it away.

"You're still pissed off," he said.

"No, I'm not."

"Your face is red."

"From bending over."

He wouldn't touch that one.

"Do these kids a favor, Billy. Stop trying to be their pal." She strode away, the mess of papers clasped in her arms. Midway across the room, she turned and drew a deep breath, her features relaxing. "Listen, I need a favor."

"Anything."

"Could you give me a lift home? My car's in the shop." She fingered the crucifix, now caught in the fabric of her blouse. "New brake pads."

"Sure," he said, trying to sound casual while his heart gave a hopeful beat. "Sure, I can give you a lift."

She smiled. "One other favor?"

"Name it."

"The costumes for the school play? They're at my place. Could you take them home with you and bring them in on Monday? I'm probably going to ride my bike."

"Whatever." He smiled back.

Claire's apartment was a mess. It looked as if she'd emptied the entire contents of every drawer, closet, and shelf onto the floor. She offered to brew some coffee, and they stood in the kitchenette, talking. He couldn't imagine sticking his hand in the sink, where submerged silverware glistened dully in the cold, milky water. There was a bag of moldy English muffins on the countertop, several filth-encrusted dishrags, a black banana, various scraps of cellophane wrapping, and the broken backs of pink Styrofoam packaging.

"I admit it, I'm a pig," she said with a laugh, spinning a bulging trash bag and tying the top with a twist tie. She set it on the floor and left it there, then led him into the living room, where she pushed her dirty laundry off the sofa onto the floor and sat down. He sat beside her, wondering when the coffee mugs had last seen soap. He wondered what kind of person could be so sloppy and

so strict at the same time. What kind of person could love children so much that she'd stubbornly resist holding their hands?

"This coffee sucks. I'm sorry." Claire got up and opened the
windows, letting in a cool breeze that ruffled the dying spider
plants. "How about some wine?"

"Really?" he said. "You sure it's okay? I mean, is this professional and everything?"

"Funny guy." She poured them both a glass of Chablis, then
sat down beside him and kicked off her shoes.

He swallowed some of the tepid Chablis, then studied her
thoughtfully.

"What?" she asked self-consciously, stroking her throat.

"What?"

"What're you looking at?"

"Just you."

"Now you're making me uncomfortable."

"I didn't mean to make you uncomfortable." The wine was
sweet.

She shot up from the couch. "Costumes are in the bedroom.
I'll get them."

"Need any help?"

"No, that's okay."

He heard her rummaging around in her bedroom and swallowed the rest of his wine. He got up and followed her in. The
bureautop was a junk pile of toiletries, and rising from this mess
was an earring tree, loops of silver and gold dangling from its
plastic branches. On the floor she'd left a heap of dirty clothes,
underpants tangled with jeans and blouses, a tossed salad of
khaki and denim and cotton. She was rummaging through her
closet, an artist's palette of color, and he could see the hourglass
shape of her backside through her clothes.

Claire glanced at him over her shoulder. "They're in here, I
swear to God." She laughed and dove back in.

His hands shook as he walked up behind her, and suddenly

she was handing him the children's costumes. When his arms were full, he asked, "What's in the red envelope?"

She swung around. "Oh God," she said, face flushing, "you don't wanna know."

"Yes, I do." He sat on the edge of her bed, sheets stirred like foam in a whirlpool.

Sitting beside him, she crossed her legs and started to cough. She coughed so hard, he was afraid she might choke. She opened her leather bag, took out her inhaler, stuck the nozzle in her mouth and sprayed three times in rapid succession.

After a moment, the coughing fit passed. She looked at him. "They're from my ex-boyfriend. We met at a rock concert. I'd just gotten out of grad school and was feeling kind of rebellious. He rode a motorcycle and drank Kahlúa straight from the bottle. He had this incredible energy, vast reserves of it, and the best pot around. I mean, he wasn't afraid of anything.

"But after we moved in together, things changed. I realized something was wrong . . . I mean seriously, terribly wrong with him. I kept catching him in these lies. At first I thought it was me, that I was out of sync somehow. Then one day he accused me of moving his stuff around."

"His stuff?"

"Things on his bureau, I dunno. I was moving his stuff around. We split up, and ever since, he's been sending me these creepy letters. Sometimes I read them, sometimes I don't. I probably shouldn't be reading them at all."

Billy's heart began to pound, a steady throbbing beat. He pictured a biker with long greasy hair, staring at his hairbrush on the bureautop. Staring at his things. Billy wanted to kiss her, and the first place he'd kiss her would be the damp, pale skin at the base of her throat. The place she kept stroking with her hand.

"What do the letters say?"

She gazed at the rug and shrugged. "I don't want to repeat it. I don't want those words getting out in the open."

"I'll protect you," he said. "I'll protect you from the red envelopes."

She looked at him and laughed. She threw her head back, and her hair got caught in the zipper of a raincoat that was spread across the bed. "Ow!" she cried, still laughing, and he dropped the costumes and reached over to rescue her. He unstuck her hair from the zipper and kissed her, but not at the base of her throat; he kissed her sweet-smelling lips. They tasted of medicine.

"Please don't act like I'm not here anymore," he said.

"I won't," she whispered, fervently kissing him back.

"Why do you do that?"

"Do what?"

"Act like you don't like me?"

"I'm sorry," she said, wrapping her arms around his neck. "I'm self-conscious, is all. I'm very aware of myself and how I'm acting, I analyze everything. I'm overly aware of everything and everybody . . . it drives me crazy sometimes. I'm an idiot."

"No, no," he said, "I love you self-conscious. I love the way you touch your gold cross and . . . how your lips curl back when you're mad at me."

"I'm not mad at you. I'm attracted to you. Don't you realize how nervous you make me?"

"Me?"

"Yeah, you."

She was hanging from his neck, licking the sweat from his neck. She writhed out of her skirt, and he kissed her greedy mouth. She tugged on his jeans, his stubborn zipper. She peeled out of her blouse and her hair hissed with static. He kissed her breasts through her skimpy bra, pawing at the straps. Gasping for air, he nipped at her lips and chin, then sniffed at her skin like an animal; suddenly he was all over her. He could barely catch his breath. They were halfway in the closet now, rolling over shoes and clothes and crumpled tissue paper. He unhitched her bra and she gasped, "Wait!"

"What?" He looked at her breathlessly.

"I can't." Her face crumpled as if she were going to cry, but suddenly she was laughing. "I'm sorry."

"What is it?"

"I'm such a jerk."

"No, you're not. You're not a jerk."

"Everything's just so traumatic for me."

"It's okay." They collapsed side by side, and the room slowly filled with their breathing.

"Everything's such a drama." She shook her head and sighed. "I just think . . . I think I need to take it nice and slow. Is that okay?"

"Of course it's okay," he said, smoothing his thumb across her downy cheek, trying to read her mind. Was this a brush-off? Maybe she didn't like the way he kissed? "Whatever you say," he said.

"Because . . . you know, the last time was such a disaster."

"Sounds like it." His chest hurt.

"I need to move slowly."

"Okay." Was she lying?

"Take it sorta slow, y'know?"

"We'll take it slow."

"I like you." She smiled, and her eyes glistened a little. "I really do."

"I'm glad," he said, wishing with all his might she meant it.

13

AT FIRST GLANCE, THE FLISS FARM LOOKED LIKE SOMETHING out of a storybook. Large white house surrounded by a picket fence, tall silo beside a big red barn. Acres of green pasture where brown cows grazed. On this Thursday morning, the second week in October, the sky was filled with streamerlike clouds, crisp autumn air popping inside her lungs. Rachel drew up the collar of her winter coat, just recently plucked from the mothballs, and knocked on the door. Neal Fliss wasn't home. "Go on down to the barn if I'm not in," he'd told her over the phone, so she skirted the house and descended a sloping backyard past half a dozen stray cats and entered the barn, where the air was warm and sweet-smelling from the alfalfa and green hay on the cows' snorty breath.

The cows were being milked, the machines making sucking sounds. Swallows darted in and out. She found Neal in a far corner over by the calf pen. When she got near enough, several calves poked their heads through the slats of the wooden fence and suckled on her fingers.

"Hey there, pipsqueak," Neal said, never one for formality. He had a great tousled head of hair and an overbite that used to be cute but that now made him look much dimmer than he was. He wore a filthy T-shirt and baggy jeans, and his hands were slick with something liquid and dark—she didn't want to know what. He wiped them on a rag and hopped out of the pen, landing hard on his muddy workboots. "We can talk in my office," he said, leading the way.

Neal's office was located in another building just off the main barn, connected by a chilly hallway. The pasteurization equipment hummed noisily, alternately cooking and cooling the milk, separating skim from cream. Neal closed the door behind them and the hum of machinery grew muffled. She took a seat in a cracked leather chair while he sat behind his desk, moving stacks of paperwork aside so that they could see one another. The office smelled of linseed oil and leather harnesses.

"So what's your liquid lifestyle?" he asked, opening the door of the mini-fridge, and she noticed his hands were callused. "Chocolate milk? Perrier? Classic Coke?"

"No, thanks, I'm fine."

"Mind if I have a beer?"

"Go right ahead."

"You haven't changed." He snorted laughter through his nose and cracked a Samuel Adams.

"You haven't either, much."

"I'll take that as a compliment. Cheers." He guzzled his beer, then wiped his mouth with the back of his hand and sat back in a relaxed fashion, except she knew he wasn't relaxed: his foot jiggled nervously over his crossed leg.

"Thanks for granting this interview."

"Anything for you, doll," he said magnanimously.

She opened her notebook. "The night you dropped Melissa D'Agostino off on Black Hill Road . . . where did you go afterward?"

"Let's see." He squinted into some middle distance. "Ozzie and Dolly took off, and me and Boomer went over to Boomer's house to play pool."

"For how long?"

"Couple hours, maybe."

"Boomer's parents were home?"

"Yup." He looked at her over his beer. "Isn't that in the report? What're you reopening the case for?"

"Because it was never solved."

"Listen, Rachel . . ." He sat forward and picked up a snow

globe from his desk, miniature Santa and sleigh and eight tiny Guernseys inside. He turned it over, making it snow. "Ask your brother where he went that night."

"I've already spoken to Billy."

"What'd he say?"

"I'm not at liberty to discuss that with you, Neal."

"Well. Ask Billy where he went after we dropped Melissa off."

"He spent the evening with Gillian Dumont."

Neal squinted at her. "Okey-doke."

Her mind raced like an anthill that's been stirred with a stick. "What d'you mean, 'okey-doke'? Are you implying he lied?"

"You're the one who's reopening the case," he said, turning to gaze out a dust-speckled window. "You know, I was born inside that house. My dad was born in that house. Grandpa, too. I didn't think I was ever gonna be a farmer like my old man, and now . . . look at me. Farmer Fliss. Weird, huh? Sometimes I feel like Gary Cooper on acid. You know what the crazy part is? I love being a farmer. Love it. And it scares the piss outta me. Because I don't know what's gonna happen in the future. I think it's gonna get rough."

She remembered how he used to chase her when they were kids, threatening to pee all over her Sunday school shoes, but he never did. She took all his curses and insults like the little love missives they were meant to be.

"You know," he said, "as a farmer, you have to keep getting bigger or you won't survive. Gotta offset the acreage. The margin income. I honestly don't know how I'm gonna keep things going."

"Neal," she said, "do you have some information you'd like to share with me regarding my brother?"

"You know," he said, looking straight at her, "I always thought that maybe you and me would get together eventually, but we never did. Isn't that funny? You felt it, too, didn't you, Rachel?"

"Yeah," she admitted, "once. A long time ago."

"Look," he said, smoothing his hand across the wide, worried expanse of his forehead, "I've got nothing to say that you don't already know deep down inside."

"Could you be a little more obscure, please?"

"You've got the same smile you had twenty years ago, y'know that, sweetpea?" He winked at her. "Talk to Boomer."

"Boomer?" Her cell phone rang. "Excuse me." Static broke up most of the words so that ". . . missing person . . ." was the only thing she heard.

FRUIT OF THE POISON TREE

THE CASTILLOS LIVED ON PUMPKIN RUN ROAD IN ONE OF THE town's nicest neighborhoods, oversized houses like symbols of potency set back from the streets, backyard swimming pools surrounded by tall cedar fences. The renovated Greek Revival stood on a half-acre clearing and had the kind of sheen and upkeep that told you its residents were well off enough to imagine they could buy peace of mind.

Rachel knocked on the door and Dr. Yale Castillo answered. Yale was the senior surgeon on call in the emergency room at Kerrins County General Hospital. They'd spoken fairly often in the ER, exchanging information about a carjacking or a stabbing. He was an old warrior with an overly proud demeanor, his dyed black hair plastered unflatteringly across his balding pate. He wore gold wire-rim glasses and his mouth was a practiced slit from years of keeping his patients' harrowing needs at arm's length.

"It could be nothing," were his first words to her, "but my oldest daughter appears to be missing." His voice was raspy, but his eyes betrayed not a hint of panic. "Please, come in."

Rachel's scalp prickled, the gravity of the situation impressing her in a new and visceral way. Claire Castillo worked with Billy at Winfield School for the Blind, and Billy had confessed he'd had a crush on her. Rachel's and Claire's lives had crossed paths early on, but then Claire was sent away to boarding school, a luxury Rachel's parents could ill afford.

The family was gathered in the contemporary-style living room with its gleaming beveled bronze mirrors, elm veneer in a light finish on the doors and drawers, octagonal glass-topped end tables and Plexiglas-cube lamps. Yale's wife sat on a long white sectional couch, her slender hands fidgeting in her lap. She had a slouchy, chestnut-colored hairdo and a stiff, prim posture. She stood nervously when Rachel entered the room.

"Are you with the police?"

"Jackie, this is Detective Storrow," Yale said. "She's here to help us."

She eyed Rachel skeptically. "She's so young."

"I've had four years on the force, Mrs. Castillo. Three as a patrol officer and one as a detective, and I can assure you that I'm not all that young."

Jackie's face was frozen in a pained smile. "We're worried about Claire. She didn't show up for work this morning."

"Claire is a creature of habit," Yale interrupted. "She calls home twice a week, rain or shine. Wednesday nights and Sunday mornings, without fail, we get our phone call from Claire."

"Without fail." Jackie turned to her husband.

"But late last night, when we hadn't heard from her, Jackie phoned and kept getting the machine. You have to understand, this is not like Claire. So earlier this morning, I went over there to check on her myself . . ."

"You have a key?"

"She gave us her spare."

"She rents an apartment on Fidelity Drive." Jackie's face was flushed. "Something's definitely wrong, Officer."

"Detective," Yale corrected his wife. "We're a bit concerned. Claire's twenty-nine years old, she's very responsible."

"Have you tried calling any of her friends?"

"Oh, yes. Nobody's heard from her since yesterday afternoon."

"She works at Winfield with your brother," Yale added.

"Yes, I know. I've met her. Let's have a seat and I'll take down some information."

A pale, pretty teenager was seated in a corner of the living room, her mouth a dot of resentment. Yale turned to her.

"Nicole?" he said. "Say hello to Detective Storrow."

"Hi." Nicole gave a dismissive wave.

Rachel took a seat opposite Yale and his wife, now pressed together like two hands in prayer on the sectional couch. "When a person goes missing, we have to consider all the possibilities," she began, opening her notebook. "Did she run away? Was she suicidal? Did she owe anybody money?"

"No, no. Certainly not." Jackie shook her head.

"No to suicide," Yale said. "No to running away. The girls know they can always come to me if they need money."

"Okay," Rachel said, removing her coat in the stuffy heat of the house. "I'll need a list of acquaintances and friends, bank accounts, hobbies . . ."

"When the girls were little," Jackie said softly, "I'd let Claire baby-sit. I knew she wouldn't open the door to strangers."

Nicole Castillo shifted on her leather wing chair and frowned.

"Any history of depression?" Rachel asked. "Was she on medication?"

"Just an inhaler for her asthma, when she needed it."

"Claire's a born optimist," Jackie said. Poised and brittle, she was having a hard time keeping it all together, and her hovering husband and distanced daughter seemed very aware of this fact. "I doubt she had an enemy in the world."

"She did have a habit," Yale said, taking Jackie's hand and pressing it firmly between his, "of frequenting a certain diner every Wednesday night . . . what's it called?" He turned to his wife. "The Homebaked . . . Halfbaked . . . ?"

"The Hurryback Cafe."

"That's it. Located downtown."

Rachel knew the place, a vegetarian restaurant on Main Street, and jotted the name in her notebook.

"She called it her 'me time,'" Jackie said. "She'd eat dinner, maybe do some shopping. Claire enjoys spending time by herself, whereas me . . . I'd go stark raving mad. I like having lots of people around."

"Claire's very independent," Yale said proudly.

"Stubborn," Jackie agreed, "like her father."

"Pigheaded like her old man." He nodded.

"I'll need a picture," Rachel said, and nervous smiles fought through the fear on their faces.

Back in her '91 Isuzu Impulse, Rachel phoned Billy at school. It took a while for the receptionist to track him down. "Billy?" she said, and the line started breaking up. "Billy, it's me. You work with Claire Castillo, don't you?"

"She hasn't shown up yet," he said. "It's kind of chaotic here."

"Her parents think she's missing."

"What?" He sounded genuinely alarmed.

"They think she's missing. She's not in her apartment and she keeps in pretty close touch."

"Jeez . . ."

"When was the last time you saw her?"

"Yesterday after school. We had a cup of coffee in the cafeteria, then I had to go pick up Porter."

"Who?"

"You know . . . my head-injured kid. I'm his volunteer. We hang out together Wednesday nights."

"Billy," she said, "do you think something could've happened to her?"

"What?"

The line was breaking up. "Do you have any idea what might've happened to her?"

"No," he said, and she sensed him getting defensive. "I have no idea where she is, Rachel. I just hope she's okay. We were gonna get together tonight and do something. Jesus . . ."

"Billy? You're breaking up . . ."

"Call and let me know, okay?"

"What?"

"Call me and let—"

The line went dead.

. . .

Flowering Dogwood straddled a bend in the Androscoggin River on the edge of the White Mountains, nestled deep in the glaciated valley of Maine's northern wilderness. Eighty percent of the state was covered with pine and hardwood and tamarack, the all-encroaching forest interrupted by occasional marshy fens and rolling hills of fields and pastures. In the distance, the mountains with their white landslide scars spiked the horizon.

Rachel pulled into an asphalt parking lot behind Claire's brick and granite apartment building on Fidelity Drive. Inside, the landlord met her in the wide vestibule and they rode a creaking elevator up to the fourth floor. She had called him from her car and he had offered his full cooperation. Fred Lake's gray hair was scraggly and long, like a wrestler's, and his myopic gaze made her uneasy.

"So Claire's missing?" he asked pointedly.

"We're still investigating."

"She's got the best unit. Top floor. Nobody over you playing fucking Mexican marimba music. Great view. Cross-ventilation." He opened the elevator doors. "Her dad's a doctor. Rich guy. You can't tell me she makes that kind of dough working with the ginks."

"The what?"

"You know. Moles. Bats."

Rachel's voice grew cold. "Thanks, I'll take it from here."

"Lemme get the door." She noticed his limp as he walked down the hallway in front of her. He fiddled with the keys, then unlocked the door to Apartment 402. "Here you go."

The first thing Rachel noticed when she entered the apartment was that the lights were off and the windows were shut. The place was a colorful mess, the home of a woman too busy and involved with life to bother with anything as trivial as housework. The large, comfortable furniture in the living room was buried beneath a snowfall of unfolded laundry, last week's newspapers, abandoned books, forgotten plates dotted with crumbs, glasses that left rings on the varnished end tables. The kitchenette was painted a sunny yellow, nasturtiums basking on the windowsill above a sink full of dirty dishes. The dishwater was cold. There was nothing in or on the stove, no plate of food left out, no half-smoked cigarette left in an ashtray that might indicate she'd been interrupted in the middle of something here in the apartment.

"You know, she had this visitor lately," the landlord said, "some guy, tall fellow, brown hair . . . kind of pie-eyed."

"What?"

"Pie-eyed, you know . . . he followed her around like a puppy dog."

"Thanks," Rachel said. "I can handle it from here."

His face grew resentful. He rattled his keys and brushed rudely past her on his way out.

The bathroom was mildewed, half a dozen towels draped carelessly over the shower curtain rod. The bedroom walls were festooned with art prints—van Gogh, Miró, Frida Kahlo. Rachel rummaged through the closet, lots of dresses and skirts, a pair of funny-looking khaki trousers with short silver zippers over each pocket and vertically down each cuff, a dry cleaning bag with a white blouse inside. Shoes and sneakers in a jumble at the bottom, scarves dangling from the shelf above, a black fedora plunked over a terry cloth bathrobe hanging from a large wire hook on the door. Aside from the clutter Jackie Castillo had already warned her about, nothing seemed amiss.

Still, Rachel was getting a bad feeling about this.

She moved to a rolltop desk made of some fine grain of wood and picked up a black leather organizer from the navy ink blotter. Names, addresses and phone numbers filled its back pages. She thumbed through the calendar section, random initials written inside the little squares: "GL . . . s . . . HC . . . c/d . . ." A shorthand diary?

Rachel flipped to last night—Wednesday, October 14th—and found several letters etched inside the calendar square, one predominant among them: "b." She felt an extended shiver run down her spine. *"b" for Billy?*

Billy had mentioned he and Claire were supposed to get together tonight, Thursday night. Inside Thursday's square, she found the notation "B @ 7." A chill came over Rachel. It seemed obvious that this "B" stood for Billy, but had Claire seen Billy yesterday, as well? Or last night, Wednesday night, the night she disappeared? Did the "b" stand for Billy? If so, why the lowercase?

She glanced at the desk's cluttered cubbyholes, eyes drawn to a thick stack of red envelopes. She slid out the packet of envelopes, some of which were still sealed, and opened the letter on top. ". . . I will slit your throat . . ." She could feel the heat of her own body as she flipped through page after page of threats and irrational accusations written in shaky block letters. ". . . I will strangle you in your sleep . . . you ruined my life . . . don't deny it, you bitch, I know what you did . . . you loosened the stitches on all my clothes while I was asleep . . . I KNOW THIS TO BE TRUE! DO NOT DENY IT!" The letters were unsigned, with no return address, and postmarked Bangor, Maine.

She jumped when her cell phone rang.

"We found something." It was McKissack. "I think you should come take a look."

2

FLOWERING DOGWOOD WAS LAID OUT ON A GRID PATTERN. IT had one movie theater and over a dozen churches. There were eight bars, including the Peaked Hills and Eleazor's Gutter, and its two main commercial streets, Delongpre and Main, intersected at the downtown business district. There were two parks and a shopping mall built in the 1970s, and the town itself was surrounded on all sides by forest, a vast wild growth. Every street ended in woods, except to the west where the interstate and dairy farms began; then you got a checkerboard of pastureland and a fast way out of town.

Several police officers were down on their hands and knees, crawling around on the asphalt of the public parking lot behind Sears on Main Street. McKissack greeted Rachel as she pulled up to the yellow police tape.

"Claire Castillo's car," he said, pointing.

A shiny red Nissan Sentra was parked in the northwest corner of the lot where the forest grew right up to the concrete. Rachel glanced around. The nearest streetlight was about fifty feet away. There had been a heavy ground fog last night, she recalled, the air pregnant with the promise of rain.

"This feels funny to me," McKissack said, refusing to meet her gaze. He always did this to her after one of their encounters, became coldly professional in order to mask his guilt. He acted as if they barely knew one another, and she deeply resented his hypocrisy.

"Me, too," she said in her most detached, professional manner. "The apartment looks okay, outside of the usual mess her mother warned me about."

"I'll send Nussbaum over to vacuum for hair and fibers and dust for prints."

"So you're classifying the case a kidnapping?"

"What do you think, Storrow?"

"I think we can eliminate the possibility of a voluntary walk-away. She wasn't on any medication outside of an asthma inhaler, she didn't owe anybody money, she wasn't depressed . . ."

"I'm classifying it as a missing persons for now." She accompanied him to his car, where a flock of starlings shrieked into the air, and she tried to connect somehow with their darting reptilian eyes, their tiny bristling heads.

"This corner of the lot's awfully dark. You think somebody could've jumped her?" she asked.

"We're scouring the area. We'll get prints off the car, hopefully before it rains." He glanced at the overcast, celery-colored sky. "I'm gonna launch a full-scale search-and-rescue."

"Good."

McKissack opened his trunk and took out an evidence collection kit containing wire cutters, pliers, syringes, plastic bags, a flashlight and measuring tape. He also pulled out a latent-fingerprint kit, then flipped through his notepad, its pages smudged and chaotic with hastily scribbled notes. "She ate at the Hurryback Cafe last night. We interviewed the waitress. Entered unaccompanied around seven P.M., ate her meal alone, then left around eight P.M. The waitress noticed nothing odd about her behavior. So far, she's the last person to've seen her alive."

Rachel arched an eyebrow. "You found a body?"

"Sorry. Slip of the tongue." There was something appealing about his unaccustomed dishevelment, something dangerous, as if his thoughts were scattered in a dozen different directions, but she knew better than to make that kind of assumption. "The Castillos give you friends and acquaintances?"

Rachel nodded. "I found this in her apartment." He still wouldn't look at her fully, and she had to thrust the organizer into his hands. "It's got initials marked all through it."

"Initials?" He thumbed through the calendar section. "Her own private code?"

"Maybe." She wasn't going to share her suspicions with McKissack unless it became absolutely necessary. Besides, her brother had an alibi for Wednesday night. He had been with his head-injured kid. "And these." She showed him the stack of red envelopes sealed in an evidence bag. "I think she was being stalked. None of them are signed. All Bangor postmarks."

"Let's get them down to the station," he said. "I want these photocopied, then sent to the lab for prints."

"I'm way ahead of you, McKissack."

He smiled self-consciously. "Don't be such a smart-ass, Detective."

"Can't help it. It's a lifetime membership."

He had slipped momentarily, exposing his human side and ruining his icy pose, but now his face hardened, and his voice, even in its lowest register, radiated cool detachment. "I want interviews. Friends, relatives, acquaintances, coworkers. Let's find out who the nutjob is."

"Jim," she said, and he looked away, color blossoming on his cheeks. "We don't have to act like strangers again, do we?"

He wouldn't answer.

"We made a mistake, and now I'm getting crucified for it."

"What am I supposed to say to that?" he snapped.

She held his eye, shook her head. "Fuck you, Chief," she said and strode away.

3

THERE WERE PEOPLE MILLING AROUND OUTSIDE THE HOUSE, and Nicole Castillo didn't know how much longer she could stand it. It was raining but the sun was trying hard to penetrate the clouds. She and her boyfriend, Dinger, were cozily nestled in the pillowed alcove of her father's study. The door was closed, the lights were off, and Dinger was holding her hand.

"I don't believe this," she said with an involuntary shiver. "I just talked to her the other day."

"I know."

"She called me yesterday."

"It's weird."

She could count every pore on his face. A big blue vein stood out on Dinger's neck, and he wouldn't look at her directly. He was taller than she by half a foot, with soft formless features, his blond hair growing out straight but ending in little waves like the ruffles on a potato chip. His fingernails were dirty and his hands were callused, and he kept glancing at her as if he expected something to happen.

"Feels like I've been bad or something," she confessed.

"Why?" he whispered. They'd been whispering all afternoon.

"I dunno." She slid another cigarette out of the pack tucked inside her sweater pocket. Her mother had promised them complete privacy, so it felt safe to smoke.

"You should quit," Dinger said.

She looked at him.

"You're gonna get cancer."

She cracked the window an inch and lit up, then exhaled long and slow. Her breath fogged the window, and Dinger drew a heart in the fog on the glass. "I don't want you getting sick," he said.

A shudder traveled through her body, making her teeth rattle together. A tiny black bug crawled up the cold windowpane, and she crushed it under her thumb. "I just think maybe there's good and there's bad," she said, "and if you do bad, then at some point in your life, you get bad. It's karma."

He smirked. "Please don't squeeze the karma."

"I'm serious." She frowned. "Don't you think it's true? Like if I snubbed somebody a couple of years back, then I'm paying for it now?"

"No."

"Well, I've done bad things."

"Like what?"

She thought for a moment. "I used to cheat in Sunday school. I ever tell you?"

"Nuh-uh."

"I never cheated in regular school, but I always cheated in Sunday school. Isn't that weird? Like I had to defy God or something."

He laughed. "I thought you were gonna say something darker than that."

She fingered the high school ring he'd given her, which she wore on a long silver chain around her neck. The amethyst ring she'd gotten for her fifteenth birthday was on an identical long silver chain around his neck. "I'm mean to children," she whispered.

"That's not true."

She deflated. "I know."

"See? You haven't done anything bad. You're good." He smoothed her long dark hair off her face. "You're like an angel or something."

"No, I'm not."

"Yes, you are."

"I've done bad things," she insisted. "I just can't remember what they are." Sighing smoke, she gazed out the window. "The police've been asking my mom all these creepy questions, like did Claire own a gun, or was she depressed, or do we have any rope in the house."

"Rope? What for?"

Her back stiffened. "Haven't you been listening? They think she killed herself! They must be complete morons. Claire would never kill herself." Her ears itched. Everything was different now, everything had changed. She wasn't the same person she'd been last week, or even earlier this morning. A small crowd of people had gathered outside the house—volunteers, her mother said. She didn't want them there. She wished they'd all go to hell.

"I hate this." She hid her face in her hands. She was wearing her purple cardigan and a Cornershop T-shirt, turquoise plastic sandals over pink ankle socks, and her mother said she looked like a clown.

Dinger put his muscled arms around her. "Don't cry, Nicole," he said, but she couldn't help herself.

"I can't breathe." Pushing him away, she opened the window

wider and tossed her cigarette out onto the grass. A wet wind blew in, and she both liked and hated how it felt on her skin. Three officers in yellow slickers were standing under an oak tree in the backyard. One was drinking coffee, shaking his head. The volunteers were gone.

"I used to believe that good people would be rewarded and bad people would get punished, but my father says life isn't fair."

"Cold?" Dinger tried to hold her.

"Don't touch me, okay?"

"Sorry." He wiped his hands on his jeans, back and forth across his knees. He looked dumb to her all of a sudden. Big-eared and dumb dumb dumb.

"I used to have this fear," she said, taking off her sweater and leaning back against the faux-gazelle pillows, "that if I opened my legs while I was asleep, then evil spirits would enter my body and take over my soul."

He squinted. "You're kidding, right?"

"So I always sleep with my legs shut, like this. Never open, like this." She demonstrated, enjoying the effect it had on him. He looked really scared and excited at the same time. He looked so silly, she wanted to laugh.

"Don't get weird on me, Nicole."

She sat up abruptly. "How come nobody tells me anything?"

"Because they don't know anything yet."

She cupped her hands around her mouth and yelled, "What's going on out there?"

Only nobody heard her. It was raining too hard.

"I feel horrible," she shuddered, "like I can't breathe." Her teeth were chattering uncontrollably now. "Do you have to go to work today?"

"I'll call and say I can't make it." He snatched the cigarettes out of her sweater pocket and crumpled them in his fist. "No more."

"It feels like I've lost something." She couldn't see him

through the blur of tears. Her nose was plugged, and her voice was coming from somewhere faraway. "What should we do?"

"Nothing." He put his arms around her, and this time she let him. "Nothing, Nicole. Let's not do anything," he whispered in her ear. "Let's wait."

4

BILLY WAS STARING AT HER. "YOU THINK *WHAT*?"

"I'm not accusing you of anything, Billy. I just have to ask . . . since you work with her . . ."

"Jesus, this is like Dad all over again."

"Cut it out. It's nothing like that."

His mouth was set against her. He wore an ancient pair of jeans with dime-sized holes in the knees, dirty black hightops and a rumpled tailored shirt. They were sitting in the lime green kitchen of his rented house, and he'd poured them both a cup of coffee that neither of them had touched. The house was one of those gingerbread Victorians that'd long since fallen into disrepair, just your basic Charles Addams mansion—dark, tall, brooding, crowned with a high, flat-topped tower. A previous tenant had painted the dark natural interior woodwork phosphorescent colors in an attempt to brighten up the place, and the results were spectacularly ugly.

"I've got a few standard questions."

His eyes grew veiled. "Go ahead."

"Where were you around seven-thirty, eight o'clock last night?"

"I already told you, my head-injured kid. Porter Powell. I spend every Wednesday afternoon and evening with him. I took him to Taco Bell, then we shot hoops out back, then I drove him to his dorm."

"At Winfield?"

"Yeah."

"And after that?"

"I drove home. Why?"

"What time did you drop him off at the dorm?"

"Nine o'clock, I think."

"You think?"

"I don't remember."

She looked at him. "Can anyone verify the exact time you dropped off Porter Powell, Billy?"

"Yeah, his aide. Russell something, I don't remember his last name. He was there in the lounge, waiting to take Porter up to his room. I signed in at the front desk. The guard saw me."

"Billy," she said, carefully choosing her words, "you might want to consider hiring yourself a lawyer."

"What d'you mean?" His face deflated. "You think I did something to her?"

"I'm not suggesting—"

"You think I'd hurt a hair on her head? I was in love with her, Rachel! I was in love with her for an entire fucking year! She's my friend, and now suddenly she's like . . . in my arms, and I'm going crazy thinking . . . Christ, I could marry this woman. I could actually marry her!"

He got up from the table, accidentally knocking over his chair. It landed with a crash, making them both jump. He uprighted the chair and sat again, red-faced. "It's really insulting that you'd even consider me a suspect."

"Did I say that? Did I say that, Billy?"

"You implied it."

"I'm giving you good advice here. Off the record. As your sister who loves you. They always consider the boyfriend, the fiancé, the immediate family first. You need to pin down your alibi."

"Alibi? What is this, fucking *NYPD Blue*?"

She sighed defeat. "Billy, I didn't come here to fight."

"This is because of those fucking cats, isn't it?" he said, his anger raised to such a pitch that everything seemed to blaze. "It doesn't matter that I'm an entirely different person now, that I was royally fucked up at the time . . . that it's taken me years to straighten myself out . . ."

"This isn't about the cats, Billy," she said, masking her own uncertainty.

"Listen," he said, "I'm going to tell you something I've never told anyone before. You don't know about this because you were too young. I've tried to protect you from the truth, Rachel, but screw it . . ."

She stared at him, not sure what was coming. Billy was prone to exaggeration and sometimes joked around and said things he'd later take back.

"Dad hurt me psychologically and physically from the time I was born until I was six years old."

She sat in stunned silence.

"You know he used to drink, right? Early on in Mom and Dad's marriage? You know Grandpa was a drunk, right? Remember how Dad used to say he never wanted to follow in his old man's footsteps? Well, that's what he meant."

"Billy . . ."

"Why do you think there was so much tension between us? Rachel, from the time I was born, I was not allowed to have a safe feeling. Can you imagine what that's like? It's different for you. You came along after he quit drinking, after he pulled his shit together . . ."

"Billy, that's all in the past. Dad loved you . . ."

"Past? *Past!*" He chucked the words at her like pieces of gravel, too small to hurt but sharp enough to sting. "I'm afraid to get close to anyone. Do you know what that's like? I'm afraid of losing control. I've lived my whole life in a prison I've been trying to either blow up or burn down . . ."

"Billy," she said, lime green walls undulating in her peripheral vision. "I don't know what to say. I wasn't there. I wish I could've helped . . . I'm trying to help you now."

He held her eye an indignant moment, then rubbed his exhausted face. His coffee was getting cold. "I've known Claire for three years," he said, "and she was like this big mystery to me. She's a strange person, Rachel. Real open, and yet real private. Before last year, I only knew her casually, the way you'd know somebody at staff meetings and stuff. Not very well. But last year, we taught class together and got pretty tight. Christ." He groaned and lowered his head. He ran his hands through his hair; he never reminded her of their father so much as when he did that. "We were just starting to get . . ." He fell silent.

"What, Billy?"

"We were just starting to get . . ."

Her knuckles whitened around her pen. He paused for so long, she thought maybe he'd fallen asleep. "Just starting to get what, Billy?"

"Close."

"How close?"

He didn't answer her directly. "You know," he said, "I've always lived my life *as if* I cared, *as if* I felt something . . . but I didn't. Not really. Not until I met Claire."

She stared at the top of his head, the swirling innocence of his brown hair. Their father's hair.

"And then something strange happened . . ."

These words shattered her self-imposed calm like rubber bullets.

"Oh God." He didn't speak for the longest time. He started to tremble. Terrified that her own brother might be on the verge of confessing, she put down her pen and rested a hand between his shoulder blades.

"What is it, Billy?" she whispered, feeling each sob like a silent hiccup. "You can tell me."

"Oh God."

"Tell me."

He sat up abruptly, as if he might hit her. Eyes blazing, back stiffening. "If something's happened to her, it would be brutal. It would kill me, it really would."

"Billy," she said, carefully choosing her words. "After you dropped Porter off . . . is there anyone who can verify your whereabouts?"

He shook his head.

"Billy . . ."

"I think I know who might've done something," he said, voice drained of all emotion. "An ex-boyfriend was writing her these threatening letters."

"In red envelopes?"

"Yeah." He looked up. "She told me he was crazy. She'd get a red envelope about once or twice a month."

"What's his name?"

"I don't know, but she said he used to accuse her of all this crazy stuff, and she finally got up the courage to leave him."

"When?"

"A couple years ago. Rachel . . ." He looked at her angrily. Accusingly. "Not everything is my fucking fault."

"I know, Billy." She reached for his hand and he let her hold it momentarily. "I know."

5

THAT AFTERNOON A FULL-SCALE SEARCH-AND-RESCUE WAS launched in conjunction with the Maine State Police. Helicopters buzzed the county, while officers with K-9 dogs searched every inch of the downtown area in a grid pattern. The dogs picked up Claire's scent at the diner where she was last seen but lost it several yards out the door, diverted perhaps by the confusion of foot traffic on Main Street and the pouring rain. The rescue team penetrated the dense forest north of town, pushing past sodden fir boughs and sliding down ravines slippery with rain. They searched the swampland west of the Triangle, the cornfields, the parks, and came up empty-handed. Claire Castillo had simply disappeared.

She'd undoubtedly come to harm, Rachel thought. This was a woman who'd hardly missed a day of work, who was in constant contact with her family. "It's the kind of case I dread," McKissack told her that afternoon over the phone, and she imagined his tense face couched in a jagged halo of disarranged hair.

"I found out who wrote those letters," she said.

"Who?"

"An ex-boyfriend. He lives outside of Bangor. I got a phone number from her parents. He's agreed to an interview."

"Go, girl."

"I'm on my way."

It was a two-hour trip. The setting sun flared across the horizon by the time she arrived in Sayerprayers, Maine, a real knees-and-elbows town. WELCOME TO SAYERPRAYERS, a sign in one of the town's many bars read, HUB OF THE UNIVERSE.

Rachel crawled along a rutted road, looking for Buck Folette's street. Ramshackle houses spread like acne across the face of this shabby old burg, muddy lawns strewn with trash—fast-food wrappers, doggie chew toys, rusting tricycles. She took a right onto the aptly named Devil's Reach Road and drove past a six-pack of silent teenagers until she reached the dead end. As she got out, a cold pocket of air snaked around her head.

Her heels clicked up the flagstone walkway. The house was dark, the rest of the street deserted. The porch floorboards creaked and the rusty screen door had fallen off its hinges. Biting back her trepidation, Rachel knocked.

A man in his mid-thirties answered. He was good-looking with red-rimmed eyes and kept sniffing, as if he'd done a few lines and wasn't afraid to let it show. He had an aristocratic nose, chiseled cheekbones and long, wavy yellow hair he pushed back behind his ears. His eyes were cunning and mean, and he resembled nothing so much as your average frat boy from hell. She detested him on sight but recalled her father's words: *You catch more flies with honey than with vinegar.*

"Officer Storrow?" He extended a tanned hand, his breath reeking of alcohol.

"You must be Mr. Folette."

"I must be. C'mon in."

The place was squalid, pizza boxes imprinted on the dirty toast-colored shag, beer bottles strewn like rose petals at a wedding, stolen hotel ashtrays bristling with butts. The TV set was on, tuned to some forgettable 1980s sitcom.

"You'll have to forgive the place, it stinks like the crack of God's ass." He flashed her a million-dollar smile. "Beer?"

"No, thanks."

"Yeah, right. Not while you're on duty." He fell backward into a pea-colored armchair, a cloud of dust puffing up around him. A path from the sofa to the kitchen had been worn threadbare in the shag rug, and the only light was coming from the TV set. She strained her eyes for a place to sit.

"Just push those magazines off," he said, pointing at a sofa covered with auto magazines. "Sorry about the mess." He stared at her, transfixed. "So what's this little visit about, Ossifer?"

A million thoughts raced through Rachel's head. She preferred to conduct interviews on tape and had brought a mini-recorder for that purpose, despite the fact that most interviewees refused to allow themselves to be recorded. Predictably, Buck declined, and so she took out her pen and a statement form. She would listen, take notes and shape a written statement for him to sign.

Since it was highly likely that Buck might become a suspect, Rachel reminded herself to read him the noncustodial rights warning, which was like the Miranda warning only with a difference: the suspect did not have the option of having a lawyer appointed for him and was advised he could cut the interview short at any time. Although he was not under arrest, the noncustodial warning would subsequently establish that she had given him every opportunity to exercise his constitutional rights.

After she'd handled these bits of business, Rachel got right to the point. "Claire Castillo has been missing since Wednesday evening."

"Oh yeah? Missing, how?"

"Missing, as in gone."

"Gee whiz." He seemed amused. "That's too bad."

"Where were you Wednesday night, Mr. Folette?"

He gave her a winning smile. "I'm Buck to my friends."

The hairs rose on the back of Rachel's neck. Was Buck the "<u>b</u>" in Claire's Day-Timer? "Where were you Wednesday night, Buck?"

"Right here." He slapped the arm of his chair and another puff of dust rose up. "Planted in front of the tube like a tulip."

"Can anyone verify that?"

"My landlady. Lives upstairs."

"Is she home now?"

He shrugged.

"Mind if I talk to her after our interview?"

"Long as you don't mind if I smoke."

"Go right ahead."

"You can trust a man with a vice, my papa used to say, but never trust the Sober, the Smoke-Free, the Slender or the Sweet-Smelling." He got up from his chair and knelt in front of the coffee table where he proceeded to roll his own cigarette. When he was done, he sat back on his haunches and sparked up. Picking bits of tobacco off his tongue, he said, "Man, that girl was nuts about me. Her old man hated my guts, though. One summer we were living in Flowering Dogwood, and her father used to spy on us. He'd drive by the apartment all the time, so we moved back here."

"Do you still communicate with her?"

"No," he said, mouth growing hard.

"Phone calls? Letters? E-mail?"

"Nope." He sat back smugly in his chair.

"Well, somebody's been sending her letters on red stationery, in red envelopes."

"Not me." Smoke bled from his cigarette.

"They're pretty abusive, these letters."

"I wasn't mean to her," he said defensively. "I never slapped her around or called her bitch or anything."

"That's not what I hear."

"Yeah, well, you know . . . we could both get pretty liquored up." He grinned at the thought. "Man, I was in love! You only fall in love for real once in your life. From day one, that girl was all over me like a cheap suit. She'd get jealous if I even looked at another woman sidewise."

"I heard you hit her a couple of times."

He stared at her oddly. "No, ma'am."

"There's a police report . . ."

"Oh. Wait. The microchips in my brain are a little rusty." He laughed. "Once. Just that one time. Cops wouldn't listen to me: I mean, if you want the truth, Claire used to beat the crap outta me. I had scratches all up and down my arms here . . . on my neck and shit . . ."

"In one such incident, you gave her a black eye. I have a copy of the police report." Rachel swallowed back the bile rising in her throat. Her feelings for this man weren't important. She needed to adjust herself psychologically so that she and Buck were in harmony. She could be hard-nosed when she had to, but the sympathy approach rarely failed.

"Yeah, well, maybe I did hit her once or twice," he hedged. "She could drive a man nuts with a capital N. Peace, love and parking lots." He extinguished his cigarette, cracked another beer. He seemed to want the conversation to end there, but Rachel persisted.

"You said in your letters—"

His entire body tensed as he leaned forward. "You read them?"

"Yes."

"Do you have them?"

"Not on me. They're down at the lab being dusted for prints. So you admit you wrote them?"

He looked away, profile bathed in TV light, and set his facial muscles into a glare.

"Look, we've all been in relationships," she said, "good and bad . . ."

"You can't just waltz into my house and completely impose yourself." His icy gaze tickled the base of her spine. This interview was on the verge of becoming an interrogation, and Rachel silently gave herself permission to try for a full confession. She wanted a confession, even if it meant he might go free later on. If a suspect confessed and supplied information about a crime, such as where the body was hidden, and if his attorney had the confession ruled inadmissible later on, then none of the evidence collected from the confession would count. This was called "fruit of the poison tree." McKissack liked to get his confessions last, once most of the evidence was in, but in the case of a kidnapping, there simply wasn't time.

"When was the last time you took a vacation?"

"Huh?" He squinted at her through the flickering TV light.

"You know, just got away from it all?"

"Not in a while." His eyes misted over. "My folks have this place by the seashore . . ." His eyebrows dropped. "Okay, so I wore the same clothes all summer long, so what? I was wasted eight ways to Sunday, too stoned to change my clothes, okay?

She made such a big deal out of it, and here she was, this incredible slob . . . you ever seen her place?"

"Yes, I have."

"You know, when it comes to other people's personal shortcomings, Claire was an idiot savant on the subject." He swallowed some beer and looked at her. "You married?"

"No." Rachel strained forward during the silence that followed, listening for any stray sound that might alert her to Claire's presence in the apartment. Soon she would ask his consent to search the premises. She'd brought along a consent form for that specific purpose.

"No, I'm not," she admitted. "I'm not married."

"Pretty cop like you?" He smiled his indigent frat-boy smile. "Never been proposed to?"

"We're not talking about me."

"Why not?"

She could feel her face getting hot. "Because."

"I got you." He grinned.

"Mr. Folette—"

"Call me Buck."

"Buck . . . in these letters, you accuse her—"

"The bitch was after me." His mouth had a bitter downturn. He looked at her and slammed his fist on the arm of the chair.

Reflexively, she thought about her gun. It was awfully dark in here. Buck probably had a weapon hidden somewhere inside the house. Welcome to Sayerprayers—guns in the homes, guns in the pickups, guns at the 7-Eleven . . .

"She wanted my soul. She kept doing things . . . plotting against me . . ."

"Like what?"

"Okay, you wanna know? She'd wake up in the middle of the night and loosen the stitches on all my clothes."

"What?"

"You heard me." He sat back, apparently satisfied.

"Why would she do a thing like that?"

"Exactly what I was wondering." He frowned, long lines mapping his face. "That's why I broke up with her."

"I thought she broke up with you?"

"No, it's the other way around."

"Well, she got a restraining order."

"I know how it looks." He became suddenly animated, like a child watching fireworks for the first time. "Ain't nobody ever told you, you can't judge a book by its cover? It's not my fault she's missing. She asked for it. She's crazy. That woman lies like a rug. She's a ballbuster with a capital B." He was speaking with the narrative speed of an excited two-year-old. "What goes around, comes around. My luck'll turn. My day will come. You can count on it, sister. One of these days I'll be God, judge, president and the goddamn high school guidance counselor. But Claire, see . . . Claire's luck flew south. She fucked with too many heads, and now she's gonna pay."

"Buck, are you on any medication?"

He stared at her sullenly, brow furrowing.

"Do you take medication?"

"What's that got to do with the price of Eggos?"

"Do you hear voices?"

He smiled and relit his half-smoked cigarette.

"Do you, Buck?"

"What, hear voices?"

"Yes."

"Well, I can hear your voice."

"Any other voices?"

"Sometimes." He shrugged. "Coming from the keyholes."

Leaning forward, Rachel chose her words carefully. "I'd like your consent to search the apartment."

"Huh?" he said with a fleshy smirk.

"I brought this consent form with me. It means you waive your right to be free from search without a warrant. Just sign here, that proves the consent was voluntary."

He drew back. "Why should I?"

"You've got nothing to hide, right? This will show you were willing to cooperate. Trust me, it can only help in the long run."

"Cut it out," he said, hand sliding between the cushions, and before she knew it, he was holding a .45-caliber handgun on her. "Quit screwing with my head."

Without thinking, Rachel drew her weapon and aimed it at Buck's chest. The world closed in around her. Stupid, stupid. How could she have let things get so out of hand? "Don't move!" she said, a tiny scream worming its way through her brain. "Drop your weapon. Now!"

"No."

"I said drop it!"

"You first."

Her hands were shaking, a sheen of sweat breaking out on her forehead. She'd been taught to fire center mass, which meant the chest, where the vital organs were. If she tried for the head, she might miss. There was less margin of error with the chest. "Easy, now. Put the gun down."

"You first." His aim was frighteningly steady.

Her heart was pounding and she couldn't breathe. Her life was in danger. She needed to remain calm. Carefully, she aligned the target in her front and rear sights. If she had to shoot to kill, she would. If forced to. If only her heart would quit leaping around inside her throat so that she couldn't breathe.

"Ease your finger off the trigger. You don't want to hurt anyone, and neither do I. Place your weapon on the coffee table, Buck." The gun was centered directly in front of her eyes and both arms were locked. Her feet were spread apart about shoulder-width, knees bent slightly, and she could feel her weight on the balls of her feet.

After an interminable beat, he finally eased his finger off the trigger and placed the .45 down on the coffee table.

She picked up the gun and was surprised to find it empty. "You're under arrest," she said, pocketing it. "You have the right to remain silent . . ."

"What for?" His pupils contracted. "I put the gun down, didn't I?"

"Is this gun licensed?"

He shrugged. A twisted lump of clothing lay on the rug at his feet, and he gingerly stepped over it as if it were a dead body.

"Stay where you are," she warned, palm growing sweaty on the checkerboard grip. His proximity was making her uncomfortable. Her balance was poor; she had automatically chosen the Isosceles stance, which put her at a distinct disadvantage. Increased recovery time, strain on the shoulder muscles.

"Put your hands on your head and turn around."

He eyed her with an odd fascination. "What for?"

"You're under arrest."

"Aw, c'mon. Can't you let it slide just this once?"

"Turn around and put your hands on your head!" She reached for her handcuffs.

He took his time tamping out his cigarette. Blood pounded in her ears, and her heart raced faster than her thoughts. She didn't want to kill another human being. She didn't want to make a mistake. Her finger was growing slick on the trigger—she couldn't feel the trigger anymore. She fumbled for her handcuffs, but before she could prevent it from happening, he darted around behind her and got her in a headlock. He hugged her throat with his powerful arm, cutting off her airway. She twisted in fear and scratched his arms, drawing blood, but he held on fast.

She was losing consciousness. Trembling with rage.

"Some people fuck with people and play with their heads for the sheer pleasure of taking them apart," he said, grunting, and Rachel drew her elbow forward and jabbed it backward into his ribs.

He cried out and released her. Twisting around, she slammed her palm into his nose, and Buck flew back and crashed into the TV set.

Down on the floor, she got one of his wrists handcuffed, but he fought her off, bucking like a bronco. He screamed obscenities at her. His face was bleeding. She dug her knee into his back and tried to twist his other arm around behind him, but he bucked her off. She went flying into the wall and saw stars. The world narrowed as he lunged for her, but she rolled out of his way, accidentally hitting her knee on the edge of the coffee table.

She heard a metallic snap as a sharp pain kicked up her leg. "Ow, shit." She could barely breathe, she was so full of fury. She wanted to rip his flesh apart with her teeth.

He lunged again, and she cracked his windpipe with her fist.

Dropping like a stone, he clutched his neck, eyes spiteful. Lying splayed, spitting blood, he gave a grunt of surrender.

She finished handcuffing him, got up quickly from the floor and called for backup. "I need an ambulance," she said, her heart gradually easing back into its normal pulse.

He stared up at her, slender fingers working his throat. "Christ's last word should've been 'Assholes,'" he said.

6

"THE PUBLIC WANTS ANSWERS," MCKISSACK SAID, UNWRAP-ping a Ring Ding, his voice both soft and fierce. "I'd like to be able to tell them that the case is moving forward."

They were all seated around the conference table—Rachel and McKissack, dispatcher Phillip Reingold, now close to retirement, Lieutenant Ted Tapper, and Detectives Ira Keppel and Steve Cavanaugh. Two weeks had passed, and they were no closer to solving the case. Fourteen days of searches, surveillance and the gathering of physical evidence, and still they had no ransom demand, no eyewitnesses, no suspects, not a clue as to Claire's whereabouts.

They had set up recording equipment for "trap and trace" at the Castillos' house, where the anguished family anxiously awaited some word, even a ransom demand. Dr. Yale Castillo publicly begged for the return of his daughter. "She needs her asthma medication," he said on all the local news stations. The family clung to hope.

"What about Buck Folette?" McKissack now asked Rachel.

"Landlady confirms she spent Wednesday night and most of Thursday with him in his apartment. Two friends called him that night, three friends visited on Thursday."

"When did they call him Wednesday night?"

"One at nine-twelve P.M., the other at eleven-seventeen P.M. Both conversations lasted over thirty minutes. The phone company's security division has supplied us with a list of all incoming and outgoing numbers. Looks like our friend Buck wasn't anywhere near Flowering Dogwood on the night Claire disappeared."

"Are you kidding? His prints are all over those letters," Ted Tapper said. Nearing forty, Lieutenant Tapper was swarthy and arrogant, his perpetually stiff expression blunting the initial impact made by his handsome features and muscular body. In Rachel's opinion, Tapper was aggressively unappealing.

"We don't need fingerprint analysis," Rachel said. "He admits he wrote them."

"Look, whoever wrote those letters definitely had something to do with Claire's disappearance, I don't care what his skanky-ass landlady says."

"He got a record?" McKissack asked.

"Antisocial tendencies surfaced early," Rachel said, thumbing through her notes. "He assaulted a cousin at age fourteen, but the family hired a lawyer who got the charges dismissed after Buck's father lied about his whereabouts. I got this from the sister. Throughout the years, the family has continued to protect him."

"What if Buck's friends are covering for him now?" Tapper asked. "What if those phone calls were actually for the landlady?"

McKissack arched an eyebrow at Rachel.

"It's possible," she said. "He and Claire Castillo were in an abusive relationship for two years, and during that time he was arrested twice for domestic violence."

"And each time," Tapper said, "the family hires this big-time lawyer, waving psychiatric reports."

"Just like they did last week," McKissack said with thinly veiled disgust. "He was booked for aggravated assault, assault with a dangerous weapon, resisting arrest and possession of an unlicensed firearm. But because the gun wasn't loaded, his lawyer was able to get the charges reduced."

"He's held for a mere five days before being released on his own recognizance," Tapper sneered.

"Mom and Pop keep bailing him out," Steve Cavanaugh said. Not fat but certainly soft-looking, Steve was an inveterate doughnut-eater and prodigious coffee-drinker who had a way with the ladies, perhaps because of his dogged earnestness. "I'm so earnest, I'm Ernest Hemingway," he was fond of saying. "So what's his psychological problem du jour?"

"His psychosis has been marked by delusions and hallucinations," Rachel said. "He started deteriorating at around age thirteen, when he growled at people and threatened to stab his parents with a butcher knife. He was prescribed an antipsychotic to stabilize his schizophrenia. Since then he's been admitted to area hospitals for treatment of psychosis and has suffered several relapses."

"There you go," Tapper said. "He's our man."

"Just because he's mentally ill, doesn't make him guilty," Rachel said.

"He attacked you, didn't he?" Tapper sneered.

"Yes." It had taken her several hours to get the adrenaline down and regain her composure. Buck was bigger and stronger, and she had survived a very dangerous situation. For days afterward, she felt grateful for every breath she took. "Schizophrenics have been known to attack when provoked."

"Go ahead, Rachel," Tapper said, "take the creep's side."

"I'm not taking anyone's side."

"Let's be civil, people." McKissack's face was heavy from pulling sixteen-hour shifts like the rest of them, yet he'd recently changed into a crisp white shirt and tie. "Is he on medication?"

"He's taking clozapine."

"Forget about it, the guy's insane," Phillip Reingold said. "He's got all kinds of psychiatrists testifying to that effect."

"I think it's bullshit," Tapper said with priggish confidence. "He's a drug addict with antisocial tendencies whose rich mommy and daddy keep bailing him out. And his junkie landlady's about as credible as that Ring Ding you're eating."

"I want him under surveillance," McKissack decided. "I know the local sheriff, he'll cooperate. Tapper?"

"I'm on it."

"I just have a feeling," Rachel said, "he's not our man."

"Such insight from a mere mortal," Tapper said, and Rachel ignored him, although her heart beat just a little bit faster.

"I spoke with his landlady personally," she said, "and I believe her story. Also, after his arrest, after he was Mirandized, he waived his rights and gave me permission to search the premises. We found nothing the least bit incriminating."

"What about the cabin?" Ira Keppel asked. Keppel was a two-dollar toupee in a polyester sports coat, a workaholic who liked to jump-start his day with a fistful of No-Doz. "I thought you said his family owned a place by the ocean. What if he's hiding the victim there?"

Tapper leaned forward, eyes intently focused. "What if she's holed up in the family cabin? We should get a search warrant."

"We don't have probable cause," McKissack said.

"Fuck probable cause, get a consent search."

"We'll see if we can secure one from the family. And let's put a car on him," McKissack said. "We're running out of time, people. J. Q. Public's getting pissed off. They watch TV, they see no arrests. They're afraid for their children, their wives, their sisters."

"I'm just saying," Rachel said, "we can't afford to focus everything on a single suspect right now."

"I'm open to suggestions, Detective Storrow," McKissack said, and her name on his lips sent a chill shuttling down her spine. His voice was so constricted, she wanted to find the choke control and ease up. "We need answers fast. The Castillos are demanding immediate action, and what do we do? We sit around nursing our ulcers."

For the first time, she noticed his hair was shot through with gray. He looked old. Drained. He'd once warned her that hypertension, ulcers and alcoholism came with the job.

"What's the status on the phone records?" he asked.

"She made multiple calls from her office and cellular phone," Cavanaugh said, pulling out the list they'd received from Bell's security division. "We've interviewed everybody she was in contact with that week."

Rachel stiffened, grateful that Tapper had been the one to interview Billy about the phone calls he'd made to Claire and about their budding relationship. They'd found Billy's prints all over her apartment, along with the landlord's, the plumber's, family members' and friends'. Tapper had pretty much cleared Billy of suspicion. Porter Powell's residential aide had seen him entering the dorm at 9:10 P.M. Billy had signed in at the guard station and chatted with the guard. Claire Castillo had disappeared some-time after 8:00 P.M., and Tapper surmised that Billy couldn't pos-sibly have gotten to the downtown area until sometime after 9:20, almost an hour and a half after Claire was last seen. Tapper concluded that Billy had an airtight alibi.

"She called over a dozen people from her office that day," Ca-vanaugh went on, "including her sister, Nicole."

"We interviewed them all," Keppel said. "Nothing unusual."

"The week before she disappeared, she made over sixty local calls from her office, cell phone and home," Keppel said. "Mostly regarding school activities. She contacted several people about a charity dance for the blind . . ."

"Sears, her landlord, the plumber, the dry cleaners, the florist, her family, some friends, parents of students. She called her mother five times, her sister ten times, her dad at the hospital twice, the plumber three times, the landlord twice about the rent being late, the gas company about a late payment—"

"She had financial problems?"

"Organizational problems," Rachel corrected. "Sometimes she'd forget to mail a check. No financial distress whatsoever."

"Daddy's a doctor, he's loaded, she's his princess." Tapper had a smirk like congealed grease.

"What about the plumber?" McKissack threw it out there.

"'Kenny G' Tarrington," Tapper said. "Fixed her leaky toilet Wednesday morning while she was at work. The landlord let him in."

"He credible?"

"Yeah, he's got a wife and kids, squeaky-clean record, offered to take a poly."

"Who'd she call on Tuesday?"

"Tuesday, specifically?" Cavanaugh shuffled through the BSD list. "Her sister, Sears, her landlord—"

"Tell me about the landlord."

"Fred Lake," Keppel said. "Older guy. Kind of a recluse. Divorced for five years. Wife moved out of state."

"He has keys to Claire's apartment," Rachel said.

"Is he cooperative?" McKissack asked.

"So-so." Cavanaugh shrugged.

"Got an alibi?"

"He went out for a six-pack and some SpaghettiOs around seven-thirty. Liquor store and 7-Eleven clerks verified."

"Background check?"

"Check forgery, decades ago."

"Something smells fishy," McKissack said.

"I agree," Cavanaugh said.

"Talk to him again. See what you think. Maybe we'll put a tail on him, too. What about Monday?"

"Who'd she call Monday?"

"That's what I like about you, Cavanaugh. You're mediocre and always on, just like television."

Cavanaugh ignored the barb. "Okay, so Monday she calls her mother, the plumber, the dry cleaners . . ." Cavanaugh shuffled through a stack of interview forms. "Picked up her dry cleaning on Monday afternoon. We interviewed the store owner."

"Blind guy," Tapper said.

"Visually impaired," McKissack corrected him, pinning Tapper with a look. "I know Vaughn. He does my dry cleaning."

"Pardon my political incorrectness."

Keppel made a snorting sound through his nose.

"She called her father at the hospital . . ."

"What about the father?" Keppel asked. "Nobody's said anything about the father."

"I've ruled him out as a suspect," McKissack said quietly, and Rachel saw the strength hidden beneath the aloof exterior. Now he turned to her, his eyes unreadable. "Anything else on the downtown area?"

"The crowd had thinned pretty much because of the rain," she said. "Of the twenty or so people who came forward who were in the downtown area that night, nobody outside the diner saw Claire leave. Nobody saw her walking back to the parking lot. Nobody heard a scream that night or saw anything unusual."

A picture of the missing woman was tacked to the wall. She had an unspoiled beauty, keen eyes sparkling with her zest for life. They had a description of the outfit she was last seen in: black lined raincoat, short black skirt, cinnamon-colored hose, short black leather boots, pink silk blouse, thin black belt, diamond stud earrings, small gold cross on a thin gold chain. She wasn't particularly religious but she never went anywhere without that necklace.

The police had in their possession X rays of Claire's chest and her left wrist where she'd broken it skiing ten years ago. Rachel feared that those and Claire's dental X rays might be the only way they'd be able to identify the body.

"What about the hotline?" McKissack turned to Phillip Reingold. "Any new leads?"

"The usual, Chief. Calls keep pouring in. It's witchcraft, it's devil worship. Couple of psychics weighed in today with their weird theories about UFOs and what have you. Yadda, yadda, yadda."

McKissack nodded. They'd already spent too much valuable time tracking down hundreds of "leads" that turned out to be false—calls from concerned residents, calls from kooks, calls from other police departments with suggestions relating to Claire Castillo's whereabouts. Strange men had been spotted all over town. They'd interviewed all known sex offenders, but the exercise had proved fruitless. In the papers, you always saw a caption under the picture of the killer, Rachel thought, and it always said "Nice guy. Real quiet."

"Everybody liked her," Rachel said. "Friends, relatives,

coworkers. She was a dedicated, hardworking teacher. Her students adored her . . ."

"We're working on the codes in the Day-Timer," Keppel said. "These notations are odd, but who's to say? This kind of thing's idiosyncratic and I guess it worked for her. So far, we've figured out that the capital letters mostly represent friends and family, people's initials. 'M&D' means Mom and Dad, 'N' stands for Nicole, and so on. Then there's lower case: 'c/d' means charity dance; 's' is for shopping; 'h/c' for haircut, et cetera. But sometimes you'll get an upper-case 'HC,' meaning Hurryback Cafe, or a lower-case 'pm,' meaning Peggy Morrissey . . . so she doesn't always stick to the rules."

"What about the day she disappeared?"

"Okay, she's got a lower-case 'pm @ 12' written down here. Peggy Morrissey confirmed they had lunch together. Then an upper-case 'HC' in the lower right-hand corner, meaning her usual Wednesday night dinner at the Hurryback. Then a 'pu C slash P' with a question mark—meaning pick up costumes, we think . . ."

"Costumes?"

"For the school play. 'P' for play, 'C' for costumes. We found them in the trunk of her car. Then she's got this big, lower-case, underlined '<u>b</u>.' It's prominent on the page."

"Buck Folette, obviously," Tapper said.

"But it's lower case."

Tapper shrugged. "She doesn't always follow her own rules. You said so yourself."

"It's problematic, because the next day, Thursday, she writes upper-case 'B @ 7,' meaning she had a date with Billy Storrow that night."

"What about Billy?" McKissack asked, and Rachel's heart pounded as he eyed her with aggressive suspicion. "He and Claire were close?"

"They were good friends."

"How good?"

"Billy was with his head-injured kid until nine-ten P.M.," Tapper reminded him.

"I'm not suggesting he's a suspect," McKissack said as his eyes explored Rachel's face. "I'm just wondering what their relationship was."

"At the beginning stages," she said as evenly as she could. "They'd been friends for over a year, and it was just beginning to turn into something more . . . substantial."

"It would've taken him ten minutes to get from the school to the downtown area," Tapper said. "That would've made it nine-twenty P.M. She'd've been walking around for almost an hour and a half by then, and yet nobody saw her after eight P.M. Not a soul. Doesn't add up."

"I know," McKissack said, eyes hard on Rachel. She could feel her body moving as she breathed. "I'm not saying he's a suspect."

"He's got a solid alibi," she said, sounding more defensive than she'd intended.

"You said something about Nicole the other day?" McKissack switched gears, sitting back and breaking off eye contact.

Rachel took a moment to compose herself, subtly wiping her palms on her knees. "Nicole's parents won't let her see her boyfriend anymore. Nicole and Dinger Tedesco have been going steady for nine months now. I talked to Jackie Castillo, and she and her husband don't like Dinger. They think the two of them are sleeping together, and in light of Claire's disappearance, they don't want Nicole involved with this young man. They realize they're being extremely protective, but they believe it's for her own good."

"What about it?" McKissack asked. "D'you think this kid could've kidnapped Claire?"

Rachel glanced around the table and could tell by all the blank looks nobody else had thought of it, either. "I talked to Dinger briefly," she said. "Asked him about his relationship with the family."

"And?"

"Left it at that."

"Well, what d'you think?" McKissack asked no one in particular.

"He's just a kid," Cavanaugh said. "What is he, seventeen?"

"So nobody's thought of it? Nobody's even considered the possibility?"

The question hung in the air.

"He's sleeping with the younger daughter, hanging around the house a lot. Claire comes over once or twice a week . . . always on weekends. He meets her. Develops a crush . . . follows her . . ."

"Dinger Tedesco?" Keppel fumbled with the Day-Timer, rifling through its pages. "I don't see any 'DTs' in here."

"So what's the kid's real name?" McKissack asked.

"Huh?"

"I'm assuming Dinger's a nickname."

Rachel scanned her notebook. "Brigham," she said.

"Brigham." McKissack held Rachel's eye.

"It's possible," Rachel hedged.

"I want you to look into it further, Storrow."

Her cheeks burned; she felt unfairly targeted.

"Now everybody go home," he barked. "Let's get some shut-eye."

7

THE FOLLOWING MORNING, NICOLE CASTILLO MET DINGER out behind the bleachers on the wet athletic field where they huddled together against a rotting wooden beam. She hadn't told him yet that she'd changed her mind. The air was misty with rain, the kind of rain you couldn't see but could feel coagulating on your skin and your clothes.

"You've gotta talk to them," Dinger insisted. "You've gotta convince them it's okay for us to see each other again."

"I can't convince my father of anything. Once he makes up his mind, that's it."

"Oh great." He threw up his hands and looked like he wanted to hit something. "Shit fuck dammit all to hell!"

"Dinger," she said tensely, "you know, I've decided to go ahead and have this baby."

"What?" His eyes grew startled, hair clinging to his scalp in a defeated sort of way. He glanced at her belly as if he could see through her raincoat. "Are you sure?" He sounded panicky, as if he'd changed his mind, as if maybe he didn't really want this baby after all.

"Fucking asshole."

"What'd I say?"

She stormed past him, her high heels punching dots in the soggy field, and he followed her into the parking lot.

"Nicole, *what*?"

"I thought you wanted me to have this baby? I thought you were against abortion?"

"I did. I mean . . . I am!"

She eyed him with suspicion. "You sure?"

"Yeah."

"You don't sound so sure."

"Of course I'm sure! You just surprised me, that's all . . ."

"Shut up and drive."

Dinger's car, a '76 Monte Carlo, smelled of candle wax and hamburgers. They blasted music while they drove into town, past cows grazing stupidly in the yellowing fields. They drove past tilting barns and grain silos and ugly, old Victorian houses. She didn't want to live here. She didn't want to spend the rest of her life in Flowering Dogwood.

They pulled into Burger King and parked. While he was getting their food, she primped in the rearview mirror, catching sight of a small hard pink pimple on her chin. "Oh great," she said. "Miss Zit-merica."

She lit a cigarette, and when Dinger came back with their food, he said, "The tip's bright orange."

"I can't help it."

"You'll fry your lungs extra-crispy."

"I don't care."

"You'll care later."

"No, I won't."

They didn't speak for a while. After he finished his burger, Dinger picked up an Etch-A-Sketch from the car floor and fiddled with the knobs. His fingernails were dirty. He drew a squiggly, angular baby, and suddenly she loved everything—rain beading down the windshield, the wipers with their rubber squeak-squeak, hot coffee smells mixing with Dinger's pretzel-smelling scalp, his fuzzy profile with its ski-slope nose. His soft features spoke of great potential, of what he might someday be-come, and she wanted to know that man.

"I love you," she whispered, throwing herself at him.

"Oh God," he gasped, "I love you, too, Nicole."

His strange gaze flitted across her face, and they kissed for a while, then she pushed him away and masked her deep love un-der an expression of disgust. "Daddy's going to kill me."

"Don't tell him, then."

"I have to tell him, Dinger! I have to tell my mother at least, and she'll tell Daddy, and he's going to kill me."

"No, he won't."

"Ugh! You're impossible. We have to figure this out," she said. "Help me!"

"I'm trying."

"Try harder." The hot coffee burned her tongue and she could feel a blister rising up on the roof of her mouth. Good. She needed this pain to remind her of Claire; needed to be scalded, always and forever, perpetual punishment for her stupid, happy thoughts. "When we were little," she told him, "Claire had this trick where she'd make Abraham Lincoln cry. She'd wet a wad of toilet paper and hold it behind a penny and squeeze, and big fat tears would drop down, and she'd say, 'See? Abraham Lincoln's crying.'"

They sat in stony silence while the rain came down. It made a shuddering sound on the roof of the car, like someone trying to break in. As if Claire were lost in the rain and desperate to get inside where it was safe and dry. Nicole looked out the window and thought about Claire making Abraham Lincoln cry, and a sour taste came into her mouth. Everything was a blur.

"D'you think she's dead?" Grief numbed her throat.

"I don't wanna talk about it." He smelled of mothballs and wool zipped up too long inside a winter storage bag.

"I think the police have given up." She shuddered. Her feet were cold. Her hands were cold. Right in front of her, raindrops clung to the doorframe of the car, their shimmering fullness like great beads of hope. One by one, they dropped. "I think my parents have given up."

"Don't cry, Nicole."

"Where could she be?" she demanded, eyes flashing, hair crackling.

"Maybe she ran off with somebody?"

"She didn't run away, Dinger. Why would she run away when everybody who loves her lives right here? She could drive you nuts sometimes, y'know? She could get kind of bossy and in your face, like she knew better than you, but I loved her so much."

"I know." He rubbed her back and she tried not to cry.

"If anything happens to her, I'll die."

"No, you won't."

"I will. I'll stop breathing."

"Cut it out." He clutched her tight, their raincoats squeaking together.

"I'll die." She sobbed, helium-voiced, her breath in the curve of his neck wafting back in her face, warm and coffee-smelling. "I swear to God, I will."

"Nicole." He shook her shoulders. "Nicole, look at me."

She blinked at him through a whirlpool of her own foul mood, her misery and fear. "What?"

"I want us to spend some time together."

She wiped her wet face with her hands.

"We've gotta find a way to be together . . . someplace where no-body'll bother us . . ."

She was shivering.

"Someplace where we can hold each other for about a million years. Don't you wanna be with me, Nicole?"

"Yeah." An icy wind licked the back of her neck.

He kissed her. He put his hand on her breast. "Oh, Nicole." His body trembled as he slid his tongue into her mouth.

Her stomach knotted, a wave of nausea sweeping over her. "Stop." She pushed him away. "I'm gonna be sick." She opened the door and leaned over the rain-soaked asphalt, but nothing happened. Rain drenched the back of her neck as she tried to throw up but couldn't.

She slammed the door shut. "I'm okay." She lit another cigarette.

"I definitely want this baby," he said. "I want us to get married and be a family."

Her knees were knocking. "I want to go home."

"Okay." He keyed the ignition. "I'll figure out a way for us to be together, like maybe for an entire night, okay?"

She wanted that. An entire night.

"Okay?"

"Yeah."

They drove into the darkening day.

8

RACHEL TAPPED HER HANDS IMPATIENTLY ON THE STEERING wheel. The light at this intersection took forever. A stiff breeze blew in through the rolled-down window and pushed her hair into her face. She didn't want to admit how angry and frustrated she was. She hardly slept anymore, and when she did, she was plagued by nightmares. The only thing that kept her going lately was the anguish of the grief-stricken family.

There had been twenty-nine homicides in Kerrins County this past year, and of those, six had occurred within Flowering Dogwood's town lines. The FDPD detective squad handled rapes, armed robberies and domestic abuse cases, in addition to homicides. Rachel was the youngest of the three detectives who made up the unit, but she had impressed the older men with her investigative and organizational skills. She'd solved two of the homicides herself—one a domestic quarrel gone bad, the other a drug-related shooting. Both cases had been cut-and-dried, but this kidnapping case . . . her brain hurt just thinking about it.

Rachel knew everything there was to know about Claire Castillo: weight, height, shoe size, dress size, favorite color, taste in movies, books and CDs; she knew every necklace Claire owned, every book she'd ever read, every piece of mail she'd received down to the last postcard. She knew what she carried in her purse: calfskin wallet containing ID and credit cards; Ray-Bans in a black leather case; a Mason Pearson hairbrush; a Mont Blanc pen; a package of Vicks cough drops; a package of Kleenex; her keys on a plastic-banana keychain; tampons; a tube of Origins Sassafras lipstick; Sudafeds, a prescription bottle of Benadryl, and an inhaler.

A lot of cops distanced themselves from the victims, the families, the corpses. McKissack did. He numbed himself to every tidal wave of grief. They'd had a running argument about her becoming too personally involved with the victims' families, but upon graduating from the police academy, she'd sworn she would never lose touch with the human element, never forget that the loved ones were in exquisite pain. She didn't want to become immune. She didn't want to be McKissack.

Rachel would never forget her first homicide. A domestic situation, a pretty young housewife beaten to death by her husband. Neighbors complaining about the noise. The stench of Richard's Wild Irish Rose. He'd beaten her so brutally, she'd miscarried on the kitchen floor. He'd grabbed an electric fan and bashed her head in. The most dangerous place in the world, it turned out, was this woman's own home. Rachel still got goose bumps whenever she drove past the weathered gray ranch behind the peeling picket fence.

Pulling into Taco Bell, she drove around back where pigeons pecked at the stray crumbs scattered around a large green dumpster. The boy was standing over by the picnic tables, looking tall and skinny and shivery cold.

"I'm Detective Storrow," she said with an outstretched hand.

"Hi, I'm Dinger." They shook, then selected one of the picnic tables.

All around them, trees swept the sky with their upturned branches. Rachel drew her coat collar around her neck. Dinger was an awkward-looking seventeen-year-old with oversized hands and feet on lanky limbs. A puppy-dog face on a fast-growing body.

"I need to ask a few questions," she began. "Try to remember as much as you can. You're not nervous, are you?"

"No," he said, biting his thumbnail.

"Okay. Where were you the Wednesday night Claire Castillo disappeared?"

He shivered inside his windbreaker. His hands were red and chapped, his cheeks crimson from the cold or nerves or both. "At work."

"Until when?"

"Seven."

"Where do you work?"

"Kellum Kleaners."

"On Delongpre?"

"Yes."

"And what did you do after work?" Rachel asked.

"I dunno. Cruised around, I guess."

"Was anybody with you?"

"No."

"Where did you go?"

He shrugged. "Just drove around."

"Nicole says she didn't see you that night."

"She wasn't feeling so hot." He fingered a delicate amethyst ring on a long silver chain around his neck.

"She told me you called her around nine."

"Yeah. I used a pay phone at the bowling alley."

"And you guys talked for about ten minutes?"

He shrugged. "Maybe less. I ran out of quarters."

"Did anybody at the bowling alley see you that night?"

"You'd have to ask them."

Rachel nodded. "Then what did you do?"

"I drove around some more."

"Past Nicole's house?"

He looked at her, chewed a ragged fingernail. "I dunno."

"You didn't?"

"No."

"Dinger," she said softly. "These questions are very important, very critical."

He looked down at the picnic table pocked with graffiti. "Maybe," he admitted.

1 7 1

"Just once?"

"I dunno. A few times. I can't remember."

"Did you drive back downtown again?"

"No." He looked at her, recognition dawning. "Why are you asking me all this stuff?" He said it innocently, sweetly, his adolescent voice breaking with naked anxiety.

"We're trying to establish where everybody was that night. It's routine."

He seemed satisfied with her answer.

"Did you talk to anybody else after nine P.M.?"

He thought a beat, then shrugged. "Nobody, really."

"Did you buy anything that evening?"

"No."

"Stop for food somewhere? Fill the tank?"

"Nope."

She looked at him. He seemed like a good kid, a bit shy and awkward, maybe, not the brightest bulb in the eleventh grade. His parents were blue-collar workers, divorced; he had three siblings and probably had to fight for everything he'd ever gotten. Her instincts told her Dinger Tedesco wouldn't hurt a flea, but he had no alibi.

"So Nicole's not allowed to see you anymore?" she asked, trying a new tack.

He cringed, looked around nervously, then pulled something out of his jacket pocket—one of those green plastic turtles whose head bobbed when you touched it. He put the turtle on the picnic table in front of them and watched its tiny head bob up and down.

"Must be rough," Rachel said. "Not being able to see her."

He looked at her oddly, and she sensed that she puzzled him a great deal. Finally, he blurted, "Yeah, it sucks."

"Do you love her?"

He glowered.

"You don't have to answer that question if you don't want to."

"What's it got to do with anything?"

"I just think people who are in love should be responsible, that's all," she said.

He met her gaze, eyes blurring with tears, although it could've been the wind.

"I am responsible," he said defensively.

"Okay," she said.

"I love her very much."

"Okay," she said. "I believe you."

"I'd marry her today if I could, but they won't let me."

Rachel nodded.

"I don't want to talk to you anymore." Dinger stood up. "Are we done yet?"

"Almost."

He stepped over the picnic bench and walked to his car, a rust-colored '76 Chevrolet Monte Carlo. "I'm sorry, but it's none of your business."

"Dinger—?"

He slammed the door and drove off.

9

KERRINS COUNTY GENERAL HOSPITAL WAS A SIX-HUNDRED-BED facility that, as its name implied, served the entire county. Rachel had followed more than a few ambulances to the ER in order to take statements from victims of gunshot wounds or stabbings. The waiting room was painted robin's-egg blue and a few rubber plants were scattered around for ambience.

Dr. Yale Castillo's cramped office on the first floor of the emergency medicine suite was tastefully decorated with antiques. He'd been the on-call supervising surgeon of the ER at Kerrins County

General for over thirty-five years now, and he and Rachel had crossed paths many times, although his brusque, official manner made him difficult to approach. He had a reputation for being a stereotype of the pompous surgeon, but Rachel couldn't help cutting him a lot of slack these days. His daughter had been missing for almost three weeks.

"Please, Detective," he said in a deep, authoritative voice, "have a seat."

"Thank you."

Yale Castillo was one of those doctors who refused to associate with the common people—nurses, clerks, orderlies. Rumor had it he'd ended up in the ER, handling any and all cases regardless of surgical potential, because he couldn't get along with the hospital's surgical staff. He and Rachel had always had a polite but remote relationship, and now he seemed to be masking his pain with an even more disdainful expression than usual. "How can I help you, Detective?"

"I need to clarify the last conversation you had with your daughter," she said, flipping through her notebook. "You spoke with her on the afternoon before she disappeared?"

"Yes, she called my office."

"What about?"

"She asked if I'd buy some tickets for the charity dance, a benefit for the school. I told her I'd be happy to."

"Did she mention anything else?"

He twisted his gold wedding band around on his finger. "Let's see . . . she spoke about her rent being late. Her rent's always late." He smiled.

"Anything else?"

"The plumber was in her apartment, fixing the toilet. She was nervous about him being there."

"Nervous? How so?"

"Just that . . . she felt self-conscious about how messy the place was. Something like that."

Rachel nodded. "Anything else?"

"Not that I can recall." He cleared his throat and his features softened, and almost against his will he added, "Jackie and I have called everyone we can think of. I must've driven around the neighborhood at least a hundred times."

"Don't worry," Rachel said with false confidence. "We're doing everything we can . . ."

"I know she'll be all right."

She could see the strain in his eyes from wanting to believe it. He must have read about his daughter's case in the papers, picked up on the growing skepticism of the media, the police, the public in general.

"We'll find her," Rachel promised, not wanting to destroy his illusion. Sometimes illusions were the only things holding us together. Besides, even if she did take a hammer to it, bam, he'd probably find refuge in the shards.

"Last night," he said, "as I lay in bed, I tried to remember her face. Only I'm afraid I've forgotten what she looks like." He blinked in the stripes of washed-out light slanting through the slatted blinds.

The silence was broken by an announcement on the loud-speaker: "Methamphetamine overdose. Male, twenty-eight years old. ETA five minutes."

Ignoring the urgency in the admitting clerk's voice, Dr. Castillo smiled wistfully and said, "She started to read when she was two. Imagine that."

Rachel's face was frozen with pity. She felt a young Claire at her side like a sudden gust of wind, imagined a bouncy, smooth-skinned child whose bright, ringing laughter momentarily drowned out the constant hum of her father's grief.

"Every day," he went on, "it gets a bit worse. You try to hang on to your optimism."

"Yes."

"She took ballet, you know. Seven years. Piano, tennis. She

was such a strong little girl. And smart." He leaned forward and rubbed the delicate skin around his sunken eyes. "Listen to me. I keep saying 'was.'"

Rachel sat still while he caught his breath. His shoulders slumped, his sad vanity evident in the long black strands slicked across his male-pattern baldness.

"Dr. Castillo," she said softly. "We're doing everything we can. We're working double shifts. Every officer in the department cares deeply about this case."

He nodded, his sorrow both soothed and fed by her words, and slowly regained his composure. "I did my clinical year at Massachusetts General." His eyes were red-rimmed. "Four years as an undergraduate, four years of medical school, six years' residency at Kerrins County." He held out his hands, spread his slender fingers. "Look at that. Rock steady. I've been told I have a gift."

Rachel shifted in the soft leather-upholstered chair, the kind you could easily suffocate in.

"The most important thing to a surgeon is eye-and-hand coordination. I know how to repair potentially lethal bleeding in trauma victims, restore cardiac function, remove life-threatening foreign bodies. I know how to be aggressive and when to hold back. I can operate for hours at a time without getting tired, and yet . . ." He looked at her with resignation. "None of that knowledge, none of that training will help me bring my daughter back."

The admissions clerk interrupted over the loudspeaker again, and Dr. Castillo's eyes turned inward. "Jackie keeps asking, is this our fault? Did we do something wrong?"

"Of course it's not your fault."

"She asks me all the time . . . was I a good mother?" His voice broke. He couldn't go on. He quickly wiped his eyes and stood up. "I'm sorry, I'm needed out front."

They shook hands. He had a surgeon's grip, rock steady.

10

"MOM! I'M LEAVING!"

Jackie Castillo found her daughter in the living room, her valentine-shaped face going all pink as she bent down to lace up her sneakers. She'd momentarily rested her bike against the wall and left a scuffmark on the eggshell-colored paint.

"I told you I didn't want you going over there."

"Daddy said I could!"

Jackie bit back her fear and anger. Nicole was getting her way, as usual, by skillfully playing one parent against the other.

"It's just a sleepover, Mom. We're gonna watch TV and eat popcorn and shit. I mean stuff." Nicole was lithe in blue Spandex tights, an oversized banana-colored T-shirt and blue down jacket, her auburn hair pulled hastily into a Pebbles Flintstone top-knot, unruly bangs held in place by two green glow-in-the-dark barrettes. She'd inherited her coloring from Yale's side of the family—same pale skin with its propensity to burn, same watery blue eyes, same restless legs and slender hands. Yale had long ago given up hope that one of his beautiful, talented daughters might pursue a career in medicine.

"Besides," Nicole said, "I'm sick of staying at home all the time just because you're a worrywart. It's not fair."

"I'm only thinking about Claire."

"All we ever do is think about Claire. It's like she's dead or something. Only I had this dream, Mom. Claire's alive. I know she is. So you can quit worrying."

Jackie fought the urge to stroke her daughter's cheek, since Nicole no longer allowed it. She held herself erect and didn't move like a child at all.

"Did you bring a change of clothes?"

"*Mom . . .*" Nicole rolled her eyes, her hand automatically reaching for her backpack. "And a toothbrush and a hairbrush and my very own shampoo . . ."

Jackie could feel the tension between them like a crack forming on black ice. "When can I expect you home tomorrow?"

Nicole shrugged and grabbed her bicycle, anxious to leave. She walked it to the front door. "We'll probably sleep late."

"How late?"

"I dunno . . . two?"

"I want you home by noon, young lady. No ifs, ands, or buts."

"All right, already." Nicole swung the front door open and stood under the yellow porch light, her translucent face glowing with impatience. Jackie stood in the doorway feeling small, diminished. She was shrinking by the minute; her life was receding just as her daughter's gained momentum.

"I love you too much, I guess," she confessed.

"Don't get mushy on me." Nicole bumped her bike down the front steps. As a tiny baby, she used to bite Jackie's breast while nursing; now she was this lanky creature with the kind of exotic eyes men killed for.

The front door poked Jackie's arm like some shy girl. Outside, the November night unpeeled before them, crows weighting the telephone lines, dark trees bleeding into a violet horizon. A ground fog was moving in. "Nicole?"

"*What?*"

"Be careful."

"Careful's my middle name."

"Almost forgot." Jackie tripped down the stairs and hijacked a kiss. "I'm still your mother, y'know."

"How could I forget?"

"I'm going to stand here until you're safe inside."

Nicole frowned. "What am I, three?"

Three years old. Jackie remembered when they'd first moved

to Pumpkin Run Road and bought the house, a white clapboard with red shutters. There was a side of her back then that desperately wanted to be Betty Crocker. She had the man she loved and two beautiful little girls, two miracles in their summer dresses. She spent her days shaking the sand out of their bathing suits, bandaging their cuts, buying them just the right kind of peanut butter—smooth, not chunky.

And where was her older daughter now with her sweet smile and adventurous spirit? Where was the little girl whose asthma occasionally crippled her enthusiasm, reducing her to a bundle of trembling limbs and wheezing coughs? Where was the sweet-tempered child who'd sit out on the front sidewalk feeding cane sugar to the ants one grain at a time?

"Noon tomorrow," Jackie said as Nicole walked her bike down the sidewalk. "Repeat after me."

"I just said so, weren't you listening?"

"Beef stew for dinner tomorrow night," Jackie added lightly.

"Ugh."

"Ha. Only kidding. Cheeseburgers."

"Very funny, you rat."

"I'm flattered. Rats are smart."

Nicole's eyes shimmered under the virulent moonlight. "Claire's coming home, Mom. I can feel it." She hopped on her bike and sped to the end of the street, where she turned into the Pattons' driveway.

Jackie waited in the shivering cold until she saw Shelly open the door, and then and only then, knowing her daughter was safe, did she duck back inside.

AROUND MIDNIGHT, RACHEL RETRACED THE ROUTE CLAIRE
Castillo had most likely taken from the parking lot to the Hurryback Cafe and back again. Somebody had left flowers in a corner
of the lot where Claire's abandoned Nissan Sentra had been
found. It would've been foggy that night, just like now. The street
lamps were fifty feet apart. If the perp had followed her with the
intention of grabbing her, he might've snatched her here, at the
mouth of the alley between the shoe store and vacant storefront.
The alley was Bible black, the windows of a nearby apartment
house sealed shut against the cold. Perhaps that explained why
nobody had heard any screams that night? Or maybe the perp
had attacked her in the parking lot, in the darkest corner where
her car was found? The forest grew dense in this section of the
lot, and the nearest street lamp was shrouded in fog.

Still, if she'd been physically grabbed, wouldn't her purse have
flown open? Wouldn't a shoe have come off? Wouldn't someone
have heard the screams? There should have been something left
of her at the scene, some sign that a struggle had occurred. A
woman had been abducted. Forced into a moving car or window-
less van. According to friends and family, Claire Castillo would
never have given up without a fight.

The scenario didn't make sense.

Turning around, Rachel walked back past the shoe store, the
vacant storefront, the diner, Dale's Discount Hardware, a couple
of clothing shops, a beauty parlor, another empty storefront, a
dance hall, a dental practice. Was it possible the perp had been
hiding in the darkened foyer of the dentist's office? Had he leapt
out and grabbed her from behind before she'd had a chance to

scream? Had he gagged her? Chloroformed her? Injected her with some swift-acting nervous system depressant? Knocked her out with a sharp blow to the head? But there were other shoppers out that night. The ground fog was thick, but somebody surely would've heard the scuffle or seen a man and woman struggling.

Perhaps it wasn't a stranger, but someone she knew? Perhaps she had been lured into a car or a building? Maybe a safe-looking stranger in a police uniform, or dressed as a minister? Hughie Boudreau? He'd once been a cop with emotional problems. Would Claire have accepted a ride from Dinger Tedesco? Certainly not while her own car was parked in the public lot. The Nissan Sentra was found to be in perfect working condition and with the exception of new brake pads, there hadn't been any major changes in the last two years. Maybe she'd accepted a lift to the parking lot from the cafe? Six city blocks could seem a lengthy walk in the foggy cold of an October night in Maine.

Now Rachel's cell phone rang, the bright sound of it jangling her nerves. "Hello?"

"It's me." The strain in McKissack's voice made her heart skip a beat. "They found a woman in the woods about five miles from Claire's apartment."

"Is she dead?" Rachel asked breathlessly.

"No, she's alive. They're transporting her to Kerrins County General. I want you to get over there ASAP."

"I'm on my way."

12

SIX HOURS INTO HIS FOURTEEN-HOUR SHIFT AT KERRINS County General, Dr. Yale Castillo woke up from a brief nap in the sleep room, gowned up and went back into the Pit. He glanced at the roomful of sullen faces waiting to be admitted. Tonight was mostly garden-variety stuff—flu, fever, miscarriage. As the senior person on call, Yale was in charge of all personnel on staff tonight, which included two interns, a moonlighting resident, a third-year emergency medicine resident, two junior residents, a pediatric surgeon, two technicians and three nurses.

"Looks like we've got a full house, Gladys."

"You said it, Doc." Gladys was the head nurse, a bighearted, matronly woman who knew enough to keep her distance, which he appreciated. "They're all coming in at once . . . laceration in Room 5, ingrown toenail in Room 12, gallstones in Room 3 . . ."

"Any urgents?"

"No immediates, seven delayeds, six totally nonurgent."

Suddenly, the EMS radio went off: "Twentyish white female with trauma to the face and chest . . . blood pressure ninety palpable . . . good vital signs. ETA five minutes."

His face flushed. He had a flash memory of five-year-old Claire hurling herself into his arms with a breathless little laugh. "I always come back to you, Daddy!"

He snapped into action. "Let's get some O-negative blood up here, stat."

"But, Doctor . . . we don't know for sure it's your—"

He was already on his way into Trauma Room 1. "Page Hurley!"

She continued babbling behind him but he shut her out, his thoughts already spiraling inward—little Claire in sweater and shorts at the beach, Claire feeding peanuts to the monkeys at the zoo—then he violently shook his head. He had to keep his wits about him. If this was Claire . . . if indeed this was his daughter, he needed to be at the top of his game. He winced in the stark light of the trauma room, tore off a joke note somebody had taped to the wall: "Just say NO to nefarious substances."

Moments later, the Emergency entrance doors crashed open and paramedics wheeled the victim past the front desk directly into Trauma Room 1. Yale heard a low, plaintive moaning as he approached the gurney, and suddenly he was smack in the middle of a vicious slice of nightmare.

Her injuries were incomprehensible. Even the most trauma-hardened ER personnel fell silent, shocked at the violence inflicted on her body. A naked young woman lay writhing on the gurney with her eyes, mouth and ears sutured shut. There was so much trauma to her face, so much swelling, her features were unrecognizable. Blood coagulated around the tight, precise stitches—simple running sutures placed at an equal distance and depth, as if to avoid strangulating healthy tissue. The patient was hyperventilating through her nose, and her right arm, held in rigid contortion, was sewn diagonally across her chest wall, the right fist clamped shut, fingers sutured together like a lumpy baseball resting on her heart.

Yale struggled for breath, knees buckling, and clutched the sides of the gurney. This grotesque creature, this mutilation was not his daughter. Couldn't be. Not in a million years. Forcefully, he reminded himself he was the attending physician and, regaining his composure, he proceeded to examine the woman's body. Her skin was cold and clammy. He checked for capillary refill, applying pressure to the palmar tip of one of the fingers until it blanched, then releasing it. A nurse timed the interval until the fingertip "pinked up."

"Let's assess tissue perfusion, not just the BP," he said. "Monitor with pulse oximetry."

The patient snorted loudly at the sound of his voice. Her hair was caked with dirt, and there was ground-in grime on her elbows and knees. He refused to admit to himself that he knew that long red hair. Knew it intimately, in fact. That he recognized, more importantly, the small dark mole on the underbelly of her chin. All those years he'd tickled it with his finger, saying, "You know what this is? It's an elf freckle. Definitive proof you're my little elf." He stood still, in shock, a tiny scream ricocheting around inside his stubborn skull.

"Oh my God." His voice barely registered.

"What is it, Yale?"

"It's my daughter."

Claire. His precious Claire. Short of breath and wheezing through her nose. He recognized the expiratory and inspiratory wheezing . . . hyperventilation, dyspnea. She was having an acute asthma attack.

"Blood pressure's up to one-thirty over ninety," Hurley, the surgical resident, said. "She's having a little trouble breathing."

"No shit. She's got asthma." Overwhelmed with panic now, un-comprehending and trembling, he started barking orders. "Draw up some epinephrine, stat! We need blood. O-negative! Monitor peak flow, oxygen saturation and respiratory rate."

The paramedics moved her body in one fluid motion onto the table, and the surgical team worked both sides of the bed, swiftly and silently placing her on a warming blanket, hooking her up to the machines. The stillness was interrupted only by the swish of the respirator and the beep of the cardiac monitor.

"Her temp is up," the nurse said. Her name, he vaguely re-called, was Casey. "Color looks okay."

"Give me 0.3 ml epinephrine, subcutaneous."

"But Doctor—" the nurse said.

"What?" he snapped.

"Her vitals are still okay."

"She's having an asthma attack!"

The nurse backed off.

"I want SC epinephrine, 0.3 ml. Hand me those scissors!"

The patient . . . his daughter . . . struggled for breath, not getting enough oxygen into her lungs. Her legs kicked in panic as two nurses pinned her down while Yale attempted to cut the sutures from her mouth. He worked by rote, his hands jerking mechani-cally in response to instructions from his brain. He worked as quickly as he could, trying to forget that this gruesome creature was his daughter, his beautiful, headstrong, adorable little girl.

"Her pressure's down to one-ten over seventy. Pulse one-ten."

The epinephrine wasn't working quickly enough. "Give me another SC epi, 0.3 ml, and a hundred-milligram bolus of IV methylprednisolone."

He managed to remove some of the sutures as she tossed her head from side to side, fighting him off. "Hold steady . . . steady, please." She moaned like a wounded animal. He wanted desperately to look into her eyes, her lovely almond-shaped eyes, but they were stitched shut, swollen and blood-encrusted. God, how awful, how awful. No time, not vital.

"Calm down, Claire. Daddy's here. You're going to be all right, everything's going to be all right, just calm down . . ."

The voices in the room grew distant as he struggled to save his daughter's life. Her exposed body was a pathetic sight, a conduit for various tubes and wires. Hurley was feeling her belly to assess for internal trauma, the X-ray techs were trying to get a chest. She became combative, kicking them away. A hideous shriek came rattling from her oxygen-starved lungs.

"Another SC epinephrine 0.3 ml. Start an IV administration of magnesium sulfate 2 g in five hundred of saline."

Suddenly she lost strength in her limbs. With rising panic, he sensed that she was inexplicably slipping away from him.

"Claire! Wake up!"

She stopped breathing. He needed to intubate. His hands were shaking violently now.

"Doctor—?"

"What?" he snapped.

They were all staring at him.

"I can intubate," Hurley said in the calm, efficient voice Yale had used himself on hundreds of hysterical patients.

"I've got it," he stubbornly insisted, somehow managing to snip the rest of the sutures from her purplish lips. He pried open her mouth and, using the laryngoscope blade to push her tongue to one side, lifted the jaw and exposed the vocal cords. He slipped the tube between the cords into the trachea, forcing 100 percent oxygen into her lungs with a bag.

A nurse took over, squirting medication directly into Claire's lungs and ventilating her with the bag. He breathed a sigh of relief. At last he was regaining some measure of control, even if it was controlled confusion.

His voice was tight. "What's her blood pressure?"

"Dropping . . . I'm getting ninety over palp . . ."

"Dropping?"

". . . down to seventy . . ."

The roomful of faces fell simultaneously.

The monitor suddenly flatlined and she went into cardiac arrest.

"Full arrest!"

Yale stared in horror at the arm sewn across her chest. "Remove these sutures, *now!*" he screamed.

Everybody grabbed a pair of scissors. Precious minutes passed as the room filled with the sound of snipping. Yale felt sickened by the intimate frenzy of the people around him. When they freed her arm, he began frantic resuscitation efforts, first hitting her in the sternum.

"The rhythm's V-fib."

"Paddles," he said, placing them on her chest. "Clear!"

Her body spasmed with the two hundred joules of electricity.

"Pulse?"

"No pulse."

"Clear!" He defibrillated at three hundred joules. "Pulse?"

"Still no pulse."

"Let's try 340. Clear!"

"Epi in. No pulse."

"Clear! Check pulse."

"No pulse, Doctor."

"Goddammit!"

"No pulse, Doctor."

There was no spontaneous breathing or movement. Her lips were blue and her pale, clammy skin was already beginning to cool. He couldn't understand what had gone so terribly wrong. They'd done everything in their power to save her, they'd done everything right. She'd been intubated, she was breathing just fine, when all of a sudden there had been a dramatic lowering of blood pressure. In an instant, he went over the entire procedure in his mind, questioning each decision in turn. Her wounds were not terminal. There were no fractures, no internal bleeding, no . . .

He glanced at the heart monitor where a faint, irregular pattern danced listlessly—electrical-mechanical disassociation, the electrical impulses of the dying heart. Her vital signs were preterminal. He knew without even thinking about it that his daughter was going to die.

"Code Blue!" he screamed. "Clear!"

His mind raced, his hands trembled. He worked on her for twenty minutes more, but she failed to respond. Everything around him seemed to slow way down. He knew it was over but couldn't stop himself, he had to resuscitate. At some point, he felt a hand on his shoulder.

"Yale," Hurley said softly.

He let go of the paddles, a sickening sense of helplessness engulfing him.

Everybody stood in silence around the gurney.

"Let's pronounce it," Hurley suggested.

Yale opened his mouth but the words died in his throat. He emitted a hissing sound, the full weight of his daughter's death crushing the air out of his lungs.

"Time is one-thirty-three A.M., Wednesday, November first," Hurley said.

The code team dispersed, leaving only Yale, Casey and the tech who cleaned the bodies and straightened the rooms in anticipation of family viewings. The tech, whose name Yale couldn't recall, braided his hair in cornrows and had the kind of disposition Yale distrusted; he never had anything bad to say about anyone and was always quoting Scripture. Yale stood watching helplessly while the tech mopped up blood from the floor and threw out used needle caps and IV bags. Casey was carefully removing the rest of the sutures. She cleaned the wounds, and Claire's face became suddenly recognizable again. Yale gazed down into the cornflower blue eyes of his first child—eyes fixed and dilated—and felt like a fraud. How had he not managed to save her?

In moments, the chaotic room was cleared.

"Excuse me, Doctor." Gladys poked her head in. "Your wife's here."

Feeling like a condemned man, Yale trudged down the long ammonia-smelling corridor toward the waiting room. When she saw him, Jackie shot up from the sofa.

"How is she?" She clutched his arm, an ugly tension in her face. "Is she okay, Yale?"

He noticed there were splotches of blood on his shoes. He'd seen lives wasted daily: babies sealed inside plastic bags, men with their brains blown out. He'd broken the news to countless families, always managing to numb himself to their externalized pain.

"She's gone," he said flatly.

"What?" She squinted up at him, uncomprehending.

"I did everything I could."

She shook her head, and suddenly he felt a thousand years old. "What are you trying to tell me, Yale?"

"I don't know what went wrong."

"So what happened?"

"She didn't make it."

"I don't understand."

His face flushed, voice going flat with anger. "She's *dead,* Jackie."

Jackie stared in disbelief. Then the raw sound of her grief filled the stuffy waiting room. She lost her balance and had to be propped upright, and Yale was forced to endure every bone-chilling, unrelenting sob.

After a while, she deflated in his arms. Became compliant. "I'm okay," she said, but she was trembling.

"I don't know what went wrong . . ." His voice trailed off. He stroked her hair, going through the motions, dead inside.

Now Casey came hurrying down the hallway toward them, holding out something for him to inspect. "Dr. Castillo?"

He looked at the object in her hand. It was a necklace, a high school ring looped through a long silver chain. Dinger's ring. Nicole's necklace. "Where'd you get this?" he demanded to know.

"It was clamped in her fist."

"Whose fist?"

"Your daughter's fist. I removed the sutures and this dropped out."

He answered her with stunned silence.

IV

OFF-DUTY EYES

1

RACHEL STARED AT THE LONG SILVER CHAIN WITH THE school ring looped through it, now coiled in the doctor's hand.

"It belongs to Nicole," he whispered. "Dinger gave it to her." His eyes were wide with raw fear. "Nicole refused to take this off. She even wore it to bed."

Rachel turned to the nurse, a makeupless, naturally pretty woman in her thirties. "Where did you find this?"

"Clenched in her fist." She demonstrated. "I was removing the sutures, and I pried the fingers open and this fell out."

The fact that the nurse had removed the sutures before the medical examiner had arrived was water under the bridge now. A more urgent issue was at stake. Turning to the stunned parents, Rachel asked, "Where's Nicole?"

They exchanged a narcotized glance.

"At a friend's house," Jackie said uncertainly. "Shelly Patton's."

"Call her." Rachel handed Jackie her cell phone, then told the nurse, "Don't touch anything else. And get the medical examiner over here right away."

The nurse hurried back up the wide corridor, scuffed white shoes thudding dully against the beer-colored linoleum.

"Hello?" Jackie Castillo spoke into the phone. "Shelly? It's Nicole's mom, could I speak with her please?" Cupping her hand over the receiver, she said with visible relief, "She's in the bathroom."

"Tell her you'll wait," Rachel instructed.

Jackie put the phone to her ear again. "Shelly? I need to talk to Nicole. It's okay, I'll wait. What?" The fine lines of her face creased like folded tissue paper. "What do you mean she can't come to the phone? Shelly," she said in a panicked, cold cadence, "let me speak with your mother."

2

SHELLY PATTON SOBBED HYSTERICALLY IN THE SPACIOUS, antique-filled living room of her home, just five doors down from the Castillos'. A petite brunette whose dull, edgeless features found their mirror image in the faces of family members gazing out of expensive frames mounted on the living room walls, Shelly spoke haltingly between sobs. "Nicole said that . . . she and Dinger were gonna . . . meet someplace secret . . ."

"Did she say where?" Rachel asked as the girl cringed beneath McKissack's steely scrutiny like some cornered animal. "Where were they going to meet?"

Shelly's thin-lipped mother stood off to one side. "Shelly," she said, "sit up straight and answer the question."

Shelly shook her head, mucus bubbles dangling from her nose.

"So you agreed to cover for her?"

"Yeah," she sniffed, daubing at her wet face with trembling fingers. "She told me they wanted to be alone for like a whole night . . . she said, 'Do me a favor, okay?' And I said, 'Yeah, okay,' and it was like . . . no big deal . . ."

McKissack loomed over the girl like a pure floating spirit of malevolence. "It's extremely important that you tell us the truth, Shelly. Nicole could be in serious trouble."

"I know," she wailed, burying her face in her hands.

"Help us find your friend."

"I'm trying!" she blubbered.

"Shelly," her mother scolded. "Look at Chief McKissack when he's talking to you."

Shelly reluctantly lifted her mottled, hysterical face. "I don't know where they went . . . someplace secret, she said!"

Rachel didn't like the look in McKissack's eyes.

Back outside in the New England drizzle, he told her, "This is about as bad as it gets."

3

SENSING HE HAD A CRISIS ON HIS HANDS, MCKISSACK ORGA-nized another full-scale search-and-rescue operation. Officers, bloodhounds and over three hundred volunteers combed the surrounding forests and cornfields in the pouring rain. The entire neighborhood within a two-mile radius was thoroughly searched. It rained all day and into the night, and didn't start to clear until the following morning when helicopters with special heat-seeking detection equipment repeatedly circled the area, spotters on board searching for Nicole's yellow T-shirt, her red backpack, a body lying in a cornfield or a swamp. Patrol cars cruised the tangled back roads, searching abandoned buildings, dumpsters and ditches on their meandering route. Patrolmen stopped to talk with the locals, displaying Nicole's picture and asking if anyone had seen her.

Around 10:00 A.M., Rachel pulled into the parking lot behind the medical examiner's building on Lagrange and met McKissack in the basement where the autopsies were performed. Archie Fortuna was pushing sixty-five but nobody wanted to get rid of him. He had the stamina of a much younger man and a mind as sharp and functional as a tack. He was corpulent, with a shock of white hair like the tuft on a cockatoo, and today he reeked of garlic and onions.

The three of them donned surgical masks, gowns and gloves

before entering the morgue. Claire Castillo's body was laid out on a steel tray on top of a gurney, lit by an overhead fluorescent lamp. Rachel could see where the blood had pooled on the underside of the body, and there were tiny holes in the flesh of the victim's chest, face and right arm from where the sutures had been. Her long red hair coiled onto the steel tray like a bolt of silk.

Beginning the postmortem, Archie examined the external features of the girl's body in minute detail before starting an internal exam. Tracing a gloved finger over the suture holes in her chest, he said, "These were simple running sutures made of non-absorbable cotton thread. The nurse saved them for me." He pointed at an evidence bag full of curled lengths of blood-encrusted thread. "The sutures were placed at an equal distance and depth and didn't strangulate any of the tissue. Knotted on the better-vascularized wound edge."

"So this guy knew what he was doing?" McKissack asked, stress showing on his face.

"Maybe. Or could be he's just very neat." Archie delicately lifted the girl's left arm. X rays of the body were displayed in light boxes mounted on the far wall. "Injuries to her wrist were antemortem."

"Ten years old," Rachel said.

"There's some sort of sticky residue on her wrists and ankles . . ."

"Duct tape," McKissack surmised.

"I'm taking fingernail scrapings now . . . looks like mud. There's dirt ground into her knees and elbows, and lots of mud and debris on her body from where she crawled through the woods."

"That's how they found her, right?" Rachel asked, the thought of it causing a tectonic shift inside of her. "Crawling out of the woods on her hands and knees?"

"All sutured up and everything, yep. Dragged herself along by one arm," Archie said, his voice cruelly matter-of-fact. "Three of her nails are broken off."

Archie switched on a Luma-Lite, which normally caused any hairs, fibers or semen stains on the body to glow. Traces of luminescent fuzz showed up around her face, neck and chest, especially in the areas of sutured flesh where fibers clung to the drying blood. "A lot of these fibers and hairs might've been picked up in the ambulance or the ER," Archie said, collecting evidence with a mini–vacuum cleaner.

McKissack stood stiffly beside Rachel, their arms touching, while Archie slowly ran the Luma-Lite down the length of the victim's body. He paused on a bright yellow splotch on the victim's left calf.

"Looks like we got lucky, Chief," Archie said, taking a sample. "I've found a small amount of what appears to be semen on her left calf. If the perp is a secretor, we can get blood type and markers down at the state lab."

"So he raped her?" McKissack asked.

"Don't know yet, Chief," Archie said. "Let's wait until we complete the internal. You know," he said, looking at them, "this little piece of equipment's the best investment I ever made."

"Expensive?" McKissack asked.

"Hell, the entire lab costs the community one movie ticket per year per person. Not bad," he said. "She was in good health overall. Well nourished."

Rachel glanced at McKissack, whose jaw was set.

"At some point, the UNSUB removed her clothes, her jewelry, everything," Archie said with a shake of his head, "even her earrings. My guess is he washed her body before driving her out to the woods. Also took his time making those sutures. They were very precise."

"He use an anesthetic?" McKissack asked.

"Without a painkiller of some sort, she would've put up quite a struggle. Let me show you something." He shone the Luma-Lite on the corpse's feet, which lit up with bright bits of grass and fiery splotches of mud. "The soles of her feet are blistered, embedded with debris . . . pine needles, dirt, pebbles . . . indicating that she walked quite a ways through the woods."

"I thought you said she crawled?"

"Crawled *out* of the woods. Walked *into* the woods." He aimed the Luma-Lite at her slightly swollen right foot, parted two of her toes, and a distinctive orange area about the size of a dime lit up. "See this spot between the toes here? If you look real close, you can see a hole slightly larger than a pinprick."

"An injection site?" McKissack asked, and Rachel felt him stiffen beside her.

"Barry? Let's take some samples."

Archie's assistant, Barry, a thin young man with wire-rim glasses, pale droopy hair and an even droopier demeanor, handed Archie a bottle and some swabs, and Archie took samples of the chemical around the site of the puncture wound.

"I'll need a syringe, Barry."

"Are you saying she was drugged?" Rachel asked.

"We won't know for sure until the toxicologist examines the blood, stomach contents, urine and liver. You know, centuries ago, they believed that the heart of a person who'd been poisoned wouldn't burn."

"So you suspect she was poisoned?"

Archie shrugged as he collected vitreous samples with a needle and syringe and placed them in the glass containers Barry held up gingerly to him. "You say the ER staff couldn't figure out what went wrong. Maybe they didn't do anything wrong. Maybe she was injected with a slow-acting poison. If she was, it should be present in the blood. Actually, the best place to find poison is in the liver, since it's the garbage pail of the body."

"What kind of poison?" McKissack asked.

"You got me, Chief. There are ten million organic chemicals, and each of those can be combined with one or more other chemicals to form an infinite number of mixtures. If you think about it, anything in great enough quantity can be toxic. Water can be toxic."

"Water?"

"People drown." He winked.

"Let me get this straight," Rachel said, trying to fathom the horror of it all. "The UNSUB held her captive, kept her well fed and in fairly good shape . . . and then, sometime late last night, he anesthetized her . . ."

"Slipped her a Mickey," McKissack suggested.

"Stripped her, washed her body . . ."

"Washing away all traces of any hairs or fibers that might later incriminate him."

"Mutilated her, stitching up her face and torso, then drove her out to the woods, where he escorted her to a specific location—"

"Whoa, wait a minute," McKissack said. "Escorted her?"

"Archie said she walked through the woods long enough to get blisters on the bottoms of her feet. With her eyes sewn shut like that, she had to have been escorted." She tried not to imagine Claire stepping over branches and pinecones and twigs, maneuvering her way past wet fir boughs with one arm sewn to her chest—eyes, ears and mouth stitched shut. "Then he forced her to lie down on the ground and injected her with some slow-acting poison?"

"This place between the toes is fairly clean, like it's been swabbed," Archie said. "All the bits of debris were wiped off, and there's cotton fibers around the site. I'm going to do a biopsy. The muscle is well preserved."

"Wait a minute. Why march your victim through the woods and *then* drug her?" Rachel asked.

"So that we'd find her there," McKissack suggested.

"But she didn't stay put. Besides, why would it matter where we found her?"

McKissack shrugged. "Why clean the body of all trace evidence, then leave your sperm behind?"

"Maybe he knows he's a nonsecretor?" Archie suggested.

"Who found her?" Rachel asked.

"Ozzie Rudd." McKissack's countenance was grim.

"What?"

"Claims he spotted her from his rig. Looks like you reopened the D'Agostino case just in time."

"Where was she when he spotted her?"

"Crawling out of the woods onto Winnetka Road."

Rachel shuddered, wondering how you could crawl anywhere with your right arm sewn to your chest, in awe of the victim's bravery.

"She's got abrasions on both knees," Archie said, taking samples. "The skin's embedded with dirt. Lesser abrasions on both elbows. Some bruising around the neck and chest, but that could've occurred in the ER."

Rachel nodded. "Intubation and CPR."

"Faint ligature marks on the wrists and ankles." Archie pointed them out. "Here . . . here . . . a slight bruising around the mouth, possibly from a gag."

"He held her captive for three weeks," Rachel said. "She must've been bound and gagged at least some of the time."

"Probably most of it," McKissack guessed. "Unless he kept her drugged the entire time."

Archie flicked off the Luma-Lite and straightened his back with a good-natured groan. "No major contusions or hematomas. No fractures."

"Dinger's not sophisticated enough to pull off something like this," Rachel said.

"Ozzie Rudd is," McKissack said.

"I hope to God those two ran away together."

"If they did, we wouldn't have the ring," McKissack reminded her. "Whoever it is, he's taunting us. He's got Nicole, all right. He's probably got them both."

Rachel choked back the outrage she'd been feeling all morning. There was no place to put it. They were impotent, playing some surreal guessing game, trying to shine a penlight into the dim recesses of a sick and twisted psyche.

"Hmm," Archie said, swabbing the vagina and anus for semen. "No evidence of rape. No internal abrasions. No visible semen stains, except for the single deposit on her calf."

"I don't get it," McKissack said. "First he kidnaps her, but there's no ransom note. Then he waits three weeks before he drops her off in the woods, where he ejaculates on her leg. But first he mutilates her face and body. This is fucking unbelievable."

"Then the other daughter disappears," Rachel picked up the thread, "and her necklace ends up in Claire's hand, tipping us off. He wants us to know what he's done."

"Maybe we should look at the father again?" McKissack said. "I mean, what are the odds that both of your daughters get targeted by the same psychopath? Let alone the fact that he's a doctor, he knows how to suture a wound."

"Yale Castillo may be an arrogant jerk," Rachel said, "but he's no psychopath. They're a close-knit family. He adores his daughters. They're the light of his life."

McKissack tore off his surgical mask. "All I know is, we've got one demented puppy-kicking freak on our hands." He stormed out of the morgue.

Steeling herself, Rachel headed after him.

4

SHE CAUGHT UP WITH HIM IN THE BACK PARKING LOT. MCKIS-sack's jacket was off, his shirt drenched with sweat. Above them, red-winged blackbirds razored the granite-colored sky.

"Time's against us with this type of intelligent, organized offender," McKissack said, eyes focused sharply on some middle distance. "This crime was well planned, not opportunistic. He's clearly from the area. We're dealing with a local."

"There's something I don't understand," Rachel said. "Why drop her off in the woods alive? After all, he'd held her captive for nearly three weeks. If she'd lived, she would've been able to identify him through his voice, the abduction site, maybe even a physical description. Why take such a chance?"

"He must've known she wasn't gonna make it."

"The injection." She nodded. "But the drug didn't kill her right away. What kind of poison doesn't take effect for several hours?"

"You took a toxicology class, right? Give it your best shot."

She turned the question over in her mind. "Arsenic is tasteless, odorless and easy to obtain. But death is slow and painful. Besides, there was no vomiting or diarrhea."

"Heroin overdose?"

"Very strong central nervous system depressant. No needle tracks, and therefore no repeat injections. No vomitus. In a typical heroin overdose, the lungs are heavy and show congestion."

"Cyanide?"

She shook her head. "There'd be localized areas of bright red livor mortis, cherry red or pink."

"Strychnine?"

"Symptoms occur within minutes. Violent convulsions."

"Insulin?"

"Takes too long. Seizures."

"Antidepressants?"

"It's possible. Confusion, hallucinations, and agitation, progressing to seizures or coma. We should be able to detect liver levels of the drug."

"Antidepressants combined with alcohol?"

"I didn't smell any alcohol, did you?"

McKissack shook his head. "We'll have to wait for the lab results. We're dealing with a sophisticated and extremely dangerous man, somebody we may have already interviewed."

"We interviewed almost two hundred people," she said, overwhelmed by the implication.

"He needs time alone in a secluded area where he knows he won't be disturbed." McKissack's eyes glistened with intense speculation. "We should expect some sort of criminal record. Assaults on women, or at least obscene phone calls. He's orderly, perhaps obsessively neat." He cleared his throat, spit on the sidewalk. "Our offender may have a record, or else there may be an unsolved rape or murder in his background. Which leads us back to our good friend, Ozzie."

She gave voice to her skepticism. "Ozzie Rudd?"

"Think about it. No evidence of forced penetration in the D'Agostino case, either, and the body was found just a few miles east of Winnetka Road." McKissack was wearing dark glasses that reflected only the sky, and it disappointed her that she couldn't see his eyes. On the far horizon, storm-strewn clouds appeared to be racing westward.

"I really think you're wrong," she said.

"So who found Claire Castillo?"

"We have to assume it was pure coincidence."

"Fat fucking chance."

"Besides, why go to all that trouble, only to cast suspicion on yourself by 'rescuing' the victim?"

"Cheap thrills? Hero syndrome?"

"He passed the polygraph eighteen years ago."

"Results were inconclusive," he corrected her. "His alibi was a scared sixteen-year-old girl, a known shoplifter." He scowled. "So now he knows he can beat the box. At least we've got the semen stain. If he's a secretor, we'll be able to match the markers."

"You've got a blood sample?"

"We know his blood type. That'll narrow it down. He'll volunteer a sample once we bring him in for questioning."

"And if he doesn't?"

"Then he becomes our prime suspect."

"Do you honestly think Ozzie Rudd is capable of something so heinous and well organized?"

"Three individuals stand out in my mind." McKissack's teeth were clenched. "Ozzie Rudd, Dinger Tedesco and Buck Folette."

"Buck Folette? I thought you put a tail on him?"

McKissack shook his head. "Local law enforcement refused to cooperate. We think the family got to them."

"What about the cabin by the ocean?"

"Family refused to sign a consent search." McKissack's eyes scanned the low-hanging clouds. "Tapper tailed him for about a week, but I needed him back here. We don't know where the hell Buck Folette was last night."

Rachel shook her head. "He drives a red pickup truck and his house is a mess."

McKissack shot her a skeptical look.

"We did profiling at the academy. You said so yourself, the UNSUB is orderly, organized. He swabbed the injection site in the middle of the woods. Those stitches were precise. Which means he's compulsive. Which means his house and car should be fairly well maintained. Orderly, compulsive perpetrators tend to buy dark-colored cars and replace them every couple of years. Buck's pickup is at least ten years old and it's fire-engine red. Also the UN-

SUB most likely has a great deal of difficulty with women. Buck Folette collects girlfriends the way a sheepdog attracts fleas."

"You may be right." McKissack shrugged. "Let's see if he's got an alibi for last night."

"I'd like to interview Dr. Castillo again," Rachel said. "I'd like to find out what happened in the ER."

McKissack nodded. "I'll talk to Rudd myself."

Sunlight shot through the clouds in slices, momentarily highlighting the rugged planes of his face. She wanted to hold him for a moment, just to keep from shivering to death.

"I never took a profiling course," McKissack said, "but I know what my gut tells me, and my gut is telling me this was a deliberate act, well planned and personal."

Rachel nodded. "Whoever did this wanted to depersonalize her. Wanted to degrade her. That's why he stripped her of her clothes and mutilated her face."

"The mutilation serves two purposes," McKissack said. "One, it caused her a great deal of pain and humiliation, so you can deduce there's a tremendous amount of anger there. And two, by sewing her mouth shut, he prevented us from finding out about his identity immediately."

"It acted like a gag until the drug or poison had time to take effect."

"He bought himself a little time. He knew she was going to die. He planned it that way. But why?"

Rachel was quiet a few seconds. "Whoever it is, I can't fathom the depth of his depravity. To actually sit there and do this meticulous work with the stitching. It's pure evil."

They locked eyes.

"Things like this aren't supposed to happen here," she said. "I'm frightened for Nicole . . . for her family . . . I don't think they can go through the trauma of losing another child. I don't think Jackie Castillo can take it."

"We'll find her," he said with determined, angry eyes. "We'll find them both alive, or I'll quit my fucking job."

All the warmth had drained from her body. She felt as cold as a corpse. "I won't be able to sleep until they're both home safe," she said.

A clap of thunder announced a sudden downpour, rain beating on their uncovered heads. McKissack's umbrella flapped noisily open, and he drew her close so they could share it, his big arm snaking around her. Rachel nestled against him, feeling terribly lonely. Most of her family was gone, her relationship with her brother was strained, all her friends had left the area years ago—Anne Marie was a lawyer in Washington, Linda an advertising executive in Manhattan. Everyone had flown the coop, and yet here she was, turning to a married man for comfort.

"My breath stinks," McKissack apologized, and she hugged him tight, needing his warmth.

5

A HEAVINESS SUFFUSED RACHEL'S LIMBS AS SHE RETURNED TO the hospital to speak with Dr. Yale Castillo once again. He hadn't taken off from work despite his daughter's death, and Rachel thought she understood.

"Why aren't you out looking for my other daughter?" he demanded to know.

She was seated in the same suffocating leather chair as before, feeling small and powerless, and that was no good. The case was complicated in a deep and murky way, and she tried to summon the mental energy she needed in order to solve it. "I'm here to find out what happened in the ER," she said, and he nodded in a resigned fashion.

"The call schedule ran twenty-four hours. It was a busy shift, the usual mix of minor trauma and accidents. Nothing to get the blood pumping. Then an announcement came over the radio, ambulance with trauma." He rubbed his hands over his cheeks. "When they wheeled her in, I didn't recognize her at first. I thought, this isn't my daughter. This is some monstrous . . . mistake. But then the hairs stood up on the back of my neck and suddenly I knew." His shoulders sagged. "It's been a singular experience for me, Detective."

Rachel's jaw ached from clenching her teeth, and she forced herself to relax.

"Claire had a history of asthma," he went on, "moderate, not severe. There was no prior need for intubation. She'd always responded well in the past to a treatment of nebulized beta-agonists and oral steroids."

Rachel shifted uncomfortably, sensing the precarious fragility in those sunken eyes. "So what happened?"

"I assessed airway and breathing. Her skin was cold and clammy and she was short of breath. I assumed her recent exposure to the cold air and intense emotional stress had triggered an acute asthma attack. For moderate cases, I usually give beta-agonists, but for severe attacks, a dose of subcutaneous epinephrine is used when aerosolized medication can't reach the target airway. So we administered three systemic injections of epinephrine, but her condition didn't improve."

Rachel could hear the controlled frenzy of the ER behind her, nurses and interns running up and down the corridor outside the doctor's office. "Was that the only medication she was given?"

"No," he continued in a hoarse whisper. "We also gave a bolus of IV methylprednisolone. When her condition failed to improve significantly, I ordered an IV administration of magnesium sulfate. But this had little effect as well, and we had to intubate.

"We used ketamine to provide sedation and bronchodilation. We used slightly smaller tidal volumes than average on a volume-preset ventilator. We assessed breath sounds and obtained arterial blood gas. But by then, her blood pressure was plummeting." Leaning forward earnestly, he said, "I can't for the life of me figure out what went wrong."

"So you opened her airway?"

"Yes." He gave a defeated sigh. "She was fine. She was breathing normally. She should've been okay. Then her blood pressure dropped to critical levels, and she lost consciousness."

"What happened next?"

Lowering his head, he cradled his broad, damp forehead in his hands. "Full cardiac arrest."

"Is it possible," she asked, "something could've gone wrong with the intubation?"

He shook his head. "I've done it a million times. I could intubate in my sleep."

They sat in stony silence. She could almost count each inky strand of hair combed across his bald spot. "My hands were shaking by that point. My hands never shake."

"You administered CPR yourself?"

"Her vital signs were preterminal. I called a Code Blue." His voice trailed off. He stroked his head as if he were petting a dying animal. "I tried to resuscitate for about twenty minutes. I refused to give up. I refused to call it. Hurley had to do it."

"Who's Hurley?"

"One of my residents." He straightened up, eyes red-rimmed and gleaming like surgical equipment. "There's an old joke. The procedure was a success, but the patient died."

"I'm so sorry about your loss," she said, getting up. "I want you to know we're doing everything we can to find your other daughter."

His face contorted, caught between a sob and his effort to control it, and he confessed, "I wake up in the middle of the night sometimes and don't know if that's me screaming."

She didn't know how to respond to such incalculable grief.

6

SHUTTING THE DOOR TO DR. CASTILLO'S OFFICE BEHIND HER,
Rachel felt a cold finger on her arm. She spun around and recognized the nurse from the waiting room, the one who'd brought them Nicole's necklace. She had an experienced grace about her, her eyes honest and direct.

"Detective Storrow? Can we talk?"

"Of course."

"Not here."

Rachel followed her out into a barren-looking alleyway between two cinder block buildings where they stood shivering beside a dumpster overflowing with IV bags and crumpled paper gowns.

"My name's Casey," the nurse said. "Casey Angstrom. I don't feel particularly great about what I'm about to tell you, the patient being his daughter and all . . . but I just can't keep it to myself anymore."

"Keep what to yourself?"

Casey's face was a slab of candor. "It wasn't an asthma attack."

"What?"

Casey paused for a moment, her moist eyes scanning the turnip-colored sky. "During the assessment period, we're supposed to provide critical interventions, including positioning and supplemental oxygen. What should've been done immediately is, we should've removed those sutures from her mouth. If we'd removed them immediately, I could have administered one hundred percent oxygen through the bag and it may not have been necessary to resort to any other interventions. Her color was good, her temp was up. She had good vital signs."

"Can you explain how you knew it wasn't asthma?"

"My brother has asthma. I know what it sounds like, those attacks. I'd know them in my sleep. The patient presented none of the symptoms of a severe attack, outside of frantic breathing. She was agitated and she was hyperventilating, but in my opinion, she wasn't *wheezing*. There's a difference. She was scared to death. Panic-stricken." She squinted at Rachel with extremely alert, intelligent eyes as if trying to impress upon her the gravity of this information. "The patient came to us with generalized swelling and trauma to the face and upper chest, but she had good vitals. She had good pressure. One-thirty over ninety. Pulse eighty-five."

"So you're saying . . . ?"

"Who wouldn't panic with your eyes, ears and mouth sewn shut? Who wouldn't have trouble breathing? It must've been terrifying."

"Are you telling me that Dr. Castillo didn't need to intubate? That he didn't have to use the procedures he used?"

"Oh no," she said, "no, something happened. I don't know what. After we administered the third injection of epinephrine, shortly after the third injection, there was a sudden, rapid decrease in blood pressure amplitude. She went into shock."

"Dr. Castillo made a mistake?"

"I don't mean to question the doctor's decisions."

Rachel was confused. "But you *are* questioning the doctor's decisions."

"All I'm saying is, there was a lot of panic in that room."

"So he misdiagnosed her original condition?"

"Gosh, I suddenly feel like I'm on the witness stand." She edged toward the exit door. "I don't know what went wrong. But I think the whole thing could've been avoided if we'd all kept our heads. When they wheeled her in, she was okay. Scared, but okay. I tried to tell the doctor."

"Exactly what difference would it have made?"

"I don't know."

"Then why tell me?"

She shook her head mutely, eyes wide, and Rachel knew she was holding something back. "I've gotta go."

"Casey . . ."

"I really have to go now . . . they'll be wondering where I am. I don't want them to know I was talking to you."

"What went wrong in there, Casey?"

"I don't know. Something awful. I never want to be that scared again as long as I live."

7

GUS ENTERED THE CLASSROOM SWINGING HIS CANE IN SUCH broad, lethal arcs, Abraham Andrews had to leap out of his way. Gus must've been crying because his eyes were swollen shut, and Abraham guessed he'd heard the ugly rumors circulating around school. Abraham was the director of Winfield School for the Blind and Special Needs, and his neck was stiff from lack of sleep. He detested being put in such a position, but Billy Storrow, Claire's teacher's aide, had called him late last night to confess he didn't know what to tell the children, didn't have a clue, and so it was up to Abraham to break the news.

"All right, boys and girls. Settle down."

The students formed a semicircle, luminous faces uplifted, heads cocked toward the sound of his voice. The room's stillness was insufferable. Claire Castillo's absence clanged like a bell. She should have been there, brushing her long, flowing hair off her face, fingering the tiny gold cross at the base of her throat.

Abraham considered Claire to be one of the best teachers he'd ever hired, but he didn't know about Billy. How could someone so bright be so lacking in ambition? What was he now, thirty-four?

Billy Storrow was leaning against the blackboard, trying to make himself invisible. Arms crossed, eyes downcast. His knees wobbled, but his feet somehow managed to plant themselves, and Abraham silently encouraged him to pull himself together. *Come on, boy, suck it up.* Abraham was there to break the news, but Billy would have to shoulder the rest of the day himself until a substitute teacher could be found.

"I'm afraid I've got bad news." Abraham couldn't keep his usually booming voice from shaking. "Some of you may have already heard about Ms. Castillo . . ." He broke off in midsentence. Their wide, expectant eyes were indifferent to the glaring sunlight, and suddenly he realized how unknowable they were in their innocence. Next to these children, he felt old. Worn-out. "Ms. Castillo passed away last night," he said simply.

The children remained remarkably silent, fingering their pencils and gazing at the sunlight slanting in through the windows.

"We've all been invited to the service this coming weekend."

"What happened?" one of the students asked. Her name was Gabie. Abraham only had to be introduced once, and the name stuck. "How come she had to die?"

Billy wilted, hands covering his face.

Abraham glanced around the room. "Her heart stopped," he said as gently as he could.

"Why?"

"Because she was very sick."

"Why?"

"I don't know, children."

"How come her heart stopped?" a tall boy named Luke wanted to know. "What happened?"

"There was . . . an accident," Abraham hedged, shooting Billy a sideways glance. No wonder he'd palmed this heartbreaking little task off on him. But it was all right. Abraham had broad shoulders.

"What kind of an accident?"

"Mr. Storrow?" Gus said. "Are you here?"

"Yes, I'm here." The children turned expectantly toward the sound of his voice as if he were an index of their despair and hope.

"What happened to Ms. Castillo?"

Abraham detected the sub-Richter shift of Billy's pupils and thought to himself, *This won't do.*

"Sometimes," Billy answered in a voice softened by sustained shock, "sometimes bad things happen to really nice people. There's no . . . there's no explanation why, really . . . there's no—"

"She was murdered," one of the children blurted.

There it was. The word hung suspended in the air. A communal gasp was followed by a stunned silence. Things had strayed far afield.

"Now, children," Abraham said, "speculation will get us nowhere."

"That's not true, is it, Mr. Storrow?" Gabie wanted to know. She had an awkward way of sitting, never resting for too long in one place, as if she were being constantly observed. "Was she murdered?"

Billy was trembling visibly now, lightning dancing behind his eyes. This wouldn't do. Not at all. Another few minutes and he'd be blubbering like a toddler. Abraham realized he'd better rearrange his schedule in order to accommodate these anxious and confused students. They sorely needed an adult around.

"Who killed her?" Gus asked, tears streaming down his battered face. They were all staring vacantly, mouths dots of despair.

"We don't know what happened," Abraham said firmly, taking

the reins. The class was his now. "All we know is that someone we all loved and cared about is no longer with us."

"Where is she?" asked a small voice.

Looking around the room, he tried to match the face with the voice, and found the tiny albino girl, the one with the key fetish. "Well, Brigette," he said, "she's in heaven now."

The children fell silent again, and he hoped they were conjuring up their beloved teacher in heaven with wings and a halo, for that was certainly where Claire Castillo belonged.

8

THE CASTILLO HOUSEHOLD WAS THICK WITH ANGUISH. RAchel crossed the dining room past an eight-person dining table and matching oak hutch into the living room, where an impeccably groomed Jackie Castillo waited for her on the white sectional sofa. "I stare at the phone and pray for good news," she confessed, her angular face streaked with sunlight. "When it rings, I practically jump out of my skin."

"I'd like to go through Nicole's bedroom," Rachel said softly, "to search for any possible clues."

"Yes, of course." Jackie reluctantly emerged from her cloud of grief. "Right this way." Her light touch wouldn't threaten a house of cards.

It was a typical teenager's room, except for the traces of fingerprint powder covering every surface: newly purchased clothes, stuffed animals tumbling off the bed, old Cabbage Patch dolls and Judy Blume books lining the shelves. There was a dusty telescope in one corner, a stack of CDs and a CD player in the other. The last album she'd been listening to was Bob Dylan's *The Times They Are A-Changin'*.

On the desktop was a Macintosh computer and printer, schoolbooks and crumpled homework pages. Tucked in the top drawer was an illicit pack of cigarettes, five dollars in change, and a love letter from Dinger Tedesco: "I will never stop loving you. You are so beautiful, Nicole. Did I ever tell you how beautiful you were? U have all the answers. Yers 4-ever, Dinger. XXXOOOXXX."

Everything—clothes, CDs, books, makeup—was accounted for, except for what Nicole had worn out of the house that night, along with her bike and backpack. Jackie described her daughter's outfit: pair of spandex tights, white sweat socks, hiking boots, yellow T-shirt, blue down jacket, the silver necklace holding Dinger's school ring, two glow-in-the-dark barrettes in the shape of stars, two tiny gold hoop earrings.

Like her sister before her, Nicole had simply disappeared. Rachel didn't know how much more of this she could take. The room spoke of the incredible promise of this child on the verge of womanhood.

Nauseated, she left the house, walked out to her car and stood in the freezing cold. Every angry thought found instant expression inside her crowded brain, where promising leads circled and collided with alibis and dead ends. She needed to vacuum her mental landscape. *Stop thinking,* she silently insisted, staring at her own papery breath smudging the bitter autumn air.

9

RACHEL VISITED THE PLACE IN THE WOODS WHERE CLAIRE Castillo was last seen alive, a rise near Highway 71 less than a mile from the downtown business district. The forest floor was wet from the recent downpour, carpeted with sword ferns and fallen leaves. Old Mo Heppenheimer's cow pasture, where Melissa D'Agostino's body had been discovered eighteen years ago, was two miles east. Rachel stood for a moment in the shadow of the tall pines and surveyed the cordoned-off area. Officers were combing the woods for clues, and so far nothing useful had been found. They'd spent the day soaked to the bone, sifting through wet leaves, overturning stones and kicking in rotten stumps in their relentless search for evidence.

Rachel trudged past a deadfall fir, with each step her heart beating just a little harder for the young woman she hadn't been able to save. She slid down a slimy incline, wondering what it must have been like for Claire on this death march through the woods. The UNSUB most likely had pulled his car over onto the shoulder of Highway 71, escorted her toward this general area, forced her to lie down, injected her with an unknown substance and then exited the area, leaving Claire to crawl out of the woods on her own. Rachel hoped against hope the UNSUB had left something of himself behind, but once again the heavy rainfall didn't help.

Rachel made a mental map of the area. Eighteen years ago, five stray cats had been decapitated in a grove one and a half miles northeast of this location, and Melissa D'Agostino had been strangled to death two miles east of here. Her heart was a fist knocking against her rib cage. The clouds were torn away, sun shining down through a canopy of golden leaves, and suddenly everything seemed crystal clear. She thought about her brother, the absence of grief in his dull eyes after their father's tragic suicide. She vividly recalled a dream he'd once had about killing a neighborhood girl. She lived on their block, and rumor had it she liked to play doctor. Billy must've been thirteen or fourteen, and he hated this girl, he said. In his dream, he cut off her head. It was the way he'd said it that stuck with her, eyes flashing, mouth a vicious blur. Just like his idea about the Old Testament God being better than the New Testament God—

brutal, bitter, avenging, murderous, the kind of deity who took no prisoners and made no excuses.

She loved her brother but didn't fully understand him. Sometimes they could be so close, yet other times he withdrew from her like a snail into its shell. Even as children, she sensed he had a secret life. He could have easily become a teacher, but instead he'd chosen to remain a teacher's aide. He'd won a scholarship to Amherst, had majored in English, had graduated with honors, and yet he'd never written so much as a paragraph as far as she could tell. He was bright and kind, the best brother anybody could ever want, yet he'd alienated himself from all his old friends and had never had a successful relationship with a woman. His one long-term relationship lasted only a few years. Gillian Dumont. She'd moved away over a decade ago and nobody had been able to locate her after she left Seattle.

Billy lived alone in a house four miles north of here, and worked at Winfield, half a mile to the northwest. Billy was obsessively neat. He owned a dark-colored car, a forest green Plymouth Breeze. He'd always had difficulties with women. He was very intelligent and organized. He'd been implicated in the murder of Melissa D'Agostino and he'd admitted to killing those cats. Disturbed individuals were known to torture animals in their childhood. Violence was generational. Billy was a local. He lived in a secluded part of town and had, in the past, rented a cabin in the woods near the Canadian border.

Rachel shook her head. What kind of desperate speculation was this? It went against everything she knew about her brother. Despite his shortcomings, Billy was no monster. It failed to make sense to her on any level, and she dropped the thought as abruptly as it had appeared.

Reaching for a tree branch, Rachel hauled herself out of a ravine and grabbed the trunk of a birch tree. There were indentations in the bark, three gnarled holes that reminded her of the holes in a bowling ball. People sometimes collected sap from these trees, drilling holes with a gimlet, then hanging a tomato can on a nail to collect the watery sap. She traced her fingers over the rough, sticky bark, then looked around at the patches of light and shadow, the sky above her a stirred-up summer blue. Exactly the kind of weather they should've had four weeks ago when Claire Castillo first went missing, instead of this relentless downpour that washed away fingerprints and fibers, hairs and precious clues, leaving no odor for the bloodhounds to track. It was cosmically unfair.

Rachel followed an overgrown trail to Winnetka Road, where Ozzie Rudd had spotted the victim crawling out of the forest. They'd already examined the marks in the leafy dirt where she'd dragged herself along, semiconscious. With her mouth sewn shut, Claire wouldn't have been able to scream for help.

The chirp of brakes snapped Rachel's train of thought in half. McKissack got out of his car and joined her by the side of the road, his face peppered with beard stubble, eyes red-rimmed from lack of sleep. He put on a pair of mirrored glasses and gripped her arm. "How are you?"

"Fine."

"Funny, you don't look so hot."

"Neither do you." She smiled back.

"No word from the lab yet about the semen." McKissack's mouth tucked around the corners. "How about you? Any luck?"

"One of the nurses at the hospital told me she didn't think Claire Castillo had an asthma attack in the ER that night. She seemed concerned about the doctor's decision to treat the patient for acute asthma."

McKissack shrugged. "Ultimately, it wouldn't've mattered what he did if she was poisoned."

"Did you get the toxicology report?"

"Not yet."

"What about Buck Folette?"

"Claims he was planted on a barstool in Laconia the entire night but can't remember which bar. We're checking it out."

"Claire's landlord?"

"Says he was home alone, mainlining *Laverne & Shirley* reruns. Tapper's taking his statement as we speak."

"I thought you put a car on him, too?"

"We did, for two weeks." McKissack sighed. "We're understaffed and overbudget. It was a judgment call."

It was starting to get bitter out. Evergreen branches stabbed at the crisp blue sky, and the sun seemed as remote and shiny as an ornament. She decided to give voice to the question that'd been torturing her all night long. "So how do two teenagers disappear into thin air?"

McKissack glanced back up the steel gray road tapering off like the tip of a knife. "Seven-thirty P.M., Nicole goes over to her friend Shelly's house. Shelly's mom goes to bed at eleven, and Nicole takes off on her bike. If anybody saw her pedaling around that night, nobody's reported it."

"You searched all the alternate routes she might've taken to Dinger's house?"

"Thoroughly. It was fruitless. In the meantime, Dinger rides *his* bike off into the sunset and is never heard from again. They both vanish into the mist."

A gust of wind twisted her coat open, and she yanked it shut. "Somebody has to have seen them."

"We're getting plenty of tips on the hotline. Usual percentage. Eighty percent crap, twenty percent promising. I'm hoping somebody comes forward before it's too late. Fuck." He stomped his feet. "I'm freezing my nuts off."

"How much time have we got, McKissack?"

"I don't know."

Her eyes blurred with tears. "I keep feeling more and more lost."

His features softened. "Maybe we've got time," he whispered unconvincingly. "Maybe we've got a window here."

"He kept her alive for three weeks," she said hopefully.

"To the day."

"When a victim's face is mutilated, especially the eyes, it suggests the assailant and victim knew one another." A faint taste of bile leaked into her throat. *Billy and Claire knew each other.* "I wish I wasn't . . ."

"What?"

"Nothing." She shook off the thought. "Maybe it's not a relative or friend? Maybe it's a complete stranger?"

"I seriously doubt that." McKissack fastened the top button of his overcoat. "We're looking at Ozzie Rudd, Buck Folette, Dinger Tedesco . . . possibly the landlord."

"Dinger got off work at seven P.M. the night Claire disappeared. He has no alibi from that point on."

"Talk to his employer. See what you can dig up."

10

THE INSTANT SHE WALKED IN THE DOOR, RACHEL REALIZED that Vaughn Kellum or one of his employees must be a tailor. Still, the sewing up of Claire didn't require skill so much as utter cruelty. Claire Castillo had all her dry cleaning done at Kellum Kleaners, but so did a lot of people, including McKissack. Those who could afford him swore by him, but Rachel preferred the cheaper places in Commerce City.

The nineteenth-century Queen Anne was painted moss green, a sign in the window reading: SATISFACTION GUARANTEED. Inside, the air was oppressive. Rachel couldn't imagine inhaling dry-cleaning fumes all day long. The walls were pine-paneled, and the view of Delongpre through the plate glass was obscured by a web of ivy growing abandoned on the windowsill. Directly across the street from Kellum Kleaners was a vacant lot, weeds twisting up through cracks in the asphalt. If you stood close enough to the glass and craned your neck, you could see where Delongpre intersected with Main.

"Mr. Kellum?"

"Please, call me Vaughn." He acquainted himself by touching her on the arm. Vaughn Kellum owned and operated Kellum Kleaners along with two old-time employees, Ray Fielding and Jose Manuel. He was in his mid-thirties, tall and slender with a charming smile and perfect teeth, his Nordic good looks marred only by the thick corrective lenses that magnified his green gaze all out of proportion. His eyes were deep-socketed and seemed to roam without purpose, suddenly settling on her with distracting intensity. He wore jeans, leather moccasins and a light blue shirt whose pockets brimmed with pens and receipts, and had a pair of flesh-colored hearing aids looped around behind his ears. "The police have been in a couple of times asking about Claire," he said. "I still can't get over it. She was such a good person."

The customer pickup counter was made of oak, the carpet was dove gray, the walls matte white. In back behind the garment trolleys, Jose was pressing clothes. To his right was a large worktable littered with facings and pincushions, measuring tape, and a tailor's ham. To his left were two dressmaker's forms—a man's suit on one, a large-shouldered lavender dress on the other.

Vaughn Kellum escorted Rachel into his office, just off the lobby to the left of the cash register. Walking through the door was like stepping into a more genteel age—rosewood tables, Aubusson carpet, faded photographs in vintage frames. There was a picture of Vaughn shaking hands with the mayor, another of him posing with the chief of police. McKissack looked ruggedly handsome in his uniform, and she felt her neck going pink. The large, impressive office was well lit and the heavy velvet curtains were drawn shut against the noontime glare.

Vaughn explored the room tactilely, lightly touching the wall as he made his way toward the carved mahogany desk. His computer was on, and in front of the large-print screen was a magnifier on a fixed stand. Braille Dymo-tape labels were stuck to every surface, and a Perkins Brailler "typewriter for the blind" affixed to a typing table was pushed up beside the desk. The computer keyboard was large-type, not Braille. Behind the desk on a bookshelf sat a small television set tuned to the weather channel. The volume was on high, announcer's voice booming into the room, "Now let's take a look at the East Coast—"

Vaughn clicked off the set. "How can I help you, Detective?"

"Please, call me Rachel."

He nodded. "Would you like some tea?"

"No, thanks. I'm fine." She opened her notebook. "Dinger Tedesco works for you part-time?"

"I hired him last March. Sweeping, discount mailings, that sort of thing." His corrective lenses were as thick as manhole covers, his gaze both luminous and unnerving.

"You're aware," she said as delicately as she could, "that Dinger and Nicole Castillo have been missing for almost a week now?"

"Yes." Vaughn's gaze may have been blank, but his face was alive with emotion, his deep concern evidenced in the wrinkle of his brow, the jut of his chin, the deepening of the parenthetical lines around his mouth. He had left the door of his office open, and Rachel could see out to the front of the shop. Ray Fielding was behind the counter, attending to business. A customer had just walked in, the intermittent hiss of the steam press punctuating their conversation.

"What are Dinger's hours?" she asked.

"Three to five, four to six. It's flexible. Sometimes if we don't have anything for him to do, he'll finish his homework in my office." His face tensed. "His parents must be going out of their minds."

"It's tough on everybody," she acknowledged.

"I think he might've left his latest chemistry assignment here." His hands explored the desktop. "Do you see it?"

Rachel got up and scanned the desk for a teenager's scrawling penmanship, but found nothing amidst the balance sheets, discount flyers, self-threading needles and stacks of invoices. "I don't see anything." She sat back down, struck by how flippantly people used terms like "see" and "hear."

"He's acing math and chemistry, but flunking English."

She nodded. "You live here, don't you? Upstairs?"

Vaughn smiled. "I grew up in this house. Dad started the business in '54. The three of us—me, Mom and Dad—lived here until Mom passed away. Then Dad had his stroke. Now it's just me."

"And you were home the night Claire disappeared?"

"It was a slow day. We closed shop at seven. I went upstairs and left Dinger sitting in front of my computer."

"He didn't leave at seven?"

"No."

"Are you sure?"

"He had an English paper due the next morning."

"When did he leave?"

"I don't know. Seven-thirty or eight, maybe."

"And we're talking about the night of October fourteenth?"

"Yes."

"Mr. Kellum . . ." Rachel hesitated. "How well do you hear?"

The friendly, unruffled reception he gave to this rather rude line of questioning bolstered her opinion of him even further. "As a child," he said, "I was diagnosed with moderate to severe hearing loss in both ears. These hearing aids are designed to correct severe to profound losses. They're very comfortable. But if I removed them, I wouldn't be able to hear you unless you shouted, and even then I probably wouldn't understand what you were saying."

She nodded.

"As long as I remember to replace the batteries, I'm fine." He waited a moment, then said, "That was a joke."

"Oh." She gave an embarrassed smile.

"By the way, Detective, I don't mind answering these types of questions. The more informed people are, the less confusion there is in the world."

"I appreciate your candor." She flipped through her notebook, anxious to change the subject. "So you close at seven?"

"Every night. Like clockwork."

"Did you hear anything unusual that night? Scuffling sounds? Screams? An argument, maybe? A shout?"

"My hearing aids amplify all sounds, but I've learned to filter out those I don't wish to focus on, just like 'normal' people do. So when I'm listening to the radio, that's pretty much all I hear. Background noises don't usually register."

Rachel nodded. "And you say you went upstairs that night?"

"Ray came over around nine. We had a few martinis. Ketel-One, straight up with an olive."

Rachel glanced through the open doorway at Ray Fielding, a blue-collar guy with a walrus mustache.

"What does Ray do?"

"He's our master tailor."

"I'd like to speak with him."

"Now?"

"After we're done." Rachel glanced at her notes, then paused. "Was Dinger still here when Ray dropped by at nine?"

"No."

"Does Dinger have his own key?"

"The door locks behind you and he knows the security code."

"And you trusted him?"

"Sure."

"What about the cash register?"

"Jose makes nightly deposits."

"How often do you let Dinger stay after hours?"

"Just a couple of times so far. Like I said, I trusted him."

"And you wouldn't be able to hear anything from upstairs, like the slamming of a door when he left, for example?"

"What are you getting at, Detective?"

"You say Dinger was in the shop until seven-thirty or eight P.M. Claire Castillo disappeared shortly after eight P.M. I'm trying to establish if there's a connection."

He shrugged. "All I can say is, Dinger's a hardworking kid, a good kid whose family can't afford a computer. I was shocked to hear what happened to Claire, even more shocked when Dinger and his girlfriend disappeared. I don't know what's happening to this town." He shifted in his chair. "I don't sleep well at night."

"To tell you the truth, neither do I."

"Are you a religious person, Detective?"

"Not exceptionally."

"Neither am I. But I find myself praying lately."

Rachel glanced through the open door again. Out front, a silver-haired woman in a camel's hair coat shot Rachel an annoyed glance. Lowering her voice, Rachel said, "Claire telephoned you several times the week before she disappeared . . ."

"Excuse me?" He tapped his hearing aid as if it weren't functioning properly.

She spoke up. "Claire made several phone calls to you the week before she disappeared . . ."

"About the charity dance, yes. She was helping us organize it. It's a lot of work. The other board members wanted to cancel, in light of what happened, but I think Claire would've been disappointed. She was very involved in community outreach."

"Did she mention anything about Dinger or her sister? Anything at all?"

He thought for a beat, hands folded on the desk blotter. "Not that I can recall."

"Your shop faces Delongpre. Did you see anything unusual on the street that night . . . ?" She stopped herself, embarrassed. "I'm sorry, I didn't mean . . ."

His smile contained a hint of melancholy. "The neighborhood kids used to call me Magoo. The term 'low vision' refers to loss of vision which can't be corrected by medical or surgical proce- dures. It's the most misunderstood disability in the United States. People think 'low vision' means you're just a 'little bit blind.' I don't use a cane or a guide dog, and I pride myself on leading a fairly independent life. But without my hearing aids or my glasses, I'd be pretty defenseless."

"I see," Rachel said, then bit her tongue. There was that "see" word again.

"With these corrective lenses, my vision's 20/150," he contin- ued. "I can spot objects and people across a room and recognize colors. I use a hand magnifier for the newspaper. The books I buy are large-print, and I can also read Braille. I have a Tell-Time VII Talking Watch, but to answer your question, no, I can't see out the window."

She cringed. "That was dumb. Forgive me."

"Please, Detective. I'm more than happy to oblige."

She closed her notebook. "Did Dinger ever confide in you?"

Vaughn nodded. "Sometimes."

"Did he ever discuss his relationship with Nicole?"

"Oh, you know. Typical teenage stuff. He was anxious to get married. I advised him to wait, that if it was true love, it'd pass the test of time. But then when Nicole found out she was pregnant—"

Rachel froze. "Excuse me?"

"I'm sorry." He looked at her sheepishly. "I thought the police knew."

"Dinger told you this?"

"A few weeks ago."

"How far along is she?"

"He didn't say."

"Did Dinger tell you that he and Nicole were thinking of running away together?"

"No."

"Was he depressed? Suicidal?"

"Quite the contrary. Now that Nicole was pregnant, he figured her parents would have to let them get married."

"Did he ever mention a secret place?"

"Secret place?"

"Someplace where he and Nicole could be alone together?"

"No. Look, this is making me uncomfortable . . ."

"Trust me, you're doing the right thing."

Vaughn took a deep breath. "Dinger was very happy until Nicole decided she might get rid of the baby."

"An abortion?"

"She was considering the possibility. She kept going back and forth with it."

"How did he react? Was he angry? Make any verbal threats?"

"I believe . . ." Vaughn furrowed his brow. "I believe if he was mad at anyone, it was Claire."

"Why Claire?"

"Because she was influencing Nicole."

"Did Dinger ever threaten Claire?"

"Certainly not." His eyes widened with concern. "Is he a suspect?"

"We don't have all the facts yet."

"Because I can't see him doing something so . . ." His voice trailed off.

"Neither can I," she admitted.

"He must've run away. They must've run away together. Dinger would never hurt anyone."

"Vaughn?" Ray called through the door. "You got a second?"

Vaughn looked at her, and she nodded. He stood up and felt his way along the wall, then paused in the doorway. "Promise me you'll find them."

"We're doing our very best," she said softly.

Out front, the silver-haired woman extended a well-manicured claw. "Vaughn, I want to share my good news! My daughter Julia's getting married!"

"She is?" he replied, sounding genuinely delighted. "Wow, that's great. When did this happen?"

11

THAT NIGHT, RACHEL MET MCKISSACK AT BIG TEE'S, WHERE they sat across from each other in a dimly lit booth. Rachel ordered a glass of wine while McKissack knocked back another scotch. He looked so beaten down, she wanted to reach out and stroke his cheek.

"I'm a prick," he confessed. "I still want you. Even in the midst of all this crap, I want you."

"Shut up, McKissack."

"I'm a bad influence."

"It's not like I'm the victim here. Your wife's the victim. Go apologize to her."

"You know what freedom is?" He slurred his words. "Freedom's when you don't give a rat's ass what other people think."

"You're drunk."

"And you're beautiful."

"Yeah, yeah."

"Beautiful and wise. Wise, but not jaded."

She looked away. "Nicole's pregnant."

That made him sit up straighter. "What?"

"Vaughn Kellum told me. Dinger wanted the baby, but Nicole was considering getting an abortion."

McKissack's eyes narrowed.

"Dinger lied to me. He told me he got off work at seven the night Claire disappeared, but Vaughn says he stayed until seven-thirty or eight doing his homework in Vaughn's office."

"Why lie about a thing like that?"

"Maybe he saw Claire as a threat."

"Okay." McKissack rubbed his eyes. "Back up."

"Claire's the person Nicole turns to for advice. Nicole doesn't trust her parents, they don't listen. They don't understand. But Claire knows about love. She understands Nicole's desires and needs. And because she lived with Buck Folette for two years, Claire also knows what it's like to be trapped in a bad relationship."

His eyes registered understanding. "And she doesn't want her little sister making the same mistake. It was Claire who advised Nicole to get an abortion?"

"Bingo."

"So Dinger wanted her out of the picture." He tossed back his scotch. "Nicole's parents never liked him, but Nicole sees them as the enemy, so they're not the real threat. It's Claire's opinion that counts."

"They'd been going together for nine months. We can assume Dinger knew about Claire's Wednesday night habit."

"He hangs out after work, waiting for eight o'clock to roll around."

"Pulls up in his car just as she's leaving the cafe."

"Offers her a lift to the parking lot. Claire tries to talk to him about Nicole, and that's what sets him off."

"He knocks her unconscious."

"Then abducts her. Where?"

"Wherever he and Nicole are hiding out."

McKissack took a moment to absorb this scenario, then shook

his head. "Three weeks, the perp waited. A seventeen-year-old kid can't wait that long. He'd be impulsive."

"Besides, where does a seventeen-year-old get poison?" Then it hit her. *"Chemistry."*

"What's that?"

"Dinger excels in math and chemistry."

"Yeah, but we don't know if it's poison yet." McKissack frowned and scooped up Rachel's hand. "We don't know shit."

She studied him a lingering beat. "How're you getting home? You sure aren't driving."

"I thought you'd take me to your place."

"Fat chance." She smiled, the threat of it flourishing in the silence that followed. Her face grew hot as he stroked her cheek.

"I wonder when," he asked, "my suit of armor fell off?"

Rachel parked in front of McKissack's house. All the lights were out. "Movies," he said, slurring his words. "They don't need me. Gotta whole life without me."

"Come on," she said, helping him out of her car. He leaned heavily against her as they walked up the gravel path toward the front porch.

"Town's goin' to hell. You notice? We're all fighting for deck chairs on the Titanic."

"Shhh."

He gazed at her beneath the yellow porch light. "Hiya, beautiful." She fumbled with his keys, turned the lock and they both tumbled inside.

McKissack's house smelled alien to her, of roast chicken and Lemon Pledge. The front hall was dark, and McKissack leaned lightly against her. "Are you flirting with me?" he asked, and she nudged him toward the kitchen.

"No, I'm leaving."

He grabbed her around the middle, wouldn't let go. "I'm

scared, Rachel," he confessed, his boozy breath warming her face. "I'm scared I'll forget how to be happy when I'm not with you."

She pried his fingers from around her waist. Her hands were trembling. "This isn't 'happy.'"

"It's the only time I'm alive."

Angry now, she pressed his face between her hands. "We're in your fucking house, McKissack. Standing in your fucking kitchen. Your wife and children *live* here."

"I don't live here. I live between your legs."

She wanted to hit him. She turned to go, but he hooked her wrist, spun her around and drew her irresistibly toward him. She fell into his arms as if she belonged there. Tears sprang to her eyes. His voice was tender. "Rachel . . ."

He kissed her.

"Don't." Her stomach rose to her throat as if she'd just stepped off a cliff.

"I love you."

"Stop."

"I want you." He kissed her as if there wasn't enough air left, and much to her dismay, she let him . . . let him kiss her . . . and started kissing back . . . when suddenly the telephone's jarring ring skittered up her spine. McKissack ignored it and the machine clicked on.

"Hey, Chief," a male voice said, "it's God speaking, pick up."

McKissack looked at her, stricken, as if they were suddenly miles apart.

"Answer it," she said.

His sweaty face sagged. "Hello?" He listened a long beat. "Right there." He hung up. "We got the lab results back on the semen stain. Our perp is a secretor. B-positive."

"Ozzie's blood type."

The world came crashing down.

12

EARLY THE FOLLOWING MORNING, OZZIE RUDD DROVE TO HIS ex-wife's house to pick up Colette and take her to school. The Gothic cottage with pink trim used to be Ozzie's house, but now it belonged to Mae. It hurt that their marriage had gone bad, that Mae hadn't been able to find it in her heart to forgive him for his many transgressions. He'd been insensitive. He was pigheaded and sometimes verbally abusive. Worst of all, he wasn't headed anywhere. He figured that was his biggest sin—not being ambitious enough for his intelligent wife.

"Thanks for doing this," Mae said at the front door. She looked confident, tailored, her well-toned stomach moving with every breath. She reached into her pockets and dug out Colette's medication, her dark glasses and a box of cough drops. "She's got a cold but she'll be all right," she said. "She's in her room. We need to talk."

"Mind if I use the can?"

Ozzie used the bathroom in the front hall, but the soap was one of those flimsy discount brands and the dirt stayed stubbornly beneath his fingernails. He checked himself in the mirror; he needed a nosehair trim.

Out in the kitchen, Mae poured him a cup of coffee. The coffee must've been sitting there awhile. "I'm getting married," she announced.

"You're what?" His heart fluttered.

"Getting married. Oh come on, Ozzie, don't look so shocked. It's been a couple of years now."

"I know . . . but it's just . . . I never figured that either of us would get married again."

"Why the hell not?"

"Let's not fight, Mae. I'm kind of in shock here, okay?"

"You've still got those damn eyes." She sounded mad as hell. "All the men in your family have those goddamn eyes."

His eyes were blue with thick lashes like rows of commas. "We've all got hairy backs, too," he said. "So who is this guy?"

"You don't know him."

"Enlighten me."

"Don't snap at me!"

"I'm not snapping."

"Yes, you are." She set her coffee cup down. "I'm not going to argue with you."

"No argument." He threw up his hands. "Sorry."

"Okay."

"Okay." He got a glimpse of his reflection in the window above the sink and sucked in his gut. His face was weather-beaten, sunburnt, and his brown hair was gradually turning silver. He wondered what it was about his muscular arms, his self-deprecating sense of humor and deep voice that Mae no longer loved.

"So who's Mr. Congeniality?"

"He's an entertainment lawyer," she said.

"A what?"

"I met him through friends."

She had friends without him now, too. She had a whole life that didn't include him.

"He's from San Francisco," she said quickly. "We're moving there."

"You're what?" The air rushed out of his lungs and he almost inhaled his coffee. "You're moving where?"

"I've given this a lot of thought, believe me . . ."

"Thought?"

"Ozzie . . ."

"How dare you?"

"I'm not going to have a scene in this house!" She stomped her foot.

"You bitch!"

"Oh great." She threw up her hands. "That's just great. And you wonder why I divorced you?"

"How dare you take my daughter away from me!"

"I think you should leave now." Her hand rested on the receiver. She'd called the police on him once before, but nothing had come of it, since she hadn't pressed charges.

"What about Colette?"

"Stop screaming at me."

"I can't believe you sprang this on me!"

"I won't talk to you unless you calm down."

"All right." He rubbed the back of his head. He was feeling disemboweled. Here he was, guts pooling over the shiny linoleum, and all she could say was "calm down." "I am calm," he said. "I'm calm."

"I refuse to get into this with you."

"I said okay."

"I swear to God, I'll call the cops."

"I'm over it." He paced the floor, taking deep, laborious breaths. His stomach ached. His skeleton tingled as if he'd been pumped full of radioactive isotopes.

"Mommy?" Colette called from the other room.

"Everything's fine, honey. Your daddy and I are just talking."

"Daddy, are you taking me to school today?"

"In a minute, sugar."

They listened for a moment more, Mae wringing her hands, Ozzie pacing back and forth. He stopped to face her.

"I guess I could move to San Francisco. I guess I could follow the two of you around like a dog. Live in the cracks and crevices of Colette's life."

"Yes, you could," she said flatly.

He wanted to slap her. His blood was on fire.

"Listen, I know it's not the best news for you. For Colette, either. But I can't help it, dammit, I fell in love. I fell in love with him, Ozzie. What else am I supposed to do?"

"I don't know."

"He's an entertainment lawyer, for chrissakes. It's not like he can open a practice here."

"Colette's school is here."

Her face went pink. "I've been looking into that. There are other schools—"

"But it won't be Winfield. All her friends are here. She grew up in Flowering Dogwood. She loves her teachers. And she loves me, Mae, as much as you hate to admit it. I'm a huge, important part of her life."

"Jesus, I know that. You think I'm stupid or something?"

He'd never felt such a burst of hatred. He shook his head violently. "I can't accept this."

"What?"

"Sorry."

"What d'you mean, you can't accept this? This is not your decision!"

"You can't take her away from me without any warning."

"I've already spoken to my lawyer, Ozzie."

"Merry Christmas, Mae! You and your lawyers."

"What am I supposed to do? I have a life. And Steve can provide for us . . ."

"Steve." He spat the name out.

"That's right."

"Great." He snagged his jacket and strode out of the kitchen, went into Colette's room and held her tight. "You ready, sweetie?"

"Yes, Daddy." She giggled. Her hair smelled of her mother's shampoo. Colette's room was filled with a soft pink light, bed overflowing with stuffed animals—Roger Rabbit, Big Bird, Raggedy Ann and Andy. A whole crowd. Ann and Andy's button eyes were pulled off so they'd be blind, too. Finger paintings covered the walls, hanging plants late-bloomed in the bay window and a fat hamster named Dibbs nibbled lettuce in his cage.

She'd always wanted to ride in an airplane. When she was little, they'd play a game where he'd lie flat on his back and lift her high in the air, prop her tummy against the soles of his feet, hold her by the arms, and she'd be flying. Laughing, giggling, squealing . . . an explosion of mirth. "I'm flying, Daddy!" Magically he made her spin, bob and weave, and all the while she'd clutch his fingers as if they were vines growing out of some slippery slope. And after a while she'd be all tuckered out, arms and legs dangling from the pull of gravity, her white-blond hair scratching his eyelids like sleep dust, and he'd gently lower her down into his arms. "No more airplane. Beddy-bye time."

At the front door, Mae's face was carved out of stone. "Have your lawyer talk to my lawyer," she said.

"Fine." He wanted to kick her. He wanted to burn the house down. His house.

"Fine." She shut the door in his face.

13

FRIDAYS WERE A BUSY TIME FOR COPS IN MOST COMMUNITIES. You had to break up bar fights and stop drunk drivers, and today was going to be no different, McKissack thought. On top of the usual mischief, they'd gotten the lab results back from the semen stain on the victim's calf identifying the perp as a B secretor with three genetic markers. Ozzie Rudd had no alibi for the night Claire disappeared. He was the one who found her crawling out of the woods three weeks later. His blood type was B-positive, same as the semen sample; they knew that from the Melissa D'Agostino file. McKissack bet it was Rudd's semen on Claire's leg and the only way to determine that beyond a shadow of a doubt was with a DNA test based on a blood or semen sample from the man himself.

Earlier that morning, armed with a warrant, McKissack and Tapper had searched Rudd's empty apartment on Maynard Avenue, then conducted raids on two homes the suspect was known to have visited. Rudd's ex-wife indicated he'd picked up their daughter at seven and had driven her to school, but Colette was marked absent, so McKissack issued an expansive radio alert over scrambled police channels, informing surrounding law enforcement agencies to be on the lookout for Rudd's truck.

McKissack was pumped. They had enough to convict, and although they hadn't found evidence of Nicole or Dinger or Claire inside the apartment, they'd swept the area with wide transparent tape to collect fibers and hairs for future prosecution. McKissack was convinced he could wring a confession out of Rudd, and along with it the location of the remaining victims, dead or alive. All they had to do now was find him.

McKissack was on his way back to the station when he spotted Rudd's Long Ranger pulling out onto Montalbanco Drive. Heart hammering in his chest, he made a U-turn and radioed in. "I've located the vehicle . . . it's traveling erratically . . . just crossed over the double yellow lines and swerved back . . ."

McKissack checked that his weapon was loaded. Rudd's ex-wife claimed he didn't own a gun, but you never knew. An officer was allowed to use whatever reasonable nondeadly force was necessary to make an arrest and to protect himself and the public from bodily harm. If Ozzie Rudd fired a gun, that would justify the use of deadly force, but then McKissack might never find out where the bodies were buried.

He'd gone to work with a gun on his hip almost every day of his life, and now it was burning a hole in his side. He could practically taste this arrest. *Just trying to make the mean streets of our community a little safer.*

14

"WHAT IF YOU LIVED WITH DADDY ALWAYS? WOULD YOU LIKE that?" Ozzie handed Colette a Milky Way, which she quickly unwrapped and devoured, melted chocolate dappling her chin. They bounced along in the cab of his eighteen-wheeler, wind roaring through the open windows, rain spattering the windshield as they climbed the hill past ancient toppling bed-and-breakfasts, heading north toward Aspen Park. In the early 1900s, preservationists had bought the land, afraid the timber companies might level the forests.

"Would you like that, sweetie?"

"You gonna move to San Francisco with us, Daddy?" She sounded excited. Her forehead was damp in the way that only Colette's skin got damp—that dull luster, as if she were glowing from inside.

"What if we moved someplace together, you and me?"

"And Mommy, too?"

His chest constricted. He couldn't explain what he'd been thinking, this thing about running away and taking her with him. Just the two of them. The details were sketchy, but the idea burned through him like Chinese mustard.

The road intersected with Aspen Park Loop, where they crossed a stone bridge and ascended a steep hill, twisting away from the valley and winding further into the woods. He tickled her under the chin and she gave a barking shriek, then grabbed his arm and held on tight. God, this unconditional love, this guileless affection was killing him.

"How about it, pumpkin?"

"You and me and Mommy?"

"No." He swallowed hard, sand trickling through his body, foot going numb on the gas. "Just you and me, cuttlefish. How about it?"

She released his arm and let out a shout—of joy? of rage? She twisted herself into a strange shape, shoulders hunched inside her jacket like two frightened animals.

"Colette?" His throat was dry and his eyes stung from the gritty wind blowing into the cab.

"No!" she shrieked, and suddenly she was crying, sobs like giddy notes blown from an old saxophone.

"Please don't cry." But she wouldn't stop, and he felt as if he'd been hit by a soft train. He searched for the nearest turnoff as she tossed her head violently from side to side. "Honey . . . Colette? Calm down now . . ."

He pulled onto a soft shoulder, tires skidding on the damp earth, and Colette flailed her arms, her fingernails grazing his cheek. Her elbow hit the door handle, the door flew open and she slipped from his grip.

"Colette!"

She tumbled out and teetered on the soft shoulder, screaming in a high-pitched voice. His little girl, lost and thrashing in this nowhere, no-walled edge of highway. She pitched toward the woods, and he tackled her, and they both went down in the drizzle.

"Colette, I'm sorry," he whispered, heart fluttering like a netted fish. He held her tight and caught a glimpse of the woods to his left, its piney undergrowth the kind of place no little girl should ever get lost in. He both loved and dreaded this faraway corner of the country with its black cherry, its quaking aspen and stunted, wind-blasted balsam firs. "It's okay, sweetie, I'll take you home. Everything's gonna be all right."

Lifting her in his arms, he dried her tears, but now his chest heaved and he was sobbing. He wept so hard, his knees buckled, and he crumpled to the side of the road. Shoulders spasming, lungs hiccuping with grief, he clung to his daughter and sobbed like a baby.

And then—miraculously—her forgiving hands reached for his face, and the next sob that escaped his lungs was like the final surrender of all his bad intentions.

"I love you, Daddy."

"I know," he whispered, holding her, holding her, knowing he was losing her with every passing breath.

"I love you, Daddy."

"I love you, too, sweetpea."

15

RAIN STREAKED THE DUSTY WINDSHIELD OF MCKISSACK'S police car as he pulled up behind Ozzie's eighteen-wheeler, hand reaching in back for one of the stuffed animals he usually carried to comfort children involved in car accidents. He got out and cautiously approached Ozzie Rudd, whose face was wet from crying, and his little girl, who clung to him like a barnacle.

"Everything okay?"

Rudd peered up at McKissack from some scary, dark place. Hollow-eyed and deathly pale. "Yeah, we're fine."

"I'm gonna have to ask you to stand up, Ozzie," McKissack said quietly so as not to alarm them.

Rudd got to his feet like an old man and took his daughter's hand. "We were just leaving."

"I'm afraid I can't let you go. There's a warrant out for your arrest."

"Arrest?" He glanced at his daughter. "What for?"

"Kidnapping and attempted murder."

Ozzie stood for a confused moment, grip tightening on his daughter's wrist until she yelped. "Oops. Sorry, honey."

McKissack took out his handcuffs and ratcheted them down on Rudd's wrists while he read him his rights, and all the while his little girl was whining and fussing, tugging on her daddy's pant leg.

"Mind if I talk to your daughter?" McKissack asked.

"If you have to."

"Only take a second."

Ozzie leaned against the truck while McKissack knelt and performed a cursory exam, inspecting the child for contusions and abrasions. She looked fine, except for the fact that her eyelashes were wet with fresh tears. A siren wailed in the distance.

"I'm Chief McKissack. What's your name?"

"Colette." She probed his face with sensitive fingers, and McKissack smiled and handed her a fuzzy pink seal. "Here, this is for you."

"Thank you." She clutched the toy to her chest.

"You okay? You've been crying."

Her lower lip crimped. "I wanna go home."

"Oh for God's sake." Rudd's mask cracked, and McKissack got a glimpse of the inner torment that drove him. "My ex-wife's getting married. She's taking Colette to live with her in San Francisco. I'm upset. Colette's upset. Been a real crappy day."

McKissack straightened. "Sorry to hear it, Ozzie."

"Yeah, well . . ." He stood like an empty grain sack, slack arms shackled behind him, and blinked so slowly, McKissack thought for a moment he might be putting him on.

Now several black-and-whites pulled up alongside the truck. Tapper got out. Keppel got out.

"One of you make sure Colette gets home safe," McKissack said, and Keppel took the girl's hand.

"Daddy?"

"It's okay, sweetheart," Ozzie said grimly. "The policeman's gonna take you home."

"Daddy, what's wrong? What's happening?"

"Nothing, pumpkin. I'll be fine."

McKissack escorted Rudd over to his car as Tapper cracked open the back of the eighteen-wheeler, evidence collection kit in hand.

"Drive carefully," Tapper told McKissack. "It's gonna get slippery."

16

MCKISSACK PREFERRED CONDUCTING INTERVIEWS IN AS PRI-vate an area as possible, free from outside interference and ringing phones. He'd decorated the interrogation room at the station himself, had even handpicked the furniture. Unlike some old-timers who preferred austere and sterile environments, Mc-Kissack believed that discomfort rarely produced the desired results. First and foremost, the room should be comfortable with a moderately official feel—pictures and certificates on the wall, soft lighting, comfortable chairs.

McKissack led Ozzie into the interrogation room, where there were no windows to distract, and sat behind a large desk piled high with folders, thus giving himself the psychological advantage. At some point during the interview, he might move away from his desk and sit in a chair opposite the one Ozzie now occupied, thereby demonstrating empathy and trust. To get a person to confess, you needed to gain their confidence. Ninety percent of the time, they wanted to get it off their chest. Whenever McKissack detected the suspect was on the verge of confessing, he'd move his chair so close, their knees practically touched.

"Make yourself comfortable," he began, uncapping his pen. "You're gonna be here awhile."

Ozzie slumped in his seat. "Do you mind telling me what this is all about?"

"We found a semen stain on Claire Castillo's leg. Just got the results back from the lab today. Secretor. B-positive blood type. We'd like a blood sample to determine whether or not the genetic markers match yours. But I can tell you right now . . . that was your semen on the victim's leg."

McKissack stared at the man he was about to interrogate. Rudd wore rain-splattered jeans and a plaid flannel shirt, a leather bomber jacket and shitkickers. The shitkickers were dusty except where fat raindrops had exploded on the yellowish leather as he'd run from his truck into the station. He had broad shoulders and a beer belly, was no taller than McKissack but heavier by about twenty pounds. He had a trucker's tan—arms and neck only—and his facial expressions ranged from don't-give-a-shit to fuck-you-asshole.

"Christ." Rudd shifted in his seat, an odd smile blooming. "That's what you're arresting me for?"

"That's right."

Rudd almost laughed. Shook his head. "You're way off base."

McKissack frowned. "Why don't you tell me your side of the story? I'll write down your statement and then you can read and sign it. Fair enough?"

"I'd be delighted to give you my statement, Chief."

McKissack nodded.

Ozzie's face grew solemn. "When she crawled out of the woods, I practically shit my pants."

"I need to know what you did the entire day."

"That was Wednesday, right?" Rudd chewed thoughtfully on his lower lip. "I was with my daughter."

"Can anyone corroborate?"

"Yeah." The muscles in his jaw twitched. "I've got an alibi, pretty much, if that's what you're getting at."

Nursing an intense dislike for the man, McKissack said, "Why don't we start with nine A.M.?"

"Okay."

McKissack wrote out Ozzie's statement as he spoke:

"I was between jobs. I slept past noon. I had Colette for the afternoon and was really looking forward to it. I picked her up after school. Her teacher can verify the time. We went out for dinner at the Drop Off. The waitress there, Suzi, knows me. Then we went back to my place and listened to some music. Colette likes Billie Holiday. Then I drove her to her mom's house.

"We got to Mae's around six-thirty P.M. She can verify the time. We had dinner together, and surprising as it sounds, we didn't argue, for once. Sort of like old times. Then after dinner, Mae said something that shocked me. She said, 'How come I'm not over you completely?' Well, you could've knocked me over with a feather. Maybe it's the hurt in my eyes that got to her? I don't know. But she invited me to stay for coffee. Then she did something totally unexpected. She stroked my arm, and her touch was . . . forgiving.

"We go outside and she walks me to the truck. She wants to see what I've got in back. 'Nothing much,' I tell her. I can't believe I'm doing this, but we climb in back together, and I gather all these packing quilts and make us a sort of nest, and we make love in the dark. She tells me it's for the last time. I can't believe this is happening, but it seems right. And while we're making love, it's almost like I'm weeping. Like I'm releasing all this anger and sadness. Like it's the right thing to do. Like it's okay for Colette to be with her. But you wanna know the real kicker?"

McKissack glanced up from his legal pad.

"I didn't know it at the time, but she'd just gotten engaged." Ozzie bit his lower lip. "To an entertainment lawyer, of all things. What the hell's an entertainment lawyer?"

McKissack wasn't going to share this bitter, ironical moment with him. "Go on."

"I left around eight and drove to Commerce City. Dropped in at the Hoary Toad for a drink. Must've been around midnight when I finally headed home. I was driving south on Winnetka Road when I spotted something up ahead. I slowed down and saw this pale figure crawling out of the woods. She was . . . naked, and there was something wrong with her. At first I thought she'd been shot, maybe, like she was clutching her chest because of a gunshot wound or something. I hit the brakes and pulled over. I sat for a moment, thinking maybe I'd imagined it. I hopped out and there she was, twenty yards back, making the weirdest sounds." He shuddered. "My heart was going a mile a minute. The sight of it just shocked the bejeezus out of me.

"I don't know much, Chief," Ozzie said, "but I do know you're not supposed to move a person who's badly injured, so I told her to lie still. I ran back to my cab, radioed for help and got a packing quilt out of the back. She was shivering, so I covered her up. Then I sat there, held her hand, talked to her a little bit. It took ten minutes for the ambulance to arrive." Ozzie was staring at him with something like vindication in his eyes. "So you see . . . I guess it was my semen. But I didn't kill anybody."

McKissack sat back. It was awfully hot in here. "We'll have to verify your account with your ex-wife."

Ozzie's eyes grew pinched and curious. "Why do you hate me so much, McKissack?"

"I don't hate you, Ozzie. I don't think about you that much."

"Oh yes, you do. It's like . . . stuck in your throat, how much you hate me. I can see it in your eyes. It's weird, because I've never done a fucking thing to you."

McKissack smiled. "Maybe I hate what you used to be, Ozzie."

"Oh yeah? What's that?"

"An ungrateful little deadbeat with an ax to grind."

Ozzie glanced away for a moment. "Can I go now?"

McKissack shook his head. "Let me give you some advice, free of charge. Hire yourself a good lawyer. You're gonna need it."

17

THE SKY'S MOLTING GRAY GAVE WAY TO VARIOUS SHAPES— clouds like rocket ships and scavenging bears. Rachel stepped into the Hurryback Cafe, where the aroma of fresh-brewed coffee mingled with frying onions, and took a seat in one of the wide vinyl booths. The waitress's nametag said *Becky*.

"I'd like to ask you a few questions, Becky," Rachel said, flashing her badge.

"You a cop?"

"Detective."

"Sure, okay. Except the cops asked me a buncha questions already." Becky had a pasty face and black-hennaed hair that emphasized the blankness of gaze. The coffee came out of the pot like hot, shimmery sand. "It's about Claire, right? She used to eat here Wednesday nights. She'd sit in that booth over there and read a book. Sometimes we'd chew the fat. I liked her a lot. She was a big tipper."

"Did you notice anything peculiar about her that night?"

"Peculiar?"

"Was she nervous or distracted?"

"No, I don't think so. Just unwinding at the Hurryback, as per usual." Becky flopped down opposite Rachel in the booth, a St. Christopher's medal riding the pulse in her throat. The diner's floral wallpaper was as faded as a bad Polaroid. "She came in here for lunch sometimes, too. Grilled cheese on rye and a Snapple. Iced tea with lemon."

The diner had a timeless, weathered feel with its potted palms and pressed-tin ceiling. A gray-haired waitress stood over by the register, staring at them. "Who's that?" Rachel asked.

"Vera." Becky waved her over. "She's a witch. Don't quote me, though. She'd give me a hot tongue, a cold shoulder and a hard time."

Vera sauntered over, arms folded across her flat chest, candy-apple uniform dotted with stains. "We're not supposed to fraternize, Becky."

"She's not a customer, she's a detective."

"Oh." Vera raised an inquisitive eyebrow. "You work with Jim McKissack?"

"Yes."

"I used to know him." Beneath the polite exterior, Rachel detected some bite. "You folks nab any suspects yet?"

"Sorry, I'm not at liberty to discuss the case," Rachel said, and Vera nodded with practiced resignation. "I would like to ask you a few questions, though."

"Ask away."

"I know the police have already spoken with you both, but it's important that you try and remember . . . did you happen to see which way Claire Castillo headed after she exited the diner?"

Vera shook her head. Rachel couldn't help feeling she was being appraised somehow. "Your name Rachel Storrow?"

"Yes, it is."

"Mm." Vera's gaze seemed to reach right inside of her.

"Do we know each other?" Rachel asked.

"No," Vera said, softening. "No, we don't."

"Claire probably went window shopping after she left here." Becky blew a ribbon of black hair off her face, but it drifted down over her eyes again. "She was a clothes horse. Her taste is kinda similar to mine. Bergman's has the best selection."

Rachel glanced out the window. Flowering Dogwood boasted the widest Main Street in New England—virtually empty now except for a few scattered pedestrians. Across the street, a young woman had her arm around an old man's waist and was gently guiding him off the curb. The old man clung to her as if she were asking him to step into a raging river. From here, you could see the time-and-temperature sign at the bank.

"Is it true what they say about Claire?" Becky asked with wide-awake eyes. "The way they found her, I mean? All sewn up like Frankenstein?"

Both waitresses stared at Rachel with fierce concentration, as if willing the rumor not to be true.

"I'm sorry," Rachel said. "I can't discuss it."

"Becky," Vera said with a wave of her hand, "we've got legitimate customers waiting."

Becky gave Rachel a disappointed smile. "I sure hope they find Nicole. She's in my sister's class."

Vera waited for Becky to leave before saying, "Don't you just hate that, telling more lies to cover up other lies?"

"Excuse me?"

Vera touched Rachel's arm lightly, confidentially. "He ain't worth it, honey. No man is."

Rachel blinked dumbly. Vera walked away.

Great, so everybody knows our business. That's just great.

Outside, Rachel headed up the street toward Bergman's, past the vacant storefront, the hardware store, the shoe store and Ruthie's Fashions. Then came Bergman's, then Gayle's Beauty Parlor and an empty storefront. An alley.

Where Delongpre intersected Main, there was Dusty's Ballroom Dancing, a dental practice, a ghostly Victorian mansion with plenty of office space available, Kellum Kleaners and the town's information center. And beyond the information center was a weedy lot, and then the woods. The woods encroached upon the town like a fungus. Every street, it seemed, ended in woods.

She turned and looked the other way: liquor store, toy store, used car lot, 99¢ store, Sears, the public parking lot. Whoever had kidnapped Claire Castillo had done so in full view of the entire town. The police had interviewed every business establishment on Main and Delongpre, but apparently no one had seen a thing. Why had she even bothered the waitresses at the Hurryback? She could have gone to the station and read the reports. The police were buried under an avalanche of paperwork.

If Ozzie Rudd wasn't guilty, then who was? It was a foggy and cold night. Claire most likely would've skipped the window shopping and headed back to her car. The UNSUB must have abducted her somewhere between the Hurryback Cafe and the parking lot. Had Dinger gotten off at eight and offered Claire a ride? Was Dinger capable of such violence? Or was Buck Folette the man they were looking for? If Buck had offered Claire a lift, would she have taken it? Had he attacked her from behind? Had he waited in an alley?

Rachel sighed, making breath clouds in the air. She had another interview to do, one she'd been avoiding. A big rig drove past, stirring the wind and making a shuddering sound as she trudged toward her car.

18

UP NEAR THE CANADIAN BORDER, ROUTE 88 BENT SOUTH AWAY from Baxter Gorge, whose densely wooded cliffs and slabs of quartzite were formed in the Devonian Age, when an immense ice sheet covering all of New England began to melt. The melting ice water drained into the Androscoggin River, a favorite for anglers seeking rainbow trout in the furious white water. Route 88 continued south down into the widening, glacier-carved valley where waterfalls splayed and forked into streams that riffled over boulders and meandered through the area of town

known as the Triangle. The Triangle sat on the site of old Fort
Hostile, erected in 1777 to protect early settlers from Native
American war parties. The fort was burned to the ground in
1783, and this was where Dinger Tedesco currently resided with
his mother and three siblings.

Rachel was sadly familiar with the area: crumbling mansions
floating on a sea of debris, screen doors busted off their hinges,
voices raised in anger, tiny bodies flung against apartment walls.
She got a lot of domestics in this neighborhood, some B&Es, an
occasional drug-related death.

Rachel took a left up a steep, poorly paved road, a silver-
painted mailbox giving away the hidden driveway: TEDESCO. The
trailer's white walls bled rust. The rusted-out carcass of an old
Dodge Charger nudged the trailer's rear bumper in the gravel
driveway. Scattered across the muddy front lawn were old tires
and children's toys.

Rachel got out of the car and approached the trailer, boots
crunching on gravel. "Hello? Anybody home?" The trailer had
miserly, dark windows. Next to the Dodge Charger was a pumpkin patch, vines growing tangled and wild, and behind that a
large chicken wire coop holding plump rabbits, their hard pink
eyes like an infestation of beetles upon their whiteness.

Rachel knocked on the door but nobody answered. Touching
her nose to the glass, she peered into darkness. "Hello?" Her
scalp prickled as she felt a distinct presence gazing back, then
detected a cluster of words. Whispered, not spoken. Somebody
was sitting in the dark, pretending not to be home.

"Police!" She thumped on the door with her fist, and finally a
small pale figure approached. The door creaked open. The boy
reminded her of an old man with his taut mouth and sour stare,
his spindly arms and legs. "Hello?" he said, peering up at her
questioningly.

"Is your mother home?"

"She's out grocery shopping."

Rachel scanned the neighborhood, pockets of poverty as far as the eye could see, and beyond this heart-wrenching poverty, the cornfields, the woods and a dirty smudge of horizon. She squinted into the murky interior where shadows danced deceptively. "Are you Dinger's brother?"

"Yes, ma'am."

"We need to talk, Mrs. Tedesco." Rachel raised her voice. "Mrs. Tedesco?"

The silence that followed was deafening; even the birds stopped singing.

"I'd like to talk to you about your son Dinger. I need to ask you some questions so we can bring him home, safe and sound."

Something stirred and creaked. There was a rustling sound, and finally a figure emerged like a whale from the soggy depths. An obese woman in a blue-floral tent dress with limp brown hair like a banana peel draped over her head said in the high voice of a sickly child, "Yes, what can I do for you?"

"Mrs. Tedesco?" Rachel held out her hand. "I'm Detective Storrow."

The woman offered Rachel a plump, limp, moist hand for her to squeeze and said, "I thought maybe you were one of them reporters." Her breath smelled yeasty. "They come crawlin' up the hill to harass us, talkin' about how my boy run off with Nicole Castillo."

"Can we talk for a minute?"

"Sure. C'mon in."

The air inside the trailer was moist and eucalyptus-smelling. Two more children were curled up on the sofa, tattered outfits revealing their bony frames. The older boy seemed more vulnerable than the other two children despite his flattop haircut and paste-on tattoos. He sat on the plaid sofa with his knees drawn to his chest, and beside him, like a frightened bird, was a little girl who cradled the sofa's musty arm.

"Would you like some Lipton tea?" Mrs. Tedesco offered, and

Rachel declined, but then changed her mind. Mrs. Tedesco disappeared into the tiny kitchenette. "My mother used to buy those pinwheel cookies, remember? I love them cookies, but you can't find 'em anywhere."

Rachel took a seat in a damp-smelling armchair beside the TV set and became the sole focus of the children's attention. There were pictures of the family on the walls in neat simple frames. Back issues of *TV Guide* and *People* were stacked on the slender coffee table. Tall plastic cups decorated with football figures littered every surface. The potted geraniums in the window were mottled with fungus.

"My ex-husband does carpentry work," Mrs. Tedesco said, a clatter of teakettle and china cups emanating from the kitchenette. "Case you need a fix-it man. Here's his card." She dug inside the pocket of her tent dress. "Oops. Had one somewhere. He's real good with his hands. Made me a computer stand with a paper tray. I'm studying computers at the community college."

"You and your ex . . . are you still close?" Rachel asked.

"Oh my, yes. He's good with yard work, all kindsa stuff. I'm his manager. I get a percentage of whatever business I can dig up." She let out a death-rattle cough. "Roger and Dinger have such a strong bond. Dinger sure loves his dad."

"Where's Roger live?"

"Over there on Carpenter Street. Funny, huh? A carpenter who lives on Carpenter Street."

Rachel took down Roger's address and phone number, then asked, "He doesn't know the Castillos by any chance, does he?"

"Oh yeah. Did some yard work for them over the summer. Worked on their pool."

"And you say you and Roger get along?"

"Like bread and butter." Mrs. Tedesco came out carrying two cups of tea. She set Rachel's down on the coffee table in front of her, then squeezed in between the pale, dirty children on the sofa. "So what can I do for you, Detective?"

"I need to ask you about the day Dinger disappeared."

"Well, he went to school, then he went to work."

"Around four-thirty?"

She shrugged. "He's got, watchacallit . . . flexible hours."

"School lets out at two-thirty, doesn't it? Where was he between two-thirty and four-thirty?"

"Over Chris's house. Chris lives with his stepdad four blocks thataway. Those two together are three stooges short of a load."

"And he borrowed your car?"

"I let him use it, long as he gasses up."

"What time were you expecting him home that night?"

"Dinger can stay out until eleven o'clock on weeknights."

"How's he doing academically?"

"Okay, I guess. He's good at math and science, but he's lousy at history, and he's failing English and social studies. He's a big kid, but he ain't interested in sports. Go figure."

"Does he own a chemistry set?"

"What?"

"A chemistry set?"

"He used to have one when he was little."

"Have you ever known him to take drugs?"

Mrs. Tedesco let out an indignant grunt. "My kids don't do drugs. Dinger can't even stomach secondhand smoke. He made me quit."

Rachel nodded and flipped through the pages of her notebook. "He took off on his bicycle that night. Why didn't he take the car?"

"I was using it. Had to go to the clinic to have a DDT or . . . you know, that thing that scrapes your insides? An IUD or something? Kind of like Roto-Rooter?"

"You mean, a D&C?"

"Yeah, sucks your insides out." Mrs. Tedesco made a sour face and rubbed her stomach. "You want a cookie? I got Yum-Yums."

"No, thanks." Rachel smiled. "Mrs. Tedesco, can you think of anyplace Dinger might have gone to be alone? Someplace private?"

"Oh gee. Lemme think. Him and Chris used to hang out in the barn that got torn down last year . . ." Her voice trailed off.

Now that her eyes had adjusted to the dark, Rachel could make out the girl more clearly—she looked twelve or thirteen, with dirty-blond hair, hazel eyes and the beginnings of acne on her cheeks.

"Do you think Dinger might've confided in one of your other children?"

"Gee whiz." Mrs. Tedesco looked at her brood. "Holy cow, kids. Who's holdin' out?"

"What are their names?"

"Sheba . . . Duncan . . . Franklin."

Rachel smiled at the girl. "Hello, Sheba."

"Hello." A mere whisper.

"Speak up, mouse fart," Duncan, the younger brother, sneered.

"Sheba," Rachel said, leaning forward, "did Dinger say where he was going last Wednesday night? The night he and Nicole disappeared?"

Sheba's eyes went wide like her mother's. "Well, um—"

"We can't hear you, goose poop!"

"Mom," Sheba whined, "make him stop."

Mrs. Tedesco pinched Duncan's thigh. "Quit teasing your sister."

"Ow!"

"Sheba," Rachel said, trying to remain focused, "your brother's missing and I'm trying to find him. Nobody's going to get into trouble here, isn't that right, Mrs. Tedesco?"

"Absolutely not."

"I need you to tell me the truth."

Sheba had a sweet smile. She drew her knees up to her chest like her brothers were doing and her clothes made a rustling sound. "Dinger said he and Nicole were gonna get married."

"Really?"

"Yeah, he said they were gonna have a baby."

A surprised Mrs. Tedesco shifted her bulk on the couch and her three children bobbed like buoys in her wake.

"It's okay, Sheba," Rachel said as coolly as she could. "No one's going to get into trouble. Your brother needs your help. Trust me, I won't get mad at anything you say."

Sheba chewed thoughtfully on her lower lip, then continued: "He said if it was a boy, he was gonna name it Brother, and if it was a girl, he was gonna call it Mercedes."

Rachel smiled her encouragement. "Interesting choices."

"When I have a baby, I'm gonna call it Portia like in *Julius Caesar,* if it's a girl. And if it's a boy, I'll call him Fabio."

Duncan made farting sounds. "Fabio! Oh Fabio! Sounds like something you'd spit up in the morning."

"Trust me," Mrs. Tedesco interrupted, "I don't know nothin' about any baby."

"That's perfectly all right," Rachel said. "Sheba, what else did he tell you? I need you to think real hard."

Sheba thought for a moment, then glanced at her mother. "Just that I wasn't supposed to tell."

"Don't worry, you're not in any trouble."

"And that if Nicole's parents found out, they'd kill him."

"Nobody's gonna kill anybody," Mrs. Tedesco said uneasily.

"And that Dinger and Nicole were gonna run away together and get married."

"Did he say where they were going?"

Sheba stared mutely at her and shook her head.

"I heard him talkin' on the phone," Franklin piped up. "He was talkin' to some guy named Billy."

"Billy?" The hairs prickled the back of Rachel's neck.

"Or maybe it was Bobby." Franklin frowned. "Yeah, I think it was Bobby."

"When was this?"

"Last week."

"Last week, before he disappeared?"

"I can't remember."

" 'I can't remember,' " his younger brother sneered, pressing his palm to his mouth and making a farting sound.

"Cut it out." Mrs. Tedesco twisted Duncan's nose, Duncan screamed in exaggerated pain, and his brother and sister giggled.

Rachel stood up. "Thanks, you've been very helpful."

"But you haven't finished your tea." Mrs. Tedesco followed her to the door. "D'you think they ran away?" she asked in an urgent, hopeful whisper. "D'you think they ran off to get married or something?"

"I don't know," Rachel said. "We're doing everything we can to locate them."

As she turned to leave, the children on the couch cried out in unison, "Sayonara!"

19

RACHEL DROVE TO THE BLIND SCHOOL WITH THE INTENTION of talking to Billy, but instead found herself parked behind Knox-wood Hall, the department for head injuries. She was feeling achy and had taken some cold medicine and now her head was groggy. It was a typically frigid November afternoon, the temperature in the thirties.

The building's furnace pumped pockets of hot, dusty air into the drafty lobby. A silver balloon floated at the far end of the receptionist's desk. Anchored to a pencil sharpener, it delicately drifted with the fickle air currents. Rachel glanced at the flowers on the countertop, a sensual yellow bouquet that aggressively greeted people as they walked in the door.

"Excuse me," she said, approaching the receptionist, "I'd like to speak to Russell Crenshaw. I'm from the police department."

The elderly woman seemed slightly out of breath. "There's a flu going around," she said, shoving the nozzle of a Vicks inhaler up her nose and squeezing. She picked up the phone and dialed. "Hi, it's me. Russell's got a visitor." She listened a beat, then cradled the receiver. "He'll be here in a minute, have a seat."

Rachel picked up a brochure and took it to the sagging lobby sofa. "Adult Services: Comprehensive Rehabilitation Programs for Head-Injured Persons 18 Years & Older." According to the brochure, there were approximately 700,000 head injuries in the United States each year. The most frequent reason for visits to the emergency room was head injury. Every year, more than 140,000 Americans died as a result, with 2,000 cases in a persistent vegetative state. The typical survivor of severe head injury required five to ten years of intensive rehabilitation, resulting in a cost of $8 million over a lifetime.

The sound of a rattling trash cart reached her ears before Porter Powell came into view. She identified him by his nametag. He had a babyish face and startled, sandy blond hair, and was taller than the man accompanying him by several inches. He hummed to himself, a tuneless groan, and shook his head so forcefully, his hearing aid fell out and began to whistle, high-pitched and insistent. The man—Russell, she assumed—followed him at a short distance.

"Hide your food," Russell said. "Porter's coming."

"Spare me," the receptionist said. "I'm going for a cigarette."

She ducked into the ladies' room just as Porter Powell stopped short of the silver helium balloon rising up from her desk. He ran his hands through his thick, stand-up hair, then poked at the balloon, which bobbed above the pencil sharpener.

"Ung!" he grunted, and clapped his hands.

"You wanted to see me?" Russell said.

Rachel stood up and they shook hands. "Detective Storrow."

"Billy's sister?"

"Yes. I have a few questions about the night Claire Castillo disappeared."

"Porter, no," Russell said firmly. He was a thin, middle-aged man in a Star Trek T-shirt. "Porter's on a mission," he explained. "It's his job. Tuesdays and Thursdays, he empties all the wastebaskets."

As if on cue, Porter rounded the receptionist's desk and found the wastebasket. He grasped the sides of the metal barrel and scanned the desk for stray scraps, his eyes as wide and blank as puddles after a hard rain.

"That's fine, Porter," Russell said, tilting back on his heels.

Porter spotted a dustball on the rug and stooped to retrieve it, his back expanding as he bent over until it was as broad as a billboard. He upended the wastebasket, shook it viciously into the trash cart and fished around for stuck pieces of tape. He returned the wastebasket to its place beneath the receptionist's desk, all the while making breathy, guttural sounds at the back of his throat.

"Thank you, Mr. Powell. Good job."

Porter didn't respond. Instead he fingered the balloon's string, and the balloon hopped anxiously up and down.

"Porter," Russell warned.

Obediently, he returned to the cart where he throttled the full trash bag, then secured it with a twistie.

"His big thing is neatness," Russell explained. "I have to stop him from carrying too many half-filled trash bags out to the sidewalk in front of the building. He's very thorough, I'll give you that."

"So I see," Rachel said with a smile.

"His one big vice is running water. He likes to go upstairs and play with the bathroom faucets. He'd run water all day long if we let him. Isn't that right, Mr. Powell? So you wanted to know . . . ?"

"Was there anything unusual about Billy's appearance the night Claire disappeared, when he brought Porter back?"

"Hm." Russell frowned. If he thought there was anything odd about her line of questioning, he didn't let on. "As far as I remember, no. Billy brought him back around nine, just like always."

"Did you two speak?"

"'Hey, man, how's it going?' Stuff like that. 'Cold out?' I probably asked him how Porter was, you know . . . what'd he get himself into this time?"

"Was there anything unusual about Porter's behavior that night?"

He squinted at her. "What d'you mean?"

"Was he more agitated than usual?"

"Porter's always agitated. A year ago, he was a normal teenage boy, headed for college on a football scholarship; then one night, he and his buddies decide to go drinking and driving, right? Big mistake. Porter's the lucky one, if you can believe it. Head trauma impact. He's lost a lot of cognitive abilities—attention, memory, reaction time, higher-level reasoning. He's got a constellation of behavior problems. Hyperactivity, irritability, impulsivity . . ."

"So you're saying . . . there was nothing out of the ordinary about his behavior that night?"

"If his behavior could be called ordinary, no."

"Would you mind if I asked him?"

"Porter?" He seemed surprised. "Be my guest."

Russell corralled Porter onto the plaid sofa, where he bounced excitedly up and down and shook his massive head.

"Porter," Russell said, "this is Detective Storrow—"

"Rachel."

"Porter, this is Rachel. She wants to ask you some questions, okay? Okay, buddy?"

"Yup." He bounced up and down, avoiding eye contact.

"Hello, Porter," Rachel said.

"Yup," he said.

"Do you remember Billy?"

"Uh-huh."

"He's your volunteer, isn't he?"

"Uh-huh."

"Remember when he picked you up about four weeks ago? It was a Wednesday night, do you remember? Middle of October?"

"Yup."

"Do you remember that night? It was sort of foggy. You and Billy went out to eat, I think. You shot hoops in his backyard. Remember?"

"Yup. Billy and me . . ."

"That's right. Do you remember what happened that night?"

"Who you sittin' in for?" Porter asked with an abrupt shake of his head.

"Excuse me?"

"Who you sittin' in for?"

She looked at Russell.

"He thinks you're a substitute teacher."

"Oh." Rachel smiled. "No, I'm a police detective, Porter."

"Police?"

"Yes."

"What's that?" He pointed at her lap.

She looked down. She had her notebook out. "These are my notes."

"What for?"

"I'm writing down your statement."

He clapped his hands excitedly and bounced up and down on the squeaky sofa, loose as a rag doll.

"You're really revved up today," Russell said. "Did you eat your Wheaties this morning, Porter?"

"Yup. What're you doin'?"

"I'm writing down everything you say," Rachel responded.

"What for?"

"It's my job."

"What's that?" He pointed at her chest.

She glanced down. Her coat was open, the handle grip of her gun exposed. She smoothed her coat shut. "That's my weapon. I'm a police detective. Don't worry, I'm not going to use it."

"On bad guys?"

"I try not to use it, Porter." She glanced at Russell, worried she might've frightened them both, but Russell only shrugged. "Porter," she said, "do you remember anything about the night you and Billy spent together about a month ago?"

He abruptly stopped bouncing and stared at the floor, making itsy-bitsy spiders with his fingers.

"Do you remember anything about that night?"

"Girls," he said cryptically.

"What's that?"

"Girls."

"What about girls?"

"We got girl."

She leaned forward. Did he mean Rachel herself? Was he still confusing her with a substitute teacher? "I'm sorry?" she said.

"We got girl." He was bouncing violently now.

"What girl?" she asked with growing alarm. "What girl, Porter?"

"Porter," Russell said, "cool your jets."

He obeyed instantly, hands steepled in front of his face. "We got girl."

"What girl?"

"Yup."

She glanced helplessly at Russell, who merely shrugged. "I doubt he remembers much of anything," he said softly. "Porter has severely limited cognitive capacity. His family has unrealistic expectations, I'm afraid."

Porter was rocking violently now, head ducking lower and lower toward the ground. Russell intervened, reaching for Porter's shoulder and gently, physically steadying him. Porter stopped rocking long enough to rub his eyes and flap his large, fleshy hands.

"I'm really disappointed in you," he said, flapping his hands as if he'd burnt them on a stove. "I'm really disappointed in you . . ."

"Okay, buddy, calm down."

He jumped up and ran across the lobby toward the counter in front of the receptionist's desk, bumping into it with his sneakered feet.

"Porter!" Russell called out.

He folded the bouquet in a firm handshake, brought the flowers to his nose and inhaled, his broad fleshy face lit by their yellowness. "I'm really disappointed in you . . ."

Russell slowly approached. "Chill out, buddy."

Porter's fingers tightened around the stems. When he released his grip, yellow petals fluttered to the floor. "I'm really disappointed in you . . ." He bolted up the stairs.

"Porter, no!" Russell took off after him.

Shivering, Rachel stood and cinched her belt. Perhaps she shouldn't have come? The stairwell shook as Porter pounded back down the stairs again. He charged toward her, breathing noisily through his nose, snorting like a bull, and for an instant she thought he might bowl her over. Instead, he made a U-turn and hammered toward the reception area.

"Yikes!" The receptionist turned right around and went back inside the ladies' room.

Porter snatched the silver balloon by its string and gave a sharp tug. The string snapped, and Porter gleefully ran with it out the front door.

Russell was hot on his heels. "Porter Powell, you come back here!"

Rachel headed after them, keeping a safe distance.

Outside, Russell grabbed Porter's shirtsleeve and the fabric ripped as Porter twisted away, surprisingly agile. He looked up at the sky and let go of the balloon. He let out an exultant cry as the balloon ascended into the wide blue yonder.

Russell turned to Rachel with an embarrassed grin. "He's been plotting that for days, I'll bet."

20

"I'LL TELL YOU SOMETHING FOR A FACT. MOST PEOPLE'S DOOR-bells don't work," Boomer Blazo said as Rachel struggled to keep up. They were walking door to door, reading meters in an area where some of Flowering Dogwood's oldest homes were located. Boomer wore a blue shirt inscribed with the gas company logo. He'd been at it for ten years now, and his wife was expecting twins soon, and he wasn't sure how they were going to make ends meet.

"You know, I like this neighborhood," he said. "I got a real juicy book today. All outside meters. I can do about fifty an hour, that's a real juicy book.

"When you have to do a lot of walking," Boomer went on, "that's a bad book. Too many busted doorbells, you gotta knock. People get mad if you knock. 'What's wrong with my door-bell?' Twenty-five houses an hour, that's a bad book."

"I wanted to talk to you about the night Melissa D'Agostino was murdered, Boomer."

"You know, Officer . . . should I call you Officer?"

"Rachel's fine."

"Rachel, I've struggled practically my entire life trying to put that episode behind me. I don't particularly like the fact that you're cracking the case wide open. I mean, this is my life now. I've got a wife and kids. I'm a decent, hardworking citizen just like anybody else. I don't think I should be harassed for something that hap-pened, hell . . . a lifetime ago, to be perfectly frank with you."

"I respect your honesty, Boomer," she said, struggling up a short hill toward a brown house where the family's laundry was draped over the second-floor balcony. "But Neal Fliss said I should talk to you about where Billy was that night."

He stopped her with a broad, ink-stained hand. He was lanky, almost gaunt, and reminded her so much of the shy, pimple-faced adolescent who used to hang out in her brother's room, smoking pot and throwing open the windows in the dead of winter to get rid of the smell. "She lied," he said, his gravel voice lowered to a whisper.

"Who lied?"

"Gillian Dumont."

"About what?"

"About afterward. When we all took off." Boomer shook his head in frustration. "First we dropped Melissa off near the exit, right? Then Neal and I drove to my house where we shot pool all night, and Ozzie and Dolly went to the Dairy Joy, and Billy dropped Michelle off, then supposedly drove over to Gillian's, right? That's what they both said, right?"

Rachel nodded, fingers gripping her pen.

"Well—" Boomer's Adam's apple bobbed as he swallowed. "They lied."

"You can prove this?"

"No, I can't." He continued up the hill, and Rachel lost her footing and nearly slipped in the mud. "Let Gillian tell you herself."

"I haven't been able to locate her." She shuffled through the Melissa D'Agostino case file, searching for Gillian's yellowed statement. "Both parents dead, no living relatives. She moved around a lot. I tracked her to Seattle, but there's no forwarding address."

"Well then, I can't help you." Boomer's hands were balled into fists. Approaching a robin's-breast-red door, he depressed the button, but the doorbell didn't work, so he knocked, knuckles scraping the peeling paint.

"Wait." She made him stop. "Tell me what she said. Tell me everything."

He worked his teeth over his lower lip, silently debating, then wrinkled his nose. "She told me—and this was years after it happened—she told me Billy never came over to her house. Not at five-thirty, I mean. He went over later on, around eight o'clock, but not earlier. She lied to the police. She would've done anything for Billy."

The sun broke through the clouds, and Rachel squinted up at him. "She told you that?"

"Years after it happened. Right before she moved to Chicago."

"And you believed her?"

"She had no reason to lie to me."

Something clutched at her, and for an instant she almost couldn't breathe. She struggled to remain calm, or at least to look as if this information hadn't rattled her viscerally. "Boomer," she said, "it's critical you remember correctly . . . if Billy didn't go over to Gillian's at five-thirty, then where did he go?"

"Okay, that's the weird part. He told her he went back for Melissa because he felt guilty just dropping her off like that. But when he got to Black Hill Road, she was gone. He drove around looking for her but couldn't find her anywhere. And Gillian believed him. He said if she didn't lie for him, he'd be in big trouble, since there was a whole hour unaccounted for."

"Five-thirty to six-thirty."

Boomer nodded.

An elderly woman opened the door. "Yes?" She eyed them suspiciously. "What is it?"

"Meter reader," Boomer announced, rifling through his logbook.

"Why didn't you ring the doorbell, young man?" she asked angrily, and Boomer gave Rachel a sly wink.

21

RACHEL FOUND THE SPARE KEY BILLY HAD GIVEN HER IN CASE of emergencies and unlocked the door. He wouldn't be coming home for several hours, and her stomach contracted sourly as she entered the chilly house. This was not what a professional did; this was not what a loving sister did.

Quickly, she searched the downstairs area, knowing full well that a warrantless search was inadmissible in a court of law. She risked tainting herself and the case in her search for answers, but this was no longer about following procedure, it was about saving lives. Her head felt swollen to twice its size and there was a knot inside her blistered heart the size of a basketball.

The chartreuse-painted living room was clean and neat, magazines stacked on an 1843 dowry chest—*National Geographic, The New Yorker, Scientific American*; pillows propped against sofa arms; remote on top of the TV set; books placed neatly back on their scrub pine shelves. Billy was an avid reader. He was a member of several book clubs and read anything he could get his hands on. His exercise equipment was located in the closed-in porch just off the kitchen: rowing machine, Nautilus. There were no dirty dishes in the sink. Everything had been put away, and the linoleum floor was dotted with Roach Motels.

Upstairs, she checked the bathroom, damp towels folded over the towel rack, then gazed at her reflection in the bathroom mirror and told herself it didn't matter; none of this mattered. Billy was incapable of such monstrous behavior. There were two dried starfish in the medicine chest, along with a dozen pill bottles—aspirin, Advil, Sudafed, Nytol, Tylenol, Sleep-Eze, No-Doz, laxa-

tives. She found a discarded razor blade and several rumpled tissues in the wicker wastebasket.

Now she'd done it. Might as well go the distance. Inside Billy's
tangerine-painted bedroom, she fished through his bureau drawers, careful not to disturb the T-shirts, socks and folded underwear. An empty cigar box with a red clay pipe inside. Her thoughts
swam without a frame of reference, disassociated words twisting
through her head. She tried to concentrate as she looked in Billy's
closet, where she found several unopened Yves Saint Laurent
shirts on the top shelf, then her fingers touched a Ziploc bag.

Gingerly, she pulled it out. Pot and rolling papers. She slid
these back into their hiding place. She wasn't there to bust her
brother for possession. The academy didn't encourage recruits to
rat out lawbreaking relatives, but rather to avoid them. To not associate with them. Down on the closet floor where shoes and
sneakers made soldierly rows, she found a box of family photos
and other memorabilia tucked behind a folded quilt. She sorted
through the photographs: herself at seven, smirking at the camera, striking a bathing-beauty pose; their parents holding each
other tenderly, laughing with their heads thrown back, eyes in-
candescent. She remembered how, when they were kids, Billy
used to tell her he could catch time in a jar. He'd sweep his hand
through the air as if he were snatching fireflies, then screw the
lid on tight. "I've got a whole hour in this jar," he'd say. It had
been Rachel's idea to poke enough holes in the lid so that Time
could breathe.

Peeking beneath the bed, she couldn't find a single dust
bunny. Her heart grew heavy. Neat, he was neat. That fit the profile. She glanced at all the books on his built-in bookshelves. The
house was a virtual library.

She sat on the edge of his bed and opened the drawer of his bedside table. Inside were his reading glasses, a box of tissues and a
small jewelry box. She opened the jewelry box. Inside was a pair
of plastic windup teeth, a miniature Godzilla and a green plastic

turtle, the kind whose head bobbed when you touched it. Something deep inside of her snapped. Goosebumps traveled from her scalp and riffled down her arms. The room spun around for a dizzying instant, then stilled. She examined the plastic turtle, which seemed identical to Dinger's in every way. "Oh my God."

The means of obtaining evidence must be acceptable to the presiding justice. You need enough circumstantial evidence to obtain a search warrant. A request for a search warrant must be supported by a police oath describing the specific place to be searched and specific items to be seized. "Probable cause" means a reasonable ground for belief, less than evidence justifying a conviction, but more than bare suspicion.

She put the turtle back in its box, a growing fury propelling her to her feet. Her scalp burned, her ears itched. "Nicole?" The lonely, frightened sound of her own voice in the huge, empty house chilled her to the bone.

The attic was cold and dusty, a few flies sluggishly buzzing against the window screen. "Hello?" she called out to the darkness. "Anybody up here?" Her scalp tingled as she half anticipated some desperate response. Billy had taken the train set from home and set it up in the attic, miniature cars and buildings under a layer of dust as thick as snow. She crawled beneath the attic eaves and pulled out boxes one by one. *"Hello? Is anybody here?"* She found a collection of bird feathers in a manila envelope, a set of daggers with ivory handles couched in a red velvet case, books and more books, winter clothes stored in mothballs. A space heater. A broken window fan.

Back downstairs in Billy's bedroom, she glanced around, hoping she hadn't left any telltale signs of her illicit presence, then went downstairs. The floorboards in the front hall were badly warped. Her face burned. She hesitated at the basement door, doorknob slippery in her hand.

The door creaked open. "Hello?" she called down the stairs. She switched on the light and descended.

The basement was damp and musk-smelling. A water heater hummed in one corner. He'd been refinishing a couple of eighteenth-century benches. His power tools hung neatly from a corkboard. Peering into all four corners, she found no kidnap victims, no dead bodies, no gruesome tableaus.

Outside, the wind ripped her coat open as she raced for her car. It beat against her uncovered face and found the narrow band of exposed skin at the back of her neck. She got in the car, slammed the door, then turned on the heater and shivered for a good long while, hating herself.

22

THAT NIGHT, RACHEL FOUND MCKISSACK IN HIS OFFICE, GAZ-ing out the window. She sought his reflection in the glass and gropingly recalled the first time they'd made love, right here in his office, late one night on the stained oak floor. The urgency of his need had been like a secret thought grown too big to contain any longer. She'd been energized by their furious love-making. Her body hummed, the thrill of it buzzing in her ears. She'd never felt so brave or dangerous or nakedly alive as on that night.

Now a strange new fear tightened its grip on her body. She had betrayed her brother, and this knowledge spread with light speed to every corner of her being, every cell. She could feel her own self-loathing coursing through her bones like the cancer that had claimed her mother's life. Certainly her father would never have approved of her tactics. Perhaps that was why he'd commit-ted suicide—to avoid finding out the truth. That Billy had a secret life? That his son might be a cold-blooded murderer?

"We got the lab results this afternoon," McKissack said. "No presence of sperm inside the vagina or anus. No indications of forced penetration."

"So she wasn't raped?"

"In all likelihood, no." He held her eye through the window's reflection. "We spoke with Rudd's ex-wife. She corroborates his story, and she has no reason to. The information hurts her, doesn't help. Plus the bartender at the Hoary Toad ID'd Ozzie from a photograph. Looks like he's clean."

"So this wasn't a sexual crime?"

"To the best of our knowledge, no."

"What about the drug screen?"

"Multiple drugs were found in her system. Four of these were administered in the ER—epinephrine, methylprednisolone, magnesium sulfate and ketamine. Epinephrine is commonly used in emergency rooms for the treatment of asthma." Swiveling around in his chair, he held her eye. "A high concentration of a fifth drug was also found. Thorazine."

Rachel drew a blank. "An antipsychotic?"

"The injection site on the foot also tested positive for Thorazine."

"He injected her with an antipsychotic? But why?"

"Antipsychotics have potent blood-pressure-lowering properties. When epinephrine is injected into an individual taking phenothiazine antipsychotics, the blood pressure can drop to critical levels."

"But I thought epinephrine was a cardiac stimulant?"

"According to the lab report, Thorazine is one of the few drugs that can actually reverse the effects of epinephrine, making it a potentially lethal combination."

Rachel's hands tingled, this new information opening up a realm of terrifying possibilities. "You mean he injected her with Thorazine knowing full well that the ER team would administer epinephrine? And that the combination could kill her?"

"Looks that way." McKissack masked his frustration and rage beneath layers of practiced restraint.

"I don't believe it." She shook her head. "Are you implying that the UNSUB somehow *knew* the ER staff would respond to Claire's asthma attack by pumping her full of epinephrine?"

"Not just any ER. Not just any doctor. One doctor in particular."

It took a moment for his words to register. She caught her breath, incredulous. "You're telling me that the offender knew Claire's father was scheduled to work in the ER that night?"

"I'm beginning to suspect it."

She shook her head in disbelief. "You're really scaring me, McKissack."

"As in . . . 'who the fuck are we dealing with here?'" He cracked a bitter smile. "I know. I scare myself sometimes."

"So he *knew* Yale Castillo would be on duty that night? That Yale would assume his daughter was having an asthma attack and administer epinephrine? Is that what you're telling me?"

"Yes."

Rachel's head swam. She had to sit. "This is insane."

McKissack scowled. "She was alive when they brought her in. In good health, Archie said. He'd been feeding her—they found fucking macaroni-and-cheese in her stomach. No fractures, no contusions." He let his fist slam down on the desktop. "He fixed it so her own father killed her."

They locked eyes.

"Dinger Tedesco is failing all subjects but math and chemistry."

McKissack arched an eyebrow.

"Nicole was pregnant. Claire knew about it. She might've threatened to tell their parents."

McKissack rubbed his chin with his thumb. "Still, he had to bring her someplace secluded and keep her there for three weeks."

"I asked Dinger's mother if she knew of any such place. She didn't."

"Three weeks is a long time. The kid's in high school. We're talking about a very sophisticated crime here."

"Who, then?"

"Buck Folette. Thorazine is an antipsychotic."

"He's not smart enough."

"He's just crazy enough."

"What about his alibi?"

"The night Nicole and Dinger disappeared? Couldn't find anybody who remembered him. He refuses to take a poly. His lawyers have already contacted us. Fucking lawyers. I'll bet you dollars to doughnuts he's our man."

"But it doesn't make sense. Nicole knew about Buck's history. She would've screamed bloody murder if she saw him coming. She would've run in the opposite direction. No way he could've dragged those two off without a struggle. Dinger's a big kid."

"So maybe he drugged them?"

"How? He never would've gotten close enough."

"Then who the hell are we dealing with here?" McKissack barked. "Who's got the fucking depravity to sew up a beautiful woman like that and make sure she ends up in the hospital during her father's watch? How do two teenagers disappear without a trace?"

"I don't know." She buried her face in her hands.

"What else you got for me, Storrow?"

She swallowed hard and looked at him. She couldn't withhold the truth any longer. "Remember you warned me not to reopen the Melissa D'Agostino case? You said you never know what you might find?"

He nodded, eyes tightly focused.

"Well, I think my brother might be a suspect."

McKissack gave no hint of surprise.

"I think Billy's involved," she repeated.

"I heard you. I'm trying to absorb this."

"Dinger's brother claims he overheard Dinger talking to a 'Billy' on the phone. Then he said, no, maybe it was 'Bobby.' But it got me thinking. So I drove over to the head-injured department at Winfield and interviewed Porter Powell."

"Porter who?"

"Billy's head-injured kid. His alibi the night Claire disappeared. He drove Porter back to his dorm around nine-ten, which means he couldn't have gotten downtown any sooner than nine-twenty, right? Well, what was he doing at eight P.M.?"

"Shooting hoops with the kid."

"What if he's lying? What if Billy picked up Claire after she left the diner *with Porter Powell in the car?*"

McKissack's eyes darted with acknowledgment. "Since this kid doesn't have the capacity to relate the experience to anyone."

"I asked Porter if he remembered that night. He kept talking about a girl. 'We got girl' were his exact words," she said a little breathlessly. "The Melissa D'Agostino case wasn't sexual, either. No penetration, no abrasions."

McKissack nodded. "Whoever decapitated those cats is capable of great cruelty."

"So I spoke to Boomer Blazo. He told me Billy and Gillian lied about the evening Melissa died. It turns out Billy wasn't with Gillian from five-thirty to six-thirty. He went back for Melissa after he dropped Michelle off, at five-thirty, but he claimed Melissa was already gone. Gillian covered for him."

McKissack squinted at her.

"And what about the lower-case, underlined '_b_' in her organizer? She was supposed to meet Billy the following night, Thursday night, and there's an upper-case 'B' in the calendar. 'B' for Billy. Could the lower-case '_b_' also mean Billy?"

"That wouldn't make sense."

"But we've proven she's erratic with the initials. What if it does mean Billy? Why is it underlined? Was she mad at him? Did they have an argument? Did they get together to discuss it?" Rachel was pacing now. "My brother sometimes rents a cabin in the woods up north. He was physically abused as a child. He's in his mid-thirties, lives alone in a big house in a remote part of town. He's obsessively neat. Hasn't had any kind of solid relationship with a woman. McKissack," she said, "he fits the profile."

He ran his hands through his hair. "Slow down."

"And I found something else. During our interview, Dinger pulled out this little green turtle. You know the kind? Those plastic turtles whose heads bob up and down? Well . . ." She took a deep breath. "I found a turtle just like that inside Billy's house. Tucked away in a drawer."

"You made an illegal search?" McKissack cried. "Rachel, this does not leave my office! Do you understand? We never discussed it."

"I couldn't help it, I had to find out."

"Look at me point-blank and tell me you think your brother's capable of something as fucked up as this." He stared at her hard. "Look at me."

"I don't know." Her eyes welled with tears. "I think I understand what my father was going through the night he killed himself. I think he figured it out. God, he must've been so overwhelmed, so—"

"Rachel, don't do this to yourself." He stood up. "You're too close. He's your brother, for chrissakes."

He put his arms around her. He smelled faintly of Old Spice. Nobody wore Old Spice anymore. She slid her arms around his thickened waist and held on tight.

"You're off the case," he said, breaking it to her as gently as he could. "I'm sorry. We'll have a sneaker car follow Billy around. Once he's cleared, *if* he's cleared, I'll reassign you."

She nodded, strength draining from her limbs.

"The search you made wasn't any good. Forget the turtle,

we've gotta find probable cause. See if anybody saw Billy and Dinger together, hearsay's admissible in the affidavit."

"What about Gillian Dumont?"

"If she's a key witness but can't be located, the prosecutor's gonna dismiss the charges. We arrest anybody on suspicion of kidnapping and possibly murder, we'll need a great deal of corroborating evidence to make the charges stick."

Rachel shook her head. "This is crazy. Billy isn't capable of something so diabolical."

"I agree. You didn't find any dead bodies, did you?"

She shook her head. "But remember the cabin . . ."

"If he goes anywhere, we'll know about it."

"My head is killing me."

"Shhh."

"I feel like I failed him," she confessed.

"Don't let it defeat you, sweetie."

"Hold me."

She felt his body stiffen.

"Rachel," he said, drawing back, but she wouldn't let him go.

"No, this isn't sexual, McKissack. It's not anything."

He relaxed against her, finally realizing she had a deeper psychological need to hold him.

"I'm scared."

"I know." He sighed, looking at her with off-duty eyes. "So am I, sweetheart. So am I."

V

TREMBLE ON THE VERGE

1

IT WAS ALMOST MIDNIGHT WHEN RACHEL TOOK HIGHWAY 71 at Bent Fork and headed south past the sprawling mall on the short drive home. She could barely keep her eyes open. Approaching the Wible Road exit, she caught a cluster of red taillights up ahead and hit the brakes. A big rig had jackknifed across the center divider, blocking all northbound and southbound traffic. Rachel radioed for help, then got out to assess the damage and offer assistance if necessary.

She quickly approached the confusion of sideswiped cars and voices raised in panic. The slick black road was eerily lit by the crisscrossing headlights of idling cars, and at the bull's-eye of these intersecting high beams was a body. A boy's body, sprawled faceup on the asphalt. Naked. Duct tape covering his eyes. More duct tape binding his wrists. Over a dozen onlookers clustered around, staring solemnly down, and Rachel noticed right away that no one had touched the body, a strong indication he might be dead. She ran the last few yards and bent over the boy, ripping duct tape off his eyes. The shock of recognition ricocheted around inside her skull like a pinball—it was Dinger Tedesco.

Leaning down, she checked for a pulse. His face was drained of blood, his lips a theatrical blue, eyes open to the night sky, the irises like fogged glass. The body was already growing cold. There was a wide tread mark across his chest and she was almost certain he was dead, but she checked his airway for obstruction anyway and tried to start his heart. Tried with a fervent, futile hope-against-hope. She straddled his legs and, placing the heel of her hand one finger-breadth above the intersection of the ribs and sternum, began the compressions, and a thick gob of blood shot out of his mouth and hit her smack in the forehead.

The onlookers gasped and stepped back, but Rachel continued administering CPR, asking between breaths, "How long has he been lying here?"

"Five minutes, give or take."

She continued with the CPR until paramedics arrived and took over, and only then did she start taking down names. It helped her to keep busy, to have something to do. She didn't want to remember the living, breathing boy she'd just met, with his soft features and awkward disposition.

Now a bald burly man wearing earmuffs and a Bulls jacket approached her. "That's my rig," he said, pointing at the jackknifed truck. "I'm the one who hit the kid."

She pulled him aside and he gave her his statement. "I was on the road for about five hours, heading for Augusta, when all of a sudden this kid jumps out in front of me. I stomp on my brakes, blast my air horn, nothing. It's like he doesn't see or hear me. He's just stumbling around in the middle of the road, singing."

"Singing?"

"Like he's drunk or something."

"You could hear him singing?"

"I couldn't hear him, no, but I pinned him in my headlights, and he looked like he was singing. You know, drunk and dancing around and, like . . . singing. So I'm trying to avoid the kid, you know . . . but it's too late." He shook his head. His mouth was tight. "Damn, I'm all shaky."

"You said he jumped out in front of you? Where did he come from?"

"There." He pointed at the woods.

Cautiously, she approached the edge of the forest while police sirens sounded in the distance. Standing on the soft shoulder of the highway, she squinted into the woods and thought she detected movement, ghostly and receding.

The voices behind her grew distant as she waded into the thickets. Twigs snapped underfoot. She paused for a moment, eyes adjusting to the darkness, ears alert to any sound. She'd seen something seconds ago—the flash of a face in the soft moonlight, a human silhouette. Now she cocked her head and listened. Behind her on the highway, two cruisers pulled up simultaneously, and the big rig's engine made a low relentless rumble. She moved deeper into the woods, further away from the noise and the lights, her service weapon drawn.

And suddenly she heard it . . . the sharp snap of a twig . . . the sound of branches slapping back . . . about twenty yards ahead. She couldn't see a thing. The woods were dark as pitch.

Lungs on fire, Rachel ran back to her car, grabbed a flashlight from the glove compartment and headed into the woods again. The bottoms of her shoes slipped on moss-covered rocks, but she righted herself and tried to get a bead on his direction. *His* . . . subconsciously, she'd assumed it was a he. She fought her way furiously through the thickets, flashlight beam dancing and bobbing, creating jumpy shadows as she ran. Her hand clutched the checkered grip of her gun while her flashlight played over gnarled tree roots, sword ferns and blackberry bushes. Above, the sky was starless because of the haze, but you could see the moon—a soft glow like a mother's admonition. Small, she felt small.

She had lost him, whoever he was, lost him in the time it'd taken her to run back to her car. She was chasing phantoms.

Her foot caught on something, the sound of roots being ripped from the ground, and she flew forward, landed with a dull thud, flashlight hurtling from her hand. It rolled downhill a short distance, highlighting a small patch of forest floor—brambles and moss and stones as big as fists and golden leaves freshly fallen. Something shrieked, a startled bird. An owl hooted in the distance. She picked herself up, brushed herself off, retrieved the flashlight and stood a frozen beat.

Above her head, the hazy moon roosted in a nest of tree branches. For the first time in forever, she wanted a cigarette. She wanted to be home in a hot bath. She wanted to get good and drunk. She didn't want this to be happening in her town. She wanted to stop suspecting her brother. She wanted her father back. She wanted a safe world, a just world, not this horrible, complicated quagmire where lonely women like herself sought out the company of married men.

A twig snapped yards in front of her. Clutching her revolver, she ran toward the sound but didn't see anything up ahead, just tree trunks, straight and imperious as nuns in her flashlight beam. "Police! Don't move!" she shouted, and her heart made a dull, bad beat.

There was no reply. She glanced back the way she'd come, a naturally occurring path the forest had already swallowed up. Where was she? She didn't have a clue.

"Police! Don't move!"

Wrestling her way through another tangle of thickets, she burst out of the forest, every inch of her wide awake and throbbing, and stood on an incline overlooking the back of Lincoln Street in the downtown district. It seemed like the saddest, deadest place on earth. A raccoon was prying the lid off a garbage can in some dank alleyway. Several buildings stood abandoned, their windows boarded up. Nobody went out anymore. People were scared. During the day, children walked in groups of two or more. Parents watched until their kids were safely on board the school bus. The hardware store had had a run on dead-bolt locks. An evil psychopath was snatching people off the streets. Women were jumping at shadows.

Now a car pulled onto Main Street, driving slowly at first, then gaining speed. A forest green Plymouth Breeze, just like Billy's. Just like Billy's.

2

BILLY'S FACE WAS FLUSHED, BUT HE MANAGED TO REIN IN HIS rabid indignation. "What the hell are you talking about?"

They stood in the front hall of his rented house, family pictures adorning the walls. Their father and mother, the four of them together. Ten-year-old Billy with his arm around Rachel, her face tilted trustingly toward his. It broke her heart, and for a moment the words wouldn't come.

"What?" he demanded to know.

"You were driving up Main Street . . ."

"Yeah, so? I was at the hardware store." From a pine sideboard, he picked up a small paper bag imprinted with Dale's Discount Hardware's logo. "Since when is it a crime to shop at the hardware store? And what the hell happened to you?"

She suddenly realized she was covered with dirt, wet leaves and grass flecking her coat, pine needles lacing her hair. Blood smeared across her forehead. "A boy was killed on the highway. I chased somebody through the woods."

"Jesus, Rachel, what's going on?" His eyes were hard on her. "Are you saying I'm a suspect?"

She steeled herself. "Where were you tonight, Billy?"

His eyes grew incredulous. *"Where was I?"* Defiant, he ripped open the bag and several dozen picture hooks scattered across the needlepoint area rug. "At the hardware store buying picture hooks!"

"And before that?"

He shook his head numbly. "I can't believe this. You actually think I killed Claire? That I . . . sewed her up? You think I'm some kind of psychopath? That I'm capable of something so twisted and perverted? Am I hearing you correctly?"

His words had a corrosive effect. She felt terrible. Despicable. What kind of person was she? What on earth could she be thinking?

"Billy . . ."

"This is about Dad, isn't it?" His eyes flashed with a slow-burning bitterness. "This is about him putting that gun in his mouth and pulling the trigger."

"No, Billy . . ."

"Just because Dad and I didn't get along . . . I mean, I loved him, man, with all my heart. But sometimes it's easier to love a parent when he's dead."

"I'm sorry, Billy. I'm exhausted. This case has got me all turned around . . . I don't know what to think anymore."

"Bullshit, Rachel." The hurt in his voice came from a really miserable place. "How can you say you love me and then turn around and accuse me of something so vile? This is fucking unbelievable."

"Billy, I'm just doing my job . . . I'm trying to figure out—"

"You're killing me!" Tears sprang to his eyes. His features contracted as he bit back his rage and pain, and suddenly she recalled how, all during their childhood, he would fly into rages, thinking everybody was against him, even her. "Dad struggled with his own private demons, we'll never know what was going on inside his head that night. Doesn't matter what kind of a hot-shit detective you think you are, Rachel, you will never find the missing piece to that puzzle. Trust me."

"Billy, I didn't mean to accuse you . . ."

"I'll take a lie detector test."

"What?"

"I want to. In fact, I insist on it. I'm not having my kid sister running around thinking I'm Ted Bundy." Crossing his arms, he shut her out, his lean, handsome face drained of all emotion. "I'll take a polygraph."

"Billy, I don't think that's advisable."

"Yeah, whatever." His eyes were streaked with hatred, and she felt the rebirth of a deep, impenetrable sorrow, like a scab being peeled off before the skin underneath has had a chance to heal. "I'll cooperate with the police."

"I think you should hire an attorney."

He stood there, waiting for her to leave, only she didn't want it to end this way.

"I can't help wondering," she said softly, "what it was like for him, Billy. Billy? I have a gun. But I'd never turn it against myself. Just a few days before he killed himself, he seemed so happy. He seemed like himself, y'know?"

Billy uncrossed his arms, coolly polite.

"And I keep hoping . . . that it was a clean shot, you know? One clean shot to the head. No pain. Because I couldn't bear the thought, Billy . . ."

"I know, Pickle." His voice was suddenly forgiving.

Tears sprang to her eyes. "I'm sorry, Billy . . . I really am."

"I'll take a polygraph. Then maybe you'll believe me."

"Billy . . ."

"It's okay."

"You know," she said, wiping her face with wet hands, "I used to see Daddy's ghost in the house. Just the whisper of him, y'know? And I'm thinking . . . maybe I was chasing a ghost in the woods tonight? Maybe I wasn't chasing a human being at all?"

3

RACHEL FINALLY ARRIVED HOME AT 2:00 A.M. AND DRAGGED herself upstairs to the bathroom, where she somehow managed to strip, draw a hot bath, and climb into the tub. A hard knot had formed in her left leg, and she worked it between her fingers. She soaked for what seemed like days, wanting to erase all the bad thoughts racing crazily around inside her brain. Stupid thoughts, jumbled thoughts.

She'd snagged a bottle of wine on her way up but had forgotten to grab a glass, so now, wrapped in a pleasant haze of steam, she chugged directly from the bottle. Just as she was beginning to feel human again, the doorbell rang.

Downstairs, wrapped in a thick terry cloth robe, she answered the door. It was McKissack, looking haggard. He said nothing, just raised an eyebrow.

She stepped aside and he came in, his agitated energy wrapped in a blanket of cold air. She didn't want him there. Shutting the door against the bitter wind, she stood with her arms folded protectively across her chest.

"You were there?" he asked.

"I was."

"So tell me about it."

"I was driving home and spotted the accident and pulled over. I administered CPR until the paramedics arrived, then jotted down some names. Then I thought I saw something in the woods."

"Like what?"

"Like a person, maybe. I'm not sure. Anyway, I chased him through the woods and quickly lost him."

"Him? It was a 'he'?"

"I didn't actually see anything other than maybe the flash of a face initially . . . I heard twigs snapping. I saw branches moving."

"So where'd you lose him?"

"I came out of the woods behind Lincoln."

"And that was it? You didn't see anything else?"

"Nothing," she lied, wondering if he could tell she was lying, since McKissack was a pretty good shit detector. "Downtown was dead."

He nodded. "So maybe this guy you were chasing—"

"Or thought I was chasing—"

"—parked downtown . . . escorted Dinger Tedesco through the woods and pushed him out onto the highway. Boom . . . instant puppy chow."

"But that's absurd. Why park downtown?"

"Exactly. Why risk it? Why not just drop him off someplace along the highway?" McKissack nodded thoughtfully, then changed direction. "Truck driver says Dinger looked drunk to him. Strung out."

Rachel nodded.

"You ripped the duct tape off his eyes."

"I thought I could save him."

"Paramedics said there was like zero chance of that. He died instantly of massive internal injuries. Snapped his neck."

"I'm no paramedic, McKissack." She wiped the gooseflesh off her arms. "When's the autopsy?"

"Archie's on his way right now. Care to join me?"

"I thought I was off the case?"

"Well, now you're a witness." He gave her a halfhearted smile. "Besides, your brother just called and said he was willing to take a polygraph."

She could feel herself blushing. "My brother?"

"Yeah. Seems you went over there and accused him of murder. Says he wants to clear things up as soon as possible. He's being extraordinarily cooperative."

She shut her eyes and sighed, not wanting to look at him anymore.

"So you saw nothing in the woods?"

"It could've been the wind, swaying branches, a million things. I'm not sure I saw anything at all, McKissack." She glanced angrily at him; he shouldn't have trapped her like that. "But when I came out of the woods, I saw a car I recognized, yes. It looked like my brother's car."

"Only one car in the whole of downtown?"

"There might've been other cars, I don't know. Nobody goes out anymore. Everyone's terrified."

"These other cars . . . you get a description?"

"No, McKissack." Her voice was harsh. "I panicked, okay? Are you satisfied? I saw Billy's car and I ran back and drove over to his place."

"And accused him of murder?"

"I told him I was having problems with the case, I told him I had some suspicions . . ."

"Jesus H. Christ."

"I had to, McKissack." Anger heated her face. "He's my brother, I thought . . ." Her shoulders slumped with defeat. "I don't know what the hell I was thinking."

"You got that right."

"Oh, and you're perfect," she found herself shouting, her limbs electrified with long-repressed rage, "coming over here and fucking me while your wife and kids are sound asleep?"

He stared blankly at her, then looked away.

"We all make mistakes, McKissack."

"He's cooperating. No harm done."

"I can't live like this." She touched his arm so that he would look at her. "I can't do it anymore."

He didn't respond. His eyes were veiled.

"I feel so vulnerable when I'm with you, and I hate feeling that way. I care so much, it hurts, Jim. I'm scared when I'm with you and scared when I'm away from you. It's absurd to be so vulnerable."

He took her hand and looked at it as if it were something delicate he was charged with protecting. He slid his thumb across the bumps of her fingers.

"I'm not sure I love you, because I can't ever have you," she continued, "because it's impossible . . . but when you talk to me, when you're nice to me, McKissack . . . I feel so tender inside. So raw. It hurts all the time. We've got to end this, once and for all."

She watched in silence as a tear slid down his cheek. He was looking very fragile, and she fought the urge to stroke his face.

"How many times have I asked you, when're you gonna share that beautiful heart with some nice young man instead of this old gizzard?"

She smiled through her tears. "These words . . . these words we're speaking right now . . . they're going to tear us apart. But that's good. We need to be torn apart, McKissack."

"I know." His voice was barely audible.

"I hate this."

"So do I."

"But we have to. My heart feels so heavy."

"Mine, too."

He pulled her toward him and kissed her. The knot in her leg throbbed. She was a bundle of little hurts today, and his kisses stung. His ears were small and endearing, and the second time they'd ever made love, inside this house, she'd kissed both his ears, making him turn his head first this way and then that, and before he went home, he'd left a pair of his shoes by the front door to frighten away intruders.

"God—" He inhaled. "You smell like soap."

She drew away from him, a guttural sound emitting from her throat as she bit back her tears. She wasn't going to break down in front of him. "So it's over?"

"If you say so."

She shivered. "Good night, then."

"Aren't you coming?" he asked, buttoning up his overcoat.

"Coming?"

"To the autopsy?" He held her eye. "I need you back on the case, Rachel. I seriously doubt your brother's a suspect, and as long as he's cooperating . . ."

"Oh." She looked around, hating this kitchen, the textbook green of its walls. "Five minutes."

"Look." He grabbed her arm. "Let's talk about this other stuff later, okay?"

"What other stuff?"

"The 'us' stuff."

"There's nothing more to discuss."

"Yeah, well, I'm not done processing it yet." He smiled. "I knew someday you'd find out what a loser I was and dump me."

She smiled back. "I've always known what a loser you are."

4

EVEN STRONGER THAN THE FAMILIAR DISINFECTANT SMELL OF the morgue was the stench of booze coming from Dinger Tedesco's split-open body. Archie Fortuna hovered over the steel tray examining the bloody pulp that had once been Dinger's internal organs. "Nothing here but kibbles 'n' bits," he announced to the room.

Rachel couldn't look. The victim had "bumper" fractures of the lower legs from where the truck had struck the tibia and fibula, the calf region. There was internal hemorrhaging and spiral fracturing of the bones, and his legs looked like overstuffed Christmas stockings.

"The truck braked late," Archie said into the microphone. "The victim was impacted, slammed down, and run over by a wheel.

There's a wide patterned tire-tread mark on his chest and a large purple abrasion on his backside from where the body scraped along the pavement as the tire passed over it, pushing it backward."

They had found at the back of Dinger's head, clamped to his hair, a glow-in-the-dark barrette in the shape of a star. One of Nicole's. McKissack stood examining it in an evidence bag.

"He's mocking us," he said. "He doesn't think we'll catch him. He thinks he's invincible."

"We'll catch him," Rachel said with certainty, heart pounding.

McKissack put down the evidence bag and shook his head. "This is looking more and more like somebody in the medical profession. Someone with access to syringes and Thorazine, who knows how to suture a wound. Somebody who's maybe got a grudge against the good doctor."

"We've interviewed almost a hundred hospital employees."

"What about patients? Some wacko who came into the ER for treatment and wasn't satisfied?"

"A patient who's got access to Thorazine?"

"Buck Folette's got access."

"I keep telling you, he also has an alibi."

"If his junkie friends are to be believed. I can't think straight. Time's it?"

"Three-thirty."

"Jesus wept."

Rachel tried not to think about Billy again. Always Billy. He had access to medications such as Thorazine at the blind school. Many of the children were multiply handicapped and some required daily dosages of Haldol or diazepam or insulin. He'd once told her that security at the nurses' station was nonexistent, that anyone could jimmy into the medicine cabinet. She tried to remember if she'd ever seen him sewing anything, then wondered if that mattered. How difficult was it to stitch a wound?

"He abducts the victim," McKissack went on, "holds her captive for a specified period of time before letting her go. He can't live in an apartment building. Too many potential witnesses. He's gotta be able to slip in and out undetected."

"Both victims were discovered late at night."

"Under cover of darkness," McKissack said, snapping his fingers. "Almost forgot. We got the lab results back on the thread today. Turns out it's all different kinds. White, blue, red, green. Thirty-three pieces altogether. No single piece any longer than three inches."

Rachel frowned. "I don't understand."

"The kind of thread you'd find around the house. All different lengths and colors."

"This case just keeps getting weirder."

"What the hell is this?" Archie shouted behind them, and they turned toward the examination table. The medical examiner rarely swore, and the surprise on his face alarmed her.

"What is it?" McKissack asked.

Archie was holding up a bloody, pulpy mass in his gloved hands. As the object came into focus, Rachel could see it was a small plastic bag with something folded up inside, a rubber band wrapped around it several times.

"Where'd you find that?" McKissack asked.

"Stomach." Archie gazed at them over his surgical mask.

"Careful," McKissack said as Archie carried the object over to the sink and rinsed it under the tap. Using a pair of surgical scissors, he snipped the rubber band in half and the plastic bag expanded, falling open. Archie handed the bag to McKissack.

With gloved hands, McKissack took out a folded piece of paper from inside the bag. It looked like computer paper. Smoothing it open on the flat marble countertop, they could see the looping, girlish script in felt tip pen.

McKissack and Rachel glanced at one another before bending over the page to read beneath yesterday's date: "Dear Mom and Dad . . ."

5

SHE WAS SUPPOSED TO BE ASLEEP. SHE'D BEEN UP FOR TWENTY hours straight and now she was supposed to be catching up on all that missed REM sleep, but she couldn't stop thinking about the letter.

"Dear Mom and Dad, please don't worry about me. I love you both very much and I don't want you guys spending the rest of your lives crying over me and Claire. I'll be with my big sister soon, and I'll be with Dinger, too. (P.S. Dinger, I love you—wish I'd told you that more often, but we'll be together soon and then I can tell you in person!) Mom and Dad, I'm pregnant. Sorry I didn't mention it sooner, but I thought you'd be really mad. Besides, I really wanted this baby. Dinger and me were going to get married and everything, but now we'll be together in heaven, me and Dinger & the baby & also Claire, don't forget. I'm sure she's smiling down on us right now. I can feel it. She's an angel. Don't cry, you guys. Be happy for me. Love always, Nicole."

Rachel bolted upright, her heart a clenched fist. She couldn't sleep. She'd never sleep again.

6

THE NEXT DAY AT THE STATION, RACHEL BUMPED INTO BILLY on his way out. "I passed," he told her without emotion.

Relief suffused her. Passing a polygraph wasn't definitive, but it was a huge leap in the right direction. "Oh Billy, that's terrific," she said, meaning it with all her heart.

"You know, it makes me all warm and fuzzy inside to detect the surprise in your voice." He brushed coldly past her, and she followed him out of the building onto the front steps of the station.

"Billy, I'm so sorry."

He spun around. "You want me to forgive you, don't you?"

"Well . . . yes," she said, eyes pleading.

"Only problem is, I can't. I'm still pissed at you, Rachel. You and Dad both."

He strode off, and she followed him with her eyes, hoping that someday he'd find it in his heart to forgive her. This case had turned her inside-out, but the truth still mattered. The world had weight. She'd made a huge mistake, but that was the price you paid. She only regretted that Billy had had to pay, as well. She felt awful about it.

McKissack breezed out of his office, his face coated with a patina of sweat. "Heard the good news?"

She smiled. "Best I've had all week."

"It gets better. Lab results came back on Dinger Tedesco's blood. They found traces of methohexital in his blood."

Barbiturates and alcohol were a deadly combination. "So he probably would've died even if he hadn't gotten hit by a truck?"

"No. I said *traces*." McKissack took her by the elbow and propelled her into the conference room where the others were waiting. "Not enough to kill him but enough to severely impair his judgment."

"The UNSUB made sure Dinger was on the highway in a very vulnerable condition," Tapper continued, picking up the thread. "He knew he'd get hit by something. Truck, car, motorcycle."

"But he could walk," Rachel said. "His legs weren't bound together, he could've run away."

"Exactly. He was betting Dinger would be so fucked up, he'd

just stagger around in the middle of the road. He's still playing mind games with us."

"Maybe he was watching?"

"I doubt it."

"Our very clever UNSUB knew that Dinger was gonna get hit, just like he knew we'd find Nicole's chain in Claire's hand, just like he knew we'd do an autopsy and find Nicole's letter inside the victim's stomach," Keppel said. "This thing's planned out so precisely, it's freaky. He planted that letter like some crooked bust."

"Let's stay ahead of him, people." McKissack sounded desperate, and they all sat a little straighter in their chairs. "Let's think the way he thinks. Let's crawl around inside his skin, let's anticipate his next move. C'mon! Heads together."

"Time sure ain't on our side," Cavanaugh murmured.

"Think!" McKissack commanded, and the room fell silent. "What's his plan? What comes next?"

"Clearly," Tapper picked up the ball, "he's gonna do something heinous to Nicole Castillo."

"Only he won't kill her," McKissack said.

"And he won't rape her. He's probably feeding her macaroni-and-cheese as we speak. Keeping her warm. He'll release her alive, but then something else will finish her off."

"Or someone else," Rachel jumped in. "First Claire's father, then a random truck driver, and now—"

"Who's the lucky person gonna be?" McKissack looked around the room as if he were accusing each of them. "Who's gonna end up killing Nicole Castillo?"

"She has no medical condition that we know of," Tapper said, "like asthma or diabetes."

"She smokes," McKissack said.

It hit Rachel like a slap. *"She's pregnant."*

The room fell silent.

"Dear God." McKissack rubbed his face hard, as if he were trying to rub through to the bone.

"An abortion?" Tapper said.

"This is going nowhere fast," McKissack said nervously. "Let's back up, people."

Rachel thought for a beat. *Did the 'b' in Claire's Day-Timer stand for baby?* "McKissack," she said, "that would bring us back to the hospital."

"What?"

"Somebody in the medical profession, you said."

"Right."

"We should go over the interviews, we should . . ." Rachel's shoulders slumped. They'd recently combed through hundreds of interviews looking for any possible leads, but nothing had panned out. Dead ends, all of them. "The nurse," she suddenly said.

"What nurse?" McKissack grew alert.

"The nurse at the hospital who told me it wasn't asthma, re-member? Her name's Casey something . . . she said Dr. Castillo misdiagnosed Claire's asthma attack."

"So who're you gonna believe?" Tapper asked with a fixed sneer. "Some nurse, or the doctor on duty who happens to be the girl's father? And what the hell does it matter anyway?"

"If she wasn't having an asthma attack," Rachel conjectured, "then they shouldn't have administered the epinephrine."

"Because," McKissack said, "combined with Thorazine, that's exactly what killed her."

"You mean," Cavanaugh said, "the good doctor made a mistake?"

Rachel nodded. "A fatal mistake."

McKissack pointed at her. "Go find that nurse. Talk to her. See what else you can dig up."

She pushed back her chair.

7

THE LAST PLACE YOU'D WANT TO EAT, RACHEL THOUGHT, WAS A hospital cafeteria. Patients hacked at rickety nearby tables, doctors and nurses rummaged through the utensil tub for knives and forks. For a moment, she imagined a host of germs permeating the humid, food-smelling air. She and Casey Angstrom were having coffee with little containers of nondairy creamer, and Rachel's stomach turned sourly.

"What prompted you to tell me about Dr. Castillo's misdiagnosis?" she asked.

Casey shrugged inside the fuzzy blue of an oversized sweater, flyaway hairs trembling ever so slightly with each beat of her heart. "I just thought you should know."

"Why?"

Her voice grew unexpectedly small. "I shouldn't be telling you this. I could lose my job."

"Casey. You could save a life here."

Her eyes widened with concern, and she took a deep breath. "He's done it before."

"Done what before?"

"Come to the wrong conclusion before."

Rachel gave a shiver. "You mean he's been threatened with a malpractice lawsuit?"

"Child endangerment. Gross negligence. Failure to recognize a lethal condition . . ."

"And this has happened more than once?"

Pause. "Yes."

"How many times?"

Casey's eyes darted frantically over the gridwork along the cafeteria's ceiling. "I don't know."

"More than a couple?"

She nodded. "It goes way back."

"Over a dozen?"

Another pause. "Yes."

The cafeteria smelled of meat loaf and chicken noodle soup and all the prefabricated foods served in public institutions from time immemorial. "Do you think Dr. Castillo would let me see those files?" Rachel asked.

Casey shook her head, a serious look on her face. "He's such a proud man. I don't think he'd want anybody to know."

"So how did you find out?"

"Last year, he was sued for willful injury to a child for misjudging her condition. He thought this little girl had an ear infection, when it was actually a virus, a serious intestinal infection. The child went into shock before she was finally given fluids intravenously. The case was thrown out by the tribunal."

"Meaning?"

"It never went to court. I had some concerns, so I spoke to the admitting nurse, and she told me about the other cases."

"Has anyone ever died under his care?"

Casey seemed to shrink from Rachel's scrutiny. "Listen, Detective, I'm not trying to impugn anyone's reputation here."

"If a patient died under his care, I need to know."

Casey shrugged. "All doctors lose patients."

"Yes, and it could provide a surviving family member with a motive." For some reason, Rachel thought of Fred Lake, Claire's landlord. She remembered his limp, his comment about Claire's father being a rich doctor. What if he'd sued once for malpractice? What if he'd lost a loved one?

"I'd like to help you, but I don't really know anything more." Casey glanced at her watch. "I've gotta run."

"Casey."

"Yes?"

"Thank you."

"I hope you find her before it's too late," she said, hurrying off.

8

DR. CASTILLO WAS IN DIRE NEED OF A SHAVE, AND THE VIOLET circles under his eyes gave him a feral look. Rachel found him in Trauma Room 3 with an elderly patient—a white-haired, starry-eyed skeleton whose legs were covered with bedsores and swollen with infection. She moaned repeatedly while Yale drew blood from her arm. *"Please please please . . ."*

"Dr. Castillo," Rachel said, "we need to talk."

"Please please please . . ."

He barely glanced up. "I'm rather preoccupied right now."

"When you get a moment."

"There is no such thing as 'a moment' in ER."

"It's related to your daughter's case."

"Oh, all right," he said, tension building in the muscles of his neck. "Give me a minute."

He quickly dressed the woman's bedsores while her complaints escalated: *"Please please please please please!"*

"That's enough, Mrs. Steussie, you're hurting my ears."

A pause. Then whimpering, *"Please please please . . ."*

A few minutes later, he led Rachel into his office, where they stood just inside the door. He kept his hand on the doorknob, impatience jerking at his limbs.

"Yes, what is it?" he snapped.

"Have you ever been charged with malpractice?"

His eyes narrowed to little bandwidths of light. "What's that got to do with anything?"

"It could have a lot to do with it," she said. "If a patient suffered under your care, it might provide motive."

He gave an abrupt shake of his head. "I doubt very much that one of my former patients would be involved in such a thing."

"Doctor, has anyone sued you for malpractice because a family member died?"

He seemed outraged by the suggestion. "Detective, let me tell you something. I am a dedicated doctor who chose to practice on the front lines of medicine because I wanted to save lives. Should a doctor be punished for attempting to help his patients?" His stern face was flushed. "Medicine isn't an exact science. We're only human. We make mistakes. We are not God."

She waited a sufficient beat before saying, "Dr. Castillo, somebody has targeted your family and I'm trying to figure out why."

They held each other's eye, then his shoulders sagged, and he exhaled sharply. "Do you need them all?"

"That would be very helpful."

A knock came on the door. "Doctor?"

"Be right there!" He turned to Rachel. "Some of them go way back. I'll have to dig them out of storage. My secretary will deliver them to you later today."

"The sooner the better," she said.

He nodded. "I understand. Now if you'll please excuse me, I have patients to attend to."

She took a shot. "Do you remember Fred Lake?"

"Who?"

"Fred Lake?"

He shook his head, confused. "Not that I recall."

"Perhaps a relative of his?"

"I don't remember any Lakes, but I've seen so many patients."

"Doctor!"

"My secretary will get the files to you by the end of the day. Good-bye, Detective."

He left her standing in the corridor, where an accident victim, strapped to a backboard with a neck collar in place, gazed up at her with plaintive eyes. Rachel smiled back encouragingly when her cell phone rang. It was McKissack.

"Rachel, we need to talk."

9

SHIVERING, RACHEL WAITED IN THE PUBLIC PARKING LOT FOR McKissack to show up. He pulled up in his Buick LeSabre and opened the door. "Hop in."

The car was warm and smelled of popcorn. "I just found out Yale Castillo has at least a dozen malpractice charges against him," she said, "possibly more. That got me thinking about Fred Lake. Hey, where are we going?"

"No place in particular." He looked exhausted, face slack, clothes rumpled, as if he'd slept in them.

Aspen Loop Road climbed steeply through lush, deciduous woodlands that offered diverse habitats for more than three hundred birds and forty mammals, including deer, red fox, mink and otter. This road dated back to 1842 when a carriage road was hacked into the slopes, its first three miles winding up through a forest of hardwoods, then switchbacking through mountain ash and paper birch. The ride was creamy smooth; McKissack had recently become a big American-car fan.

"What's wrong, Jim?"

"I'm leaving my wife."

She felt as if she'd stepped onto a rocky boat. She couldn't catch her breath.

"Listen to me, okay?" He held her eye, and a deer darted in front of them, and Rachel screamed.

McKissack slammed the brakes and the deer made a graceful

swan dive into the woods and disappeared. The car swerved, tires shrieking, and they came to a dead stop in the middle of the road.

He was breathing heavily. "Holy Christ."

Rachel could hear her own heartbeat in her ears. "Jim," she said, voice shaky. "This is crazy."

"No, let me talk." His grip tightened on the wheel. "I can't find the chemical in my brain that says it's wrong."

"You're just going to leave her?"

"I don't have some big overall plan," he admitted, putting the car in reverse and backing onto a soft shoulder. He jerked the emergency brake, then turned to her. "All I know is . . . you're so much a part of my life, you're like my legs or something."

She was tempted. Sorely tempted. "You're making a big mistake."

"It's not like I haven't thought this through, Rachel. I was raised under an iron code of discipline. There were some things you didn't do, and divorce was a biggie."

She shook her head. Refused to meet his gaze. The car's heater hummed, and she could see the forward edge of the hood and its integral grille where the deer's hoof had tapped the surface.

"I love you, Rachel. I love you and I want to be with you."

"What about your kids?"

The question mark dropped away, revealing a simple truth. McKissack gazed out the window at the woods. Neither of them spoke. The heated air grew stuffy, and Rachel's thick woolen coat chafed her skin.

"Take me back, McKissack," she said.

"What is this, National Hero Day? We have to be so good? We have to be so perfect? We've gotta fix everybody else's feelings and forget about ourselves?"

Heart aching, she held his eye. "We have to try."

"Look, I've been over and over it . . ."

"You'll end up hating me."

"No," he said angrily. "You're the one who'll hate me. My kids will forgive me before you do."

It was true. She wouldn't let him leave his family because that would make her a murderer, in some sly way.

His eyes were bitter. "Nobody's interviewed Roger Tedesco yet," he said, pulling back onto the road. "I want you to do the honors."

"What about Fred Lake?"

"I'll take care of it."

"McKissack," she said, "I know what you are."

"Oh yeah? What's that?"

"One of the good guys."

He glanced at her and cracked a smile. "Don't squeaky-clean me, Rachel. I'm as selfish a prick as anybody else."

10

ROGER TEDESCO LIVED IN A DILAPIDATED SHACK IN A REMOTE part of town just east of the Triangle. The living room lights blazed, the windowpanes rattled from an ill wind, and Roger Tedesco, an obese man with a gray goatee and a kind, open face, occupied most of the couch, propped up by a multitude of pillows. He was alone in the house, submerged in grief, a box of tissues clutched in one hand, a picture of his son in the other.

"Siddown," he said with a congenial wave.

Rachel sat in the captain's chair with its spongy seat cushion. A nearby space heater stood dangerously close to a pile of old newspapers. Roger clamped a wad of tissues over his runny eyes, and she gave him a moment to collect himself. His broad shoulders convulsed several times before settling, then he blew his

nose and tucked the used tissues into a cardboard box full of ac-
cumulated litter.

"Mr. Tedesco . . ." She almost couldn't look into his eyes, two
pinpricks of grief.

"Call me Roger. Everybody does."

"Roger, I have to ask, it's procedural . . . where were you on the
day of your son's abduction?"

"Working," he said. "I'm a carpenter who lives on Carpenter
Street." He snorted laughter, then dissolved back into his watery
grief. "I was doing some work for the Pooles. You know the Pooles
of Hanover Road? They're renovating their kitchen."

She set her notebook down. "Do you know who might have
done this to your son? Who might have wished him harm?"

His eyes welled with a magisterial sadness as he plucked several tissues out of the box and pressed them to the sweaty veins
of his temples. "No, I don't. Everybody loved that kid. He's as
good as they come."

"Do you think—"

"You wanna know what I think? You really wanna know what I
think?" He glared at her. "I think there's a serial killer loose,
that's what I think."

"We don't know that for sure," she said calmly, carefully.

"Yes you do." He pointed a large soggy index finger at her. "You
know. We've got a serial killer in Flowering Dogwood and he's
killing innocent kids."

"Mr. Tedesco . . . Roger . . ."

"And if you goddamn cops were out there doing your job, you
and me wouldn't be sitting here talking right now. I told his
mother not to let him stay out all hours of the night, but she's so
goddamn lenient. Everybody's too goddamn lenient nowadays.
Everybody acts like life's just one big bowl of Jell-O. Well, I've got
news for you, baby. I've got news for you. This world ain't one
stitch safer than it was a thousand years ago when people were
getting gobbled up like pretzels by great big hairy things."

The living room was drafty, warmth from the heater dissipating almost instantly into the chilly night air. Rachel drew her coat, now draped over her chair seat, back around her shoulders. It was raining again. Rain spattered the rattling windowpanes.

"I'm sorry for your loss, Mr. Tedesco," she said as sincerely as she could, "but trust me, down at the station, we've been working sixteen-hour days. Support staff, detectives, state police. There's a task force working around the clock. There's a $20,000 reward. There's a twenty-four-hour hotline. We've scoured the neighborhoods, interviewed friends, acquaintances, known criminals. We've eliminated all of them, either through polygraph examinations or alibis. None of us sleeps, none of us eats. Trust me, we did everything we could to find your son, and we feel terrible that we failed. We take it to heart, Mr. Tedesco. So please don't tell me we aren't doing our job."

He watched her a dull beat, eyes mellowing. "You know," he said, "I appreciate that, Officer."

"It's okay."

"I really do. I appreciate that. You know, it gets pretty isolated in these parts. I could count my nearest neighbors on one finger. Nobody drops by. Dinger used to drop by." His voice broke off and his jaw muscles stiffened. "I always suspected there was something darker going on in this town. Something evil. You know what I'm talking about, Officer?"

"Not exactly."

"Drug activity. Marijuana, methamphetamine labs. Stuff like that."

She sat forward. "Did Dinger take drugs?"

"I don't know. Maybe. Just maybe."

"Have you come across any drugs in his possession?"

"I smelled marijuana on him a coupla times."

"Do you think this crime might be drug-related?"

"Hell, yeah." He ran his fingers through his peppery gray hair. "Hell, yeah. Drugs. It's definitely drug-related."

She decided to approach it from a different angle. "Did he have any enemies, Mr. Tedesco?"

His voice was indignant. "Dinger have enemies?"

"Well, did he?"

He snorted laughter. "Enemies? Who the hell has enemies besides politicians and gang-bangers?"

"If he was smoking marijuana, he must have bought it from someone. Drug dealers make fearsome enemies . . ."

"Absolutely not. No enemies. Dinger was a good kid. He was a bright kid. You see his smile?" He showed her the picture clenched in his fist, a Polaroid in a cheap plastic frame. "This kid was going places. He was on a straight trajectory. He's my pride and joy, this kid." His shoulders heaved, and he was sobbing again, massive arms and legs shaking as he tried to shrug off his world-sized grief. She waited until he'd composed himself.

"Did he ever mention a man named Fred Lake?"

"Fred who?"

"Lake."

"Doesn't ring a bell."

"What about Buck Folette?"

"Nope."

She hesitated. "Billy? Does he know any Billys?"

He squinted at her. "He just might know a Billy. I can't recollect."

"Any kids he didn't get along with at school? A teacher he disliked? A run-in with some adult? Did you and he fight?"

"What?" She could see his eye-whites. "Me and Dinger?"

"It's a standard question."

"Yeah, sure. Yeah, sure, we fought once in a while. What father doesn't fight with his offspring once in a while?"

"None that I know of." She smiled. "What were the arguments about?"

"Oh, you know . . . self-reliance."

"Excuse me?"

"Self-reliance. That's the biggest lesson a kid can learn. Taking on responsibility. Becoming self-reliant. That's how a boy becomes a man, I told him. I have this story." He wiped his nose with a fresh wad of tissues. "It's about this blind guy, see. His name's Henry. And Henry grew up in this small town way up the coast of Maine, near Bar Harbor. And Henry was a gearhead. You know what a gearhead is? He works on cars all the time. He knows cars frontwards and backwards. He eats, lives, breathes and shits motor oil, pardon my language. And most strangers never suspected he was blind."

Outside, the wind picked up, shivering through the rafters.

"So one day, it's spring, see . . . he goes into the woods to pick blackberries. Deep into the woods. He knows where the best blackberries are. But when he doesn't come home for supper, his folks get kind of worried. So they report him missing, 'cause he's blind, see.

"And the police go to find Henry, see, who they think is lost. And a cop bumps into Henry in the woods. And Henry asks him, what's up? And the cop tells him somebody's lost in the woods. So Henry offers to help out. 'What's this guy look like?' he asks. And the cop says, 'All I know is, he's blind.' And suddenly, Henry realizes that he's looking for himself." Roger squinted at her. "Now how do you suppose a blind man finds his way through the woods?"

"I don't know," she said.

"He carves notches in trees."

Rachel was struck dumb by the story, blood pounding in her skull as she recalled the three holes she'd found in the bark of the birch tree in the woods where Claire Castillo had been found. Three indentations, like the holes in a bowling ball, long overgrown. Notches carved into the bark of a birch tree many years ago. *Of course*, she thought, *of course . . .*

She knew who the UNSUB was.

11

RACHEL SPED OVER TO CLAIRE'S APARTMENT BUILDING AND scaled three flights of stairs, since the elevators were broken. Winded, heart thrumming in her ears, she unlocked the door of Apartment 402 and ducked under the yellow police tape.

The place was like a photograph, trapped in time, just the way Claire had left it the morning of the day she disappeared. Rachel felt like an intruder as she walked through room after room, flipping on lights. Traces of fingerprint powder covered every surface, and her shoes clacked on the hardwood floors, indecently loud.

All that remained of Claire in a physical sense—the vibrant mess inside her apartment, the shimmering clutter of it— brought the victim momentarily back to life. Books scattered across every surface reflected her interest in art and architecture, theater and literary fiction. Her coquettish, perhaps insecure side was revealed by the number of *Cosmo*s and *Glamour*s scattered about. Bags of exotic pastas alongside carefully selected bottles of wine were reminders of her sophisticated culinary tastes. She was something of a paradox—sloppy at home with her personal items, organized at school with teaching schedules and grade books, her appointments and Day-Timer.

In the bedroom, Rachel flung open the closet door and whipped out the dry cleaning bag with the white blouse inside. She tore off the receipt and studied it. There it was. How could they have been so shortsighted?

Hastily scribbled on the receipt was "One white linen blouse, one blue silk blouse." The pickup date was Monday the 12th, the

Monday before Claire had disappeared. Rachel searched the closet for a blue silk blouse. She pocketed the receipt and rummaged through Claire's bureau drawers. She ducked in the bathroom, ransacked the clothes hamper. There were no blue silk blouses anywhere inside the apartment.

Claire had been wearing a pink silk blouse the night she disappeared. The blue silk blouse was back at the dry cleaners.

Now Rachel's cell phone rang. "Hello?" she said, breathless with discovery.

"Rachel? It's Phil." Phillip Reingold, the dispatcher down at the station. "You just got a package. Hand-delivered."

"Be right there."

12

THE POLICE STATION WAS UNUSUALLY QUIET FOR THIS TIME OF night. Rachel picked up the package and went upstairs to her office. An enclosed note summarized what she was about to discover: "Dear Detective Storrow, Please bear in mind that the enclosed spans my entire 30-year career as an ER surgeon, and that most of the 16 charges filed against me were dismissed by the tribunal. Only three reached the settlement stage. I hope this proves useful to you. Sincerely, Yale Castillo."

It was happening so fast, the puzzle pieces falling too conveniently into place. She couldn't prevent her hands from shaking as she riffled through the files, searching for his name: *Vaughn Kellum. Born 1963.* One year older than Billy. She opened the file folder and a snapshot of a young boy fell out, plaintive green eyes staring out of a sad little face. She began to read:

ALICE BLANCHARD

FORMAL REPORT OF VAUGHN KELLUM

CAPTION: Vaughn Kellum vs. KCGH, Inc.
FILE NO: 33-288-000
LOSS DATE: April 3, 1971

1. CLAIMANT DATA

Vaughn Kellum was born on March 1, 1963. His mother, Mary Kellum, is a housewife. His father, Tito Kellum, owns a dry cleaning establishment. Vaughn has no brothers or sisters and medical records indicate Mary Kellum has had three miscarriages since his birth.

2. STATUS OF CLAIM

Active. We have received both a request for medical records and a letter of representation from an attorney at Blum, Tysdale and Papish. The attorney's name is William Papish, Esq.

3. DESCRIPTION OF FACTS

Vaughn Kellum had twenty-one office visits and nine emergency room visits during his first eight years of life. The only illnesses were diaper rash, colic, flu, mumps, and the like. Emergency room visits were mostly for sprains, contusions or abrasions attributed to the child's clumsiness.

One month after Vaughn turned eight, his mother noticed "flulike symptoms." She administered baby aspirin and fluids and put the child to bed, hoping he would feel better in the morning.

The next day, April 2, 1971, the child vomited and was lethargic and feverish. At approximately 11:00 A.M., the mother brought the child into the emergency room at KCGH where the patient was treated by Dr. Yale Castillo. Dr. Castillo examined patient and attributed the fever to a benign viral infection. He prescribed baby aspirin, recommended bed rest, and advised the mother to bring the child back if the fever persisted.

On April 3, 1971, at approximately 10:00 A.M., parents called Dr. Castillo and told him that although the child had initially improved, he was now having trouble breathing. Dr. Castillo instructed them to let the child rest and see how he fared.

On April 3, 1971, at approximately 12:00 P.M., the parents called Dr. Castillo and told him that the child was having shallow respirations. The mother was troubled that the child's eyes appeared to be "sinking in."

Dr. Castillo instructed them to bring the child in promptly. They did so, and Dr. Castillo noted that the child had developed chills, was lethargic, and had sluggish capillary refill. The mother insisted that the child "looks terrible, doesn't look like himself." Dr. Castillo performed a blood test and diagnosed a gastrointestinal ailment, gave the child Pedialyte, an electrolyte solution to prevent dehydration, then ordered a tepid bath and a chest X ray. The emergency room was busy and Dr. Castillo probably saw ten to twenty patients during the time the child was there. Family asked for "some kind of intravenous or something." Dr. Castillo explained that the child's tongue was wet, so he was no longer dehydrated.

It was at this point that the child had his first seizure. Dr. Castillo administered an antiseizure medication, Dilantin. The dosage used was 50 mg per kg of body weight per day with plasma levels of approximately 70 micrograms per ml.

After four hours in the emergency room, at the parents' insistence, the child was placed in-patient for observation and to stabilize his medications. Dr. Castillo attended to the child in consultation with Dr. Selby. The child's parents noted that the child appeared not to respond immediately when spoken to, and also that he no longer looked at them directly. After examination,

Dr. Selby discovered that the child had marked nuchal rigidity and could not completely extend his leg from a position of 90 flexion at the hip when supine. His oral temperature was 103.6F. Based on the presenting symptoms, Dr. Selby suspected meningitis.

At 4:30 P.M., the patient was placed in an isolation room with staff observing proper precautions: gown, gloves, and mask. A lumbar puncture was performed and Dr. Selby's suspicions were confirmed, meningococcal meningitis.

Before beginning antibiotic therapy, Dr. Selby administered steroids to reduce any subsequent neurological sequelae. The Dilantin was discontinued and diazepam was administered to control the seizures. Penicillin was administered in divided IV dosages and was proven to be highly successful.

Since meningococcal meningitis is a highly contagious form of bacterial meningitis, health care team and family members were administered a prophylactic treatment of rifampin 600 mg BID for two days.

4. POTENTIAL AREAS OF LIABILITY
It is doubtful that the plaintiff could prove medical negligence, since bacterial meningitis is highly unpredictable and the child was receiving the best of care at KCGH. Not every patient will display the signs or symptoms of meningococcal meningitis, and frequently patients will appear healthy only hours before they develop symptoms and die.

5. INJURIES/DAMAGES
When last investigated, the child's vision was "poor" and it was not clear how he was able to interpret what he saw; also he had a hearing impairment that could perhaps be corrected with the use of hearing aids.
Visually impaired, hearing deficit.
Developmental damage, as yet unknown.

6. INVESTIGATION

Potential defendants: Yale Castillo, M.D., attending physician of emergency medicine at KCGH.

7. COVERAGE

BC/BS Trust

8. UPDATE

Vaughn Kellum is currently under the care of Dr. O'Brien at St. Mary's Hospital, where he is being treated for visual/hearing impairments. He has been seizure-free for four months. He has been diagnosed with moderate to severe hearing loss and is visually impaired, but with the use of corrective lenses, he can spot objects and people across a room. To date, it is not known what cognitive or developmental delays may have occurred, although he seems bright and responsive. Plans are under way to enroll him in Winfield School for the Blind and Special Needs, where he will receive specialized treatment for his multiple handicaps.

She stared at the sheets of paper describing in matter-of-fact detail what would turn out to be the seeds of a murderous rampage. How could Yale Castillo have known that this tiny child he'd so negligently treated would grow up to be a hate-filled monster bent on vengeance?

She shoved the files back inside the large manila envelope, locked the envelope in her desk drawer. Checking that her gun was loaded, she went to knock on McKissack's door. He wasn't in. The station was spectacularly quiet. She practically flew down the stairs.

Phillip Reingold was reading *Interview,* sipping his first in a probable succession of espressos. "Phil?"

He delicately set down his cup and blinked at her. "Rachel, you scared the bejeezus out of me."

"Where's McKissack?"

"They all left about twenty minutes ago. Went to pick up Buck Folette."

"What for?"

"Apparently he's ready to talk."

"Talk?"

"Good news, honey," Phillip said, "we've got our man."

"No, Phil. Buck Folette didn't do it, Vaughn Kellum did."

He screwed up his face. "The dry cleaner?"

"Tell McKissack I'm going over there. I think I know where Nicole is."

13

VAUGHN KELLUM'S FINGERS RESTED LIGHTLY ON THE DOOR-knob. His magnified eyes through their corrective lenses made her think of clouds. She didn't know why. Green as kale, they searched for the shape of her. "Guess winter's come a little early this year," he said with an expansive smile. The porch light cast sinewy shadows into the dim recesses of the dry cleaning establishment. It was half past seven. Vaughn's employees had all gone home; business was done for the day.

"May I come in?" Rachel asked.

"Watch your step." He graciously stepped aside. The shop smelled of cinnamon tea. Spicy. Pleasant. She experienced a twinge of self-doubt. What if she was mistaken? More than that, what if she was egregiously wrong? This tall, suave, graceful man, this pleasant visually challenged/hearing-impaired person couldn't possibly be the psychopath she was looking for, could he?

"Tea?" he asked as they entered his office.

"Love some." She tried to steady her breathing.

Water boiled on a hot plate in a corner of the room. Vaughn found a mug and spoon, poured her a cup of tea, then felt his way along the wall toward her, fingertips skimming over the white paint, his opalescent eyes straining to read her face. "This'll warm you up." He walked back to his desk and took a seat. "So what brings you out on a night like tonight, Detective?"

"Murder," she said softly.

He cocked his head, lips frozen in a thin smile. "What's that?"

"Murder," she repeated, spoon clinking against china. "Claire Castillo's murder. Dinger Tedesco's murder."

"Ah." He sat back and waited. His handsome, inscrutable face was dominated by those distorted eyes, and she recalled how she and her friends used to make fun of anyone even the slightest bit different. "Retard" was about the worst insult you could hurl, and Rachel bet young Vaughn Kellum had gotten "retard" a lot. That it had shaped him.

He was wearing a red flannel shirt, khaki trousers, and leather moccasins—perfect, she thought, for walking through the woods. Vaughn's shirt pocket contained a number of stubby pencils and dry cleaning tickets he'd forgotten to remove, now that his shop was closed for the night. Her eyes came to rest on one of the Braille Dymo-tape labels, a series of raised dots that signified letters of the alphabet, numbers. She was certain that, if she looked hard enough, she could have located the configuration of three dots she'd found on the birch tree that day.

"How can I help you?"

She removed the dry cleaning receipt from her pocket. "We found this stapled to a dry cleaning bag in Claire's closet, but there was only one blouse inside."

She handed him the receipt and he rustled it between his slender fingers, then brought it almost to his nose. Opening the top drawer of his desk, he took out a hand magnifier. As he examined the receipt, she caught a glimpse of his left eye magnified to the size of a baseball.

"Do you see what it says there?" she asked.

"I think this is Jose's handwriting."

"'One white linen blouse, one blue silk blouse,'" Rachel said. "There were supposed to be two blouses inside the dry cleaning bag, but we only found one. The white linen blouse."

"Maybe she took the blue blouse out of the bag?"

"I couldn't find it inside the apartment. And the night she disappeared, she was wearing a pink blouse."

He put the hand magnifier down and passed her the receipt back. "I don't know what you're driving at, Detective."

"Claire picked up two blouses from your shop on Monday, October 12th, two days before she disappeared. She picked up two blouses, but there's only one blouse inside the bag."

His head moved ever so slightly, as if he were responding to some inner rhythm. "Maybe a friend borrowed it? Her sister, perhaps?"

Rachel wavered for a moment, then shook her head. "I don't think so." The '<u>b</u>' in Claire's Day-Timer hadn't meant <u>Billy</u> or <u>Buck</u> or <u>Brigham</u> or <u>baby</u>, it'd meant <u>blouse</u>. *Pick up blouse.*

"You see," Rachel said, "I've learned a lot about Claire Castillo. She was kind of sloppy, kind of careless with her belongings, not the type to inspect her dry cleaning in the store. She brought two blouses home, only to discover one of them still had stains on it. She'd asked you to remove the stains, but you hadn't done a very good job, and when she called you up to complain, you said you'd take care of it. She brought the blouse back the following day, Tuesday, then made plans to pick it up on Wednesday night. You knew she ate dinner at the Hurryback Cafe every Wednesday night, it was convenient for her to pick up the blouse afterward. She trusted you. You've been her dry cleaner for years. You two have worked on charity events together. There's no reason in the world why she shouldn't trust you."

"I honestly don't know what you're getting at," he said, upper lip beading with sweat.

"Your shop . . . this house is recessed from the street," Rachel continued. "The nearest street lamp is twenty yards away. Kellum Kleaners is wedged in between a vacant lot and the information center, which closes at five. The whole town shuts down by eight or nine P.M. most weeknights, this time of year. The woods press right against your back door. You could easily slip in and out unnoticed, under cover of darkness."

His lips stretched thin and pale over his teeth. "This is silly."

"You spent years stealing pieces of thread from Claire's clothes, her father's, her mother's, her sister's, maybe even her ex-boyfriend's. Buck Folette complained somebody was loosening the stitches on all his clothes. You often listen to the weather channel. You know when it's going to rain, when there's a ground fog. You have easy access to syringes and antipsychotics from the nurse's office at the blind school—where you went to school, where you remain actively involved and are always welcome. You were seventeen, a junior at the blind school, when Melissa D'Agostino was strangled. The school abuts the woods that run down to Old Mo Heppenheimer's cow pasture near the swamp where Melissa D'Agostino's body was found.

"The woods are the key. I couldn't figure out why the perp would drop his victims off so close to town. The answer is, you didn't drop them off. You walked them through the woods. You've been at Winfield since you were eight years old. I bet you had a habit of sneaking off campus whenever you got homesick. You've probably wandered back and forth between this house and Winfield hundreds of times. You know the lay of the land by heart. You use landmarks, reference points . . . you carve notches in trees. Braille directions.

"Dinger Tedesco and Nicole Castillo started going together nine months ago. That's two months before you hired Dinger to work for you part-time. Dinger trusted you. You were the only adult who understood. You sympathized. He could count on you to keep a secret. On the night Dinger and Nicole disappeared, they'd decided to meet someplace secret, someplace where they could be alone together. Where else but inside this house?" Rachel sat forward, blood coursing through her veins. She couldn't hold back any longer. "Where is she, Vaughn?"

He stood up, laughing, as if the question were absurd.

Rachel's heart beat hard and fast. *You must appear open-minded about the situation, project neutrality.* "I understand how difficult it must've been for you, Vaughn. Children can be cruel. Nobody gets a prize for being different."

"Now you're an expert on the low-sighted and hearing-impaired."

"I don't pretend to know what it's like. But I do know you were a victim of medical malpractice. That you suffered for someone else's mistake. Not only did Dr. Castillo fail to recognize and treat a life-threatening condition, he tried to preserve his reputation instead of admitting any wrongdoing. You suffered the consequences of his misdiagnosis, yet the state medical board wouldn't think of revoking his license. It's so unfair. Your parents must've been heartbroken."

"My mother," he said quietly, "never recovered."

"What happened? Did your parents settle out of court?"

"They hired an attorney who asked the tribunal, 'What is the price for the pain and suffering of a little boy?' The doctor admitted no guilt, and the lawyers decided fifteen thousand dollars should be compensation enough for the future distress engendered by an extreme departure from standard care."

"Fifteen thousand dollars?"

"Minus lawyers' fees, of course."

Her arms and legs felt weighted by rocks; she had his full attention now and didn't want to lose him. "I saw a picture of a little boy recently," she said, carefully choosing her words. "He looked about eight years old. Blond hair, green eyes. Small scar on his forehead. Two crooked bottom teeth."

Vaughn was breathing heavily through his mouth, studying her closely.

"In this picture, he wore a blue T-shirt with red sleeves, blue shorts and red hightop sneakers. And he had on those thick glasses other kids make fun of. And he looked . . . hungry . . . and lost . . . and very sad."

He wiped away the sweat from his upper lip.

"And I sensed something about him . . . that he'd been . . . I don't know how to put this . . ."

Vaughn smiled sourly. "Routinely beaten for minor infractions? Held to a standard of cold perfection?"

She paused a heart-stopping moment. "Your father beat you, didn't he? All those trips to the emergency room. They said you were accident-prone."

"Accident-prone?" She could feel the groundswell of his long-suppressed rage as his face reddened and his voice grew tight. "He turned the savageness of his contempt on me. Beat me with a belt buckle, with a mop handle, slugged me in the eye, twisted my arms, choked me to unconsciousness." He paused, and everything became very quiet. "You can't see it from way over there, Detective, but I'm just so horribly damaged."

Rachel pushed her coat open so her shoulder holster was exposed. "I need your help, Vaughn. We need to bring Nicole home."

His face went flat, expressionless. He inched along the wall to her right where the door to the office remained open.

She drew her weapon. "Don't move!"

"Am I under arrest?"

"All I want is Nicole. Tell me where she is."

His hand groped for the doorway.

"Don't move!"

"What are you going to do, shoot me? You come into my place of business, and now you're going to shoot me in cold blood?"

"Stay right where you are!"

He stopped about a foot from the door and smiled at her. "Did you know Helen Keller was a poet?"

"Please don't move," Rachel said, fear crawling up her spine.

"'They took away what should have been my eyes, but I

remembered Milton's Paradise,'" Vaughn recited in a deep, lilting baritone. "'They took away what should have been my ears, then Beethoven came and wiped away my tears. They took away what should have been my tongue, but I had talked with God when I was young. He would not let them take away my soul—possessing that, I still possess the whole.'" He flipped the light switch and everything went black.

The drawn velvet curtains were supremely effective in shutting out all light. She stood in total darkness, heart knocking in her chest. Frantically, she felt her way toward the wall, bumping into furniture, and finally found the light switch, but just as she flicked the lights back on, there was a blue flash and the room went dark again. The air chilled. Sweat poured from her body. He must've gotten to the fuse box.

"Nicole!" she screamed, skin around her eyes pulling tight. "Where are you!"

No answer. Just a lot of thumping and bumping in the dark and suddenly a hand groping past her head, and something heavy landing on the back of her skull. The bone-crushing blow sent her careening across the carpeted floor, gun flying out of her hand. She lay sprawled across the carpet in the lobby, a low insectlike hum filling her brain.

Groaning, she swore her way through the pain. She'd bitten her tongue and could taste blood. Now a pair of rough hands grabbed her ankles. "No!" Vaughn Kellum was dragging her across the carpeted floor, her clothes bunching underneath her. Her eyes bulged in the all-encompassing darkness. She scratched at the rug, kicked her legs, flailed her arms, and suddenly, miraculously, her outstretched hand touched something cold and metallic, and her fingers closed around the barrel of her Smith & Wesson.

She aimed the gun in Vaughn's direction and fired. The shot lit up the night. She saw for an instant his startled face as he dropped her legs and clutched his arm, just a fraction of a second—his shocked face, his clasped hand . . . then nothing.

Scrambling to her feet, she aimed her weapon at any stray sound. The rusty clang of the radiator pipes. Wind whistling through the rafters. She felt him behind her, beside her, goose bumps popping out on her flesh. She wildly clawed at empty space until she hit a wall, then groped along it until her hand clutched velvet. Yanking open the curtain, she found the lift cord for the venetian blinds and tugged, and the distant street lamp flung its steely gray light into the house, just enough for her to see. She spotted him as he threw open the back door and disappeared into the rain.

"Nicole!" Her lungs were raw. She made a quick search of the shop, then found the basement door. Kicking it open, she took the creaking stairs down into darkness.

"Nicole?"

Feeling along the wall for the fuse box, she steadied the gun before her, worried he might come back and lock them both in the basement.

"Nicole!"

She found the fuse box, powered up. Light flooded the cavernous space, piled high with firewood and old dressmaker's forms laced with cobwebs. Near the thrumming furnace was a workbench, to the right of the workbench a width of corkboard covered with power tools. Once she'd satisfied herself that Nicole wasn't in the basement, she headed back upstairs.

"Nicole!" She took the stairs to Vaughn's private residence two at a time. The banister was burnished mahogany. The door at the top was locked. She shot out the lock, wood splintering, and searched through the large empty rooms in the upstairs residence. The dark woodwork cast an aura of gloom. Yellow-tinted pictures hung on the walls, exquisite plaster rosettes and moldings adorned the twelve-foot ceilings. The bedrooms were empty. The bathroom with its old-fashioned claw-footed porcelain tub was empty. "Nicole!"

Finding the door to the attic, she heard a muffled cry, the

sound of it producing a shock like a dash of cold water. She jiggled the doorknob, then called out, "Step away from the door!" She fired off a round and tugged until the door burst open. She hurried up the narrow attic stairs, her throat so dry, it was difficult to breathe. "Nicole?"

At the northern end of the attic was a small enclosed room with a padlocked door. Somebody was making an awful racket on the other side.

"Help! Get me out of here!"

"Stand back. Stand back! I have to shoot the lock."

It took several rounds, splintering the wood, before the lock gave way and Rachel holstered her gun. From inside a narrow, dark, smelly space leapt a ragged, trembling figure, and suddenly Nicole Castillo was in her arms, clinging like a child who'd just awakened from a nightmare. "Thank you, thank you," she whispered in Rachel's ear, "thank you, thank God, oh thank God . . ."

14

RACHEL CHECKED NICOLE'S VITAL SIGNS, WRAPPED HER IN A blanket, called an ambulance, called for backup. She locked Nicole inside her car with the cell phone and car keys and grabbed a flashlight out of the glove compartment.

"Where are you going?" Nicole clutched her arm.

"I can't let him get away."

"No! Please don't leave me!"

"They'll be here soon, I promise."

Her shoes crackled against the gritty asphalt as she took off across the street. The cold ate into her bones as she moved around behind the house. An eight-foot chain link fence surrounded the backyard. She headed up an incline into the piney woods, eyes straining for any sign of him, hand flexing on the checkerboard handle of her gun. There was no movement in the woods ahead. She was afraid she'd lost him.

Looking back, she noted the street was shrouded in fog, the nearest street lamp a distant halo. Her breath made cottony plumes. The sky suddenly opened up and the slishing sound of rain surrounded her.

Rachel moved into the woods, past gold birches and evergreen trees, their branches weighted with rain. The ground fog thickened as the woods closed in around her. Her throat constricted, throttling a rising panic. She fought to keep her wits about her, fought the urge to run as she slogged through the glistening sword ferns.

A bird shrilled, and she spun at the frantic fluttering of wings. It streaked past her head and was gone, swallowed into the mist. She stood rock steady as tendrils of fog circled the space where the bird had just been.

The ground was soggy underfoot. She couldn't see very far in front of her, perhaps ten feet. She scaled a stone wall, the soles of her shoes slipping on wet rock, then crashed through a knee-deep bed of ferns. Her clothes felt heavy, the frozen fabric scuffing together. Her legs ached, her blood dragging through her veins.

"Oh God," came shivering out of her, and she suddenly recalled something McKissack had once told her. The first thing the victim said was "Oh God." The last thing she said was "Oh shit."

Frightened now, but still not admitting it to herself, Rachel trudged through a pine grove, soggy needles crunching underfoot, then paused to listen—arteries throbbing, ears straining past the thick sibilance of rain falling on leaves. She aimed her flashlight at a dense maze of swaying conifers—larch, fir, spruce. Fat droplets collected on the purplish cones and white needles until they became too full and dropped, pelting her like water balloons.

Now she heard a rustling sound and, locating its source, moved swiftly toward it, out of the pine grove and into a stand of birch trees. White, gold, silver, majestic, magnificent. She slid between trees growing too closely together and heard it distinctly now—the crisp snap of a twig, the rustle of undergrowth. He was close.

Arffffff!

A dog leapt out of the wet tangle like a menacing growl with teeth. Rain streaked across her flashlight beam, making everything seem as scratchy and distant as an old home movie.

"Good dog. Heel!" she commanded, but the dog stood its ground, collarless and malnourished. She could see the ribbed skeleton beneath its matted fur as it gave a weakened bark.

Holding herself tightly reined, she moved on. Her breathing was labored, despair and exhaustion about to set in. Her bones felt brittle. Petrified. She wanted to lie down for a moment, right here, right now, to catch her breath, but she was somehow able to draw on an unfathomable font of strength and keep moving. Keep slogging through these black wet woods.

She no longer knew where she was. The cold damp air burned her lungs, and her flashlight danced over trees—bunchberry, tamarack, flowering dogwood. Dogwood leaves with their curved, parallel veins and delicate pink flowers bearing ruby red fruit in the spring. She leaned against the dense compact bark of the dogwood and thought she'd rest awhile. Just for a moment. She switched off her flashlight and lifted her face to the rain, a steady sprinkling downpour that caulked every crevice. She recalled what they said about drowning, how it was supposed to be painless. We started out in water; in the womb, we had gills. Perhaps death was a mercy? She listened to herself breathing, in and out. In and out.

The hand came out of nowhere. A quick grope, and then a hammer punch to the head. Her knees noodled and she went sprawling. Gun and flashlight flying out of her hands. She tried to force her arms and legs to move, then everything rocketed away. She saw a blinding light, the kind projected onto a movie screen after a piece of film has broken. A purifying, white light.

And then, clotted darkness. Hissing silence.

When she opened her eyes, she wasn't sure how long she'd been out. Seconds? Minutes? Her eyes slowly focused and she could see him through the fog. Condensation clinging to his glasses. He loomed over her with his hundred-year stare, then started kicking—heavy, hateful blows landing against her abdomen and ribs.

She barrel-rolled to avoid the next kick, tumbled through the wet leaves. Now he was gone, lost in the fog. Visibility zero. Lurching to her feet, she circled the small clearing, heart racing, eyes darting. An arm flung out and caught her on the chin. She stumbled away. Roaring, he charged after her. She squatted on the ground, thrust one shoulder forward and, bracing for impact, caught him on the knees. He grabbed her on the way down, knocking them both to the wet earth.

Now she was at a distinct disadvantage as he climbed on top of her and wrapped his hands around her throat. He was going to choke the life out of her. His rage was deep, he drew strength from it. Even in the darkness she could see the cold contempt in his eyes. The eyes of an eight-year-old boy whose mother saw him beaten, saw him hungry, saw him tormented, but never intervened.

Her insides burned. She felt tiny and breakable. She'd forgotten to eat her spinach, and now Bluto was going to stretch her limbs apart like strings of taffy. He slung her about like a mouse. Not about to let this happen, she leaned bravely into the chaos she was about to create.

Adrenaline jump-started her body and, snaking her arms through his, she broke his grip. They tumbled down an incline together, bumping over rotten logs. She caught a sharp rock with her hip and the pain of it shot up her spine. At the bottom of the incline, her head hit something metallic and tubelike, and her hand closed around her flashlight.

As he lunged forward, she threw a punch with blinding speed, flashlight connecting with his chin. A wet sound. Before he could react, she started beating him on the head with the flashlight, its impact like a metallic sneeze. There were fireflies behind his head, sparks going off in the sky. What was that? She squinted. Tiny distant flashlight beams scanned the woods and illuminated the canopy of branches above their heads. She'd never seen anything so beautiful in her entire life. Beams of light sparkling on wet leaves.

"McKissack!" she screamed. "Over here!"

"Rachel?" came a distant male voice. McKissack's voice.

Enraged, Vaughn started throwing punches so fast his arms blurred. He scooped up a fistful of dirt and plunged it into her mouth. Wet earth gritted her teeth and clogged the back of her throat, making her choke. Tears sprang to her eyes, and she couldn't see. Gagging, she blindly thrust her palm directly upward into his chin, knocking his glasses off his face, and he reeled backward and clutched his nose, blood spurting through his splayed fingers.

She struggled to her feet, gagging on matted clumps of earth, her stiff overcoat slowing her progress. He hurtled forward, bloody hands outstretched. Exploded like a popcorn kernel. He groped the air for the shape of her and let out a bloodcurdling shriek, his breath making cloudlike bursts.

She ducked and ran behind him while he flailed and groped for her. She searched for her gun, found it, leapt for it like a lioness, fingers clamping gratefully around its checkerboard grip. She grew instantly calm. Amazingly calm. Aiming her semiautomatic at Vaughn Kellum, using the Weaver stance, she said, "Police! Don't move!"

He turned toward the sound of her voice, his hearing aids secure. His glasses were gone, though, lost in the fallen leaves.

"It's over, Vaughn," she said. "Put your hands on your head!"

The flashlight beams were closer now, jogging and circling. McKissack's voice, a little louder. "Rachel! Where are you?"

"Over here!"

Vaughn Kellum started to walk directly toward her, guided by the sound of her voice.

"Don't you move a muscle! Stay where you are!"

He paused for an imperceptible moment, then smiled defiantly in her direction. This icy, contemptuous smile was meant for her.

"I never really cared anyway," he said.

"Stay where you are, Vaughn!"

He tugged both hearing aids out of his ears. With a simple flick of his wrists, he flung them in different directions far into the woods. Now he was both profoundly deaf and blind as he continued in her direction. His pace increased.

He was moving steadily toward her, arms flailing, torso twisting and shrinking to less than half its width with each antagonistic body movement. She couldn't get a bead. She didn't want to kill him. He was unarmed and she had no business shooting him. She tried to find a nonfatal target—pelvis, leg—but the dark and the rain and the limited illumination from her flashlight only added to her confusion.

"Stop!"

If you lose your cool, you lose the fight. Her life was in danger. She had to hit the target in order to stop the threat. All her training had concentrated on staid, static range drills. McKissack was the only one who'd explained to her that perfect shot placement might not suffice in real life, might not stop the threat.

"Freeze! Don't move!"

Her arms trembled as she tried to hold the gun steady, but he continued moving swiftly toward her, arms thrashing, fingers groping, a feral look on his face. He swung at the air, vicious and determined. She backed away. "McKissack! Over here!"

Vaughn Kellum lashed angrily at the space in front of him, and she took a step backward. Another. Another. To her right and left, dense woods. She was boxed in. She couldn't swallow. Her heart raced. He was forcing her hand, moving relentlessly toward her.

"McKissack!" she screamed, taking another step backward.

Legs braced. Distant flashlight beams revolved in the canopy, circling as though they were lost.

"I'm over here! Hurry!"

She took another step back and her heel hit something hard, and she flattened against a dogwood tree, its smooth, dense bark supporting her spine.

"McKissack!"

Gasping for breath.

Vaughn's arms swung like scythes, his eyes roamed aimlessly. He swiped at the air, inches from her gun. She took another eighth of a second to make sure of target acquisition, sight picture, backstop . . . fuck it . . . she pointed the gun at his head.

He grabbed the barrel.

"Oh shit!"

She fired.

The bullet penetrated his skull and blew out the back of his head, and he rag-dolled in front of her. Sprawled dead on the ground at her feet.

15

THE FOLLOWING MORNING, THE SUN PEEKED OUT FROM BE-hind cumulus clouds like great gray brains exploding across the sky. Rachel met privately with Dr. Castillo in his office to explain the unexplainable.

He eyed her solicitously. "How are you feeling, Detective?"

"Bruised. Some cuts. A few broken ribs." She fingered a marble-sized lump over her right eye. "But I'll live."

"My wife and I are extremely grateful," he said. "Words can't express how indebted we are."

"How's Nicole?"

"Recovering."

She leaned forward in her seat. This little meeting had been her idea. She wanted to tell him in person, let the words fall like a cold rain upon his head.

"Vaughn Kellum's been planning this for years," she began. "We've traced one of the threads all the way back to Claire's ex-boyfriend, three years ago. Three years, Vaughn Kellum's been collecting thread from Claire's clothes, Nicole's clothes, yours, your wife's. The ex-boyfriend's, like I said."

Yale's hands lay flat and lifeless on his desk. "But why would anyone do such a terrible thing?"

Rachel didn't answer right away, filled with an aggressive fury she didn't quite know what to do with. "Claire left the diner at eight o'clock on Wednesday night and walked through the fog to Kellum Kleaners," she said. "According to Nicole's own experience, they probably had tea together and talked about the charity dance. Claire liked Vaughn. He was her friend. She never suspected he'd laced her tea with chloral hydrate."

"The knockout drug."

"The attic room was well insulated, like a recording studio. Nobody could hear you scream. There was a mattress on the floor, an overhead light, a portable toilet. We found books, reading matter. He kept Claire drugged, bound at the wrists and ankles for long periods of time, same as Nicole. But at night, after the shop closed, they'd eat dinner together and talk. I'm sure he told her everything."

"Everything?" He seemed confused.

"I've seen his school transcripts, Doctor. His IQ was in the superior range, above 130. He came from a dysfunctional home, both parents were alcoholics. He suffered physical and emotional abuse at his father's hands. His mother apparently blamed you for their troubles."

"Blamed me?"

"He was torn away from home at the age of eight, and his

mother died shortly thereafter. He lost much of his sight, most of his hearing, couldn't run like the other boys, couldn't play ball anymore . . ." She detected the rapid pulse beating in her own throat and swallowed hard, sitting on a deep desire to hurt him. "Claire went over there to innocently pick up a blouse, and three weeks later found herself walking through the woods, where Vaughn knew every tree, every stone, every grove, every ravine. He took her to a place he knew she would instinctively crawl out of, toward the traffic sounds, and injected her with an antipsychotic. He injected it between her toes so it wouldn't be immediately detected."

Anger flared in Yale's eyes. "Yes, well . . . thank you for stopping by, Detective. I'm sure you're very busy, and I've got patients to attend to—"

"I'm not finished, Doctor," she said. She couldn't help herself, she'd lost her professional distance. Her hands were trembling. "I read the files. Throughout the years, you've been accused of gross negligence, misdiagnosis, extreme departure from standard care, failure to realize the seriousness of an illness, administration of incorrect dosages, administration of incorrect blood type, failure to summon help from another physican because you didn't want to admit you'd misjudged the patient's condition, caring more about your reputation and ego than the health of the patient. At least four of your patients suffered permanent, irreversible damage as a result, while an elderly woman died of dehydration in your care. Of the sixteen charges of malpractice—"

"Alleged medical negligence," he coldly corrected her.

"Three were settled and the rest were thrown out by the tribunal. Vaughn Kellum's case was settled. Fifteen thousand dollars minus lawyers' fees. In misdiagnosing a little boy's symptoms twenty-seven years ago, you affected the course of his life, and in doing so, you affected the course of your own life."

"I tried my best to help that child." He sat rigid in his seat, breathing hard. "May I remind you, Detective, that death in the emergency room is not uncommon . . ."

"You've been charged with malpractice sixteen times, Doctor. How did you manage to keep your license?"

"It was never my intent to harm that child. I'm sure you can understand what it's like to make a judgment call, or a series of judgment calls. They alleged medical negligence, well I've got news for you, Detective. Medicine is not an exact science."

"Oh come on, Doctor. You botched it big-time. I read the file. Vaughn Kellum's parents brought him into the emergency room twice, and each time you denied that the child was seriously ill. Each time, you misjudged his condition. You only consulted with another physician after his parents insisted, and even then you misled Dr. Selby and tried to cover up your mistakes in a three-page addendum inserted into the child's medical records."

He stood, red-faced with indignation. "You can't possibly blame *me* for what happened to Claire!"

"Do you understand the depth of his hatred?" she asked, out of breath and agitated. She'd lost control. She'd lost her head. This was no good. "Don't you get it? It took him *years* to collect all those pieces of thread. *Years* to construct the room in the attic. *Years* to befriend Claire and Dinger. He was exceedingly patient. Brilliantly patient. Fanatical in his desire for revenge."

"But this has nothing to do with me. Nothing!"

"Your daughter died because of mistakes you made almost three decades ago. The least you can do is accept partial responsibility for her pain and suffering."

He gazed at her helplessly, his face a twisted slab. He reminded her of a photograph she'd once seen in a museum, a black-and-white photograph of a Nazi guard in a concentration camp who'd been forced to dig up the dead.

"Three weeks, she lived in that room. I was there. It's the size of a walk-in closet. The walls are padded, there's no way out, it stinks of urine and fear. She lay on that mattress for twenty-one days, scared out of her wits. Not knowing whether she'd be dead tomorrow, or whether he'd rape her tonight. This man she had once called her friend. Then one night, he unlocks the door and walks into the room with some pills, a needle and thread. I can't imagine what was going through her mind."

"I did nothing wrong. Anyone could've made the same mistake. I was vindicated. We settled without an admission of guilt."

"He sewed her up," Rachel continued without mercy, "and escorted her through the woods in the middle of the night in the pouring rain. He injected her with Thorazine and left her there to die, she probably thought. But no, he saved that little task for you. He knew you'd misdiagnose her symptoms. He knew you'd make another mistake, and that it would be lethal."

Yale's shoulders spasmed. He choked back the tears, and she suddenly felt like a criminal.

"He knew your schedule. He knew you were in the middle of a fourteen-hour shift. And he'd just sewn thread from your Brooks Brothers suit into your daughter's face."

He groaned and dropped his head in his hands, and her heart froze. Her gut seized up. She'd been incalculably cruel. He'd lost his daughter. That was enough. Punishment for a lifetime.

"He knew you would misdiagnose your daughter's symptoms," she said softly, "just as you'd misdiagnosed his. He was a sick man, bent on revenge."

"Please," he begged, "no more . . ."

"There isn't any more." She stood up. "Vaughn Kellum is dead. It's over."

"Thank God for that." He slouched in his seat, mouth an anguished gash. "Thank God . . . thank Christ . . ."

She felt dirty. She hated herself for lashing out at this defenseless man, this bereft father. The window behind his desk revealed a sky sharpening to crystal blue.

She opened the door to his office, then turned for one last thought. "Three weeks she lived in abject terror, knowing she was there because of you. And you know what? I bet she forgave you."

She shut the door in his stricken face.

16

MCKISSACK FIT IN SO PERFECTLY WITH THE SMOKY ATMOSPHERE of the bar, she felt certain she must have conjured him up out of the red vinyl booths, the spilt beer, the sticky wooden floor. He was wearing his civvies—plaid flannel shirt, jeans, cracked-leather biker jacket—and his eyes were full of bitters. "I'm behind you a hundred percent, Rachel. I'm not gonna let anything happen to you."

"I shot an unarmed suspect at point-blank range," she said, finishing her wine. "A blind man. The department's being sued."

"By some distant cousin who probably didn't give two shits until this happened." McKissack signaled the waitress for another round. "Let's drink to your first unpleasant brush with bureaucracy. Unfortunately, it won't be your last. Remember those bank robbers in L.A. who terrorized an entire community with their arsenal of automatic weapons? They sprayed buildings and houses with armor-piercing bullets, but when the cops shot one of them and he lay dying on the ground, the press raised holy hell because an ambulance wasn't called fast enough."

"I shot a defenseless man, McKissack."

He fell into lecturing mode. "A person in a rage with the perceived intent of attacking an officer and failing to respond to said officer's orders to stop—"

"He was profoundly deaf without his hearing aids," she reminded him.

"—creates a clear situation in which the officer must act quickly to stop the attacker. An officer may use deadly force to protect himself against deadly force." He sighed. "Vaughn Kellum grabbed your gun. His prints are on the barrel."

"I failed to properly Mirandize him. The D.A. wants to get reelected."

"The guy was guilty as sin. Nobody's arguing with that. He deserves to spend eternity in the lowest levels of Dante's hell."

She tried to let these words soothe her but knew that, ultimately, McKissack couldn't save her. She'd surrendered her gun and shield, was on temporary leave from the department. Once an internal investigation was completed, and assuming she was exonerated, she would get her badge and weapon back. But the nightmares that had started shortly after the shooting hadn't let up. It wasn't a nice feeling, killing another human being.

Now she let her gaze wander over McKissack's face. "Have you ever been in front of a jury, Jim?"

"Yeah, way back when Moby-Dick was a minnow. Just remember, stay calm, speak in a deliberate voice, and give your lawyer plenty of time to object."

She wanted to get drunk, really drunk for a change. She wanted to lose control. She'd never felt so damaged. "You know, I get the shakes. I'll be sitting there, and something will trigger it."

His eyes were kind. "Just get ahold of yourself."

"How?"

He shrugged. "Stop tormenting yourself. It's not like you'll ever get used to it." McKissack tilted his head to drink, then looked at her, jaw muscles bunching. "I'm just glad you're okay. The guy was six two, one-ninety. That's some fierce struggle. I'm proud of you, Rachel." He stroked her bruised cheek. "You okay?"

"It only hurts when I cry."

He smiled but his eyes were sad. "You had my heart going."

"Serves you right for all the times you've had mine going."

They both fell silent. It was difficult, letting go. Her ribs were tender, the back of her head was still sore, and every aching joint in her body reminded her of Vaughn Kellum. She couldn't get away from him.

"He won, McKissack," she said softly. "Even in death, he won."

He gave her a skeptical look. "What?"

"I was his last victim."

"Bullshit. You're no victim."

"Maybe not, but somehow he managed to destroy my career, not to mention my peace of mind."

"It was suicide by cop. Nothing more. Nothing less." He stroked her hair, but she drew back slightly, and he rested his hands on the tabletop, one over the other. "We're looking more closely at Melissa D'Agostino. It might've been a crime of opportunity, his first, perhaps. One of his wanderings through the woods. There's a couple Unsolveds we're checking out."

"According to his social worker, his father once held a pillow over his face and only stopped when Vaughn pretended to be dead."

"Lots of people have miserable childhoods, that doesn't mean they all turn into psychopaths. The guy was sadistic and monumentally self-indulgent. It makes you want to handcuff your kids to your wrist and never let them out of your sight." Leaning forward, he kissed her. "I love you, Rachel. I always will."

She opened her mouth to protest, but he rested his finger against her lips. "Shhh. I know. Just keep this on the back burner. I'll always be there for you."

She slid out of the booth and stood on unsteady legs, drunker than she expected. "Me, too, McKissack," she said. "I'll always love you, too."

17

THE D.A.'S OFFICE LIKED TO CLAIM A HIGH CONVICTION RATE. As aggressive as he was, however, District Attorney Hubert Blum failed to make the charges against Detective Third Grade Rachel Storrow stick after her counsel proved, through a legal defense called justification, that she was allowed to use deadly force. Subsequently exonerated, she was reinstated to her post.

On the Saturday following the verdict, Rachel drove to her brother's house to say good-bye. Billy's U-Haul was packed. They stood on the front lawn in the crisp February air, assessing one another's feelings. She gazed into his frost-colored eyes, reminded of all the good things from her childhood.

"Well," he said, "I left you some stuff in the front hall. Microwave. Blender. It's all packed. Mom's good silverware. Dad's old army blanket. Remember that?"

"Yeah." She smiled. "He made us tuck in the corners so tight you could bounce a quarter off the bed."

Billy laughed, the sound of it lifting her spirits.

"I love you, Billy," she said, wrapping her arms around him, and they held each other for a while. She would miss his laugh, his smile, his voice, the reassuring length of him. She could hear his heartbeat through layers of wool. With great reluctance, she let him go.

"I'm glad you got your job back," he said.

"I'm not so sure I want it back."

His eyebrows lifted in surprise. "What'll you do?"

She glanced around, uncertain. Blackbirds circled the power lines that ran down behind the house. A neighbor's dog barked at its own shadow. "I majored in psychology," she said. "The world could use a little therapy, don't you think?"

He smiled at her. His hair was clean and shiny and their childhood seemed a million miles away.

She couldn't keep the sadness from creeping into her voice. "Billy, I'm sorry about what happened."

"Forget it." He shrugged as if it were nothing, then tweaked her nose. "Who's my little pipsqueak?"

"I am." The corners of her mouth curled up. "I'm going to miss you, big brother."

"I'll call when I get to Seattle." He'd found a new job working with blind adults. He couldn't stay at Winfield, he told her. It reminded him too much of Claire. "Don't worry about the rest of the junk inside. Landlord's gonna take care of it."

"Okay." She didn't want him to leave. Regret boiled up around her. She needed more time. Needed to prove how much she loved him. How much she trusted him.

"Well . . ." He had a winning smile. "Guess this is it."

She clung to him, not wanting to let go. His grip was muscular from lifting weights. He'd always protected her. He'd always been there for her. Now what was she going to do? Her family was gone. There was nothing left but memories.

He kissed her good-bye and got in his car. He waved as he pulled out onto the road, gravel crunching under his tires. She stood for a long while on the ice-slick driveway and followed the U-Haul's progress into the dazzling landscape. Then the milky woods absorbed him and he was gone.

Inside, four large cardboard boxes waited by the front door. The cavernous rooms were empty except for a carpet rolled into a corner of the living room, a broken broom, rejected paperbacks, a few moldering pieces of furniture.

Rachel took the boxes home and unpacked them in the living room as the setting sun streaked the sky pink through the windows. Besides the silverware and army blanket, he'd left his old baby clothes, a teething ring, a lock of golden hair. He'd left the family photographs, letters and birthday cards she and her mother had written to him at various addresses—Albuquerque, New Orleans, Nebraska . . .

Tucked inside the microwave was a book of poems by William Blake, a yellow Post-it stuck to the front cover. The note, in Billy's scrawling handwriting, read: "Rachel, Remember what Dad used to say about keeping a light heart? There's also a line from Blake: 'A truth that's told with bad intent beats all the lies you can invent.' Don't ever forget me, Billy."

The book fell open in her hands, and pressed between two

pages like a flower was Melissa D'Agostino's friendship bracelet. Yellow and red yarn woven together in a diamond pattern.

Rachel's feet turned to stone. How could she have been so stupid? A shriveling wind whistled through the rafters, but the blood rushing in her head drowned out all sound. Yellow and red flashed before her eyes. Her brain felt broken. Her eyes scanned down the page, pausing on a single highlighted passage:

> "Father! father! where are you going?
> O do not walk so fast.
> Speak, father, speak to your little boy.
> Or else I shall be lost."

She could feel him in her arms, her big brother, tall and strong, could smell his warm breath against her cheek, and she wanted him back. *Bring him back.* She wanted her brother back, but it was too late.

The truth was curled like a caterpillar in her palm.

18

BY MID-MARCH, RACHEL WAS READY TO GO. EVERYTHING WAS packed. She was leaving Flowering Dogwood for good, driving down the coast to Cambridge, Massachusetts, where a friend needed a third roommate. McKissack had expressed shock and disappointment at her decision to leave the department, but it was too late. She'd made up her mind.

Billy had evaporated into thin air. There were no phone calls. There was no forwarding address. No job with blind adults. Alone in the house, she took her gold shield out of her pocket and hefted it in her hand. McKissack knew nothing about her real reasons for leaving. He hadn't a clue what rested in the balance. The price she'd have to pay in order to stay.

The floorboards creaked as she walked through the empty rooms, memories reaching out at every turn. There, she broke one of her front baby teeth running. There, she and Billy had played monster that time, and he'd scared her so much she couldn't stop hiccuping. There was where they set up the Christmas tree every year. She inhaled deeply, the house filling momentarily with laughter. Birthdays, Easter egg hunts, family reunions, her parents' anniversaries . . . that was enough. She could block out the rest. She wasn't going to drag all the bitterness and grief out the door with her.

At the front door, she turned to take one last look at the kitchen where they'd shared their meals. She wouldn't be back.

Outside she picked up her pace, striding briskly past the For Sale sign on the front lawn. Ice and snow glittered like crushed glass in the moonlight. She walked past the barbecue pit, the icicled hammock, the woodshed . . . down to the back field. In the spring, the wild turkey would mate when the redbud trees bloomed, and the buck moth would hatch, and she'd miss them all. Green ash, spruce, fir, white birch. She scaled the barbed wire fence, then stood in the crusted snow and faced the swamp.

This valley was called Wuchowsem after the spirit of the benign night winds. She gazed at the bog with its stunted, spindly trees, its sheep laurel and dwarf huckleberry—a web of branches and brittle dead leaves coated with a fur of snow, now twinkling in the moonlight. The seasons changed swiftly here, dramatically, from soft to tempestuous. Northerly winds blew needlepoint frost across this great land, and the winter snows soon followed, burying everything beneath a thick icy crust.

Rachel held her shield to the moonlight. Breath clouds crackled from her lungs and the yarn bracelet danced in the biting wind. It wasn't too late to turn her brother in. Either way, she knew she'd be haunted for the rest of her life.

Her eyes blurred with tears. Her head beat with the sound of a thousand drums. The immensity of the sky floored her. She could almost feel ice crystals forming in the black air high above her head, and the cold stung her nostrils. She had never felt so all alone. She was alone on the planet.

Father! father! where are you going?

Fingers raw and numb, she tied the friendship bracelet around the shield, making several stiff knots. It was up to fate, she decided. If some stranger happened to stumble across this definitive proof of her family's guilt, so be it.

Her heart roared. The ground was made of paper. The fields were blue in the moonlight. The swamp was salt-dusted, foam-flecked, its pools covered with a skin of ice. With the passage of time, the elements would rinse the earth of evil.

Frozen weeds crunched underfoot as she shifted her weight. With a grunt, she pitched the shield as far as she could into the swamp. It hurtled through the cold night like a final thought and landed in the thickets where, unknown to her, it fell through wrinkles of snow and came to rest upon a clump of huckleberry roots embedded in fissures, roots like congealed veins growing in and around the decades-old cat bell. Rust had crept like frost around the circumference of the tiny silver bell, rust blossomed on metal, and the sleeping roots whispered of long-ago glaciers.

ACKNOWLEDGMENTS

Heartfelt thanks to my agent, Wendy Weil, and my editor, Beverly Lewis, for their great wisdom and support; to Irwyn Applebaum for his enthusiasm and generosity; to my teachers Chris Leland, Peter LaSalle and Mameve Medwed for their love of writing; to Doris Jackson, whose dedication to the truth once turned my life around; to The Group (Lori, Helen, Jane, Nancy and Ali) for its irreplaceable fellowship; to Marnie Mueller for her writer's eye; to Elon Dershowitz, Kevin Brodbin and my talented brother, Carter Blanchard, for their invaluable input; to all my friends for their encouragement when times were tough; to the good people of CRC; and last but not least, to my husband, Doug Dowling, for his brilliance, his inspiration and unshakable faith.

Alice Blanchard won the Katherine Anne Porter Prize for Fiction for her book of stories, *The Stuntman's Daughter*. She has received a PEN Syndicated Fiction Award, a New Letters Literary Award and a Centrum Artists in Residence Fellowship. Her fiction has appeared in such quarterlies as *Turnstile, The Alaska Quarterly* and *The William & Mary Review*, among others, and has been broadcast on National Public Radio's "The Sound of Writing." She lives in Los Angeles with her husband.